Promises, Promises

ERICA JAMES

First published in 2010 by Orion Books,
an imprint of The Orion Publishing Group Ltd
Orion House, 5 Upper Saint Martin's Lane
London WC2H 9EA

First published in Great Britain in 2010 by Orion Books.

An Hachette UK Company

1 3 5 7 9 10 8 6 4 2

Copyright © Erica James 2010

A CIP catalogue record for this book
is available from the British Library.

ISBN (Hardback) 978 1 4091 0186 4
ISBN (Export Trade Paperback) 978 1 4091 0187 1

Typeset by Deltatype Ltd, Birkenhead, Merseyside

Printed in Great Britain by Clays Ltd, St Ives plc

The Orion Publishing Group's policy is to use papers that
are natural, renewable and recyclable products and made
from wood grown in sustainable forests. The logging and
manufacturing processes are expected to conform to the
environmental regulations of the country of origin.

www.orionbooks.co.uk

To Edward and Samuel –
The A-Team in all respects.

Acknowledgments

Thanks to Carol Hutchinson who introduced me to the world of specialist painters.

Huge thanks to John and Victoria who yet again helped me.

As is so often the case, I've pinched a real place and bent it to fit the story. Please don't go looking for the overpriced fish and chip shop; it doesn't exist.

Promises are either kept or broken. (Proverb)

A bold heart is half the battle. (Proverb)

Chapter One

The Lilacs was as quiet as the grave. Just how Maggie Storm liked it, especially after all the noise and chaos that had gone on at home before she'd set off to come here.

The washing machine had gone on the blink mid-cycle and no matter how politely she coaxed or not-so-politely thumped it, it simply would not work. Then Dave had taken a screwdriver to it and surprise, surprise he had flooded the kitchen. She had been telling him for weeks that there was something wrong with it, but he hadn't listened.

Not that he ever did listen. Seventeen years of marriage and he still asked how many sugars she wanted in her tea – that was if he ever got off his backside in the first place to make her a drink. 'I DON'T HAVE SUGAR IN MY TEA,' she would reply through gritted teeth. 'ONLY IN COFFEE.' Increasingly she was finding herself speaking to him in capital letters. Very big capital letters. Underlined, sometimes. If she ever complained he would accuse her of nagging and say that she was lucky to have a husband who made her a drink and that it wasn't his fault that he couldn't keep up with her faddy likes and dislikes. 'But that's women for you,' he'd add with an annoying roll of his eyes and an even more annoying puff of breath that said, *Pah! Women! Always changing their minds.*

Lucky. Yeah, she was lucky all right. Just think of all the worse husbands she could have ended up with – that sick Austrian bloke who kept his poor daughter in the cellar all her life, for one.

But lucky her: at the age of nineteen she had married Dave

Storm who had all the magnetic charm, sophistication and understanding of Mr Blobby. She was now so used to referring to him as Mr Blobby in her head, she was sure that one day soon the name was going to slip out. Give Mr Blobby a lager in his hand and an audience of his mates from the garage where he worked as a mechanic and he thought he was so funny. Downright hilarious. A real Jack the Lad. There must have been a time when Maggie had thought he was funny, but now he mostly made her grind her teeth. Sometimes she had cartoon-like fantasies of taking a swing at him with a frying pan. Not to kill him, of course, merely to knock some sense into him. *I don't take sugar in my tea ... Bang! I don't like being called Mags ... Bang! I hate the way you sniff for no real reason ...*

Sometimes, when she wasn't imagining herself with a frying pan in her hands, she pictured herself screaming, her mouth wide open, her eyes bulging nearly out of their sockets. The temptation to scream was growing harder to resist. But she mustn't give in to it. Do that and she might lose it and never stop screaming.

Not Losing It was one of her New Year's resolutions. Along with:

> Do Something New.
> Learn To Stand Up For Myself.
> Lose Weight.

Other than Not Losing It, she had done nothing about the resolutions, but it was only the third of January, so early days.

It was her first day back at work after the Christmas holidays and, to be honest, after a week of being cooped up with Mr Blobby, Blobby Junior, and Brenda – the mother-in-law from hell – it was a relief. Paid to clean other people's houses, she made their lives easier. A shame no one did the same for her. If she was paid by the regret instead of by the hour, why, she'd be richer than the Queen!

She finished cleaning the loo and then sprayed the glass bowl hand-basin with Cillit Bang and wondered if the Queen had even heard of Cillit Bang, much less used it. 'What does one do with this?' she imagined her, thoroughly baffled, asking one of her flunkies.

Maggie had been working for the family that owned The Lilacs for four years now. Whilst she felt she knew a lot about them – as their cleaner she saw herself as all-seeing and all-knowing – they knew very little about her. For instance, she knew that Mr Edwards (Please-Call-Me-Ethan) was forty-six and ran his own bed linen company. He wore Armani aftershave, Hugo Boss and Paul Smith suits, size eleven shoes and a fifteen-and-a-half-inch shirt collar, and suffered with stomach problems (there was a ton of antacid products in his bathroom cabinet). He preferred boxers to Y-fronts and had a massive CD collection in his office, which he liked to listen to when he was working from home. Sometimes he played his music so loud it made the pictures on his walls slip. She was always having to straighten them. If his wife was around, he listened to his music through headphones.

With six bedrooms and three bathrooms, a dressing room, a lounge (sorry, sitting room), a dining room, a conservatory, a TV room, an office and a kitchen the size of a tennis court and a laundry room with a loo and shower off it, The Lilacs was the biggest house in Lilac avenue. She couldn't begin to think how much money Please-Call-Me-Ethan had to earn to run it. Lately he looked tired and fed up, which was a pity because he was a really nice bloke. He had dead gorgeous dark-brown eyes and a really lovely smile. He had a great body, too, a body she certainly wouldn't turn down if it came at her in the middle of the night the way Mr Blobby's did. He was always nicely dressed, whether it was jeans and a T-shirt or one of his expensive suits. And he had the most amazing hands – square strong hands with the nails all neatly trimmed and very clean. Unlike Mr Blobby's. But then Mr Blobby was a car mechanic, so that was hardly something she could complain about. She suspected that Please-Call-Me-Ethan was not entirely happy or entirely faithful to his bitch of a wife. Maggie didn't blame him.

Mrs Edwards (Please-Call-Me-Mrs-Edwards) was forty-one and had probably never done a day's work in her life. She was a member of an exclusive fitness and spa centre, where she spent most days flexing and toning and having her hair and nails done. No wonder she always claimed to be exhausted. She was a minuscule size eight and wore nothing but designer clothes. Her walk-in wardrobe was bigger than Maggie and Mr Blobby's bedroom and was laid out with shelves, drawers and hanging rails. Nothing was ever out of place; coat hangers all faced the same direction and shoes were carefully stored in their original boxes.

Recently Mrs Edwards had started visiting a clinic for Botox injections on the quiet. Maggie had the feeling that no one, including Ethan, was supposed to know about the clinic, but all-seeing, all-knowing Maggie knew about it. She had seen the bill for the last visit, a bill dated for the morning when Mrs Edwards had said she was going to the dentist. The bill had been in the pocket of the Prada jacket Maggie had been told to take to the dry cleaners. When she had found the bill and handed it over, saying, 'I think this belongs to you, Mrs Edwards,' the woman had turned very red and very pouty. Careful, Maggie had wanted to warn her, we don't want to undo all the expensive work on that face of yours, do we?

The Edwards had only the one child. She had just turned fifteen, and as spoilt brats went, Valentina Edwards was right up there with the very worst. She was a monster. A mouthy madam. It was plain for anyone with a pair of eyes in their head to see that she took after her mother in almost every way. Whatever she asked for, she was given. Her latest demand, which Maggie had overheard two weeks ago, was for a pair of shoes for a party she had been invited to. And not any old shoes; she wanted a pair of Gina shoes as worn

4

by all the WAGS. They cost the best part of four hundred pounds. Maggie had heard her father, who was working from home that afternoon, say he was sure she already had plenty of perfectly good shoes in her wardrobe. Failing that, and seeing as they now had the same size feet, she had her mother's extensive shoe collection at her disposal, because as they both had to be aware, there was a recession on and he wasn't made of money.

Maggie had often heard Ethan try to be the voice of reason, but in this instance – unable to avoid hearing every word of the argument while she polished the granite work surfaces in the kitchen, but sadly not within viewing distance – he was being out-shouted from all sides. Mother and daughter had ganged up on him and accused him of being mean, of depriving a poor girl of a measly pair of shoes for a party. 'What next, Dad?' Valentina had screeched, probably with a toss of her Goldilocks long blonde hair. 'Will I have to stop having my legs and bikini line waxed because of some stupid recession?'

'Since when did you start having your legs waxed?' he'd asked.

'Oh, for heaven's sake, Ethan, she's been having them done since she was thirteen! If you took a bit more notice of your family, you'd know that.'

'Pardon me, I'm just trying to keep a business going so I can fund your waxing and God knows what else!'

'Now you're being petty.'

'And you're both treating me as a walking ATM.'

'Like, hel*lo*, can we stick to the point, Dad? Can I have the shoes, or what?'

The bare-arsed cheek of the girl!

As she lugged the vacuum cleaner upstairs, Maggie wondered why someone as nice as Ethan stood for it. Why didn't he just walk out of the door one morning, climb into his car and drive away for ever?

On the landing, she pushed open the door of Valentina's

bedroom. It was its usual pigsty mess: clothes, shoes, boots, tights, magazines, handbags, scarves, CDs and make-up tossed any old how. Thankfully Valentina wasn't around; she was next door with her friend Katie Paxton. For her sins, Maggie also cleaned for the Paxtons. They had moved into the avenue a year and a half ago and since then Mrs Paxton had become Mrs Edwards' best friend. The two women had a lot in common, both having been cut from the same cloth.

So whilst it was safe to say that Maggie knew quite a bit about her employers at The Lilacs, she was sure they knew absolutely nothing about her. They certainly would have no idea that every week, during her secret afternoon off, she would go to Kings Melford library and lose herself in a book. She had never told anyone about her afternoon off; it was her special time, the only time she had to herself. For three hours, when no one expected or demanded anything of her, she would sit in a comfortable chair and lose herself in a romantic novel – one of those bite-sized ones, as she called them. And as if carried away on a magic carpet, she could imagine being in another world and another life – a life of love and romance where candles flickered and hearts were always beating faster.

Of course she knew it wasn't real – she wasn't stupid – but where was the harm in wanting it to be real? Where was the harm in dreaming of a sexy hunk of a man who would hold her in his arms and tell her she was beautiful?

Because one thing was for sure: not in a million years was it going to cross Mr Blobby's gormless mind to do that!

She went over to the window and opened it to shake out the duster. A blast of freezing air hit her, and as she withdrew her hand and started to close the window, she heard a car coming down the avenue. She watched it slowly approach The Lilacs and when it was level the woman driving the car stopped it; she appeared to be checking if she had the right address. The car then turned onto the drive and stopped behind Maggie's Fiat Panda. Not wanting to be caught gawping, Maggie closed the window and stepped away. Less than a minute later the front doorbell rang, followed by the sound of Mrs Edwards' shoes on the limestone tiled floor of the hallway downstairs.

Chapter Two

First impressions are lasting ones and Ella Moore hated Mrs Edwards on sight.

Usually she gave her clients the benefit of the doubt, but one look at this particular client and Ella would sooner say the world had got it wrong about Hitler, that he had been a much-maligned and misunderstood man. There would be no misunderstanding this woman, however. Her first words to Ella when she had opened the door had been: 'You're late.' Ella had immediately apologized. She had explained that there had been a lot of traffic. An accident on the bypass. She was sorry. Very sorry. Mrs Edwards had tutted and given her a steely-eyed look as if to say: And what precisely does that have to do with me?

With the pleasantries out of the way, Ella was now following Mrs Edwards and her unfeasibly pert bottom – a bottom that was wrapped tightly in a pair of fuchsia-pink trousers – as it sashayed through the house, four-inch heels clicking on the limestone and beating out the message, *I'm the boss and don't you forget it*. Ella warned herself that if she took this job it would require a lot of tact, a lot of diplomacy and a heck of a lot of patience.

Much of the ground floor appeared to be showroom perfect; all was as neat and tidy as a polished new pin. Which meant it was a soulless homage to upscale concept living. Interestingly, there was no sign that Christmas had been embraced here – the decorations, if there had been any, had already been banished.

When the clicking of Mrs Edwards' heels fell silent, Ella found herself standing in the extra-wide doorway of a large dining room. A long marble table with twelve cream chairs around it dominated the space. A colossal glass vase of peonies stood in the middle of the table. As silk flowers went, they weren't bad. Beyond the table were French doors framed with gauzy muslin drapes, the bottoms of which lay artfully bunched on the pale oak floor – a design concept Ella had never thought much of. She was too practical and too pragmatic to approve of such wanton froufrou-ness. The glass doors opened onto a terrace and the garden. Ella's critical eye came to rest on what was the focal point of the garden for this particular room: a water feature. It was the ugliest water feature she had ever seen, and she had seen some sights in her time. This one was made of metal, all sharp angles and spiky protuberances. She couldn't be sure, but at a guess it might have been a modern twist on Botticelli's Venus rising from her shell. If it was, water was spouting from Venus's mouth in an arc of abject disgust into the pool beneath, a pool that vaguely resembled a shell. Poor Venus; what would she have thought to be thus paraded? At least she had been spared the indignity of water spurting from her breasts – two vicious spikes that could have an eye out no problem.

'It's quite something, isn't it?' Mrs Edwards said rhetorically, following Ella's gaze. 'Everyone always stops to stare at it. It's Botticelli's Venus. I had it placed there so it can be seen perfectly from this room. At night it's illuminated. The lights change colour, too.'

'Lovely,' murmured Ella.

'I bought it at Chelsea last year. I always go.'

'Lovely,' Ella murmured again, forcing a smile to her lips. She turned her attention to the room they were standing in. 'Now, what was it you had in mind exactly for here?' she asked. If the water feature was anything to go by, Lord only knew what horror she was in for. Yet, water feature aside, the little she had observed of the house so far wasn't too awful.

Okay, there were some over-splashes of decoration here and there, which she recognized as the folly of flicking through too many interior design magazines in search of inspirational latest trends, but at least the damage was minimal. In the course of her work as a decorative paint artist, she had encountered the weird and the wonderful many times over. A recent client had wanted her to turn the bedroom walls of his bachelor apartment into a scene out of a Bacchanalian orgy. Each to his own, she had thought.

The woman handed her a weighty magazine. A double-page spread revealed the interior of a large sun-filled room, the walls of which had been covered in fairytale castles, mountains and meandering streams. It was pure Disney schlock. It was also, according to the caption, the dining room of some Hollywood starlet Ella had never heard of.

'That's what I want,' Mrs Edwards said, pointing with an unnaturally long fingernail. 'I want just the same thing. Can you do it?'

In my sleep, thought Ella. But instead of answering, she gazed studiously at the walls, as if carefully assessing their potential. She went over and tapped the wall above the sideboard as though checking for its suitability, gave it a little pat and sweep of her hand for good measure. What she was doing in actual fact was gathering clues as to what kind of household The Lilacs was. With Mrs Edwards' rudeness, her pert little bum that probably had trouble filling out a pair of size eight trousers, her clickety-click heels and her suspiciously line-free complexion, Ella had a pretty good idea of the set up, but a silver-framed photograph on the sideboard next to a tray of cocktail glasses and a chrome shaker had the potential to tell her more. As she moved in closer to take a surreptitious look, a telephone rang from somewhere else in the house.

While Mrs Edwards went to deal with it, Ella made the most of the opportunity. Staring back at her from what was evidently a professionally taken photograph was a carefully posed Mrs Edwards with her head tilted over so that her sheer dark hair cascaded prettily from one side to give her an air of fragile coyness. It didn't fool Ella. The woman was as fragile as a wrecking ball. To her left and slightly in the foreground was a teenage girl who had adopted almost the same pose. Like mother, like daughter. No doubt about it. The only difference was that the daughter was blonde. Behind them stood a tall, dark-haired man. Presumably Mr Edwards. The husband. The father. Tanned and dressed in a pale pink, open-necked shirt, he was undeniably good looking. In Ella's experience any man who had the confidence to wear pale pink and was that attractive had to be a whole lot of trouble. The three of them together made an arresting-looking family unit. They would easily outshine most other families. Not that there was anything particularly sunny about their disposition.

From above came the distant sound of a vacuum cleaner starting up. Unless that was the daughter helpfully doing the chores for her mother upstairs, or the handsome hubby doing his bit, Mrs Edwards had a cleaner working for her. That would explain the rather battered old Fiat Panda Ella had parked behind on the drive. But of course a house of this size would have a cleaner. A full-time cleaner maybe. A gardener too. Any number of hired helpers. To which Ella was about to be added. She had no illusions as to how Mrs Edwards would treat her: she would be nothing more significant than a lowly tradesman, an outsider.

But Ella was used to that, and not just in a work capacity. For seven years she had been in a relationship that had ultimately crumbled to dust because of one indisputable fact: she was never going to be fully accepted. For one person in particular, she wasn't just an outsider, she was the enemy.

Stupid, stupid, *stupid* idiot that she had been, Ella had made the mistake of falling in love with a man who had been married before. Not just married, but widowed. She had learned the hard way that there was nothing more dangerous than a recently widowed man. Forget the threat of an ex-wife – a living ex-wife with whom you could openly engage in combat

– a dead wife is far more lethal. A dead wife never leaves the marriage; she's there for eternity, immortalized, sanctified, an untouchable, ruthlessly divisive meddling force. From the grave she constantly reminds her replacement that she can in no way make the grade.

The plain fact of the matter is there can be no substitute for wife number one. Not if she has had the misfortune to die tragically of breast cancer with her life all before her. Not if she heroically battled to the very end to fight the deadly disease because she simply could not bear to leave her beloved family. Not if she took up marathon running to raise money for the local hospice where she eventually lost her fight to stay alive.

Who could possibly compete with such a saint? Certainly not Ella. She had been informed of this the very first time Lawrence had taken her home to Mayfield and introduced Ella to his two children. 'They'll love you,' Lawrence had said when she had suggested it wouldn't do to rush things, after all, his wife – Abigail – had only been dead a year. 'They'll love you because I love you,' he had assured her. 'They'll want me to be happy, and you make me exceedingly happy.'

Imagining herself as a pink Mr Kipling fondant, Ella had gone along with his wishes. His son, Toby, who had been twelve at the time, had been reserved but polite with her. He had formally shaken her hand and smiled hesitantly. She knew from what Lawrence had told her that Toby was quiet and thoughtful, a shy, anxious child who felt things deeply. Ella had liked him on sight and had been overcome with the extraordinary desire to wrap him in her arms and tell him that she would make everything all right for him again.

A precociously bright girl, Alexis had been a different matter altogether. It was obvious, despite being only nine years old, that she had assumed the role of head of the household. After giving Ella no more than a cursory glance during that first uncomfortable introduction, she had started bossing her father around, informing him that he had forgotten to sign a form for school that morning, that they'd run out of washing powder, and had he remembered he'd promised to take her shopping for a new duvet cover for her bed? He'd *promised*, she reminded him. Promises were meant to be kept. She had said this so pointedly, staring straight at Ella and at the same time slipping her hand through her father's, that Ella could have sworn the girl was saying it specifically for her benefit: *My father made a promise to my mother, that he would always love her. Don't think for one moment he could love anyone else.*

It was when Lawrence had asked Alexis if she wanted to take Ella upstairs to see her bedroom – *big mistake, Lawrence; you should never have left her alone with me!* – that Alexis had seized her moment and made it very clear how things were. And how they were going to be. Sitting on her bed, Alexis had picked up the framed photograph of her mother from her bedside table and shown it to Ella. Then she had taken down a photograph album from a shelf and, flicking through the pages, she had revealed herself to be the official custodian of her mother's memory. Far worse than that, she was setting herself up to play the part of Mrs Danvers to Ella's second Mrs De Winter. 'You know, don't you, that Daddy loved Mummy very much, and still does,' she told Ella. 'He was always telling her he could never love anyone else. He won't ever love you. Not really. He'll only pretend he does.'

Quite possibly the girl had been right all along, because in the end, Lawrence hadn't put up much of a fight to make her stay. Perhaps he had been pretending to both her and himself that he loved her.

She was now thirty-eight and gone in a flash were seven years of her life. Gone too, in all likelihood, was the chance of her ever having a child of her own. There had never been any question of having a child with Lawrence – he had had a vasectomy after Alexis's first birthday, and who could blame him for that? – and he'd baulked at the suggestion of having the operation reversed. But if Ella was honest, it would have been irresponsible to introduce a defenceless baby into the household; it didn't bear thinking how Alexis would have reacted to it.

Finally enough was enough and Ella had thrown in the towel: she could not go on. She had shown almost as much strength of character and determination as Abigail had shown when fighting her battle against cancer. But the crucial difference in Ella's case was that the deadly disease threatening her life was Alexis. Ella had walked away alive, although there had been occasional moments when being buried six feet under had had its attractions.

She had left Lawrence six months ago and despite all her fighting talk that she was once more back in control of her life, and no more did she have to don the armour of compromise, it still hurt. You couldn't stop loving someone overnight; it took time for the sense of loss to lessen. It was the depth of her love for Lawrence that had made her try again and again to win Alexis round. Her friends and family had warned her that what she was taking on would not be easy. But love and her conviction that it always wins out played her for a fool and she was blinded by her unshakable belief that she had what it would take to mend Lawrence's broken heart and cure his children of their grief. For wasn't it grief and grief alone that caused Alexis's cruel treatment of her?

It hadn't only been Lawrence who had stolen her heart; Toby had as well. She could not have loved Toby any more had he been her own son. He had been a simple, straightforward joy in her life and she knew that she had helped him to recover from the loss of his mother. He was nineteen now, in his first year at Durham University and still very much a part of her life. He called and texted her regularly, shared jokes with her, confided in her and constantly wanted to know that she was all right since the split with his father. Always quick in her desire to reassure him but never wanting to patronize him by lying, it was a difficult balance to convince him that she was indeed all right.

She was meeting him this evening and was looking forward to catching up with him. She knew that he had been home at Mayfield for Christmas, then away with friends for New Year and now he was coming back for a few days before returning to Durham for the start of term. When he'd told Ella of his plans she had offered to fetch him from the station this evening and drive him to Mayfield. 'I can easily take a taxi,' he had said. 'And so you could,' she had countered, 'but it's always nicer to be met by a familiar face. Besides, it'll be nice to see you.' He'd agreed and not for the first time he had said his father was a fool to have screwed things up with her. Privately she agreed, but she would never ever criticize Lawrence to his children.

There had been something so vulnerable about Lawrence when she had met him. Just as she had longed to make the world a better and happier place for Toby when he'd been a young boy, so she had with Lawrence. That was her first big mistake according to her sister, who was not slow in expressing her opinions. Her next big mistake, according to Catherine, was to ignore the warning signs that had been so clearly laid out, warning signs that everyone else had seen except for Ella. *Trouble Ahead! Turn Back Now! NOW!*

But as ever, Ella had known best, her impulsive nature guiding her on. She had quashed the concerns of her family and friends and ploughed ahead, ever misguided that she knew what she was doing.

The assertive clickety-click, clickety-click of approaching heels – *I'm the boss and don't you forget it* – shook Ella out of her thoughts. To business. She had a potential client to impress.

'Well?' demanded Mrs Edwards, hands on sickeningly tiny hips. 'Can you do the job for me or not?'

Ella summoned her best ingratiating happy-to-do-your-bidding smile and said, 'I'd love to do it for you.'

Chapter Three

His face turned up to the powerful jets of punishingly hot water, Ethan Edwards stood in the shower trying to wash away the last hour.

It was the third of January and already he had crashed through the good intentions of his New Year's resolution.

No more women, he had promised himself. Which bit of that simple instruction did he not understand? he asked himself.

Why did he do it?

Because he could?

Because it was so easy?

No, it was none of those things. Absurdly he had thought it would be different, that this time it might be okay, that it might also mean something.

He had known straight away that the attractive woman wouldn't say no to him when he had invited her to join him for a drink in the bar of the hotel where they had both just checked in. Two drinks later, when her hand was brushing against his, he had known that she wouldn't refuse his next invitation. He asked to meet up with her the following afternoon, apologizing that that evening he would be busy with a client whom he had to wine and dine. There had been no pretence between them as to what he was inviting her to do and she had been more than happy to agree.

It really wasn't something that he dwelt on, and it was contrary to what people said of him, but he had only ever considered himself to be moderately good looking. However, over the years he had been frequently told that there was a strong sexual magnetism about him, the general consensus being that it was a result of the way he carried himself. Apparently he had a confident and naturally relaxed manner that put women at their ease. It was possible there was some truth in this theory because ever since he could remember, women had been attracted to him.

His very first experience with the opposite sex, and therefore one of the most memorable, had been a day before his fourteenth birthday. The girl, whom he'd fancied for some months, had been two years older than him and it had been an embarrassing débâcle; he hadn't a clue what he was doing and in less than three minutes it was all over.

Four months later he found himself being shown the ropes by a twenty-nine-year-old woman for whom he was doing weekend gardening work. Her name had been Lynette and in the beginning she had watched him from the kitchen window while he cut the lawn, dug over the flowerbeds, or did whatever task she had instructed him to do. Then one hot summer's day, when he was up a ladder hacking branches off a cherry tree, she crossed the lawn in her bare feet and brought him a glass of cider. She had asked if he would like her to teach him everything he would need to know to be the perfect lover. What fourteen-year-old boy would have turned down an offer like that? Life skills, she had called their lessons in bed together. 'I'm teaching you skills that will serve you well all your life,' she told him. 'Think of it as me teaching you to dance properly; a good dancer is never short of partners.' He supposed nowadays she would be put on the sex offenders' register.

He turned off the shower, grabbed a towel from the heated rail and did a quick mental calculation: he was forty-six years old, which would make Lynette sixty-one. Towelling himself dry, he wondered whether they would even recognize each other if they passed in the street now. Unlikely.

He used a corner of the towel to wipe the mirror above the

basin. All around the basin and lined up on the glass shelf were female toiletries and make-up. They were expensive brands, nothing cheap. He was reminded of his wife.

He looked at himself hard in the mirror. He was in relatively good shape; he hadn't started filling out or turned all jowly like so many men of his age. Nor was he losing his hair, or his teeth for that matter. Nose and ear hair was under control and the gathering lines around his eyes weren't too deep. His only real physical surrender to the passing of years was a smattering of grey hairs and the recent need for glasses, though he often alternated with contact lenses. He was careful what he ate these days – not too much red meat, not too much booze and he'd never smoked, so health-wise he was doing okay. Well, apart from the indigestion problems, which were definitely getting worse. But mentally he was in bad shape. Mentally he felt weary and jaded. Mentally he felt as if the best years of his life were behind him. They probably were. Which depressed the hell out of him.

From the other side of the door, he heard a voice calling for him. Oh, hell, he couldn't remember what the woman's name was. Jo, was that it?

Glasses.

Grey hair.

Bad memory.

What did that say? Nothing good. But there was another, far more insidious sign that maybe the years were not merely catching up with him but overtaking at a disturbing rate. Lately he'd started having a more worrying problem.

Kate? Was that it?

Whatever her name was, she hadn't been able to hide her disappointment at the way things had panned out in bed. He'd made light of his inability to climax, saying that it was more important to him to know that he had satisfied her. Which he had. Thanks to Lynette he had no trouble in finding the right buttons and knowing precisely how to press them. It was as easy as ABC.

He knew that any doctor would diagnose stress as the cause of what was going on. Or not going on, to be more accurate. But then he didn't need anyone to tell him he was under a lot of stress; he had it in shed loads. It was his constant companion these days. It was a miracle he could get up of a morning sometimes, he felt so weighed down by it. Not surprisingly, he was having problems sleeping, too.

Was it any wonder he couldn't remember that wretched woman's name? God, he was lucky to remember his own name!

The so-called experts kept talking about the green shoots of recovery, but the recession seemed a long way from coming to an end in his opinion. His business – Lamont Devereux Ltd – had taken a massive hit in the last year and all he could do was keep his head down and his hopes up in the belief that if he could just hold on and keep things ticking over, he would survive.

He'd been through tough times before. Back in the mid-nineties when the price of cotton had skyrocketed, it had been bloody awful. But by the skin of his teeth he'd survived. He'd ridden the storm out by switching from buying cloth from Italy for his bed linen and having it finished here in the UK, to using Portugal for the entire process. When things had got sticky again in 1999, he had moved production to the Far East. Now, of course, everything was produced in China. Along the way, he'd stayed the course so successfully he'd been able to scoop up some of his competitors when they'd failed to adapt to the rapid changes facing the industry. What he'd wanted when he'd bought them out had been their clients: the blue-chip prime accounts, such as Selfridges and House of Fraser.

However, right now, the heady days of plenty seemed like a distant memory. Orders were twenty-five per cent down on this time last year and the mid-range retailers were dropping like flies. He'd had to lay off two members of staff last month and he'd hated having to explain that he could no longer afford to pay them. There had been tears from both, but thankfully no recriminations. He had promised that when things picked up, he would be in touch; they would be his first port of call, no question.

But try telling his wife – and his daughter for that matter – that there was a recession on. Francine simply didn't have a clue. She had scorched-earth tendencies when it came to shopping. He felt like getting a T-shirt printed with the words: *We're going to hell in a handcart, but no worries, my wife will be wearing Prada when we get there!*

As far as Francine was concerned, the recession was something that affected other people. She seemed to think they were immune to what was going on in the world. How stupid would you have to be to think that? Yet Francine was far from stupid. She was shrewd and calculating and knew how to fight dirty. He knew from bitter experience just how dirty she could fight. The worst of it was he had only himself to blame. He should have been more careful. Or better still, not had that wretched affair. Well, he'd paid for it dearly, and would continue to do so for some time yet.

His name was being called again. The door handle jiggled, but the door didn't open; he'd locked it. He always did.

'You all right in there?'

'Won't be long,' he called out.

He put on his glasses, picked up his watch from the side of the basin, saw how late it was and hurriedly strapped it on. Time to bring matters to a close. He wrapped the towel around his waist and unlocked the door, smile firmly in place. He hoped to God she wasn't going to suggest they stay in touch.

The seven twenty-five Friday evening West Coast train from London was full and he was lucky to get a seat when it pulled out of Euston Station. He opened his laptop and prepared to spend the two-hour journey home to Cheshire checking the orders he'd landed. For small existing accounts, Ethan had a three-man team of agents who did the rounds of visiting the clients, but when it was one of the big accounts, he or Chris, his sales director, would make the visit and schmooze the client. He could have sent Chris for this particular client, but he'd decided to do the job himself; he'd felt the need to get away for twenty-four hours. Without his office to escape to it had been a long and torturous Christmas.

The orders that had been placed were disappointing, though. He had tried hard to squeeze more out of the client, but had held back from pushing too hard and offering too many concessions. It would have smacked of desperation and that was never a good approach.

But he *was* desperate. He was bloody desperate. He needed things to improve. And fast. Fearing just how bad things could get, he felt the by-now familiar burning sensation in his stomach. He winced and closed his eyes.

Chapter Four

If there was one thing guaranteed to make Ella furious it was a tailgating jackass. And if that jackass was the type who flashed his lights at her repeatedly whilst trying to engage the bumper of his tricked-out penis extension with the boot of her Toyota Rav for a mile and a half and then gave her the finger as he overtook on a dangerous bend, her dander was likely to be well and truly up.

It was thanks to this particular species of tailgating jackass that when she pulled into the station car park five minutes later, she misjudged the distance at the barrier and clipped her wing mirror with a loud and disagreeable clunk. She lowered her window, snatched the proffered ticket from the machine and swore with great feeling.

She parked next to a shiny black Mercedes, rattled off a silent prayer that the damage would be minimal, and got out to check what the jackass was responsible for making her do. She saw nothing irrational in blaming him for what had happened. Nothing whatsoever.

She was relieved to find that she needed to do nothing more than straighten the mirror back into place. Her mood, however, was not so easily straightened and as she locked the car and hitched her bag over her shoulder, she wished plague and pestilence on the jackass. Well, a flat tyre at the very least on his way home. But not if it meant anyone else would come to harm. Her well-behaved conscience wouldn't allow for a catastrophic pile-up.

She hadn't gone far when she saw the outline of a man

coming towards her in the dark. She slipped her hand inside her jacket pocket. Ever since last year when she had been mugged in a multi-storey car park in Manchester and had subsequently gone on a self-defence course, she was always alert to danger, always on her guard. In her current frame of mind, she was more than ready to defend herself. Yet as fast as she had reached for her weapon of choice she registered that the approaching man was smartly dressed, lugging a laptop bag and had another bag hooked over a shoulder. He was also talking on his mobile, his head nodding in that way all mobile users' heads nodded when they were deep in conversation and oblivious to their surroundings. She immediately dismissed any thought that he was a mugger and relaxed. But a sudden movement in the shadows to the man's right had her tense and alert again. As if in slow motion, she watched a hooded figure emerge from behind a van and pounce on the unwary man. There was a loud, startled cry and then the man went down. Ella didn't hesitate. She let out a bloodcurdling scream, sprinted like a rocket being fired and launched herself at the hooded figure. Having successfully taken him by surprise she jabbed him hard in the face with her keys. She then aimed a vicious kick at his shins. And another for good measure. Yelping like a wounded dog, he turned and hobbled away.

'You okay?' she asked the man as she helped him to his feet.

'I ... I think so. Thank you. Thank you for wading in like that.'

'It's what anyone would have done.'

He readjusted his glasses, which had become dislodged, and dusted himself down. 'I wouldn't be so sure about that. He had a knife, you know.'

'Yes,' she said matter of factly. She picked up his mobile phone from the ground and gave it to him. 'Do you want me to call the police?'

He looked about him. There was no sign of the hooded figure.

'No,' he said. 'What's the point? It could be ages before anyone gets here.'

'Up to you. By the way, you're bleeding. Quite a bit by the looks of things.' The collar of his white shirt was turning very red.

He put a hand to where she was indicating and it came away from his neck covered in blood.

'Here,' she said, after delving in her bag. She passed him a tissue from a small packet. 'Does it hurt?'

'Not really,' he replied with a shake of his head. She could see, even in the dark, that he looked pale and dazed. She could also see that he was extremely good looking. Strangely there was something familiar about him. He removed the tissue from his neck and looked at it; it was sodden with blood.

Worried, she said, 'Let me see. If that toe-rag has cut a vein, you need to get to hospital fast.'

He turned so that she could get a better look.

On closer inspection she could see that it was in fact his earlobe that was bleeding. 'It's your ear,' she said, 'so nothing too serious. I still think you should get yourself checked out.'

He shook his head. 'I'll survive.'

'It could have been a dirty knife. A tetanus shot might be a good idea.' She handed him another tissue.

He took it from her and managed a small smile. 'I bet you were a girl guide with an armful of badges, weren't you?'

'Wrong. I was kicked out after only two weeks for insubordination.'

'Insubordination?'

She laughed. 'You don't want to know. Now give me your bags and I'll help you to your car. You're sure you're okay to drive?'

'I'll be fine. And there's no need for you to help me to my car. My wounded pride is suffering enough as it is.'

'Don't be silly.' She took hold of his bags. 'Where are you parked?'

'Are you always this—' He broke off to dab at his ear again.

'Helpful?' she said, helpfully.

'Insistent, I was going to say. And please don't think I'm not enormously grateful that you were around in my hour of need. I am.'

'But you feel wrong-footed, is that it? Your masculinity has been called into question because the poor wee damsel saved the knight in shining armour?'

'Something like that, yes.'

'Then get over it.'

'Wow, you're very direct for a poor wee damsel.'

'Trust me, I'm at the top of my game when it comes to directness right now; it was one of my New Year's resolutions. Come on, where's your car?'

'Don't you have a train to catch? Or someone to meet?'

'I have a few minutes to spare before I'm due to pick someone up.'

'A husband?'

'No.'

'A boyfriend?'

'No.'

He came to a stop a few feet away from the shiny black Mercedes that only moments ago she had parked next to. 'This is my car,' he said.

'I'd figured that out for myself, since the other one is mine.'

He looked at her. 'What are the chances of that? My guardian angel parked right next to me?'

'I'd say it was spookily coincidental,' she said. 'Do you have your keys?'

He fished a bunch of keys out from his coat pocket. 'I can honestly manage from here on,' he said with a smile.

Once again Ella was struck by the nagging familiarity of him. Where on earth had she seen him before? 'Well, if you're sure you're all right, I'll leave you to it.' She gave him his bags conscious that Toby's train would be arriving any minute.

'If the circumstances were different, I'd offer to take you for a drink,' he said as he opened the rear passenger door of the estate car and stowed his things inside. 'As a way of saying thank you.'

'And I'd refuse on the grounds that you're a perfect stranger. But I'd dress up the refusal by saying I have someone to meet, so as not to hurt your feelings.'

He smiled again. He was looking a lot less dazed now. And rather too attractive for his own good. 'But at least you think I'm perfect,' he said.

And much too charming for your own good, she added mentally. He probably saw a green light with every half-decent woman he met. 'Two pieces of advice,' she said as she began walking away. 'One: never talk on your mobile when you're alone and in the dark; it makes you the perfect victim.'

'There's that word again: perfect. You've got my number straight off the bat.'

She ignored the interruption. 'And two: get a doctor to look at that ear of yours; you might need a couple of stitches. Goodbye.'

She was halfway across the car park when she heard a car behind her. It slowed and drew level; the window slid down.

'Is this totally emasculated knight in tarnished armour allowed to know the name of the poor wee damsel who may well have saved his life?'

Amused, she carried on walking. 'Don't you worry your pretty little head about my name. I'm sure you have plenty of other names with which to concern yourself.'

The car kept pace with her. 'No, really, I want to know. If it wasn't for you, who knows what may have happened to me?'

He was a trier, she had to give him that. 'Just call me the Dragon Slayer,' she said with a laugh.

*

With a tissue pressed to his ear, Ethan watched her go. If he was honest, he was still feeling a bit shaky. As muggings went, he had got off lightly. He'd had nothing stolen and had suffered nothing more serious than a cut ear, but it was what could have happened that really put the wind up him. A single thrust or slash of that knife and he could have been killed. It made him realize that if there was one thing he didn't want, it was to die before he was good and ready. There was still so much more he wanted to do with his life. So much more he wanted to get right.

But that woman had been amazing in what she had done. Had she stopped to think of her own safety? Probably not – it had all happened so quickly. She must have acted on instinct. Maybe she was always as impulsive. He liked that in a person. Perhaps because it was the way he'd always been.

He turned right to where the exit barrier was and after hunting through his pockets for his ticket, he inserted it into the machine; the barrier went up and he drove out onto the main road. Ahead of him he saw the Dragon Slayer, as she had called herself. She was crossing the road to the station entrance. For the first time he took in her appearance. She was tall with a long stride, which gave her an immensely purposeful manner. He could be wrong, but the way she was dressed implied that she was a person who didn't like to conform too much. She was wearing a red woolly hat pulled down tight over her head, with a red and purple striped scarf wrapped around her neck. She had on clumpy black boots, an above-the-knee black skirt and a purple corduroy jacket with large, over-sized red buttons. It was a colourful and in-dividual ensemble. Was it what they called Boho chic? Or was it Vintage? He didn't know. He didn't even know if there was a difference. What he did know was that it was the antithesis of the way his wife dressed.

As he waited for the traffic lights to change and watched the colourful figure disappear inside the station he contemplated what he was going to do in the morning. Whether she liked it or not, the Dragon Slayer was going to be thanked properly.

The lights turned to green and he pulled away. Just what had she meant by him having plenty of other names with which to concern himself? She had said it as if he had been coming on to her. Which he mostly certainly had not. She was not his sort. In fact she couldn't be further from the type of woman he normally went for. All he wanted to do was thank her.

Chapter Five

Bug-eyed and sprawled on the sofa, Mr Blobby was back from the pub.

With a fried egg sandwich in his hand and a dribble of egg yolk running down his chin as he channel-hopped at dizzying speed, he was in a world of his own, snorting and shouting at the telly, letting it know that there was nothing pigging on despite him pigging well paying through the pigging nose for a pigging load of pigging useless channels.

But that was all right because Maggie was also in her own world. She was on a tropical beach, lying on the hot white sand in the dappled shade of a coconut tree and her lover was telling her he couldn't live without her. Holding her tightly against his taut, muscular, tanned body, Miguel's eyes were dark and blazed with desire for her. His hands were gently caressing her like the waves of the warm ocean they had just swum in. 'I love you, Maggie,' he whispered huskily in his sexy foreign accent – she hadn't yet pinpointed exactly where he was from, but it was somewhere hot and dusty, one of those Latin American countries where he rode around on a horse, his ruffled white shirt open, his eyes squinting in the dazzling sun. 'Say you'll never leave me, my darling Maggie,' he begged her. 'Say you'll always be mine.' 'I will,' she replied breathlessly. 'I'll always be yours.'

'Yer what?'

Maggie leapt up guiltily from the hot white sand. She glanced over to the sofa where Mr Blobby had finished chomping on his egg sandwich and was now opening a can of Heineken: it frothed messily over his hand. Frowning at her, he let rip with one of his disgustingly loud belches. Whoever said a man couldn't do two things at once had never met Dave Storm. Frowning and belching at the same time, he had it down to a fine art, a real Master of the Universe.

'What did yer just say?' he asked after he'd licked the froth off his hand. See, there was no end to his talent.

'Nothing,' she murmured. She picked up the holiday brochure that had been lying on her lap unread for the past half hour and hid behind it. Clear blue skies and the promise of a week in the sun had whipped up Miguel from her imagination. But a cut-price package holiday to the Costas or some cheap Eastern European country where they were still digging bullets out of the walls, was a million miles from the dream she dared to dream. For a start her husband wouldn't be with her. There was no place for him in her dreams.

Daydreaming aloud, though – she would have to watch that. She could get herself into all sorts of trouble.

After a few minutes had passed, she cautiously lowered the brochure and peeped over the top of it at Dave. His attention was once more focused on the television; he had found something to his liking: *Ross Kemp on Gangs*. Great, the perfect cultural high spot for their Friday evening.

Not for the first time in the last year Maggie wondered how she had ended up married to a man who scarcely noticed her, never mind cared about her. When had she become invisible to him, other than when he wanted her to fetch and carry for him? And why, lately, had her mind become so disloyal and so badly behaved?

Everyone used to say she was an easy-going roll-up-her-sleeves-and-get-on-with-it kind of woman. True, she got on with things – what else were you supposed to do when the sink was blocked, the tea needed cooking and the washing basket was overflowing? – but the easy-going bit was way off the mark. It was an act. She had learned long ago to pretend that nothing bothered her. It was how she had dodged the shame of not being able to read and write.

When she was twenty-four, when Dean had started school, she decided to take the plunge and joined an adult literacy class. In the first lesson the teacher had explained that children and adults who can't read develop all sorts of coping strategies. She'd had no idea what the teacher had meant by that, but then he'd gone on to say that her pretending nothing bothered her was a coping strategy, a way of protecting herself. The teacher had then said that in reality everyone did it, everyone pretended all sorts of things; happiness was often the biggest pretence of the lot. Sitting here with Mr Blobby – he was now scratching the top of his head like a monkey – Maggie knew all about pretending she was happy. Her fear was that one day she would stop pretending. That was why she had made Don't Lose It one of her New Year's resolutions. She had to keep it in mind at all times.

A full-throated belch from the sofa made her wince. How she longed for just a little refinement from Dave. She wasn't talking la-di-dah fancy ways and talking all posh, but couldn't he just ...

Just what?

Change! She wanted to scream back at herself. Say it, Maggie! Speak the truth for once! Admit you want him to be a completely different man. A man who actually appreciates you. A man who doesn't belch and scratch his bum in public or poke about in his nose as if hunting for something he's stored up there for safe-keeping.

She thought of Mr Edwards at The Lilacs. Now there was a man who had impeccable manners. Charming, handsome and always polite, what a waste he was on that bitch of a wife of his. The woman just didn't appreciate what she had. Maggie knew what would shake her up – a week of walking in Maggie's shoes. Force her to live with Mr Blobby, just like on that *Wife Swap* programme, and within twenty-four hours she would be on her knees screaming to be allowed home, promising that she would never again criticize her husband or take him for granted. Never again would she lie to him or manipulate him.

What a belter of an idea she'd come up with! Maggie could hire out Mr Blobby as a way to prove to other wives just how lucky they were. Husbands like Mr Edwards would pay good money for that.

Like he was probably going to have to pay good money for Mrs Edwards' latest whim, having the dining room redecorated when there was nothing wrong with the way it was.

Hearing how Mrs Edwards had spoken this morning to the woman who was going to do the redecorating work, Maggie wouldn't have blamed her if she'd told Mrs Edwards where she could stick the job. But like most people in this world, she probably had a living to earn. Funny though, she didn't look like your average painter and decorator.

The ringing of the telephone put a stop to the flow of her thoughts and knowing there was about as much chance of Mr Blobby rousing himself from the sofa as there was of her imaginary sexy lover Miguel being on the other end of the phone, she went to answer it.

'Get us another beer on your way back, will yer, Mags?' Mr Blobby called after her.

It was Lou, Maggie's mum. 'You still on for bingo tomorrow evening?' she asked.

Every now and then Maggie joined Lou and her friends – The Sisters of Fun – for a night out. The Sisters were Betty Best, Pegs the Legs, Mo-Jo and Foxy-Loxy, otherwise known as Lou. They were all in their early sixties and took great pleasure in behaving as badly as they could at every opportunity they got.

An evening at the Plaza Bingo and Social Club wasn't Maggie's favourite form of entertainment but as her mother repeatedly told her, if she didn't do that she wouldn't go anywhere of an evening. 'Yes, I'm still up for it,' Maggie said. 'What time do you want me to meet you?'

'Seven o'clock. And wear something a bit more special than you usually do.'

'Why?' Maggie asked, trying not to feel narked by Lou's comment.

'It's Peggy's birthday. We're going dancing afterwards.'

Maggie knew perfectly well that 'dancing' was a euphemism for going on the pull. Peggy was her mother's oldest friend; they'd met more than forty years ago when they'd worked on the production line at a plastic moulding factory. As with the rest of the Sisters, a steady stream of husbands and boyfriends had come and gone like rainy days; the Sisters were constantly on the hunt for a new man in their lives. Peggy's last boyfriend – Ali the Turk – had been fifteen years younger than her; she'd met him on holiday in Istanbul where he'd been working as a waiter in the restaurant next door to the hotel she'd been staying in. The romance had gone from strength to strength until Ali had come to live with Peggy in Macclesfield and a month later she had discovered him in bed with next door's twenty-two-year-old daughter. He was packed off back to Turkey faster than you could say doner kebab. Despite the experience, Peggy said she still wanted a younger man, a bloke with a bit of go in him.

When Maggie came off the phone she heard Mr Blobby shouting for his beer. *Get it yourself, you idle skunk!* she answered back silently. She wondered if Peggy would be interested in taking him off her hands. Dave didn't have much go in him, but he did at least fit the bill of being younger.

She went into the kitchen for a face-off with the washing up. She could have cheerfully smashed the lot and taken it outside to the wheelie bin. Except the local Nazi council would take her to court for misuse of the bin.

No glass allowed.

No paper allowed.

No *tins allowed.*
And under no circumstances whatsoever, no china smashed
in a fit of desperation allowed.
Life was bloody unfair.

Chapter Six

A large five-bedroom Victorian semi-detached house a two-minute walk from Crantsford town centre, Mayfield had been Ella's home for seven years. However, it had never been a real home to her. How could it have been when Lawrence and his wife Abigail had bought it the year Toby was born?

On the other hand, her modest three-bedroom end-of-terrace Georgian house here in Kings Melford had felt like home to her from the day she moved in four months ago. When she had left Lawrence, her sister and brother-in-law had invited her to live with them in Derbyshire until she got herself sorted. As grateful as she was, she had decided to stay in Cheshire. Having built up a good business here she didn't feel she had the energy to start over somewhere else.

So after only two months of renting, she completed on the irresistibly named Tickle Cottage and set up home. She had now very nearly redecorated the entire house to her exacting taste. The only room she had yet to transform was her bedroom and that would have to wait until her neighbour, Phil, had made her some fitted wardrobes. She and Phil had worked together on many jobs in the past – he was a much-in-demand joiner – and it was he who had tipped her off that the owner of the house next door to his wanted to sell. By cutting out an estate agent, Ella and the vendor were able to come to an agreement over the price and as she was a cash buyer and there was no chain involved either end, the purchase went ahead without any hitches.

She was happy here. Surprisingly happy at times. Tickle

Cottage was the sort of welcoming house that wrapped itself around you when you stepped over the threshold. It was warm and cosy, like a hot buttered crumpet on a cold winter's day.

One of her abiding memories of when she moved in with Lawrence at Mayfield was the perishing cold. He and the children were immune to it, perfectly used to the Arctic temperatures caused by rattling windows that didn't fit properly and a boiler that was far too small for such a substantial house. It was also as fiendishly temperamental as Alexis.

Just as Ella had never won Alexis round, she had never grown accustomed to the cold. Nor had she ever made her mark on the house. If it had been hers, and if she had had the money, she would have taken that large, draughty house by the scruff of its Victorian neck and turned it into something truly beautiful, but whenever she had suggested making any changes – just little changes, such as a fresh lick of paint here and there – Alexis had been quick to accuse her of wanting to rid the house of her mother's beloved memory. Ella should have known from the start that this was how it was going to be. An obvious clue had been there in the hall the very first day she had visited Mayfield. Propped against a wall, with a tin of paint beside it, had been a ladder. Intriguingly they were both still there when she returned a week later. And still there several months later. It turned out that the ladder and the pot of paint had been there for nearly two years – Abigail had been about to paint the hall when she learned that the cancer that was slowly but surely destroying her had spread and she had to go into hospital. The ladder and pot of paint had never been moved since that day. Not until Ella caught her elbow on the ladder and brought it crashing to the ground. With no one around, she furiously consigned it to the garage and to hell with the repercussions. Predictably Alexis threw a tantrum when she came home from school and saw that it was gone. For once Lawrence backed Ella up, claiming safety had to come first. Alexis refused to speak to Ella for a week.

The only rooms Ella had been allowed to redecorate had

been her workroom in the basement and Toby's attic bedroom, and his had only come about because the roof had leaked and the existing woodchip wallpaper, which the previous owners had put up, peeled away from the wall beside his bed.

Right now, Saturday morning, Toby was asleep upstairs in Ella's spare room. Luckily his train had arrived a few minutes late last night and so she hadn't kept him waiting after the unexpected incident in the car park. She wondered how the man she had helped was feeling today.

When she had been mugged – her assailant had managed to snatch her handbag as well as give her a black eye and a subsequent dislike of multi-storey car parks – she had felt horribly violated the following day. She had been outraged, too. How dare that feral bastard do that to her! For about a month she was suddenly all in favour of capital punishment, even for the pettiest of crimes. Hang the bloody lot of 'em, she would mutter whenever she read or heard of someone being robbed in the street or attacked in the supposed safety of their own home. In time she reverted to her normal more reasoned and liberal-minded self, which advocated getting to the root of the problem.

Her breakfast made – tea, toast and marmalade – she sat at the kitchen table and read through the notes she had made yesterday whilst at The Lilacs. She would put together a quotation over the weekend and post it to Mrs Edwards first thing Monday morning. She had suggested emailing it, as she often did these days for her clients, but Mrs Edwards had made it very clear that she didn't sully herself with such a means of communication. 'You can post it to me,' she had said. 'Or better still, drop it off on Monday. And make sure you address it to me,' she had added.

Ella knew what that meant: Mr Edwards at this stage was to be kept in the dark about how much the work was going to cost. It was always a risk playing along with a client who wanted to do things this way, as there was a danger there would be quibbling later on when it was time for her fee to be fully paid. It was why she always asked for a hefty initial payment up front. If the client didn't agree to that, Ella wouldn't take the job. She was fortunate enough to be able to pick and choose. To a degree. After all, she did have to keep a roof over her head.

She hadn't set out to make a career of specialist paint finishing work, but as with so many things in life, she had drifted into it by accident. Having studied art and textile design at Manchester University she had got a job as a textile designer down in London working for Liberty. From there she went to work for a firm that she believed would give her more artistic freedom. For three years she couldn't have been happier, but then the firm went bust and suddenly she was in trouble, jobless with bills to pay, including the rent on a basement flat that she shared with a friend. One day her friend's well-heeled parents came to visit and when they saw the cheap second-hand bedroom furniture that Ella had bought and transformed by stripping and repainting in a cheerful blue and yellow Provençal style – that was the phase she was going through then – they immediately commissioned her to source and paint furniture for a farmhouse in Tuscany they were in the process of restoring. Ella couldn't believe her luck, especially when they said they wanted her to go to Tuscany to source the furniture and paint it in situ in their farmhouse. The commission didn't stop at furniture; she was later asked to decorate the entire house and from there other commissions came in from neighbouring Brits in the area, as well as some Italian neighbours. It had been an extraordinary turnaround; one minute she had been facing penury and the next she had landed a peach of a job. She had more money in the bank than she'd ever had and she was living a dream life.

She had been in Tuscany for two years when she met Lawrence. He was on a trip to the area to visit a vineyard and their paths crossed at the airport when she was on her way home to England to visit her sister, Catherine. He had caught her attention because he was a dead ringer for Colin

Firth. The resemblance was uncanny. The same strong jaw, the same chin, even the same slightly ruffled demeanour. They got talking at the check-in desk when they discovered they were on the same flight to Manchester and that it had been delayed by an hour and a half. After a moment's hesitation he asked if she would like to join him for a coffee to while away the time. By the time they were boarding the flight, he had explained that he had been widowed for a year, he had two children and lived in Crantsford, which was about an hour from where Catherine lived. She decided she liked him. She liked his hesitancy, the way he lowered his voice and appeared to choose his words with extra care. She liked his quiet subtlety. He looked and sounded more like a stereotypical college professor than a wine importer. Although, not having met any wine importers before, she wasn't really sure what one was supposed to look like. But Lawrence gave the impression of being bookish and thoughtful, a man who internalized strong feelings. He had sad eyes and unruly collar-length hair that needed cutting. He looked altogether in need of some tender loving care. What woman could resist?

They exchanged telephone numbers during the flight and two days later he called her. He sounded even less sure of himself on the phone, as if it had taken all of his courage to ring her. She had found herself trying to make it easier for him, oiling the wheels of their conversation by assuming an exaggerated air of cheerfulness. After a great deal of rambling around the houses, he had eventually asked her out for dinner. She had accepted happily.

She saw him three times during her ten-day stay with her sister and when it was time for her to return to Tuscany he drove her to the airport. It was there, just yards from where she had to go through passport control, that he kissed her for the first time. Up until then there had been nothing more than a shy peck on her cheek. But at the airport he kissed her very publicly and very surely. He held her tightly, as if he couldn't bear to let her go. She had felt deeply touched. It was then, wrapped in each other's arms, that they decided – despite the obvious difficulties of conducting a long-distance relationship – that they wanted to continue seeing each other.

Whenever Lawrence needed to visit one of his suppliers in Italy, which was about once a month, they would meet up and occasionally, work permitting, Ella would fly to England to see him. Most of their relationship was conducted by telephone or email and she didn't meet his children until eight months later, by which time she had fallen in love with Lawrence and he with her. He told her that he hadn't believed himself capable of finding anyone else who would make him as happy as his wife had, but Ella, he said, made him happier than he thought possible. He described himself as a broken man whom she had put back together again. Knowing that she had had such a powerful effect on him made Ella love Lawrence all the more. What more potent force in the world was there than knowing you were responsible for turning someone's life around?

A year after they had met, one hundred per cent certain that she was doing the right thing, regardless of the advice from her sister and parents, Ella gave up her life in Tuscany and returned to England to be with the man she loved. She didn't delude herself that it was going to be plain sailing taking on Lawrence's children, but the challenge appealed to her.

She had never been afraid to take a leap of faith, but this particular leap proved too much for her in the end. She wasn't a quitter by nature and it still rankled that she had failed. What bothered her most – and she had never dared utter such a guilty confession – was being forced to accept that Alexis, a child, had got the better of her.

Forgiving Alexis was one of her New Year's resolutions. It would not be easy. The girl, sixteen years old now, had caused Ella the kind of bitter heartbreak that would take a long time to recover from. But Ella knew that the only way to put Lawrence truly behind her was to forgive Alexis for sabotaging their relationship. The wretched girl had done it systematically from day one, pitting herself against Ella in the full knowledge that Ella couldn't fight back. How could she reprimand the girl for bursting into tears whenever Lawrence so much as put his arm around Ella? How could she tell the girl that her father had moved on, that he had a new love in his life now? No, Alexis had cast her in the role of wicked stepmother and there hadn't been a damned thing Ella could do to change things.

But she wouldn't make that mistake again. Which was why her second New Year's resolution was that her head had to rule over her heart. Never again would she invest herself in a relationship that had disaster written all over it.

Being direct – as she had told that man last night – was her third resolution. It came under the heading of Spades and Shovels. From now on she would speak her mind. She would be forthright and candid. There would be no more tiptoeing round any important issues.

When Toby finally surfaced – hair tousled, face crumpled, chin unshaven and stomach rumbling – Ella fed him scrambled eggs on toast followed by a large piece of Marks and Spencer Christmas cake. When he'd finished eating he helped put away her Christmas decorations in the loft and then she drove him home to Crantsford.

'So what's new chez Mayfield?' she asked him. Last night he hadn't said a word about his father or sister, even when she had prompted him as to how Christmas had gone. Instead he had talked about his new life at university; he was clearly enjoying himself with a whole new circle of friends and interests.

'Do you really want to know?' Toby asked after not replying straight away. 'Or are you just being polite?'

'A bit of both, she said, turning briefly to look at him. He was the spitting image of his father. Only slightly bigger. At six feet two inches, he had the strong, muscular physique of an athlete in his prime, which of course, at nineteen, he was.

He had taken up rowing when he'd been in the sixth form at school and had continued the sport at Durham. He had been picked to row for his college and was training every morning at some unearthly hour. She could see that his shoulders and chest had noticeably broadened since she had last seen him.

'I wasn't going to tell you, but Dad's started seeing someone new.'

'Someone new? What happened to ... to what's her name? The one with the fox terrier?'

'It was a Jack Russell and it bit Alexis.'

Ella kept her gaze fixed on the road ahead and the car she was following; she didn't want Toby to read her expression. *Did it bite Alexis very hard? Please say it did.*

'I know what you're thinking,' he said with a laugh. 'The dog had discerning taste.'

'I was thinking no such thing.'

'You're a terrible liar, Ella.'

She couldn't help but laugh with him. 'Okay, so exit stage left Ms Jack Russell. Who's replaced her?'

'For a couple of weeks he saw a woman whose name I can't remember and then there was some woman called Debbie. Now there's a Sue on the scene.'

'That's quite a rapid turnaround in girlfriends in six months. What's he done, joined a dating agency?'

'That's what I said to him. He says he hasn't.'

'However he's meeting all these women, he's certainly not letting the grass grow under his feet.'

'He's being an idiot. He's trying to convince himself he can easily replace you.'

'You can't blame him for trying. It's what most people do – a few rebound relationships to get back in the game.'

They drove on in silence. When Ella stopped at the traffic lights in Crantsford by the dental practice where she was still on the patient list, Toby broke the silence. 'How about you?' he asked. 'Have you met anyone? To get back in the ... game?' he added after the smallest of hesitations. Thoughtful hesitation was something else he had in common with his father.

Again she laughed. 'When would I have time to meet anyone? More to the point, where would I meet anyone? Anyway, I'm a lost cause.'

'No, you're not. But I think it's good that you're not rushing into a string of meaningless relationships like Dad. He's the biggest fool going right now.'

'Don't say that. And for the record, when I used the word "game" I wasn't trivializing the relationship I had with your father. How's your sister coping with all these new girlfriends?'

'How do you think? She hates them all.'

Ella might have expected the opposite from Alexis, spitefully greeting any replacement of Ella with open arms. But apparently not. Alexis wanted her father to herself; anyone who might threaten that was going to be considered the enemy and would be treated accordingly. She should have grown out of this behaviour by now. It was dangerously destructive. To Alexis most of all.

When Ella had arranged to collect Toby at the station last night he had told her that his father and Alexis had gone to Norfolk for New Year to stay with Lawrence's parents. She had hoped they wouldn't have arrived back yet, but as she pulled onto the drive she saw that she was out of luck: Lawrence's car was in front of the garage. Through the sitting room window she could see fairy lights twinkling on the Christmas tree.

'You'll come in, won't you?' Toby said, already opening the door to get out.

Her heart sank. To refuse would make her seem petty and cowardly. 'Just for a few minutes,' she said with forced brightness. 'Just to say Happy New Year.'

Chapter Seven

Ella could not believe it.

Mayfield had undergone a makeover. Or at least a partial makeover. The hall, the sitting room and kitchen had all been redecorated. But not very well. Quite badly, in fact. There was some new furniture, too, although some of the worst offenders were still occupying the same position they always had. The standard lamp with the purple dented shade that she had longed to take to the tip from the very first moment she had set eyes on it had survived the purge and was currently adorned with a few straggly lengths of Christmas tinsel. The two ugly armchairs with the wooden armrests had also been spared. But the threadbare brown corduroy-covered sofa had gone, as had the wrought iron coffee table with the Spanish-style tiled insert. In their place was a black leather sofa and a sleek glass table. The floor-to-ceiling Formica white book shelves, laden so heavily they had sagged hazardously in the middle, had also been replaced with a combination of Billy bookcases. As implausible as it was, it looked very like Lawrence, aeons after everyone else, had discovered IKEA. Gone too was the Sanderson wallpaper with all its overblown pink and cream roses. The walls were now a cold shade of mint green. As if the temperature and atmosphere needed making any chillier.

Abigail had been responsible for decorating and furnishing Mayfield and it had to be said, even if it was wrong to criticize the dead, especially a sainted dead wife, her taste had been questionable if not downright criminal. She had been one of those vegetarian bohemian types, lots of nut roasts and eco-friendly credentials, who rummaged through car boot sales and junk shops looking for a 'find'. Ella had no problem with junk shops – they had served her well over the years – but the point was you had to disregard the junk and discover the 'find'.

Abigail had excelled in picking out the dross with an unerring eye. Mayfield had been full of the stuff – clumping great wardrobes and dressing tables upstairs, a rickety coat stand and a gruesome commode in the hall, a wicker basket chair and a patchwork leather pouffe from India with the stuffing oozing out of it in the conservatory, and in the dining room an oversized 1930s table surrounded by half a dozen mismatched chairs from the sixties and seventies. As she and Toby had passed the open door of the dining room a few seconds ago, Ella had noted that the hideously cumbersome sideboard with the missing leg was still lopsided and was still propped up by two bricks.

The inexcusable mishmash was a proud testament to Abigail's appalling taste. Or rather it had been. Now it was an even worse mix of atrocious bad taste. Shabby junk shop tat and shiny new flat-packed IKEA did not combine well. It curdled badly. Eclectic was all very well, but you had to do it with a firm hand on the tiller. A careless slip and you ended up with a mess like this.

'Do you like what we've done, Ella?'

The question was from Alexis. They were in the kitchen where Lawrence was doing an impressive job of making coffee whilst avoiding any eye contact with Ella. But then he had mastered that pretty well in the days and weeks before she left him, in the days and weeks before either of them had the courage to say what they were really thinking.

'It's great,' Ella managed to say, taking in the walls – one end of the kitchen was a sickly shade of yellow and the other was a vicious lime green. The two colours could not have clashed with more jarring clarity. 'It's very colourful,' she added. 'What made you do it?' This she had to hear. In her futile attempt to try and instigate just the smallest of changes, and in the face of what she was now seeing, she felt as if she had wasted every single one of the days she had devoted to this family. A kick in the teeth. A slap in the face. It was there in every brushstroke of paint on the walls.

Alexis went over to her father and put her arm around him; she rested her head against his shoulder. 'We decided it was time for a change. Didn't we, Dad?'

He smiled indulgently at his daughter. 'That's right,' he said. 'We decided it was high time we got ourselves shipshape.' He went back to pouring the coffee, his eyes still not making contact with Ella.

Having taken his rucksack upstairs to his room, Toby re-appeared. 'You've changed my bedroom,' he said. He sounded annoyed. He certainly looked annoyed. His brow was drawn and his jaw was squared. 'Why?'

Alexis tutted as if he was the stupidest of simpletons. '*Durr*. Why do you think? Because it needed doing.'

'No it didn't. When did you do it?'

'The decorators came yesterday when we were at Nana's. I chose the colour. Do you like it? It's called Perfectly Taupe.'

'You mean it's perfectly awful, and no I don't like it. I liked the colour it was before. Why couldn't you leave well alone? Is it because Ella painted it? Is that it?'

Everyone looked at Ella, as if suddenly remembering she was still there. Even Lawrence stared at her. For all of two seconds. 'Coffee's ready,' he said quietly.

Ella drove back to Tickle Cottage thoroughly out of sorts. So much for her New Year's resolution to start thinking well of Alexis. Forgiveness felt a long, long way off.

She had been at home for no more than a few minutes when there was a ring at the doorbell. From the window she could see a small florist's van parked outside. She opened the door. A woman was holding an extravagantly large bouquet of flowers. 'Are they for one of my neighbours?' Ella asked, assuming the woman needed her to take them in for safekeeping.

'The address is for Tickle Cottage,' the woman said. 'This is Tickle Cottage, isn't it?'

'Yes.'

'Then the flowers are for you. Lucky you.'

Ella took the bouquet through to the kitchen. Curious, she opened the small envelope that was stuck to the cellophane and read the card.

> *To the Dragon Slayer,*
> *Thank you for coming to my aid last night.*
> *From a very grateful,*
> *if slightly inept, knight.*

She smiled. What a lovely thought. But hang on. How did he know where to send the flowers?

Chapter Eight

Ethan had the feeling that if Adam Paxton could have found a way to do it and not look a total prat, he would have donned his sunglasses – despite the dark – climbed into his car and driven the short distance from next door so as to show off his latest purchase, a mighty gas-guzzling Range Rover. The way he was going on and on, you'd think he'd just invented the motor car. What he'd actually done was blow nearly seventy grand on something that in Ethan's opinion had all the aesthetic appeal of a breadbin on wheels. If he could get a word in edgeways, it was on the tip of his tongue to trot out the old joke: What's the difference between a Range Rover and a hedgehog? Answer: The hedgehog has pricks on the outside and the Range Rover has them inside!

But there was no chance of getting a word in edgeways; the man was determined to bore Ethan to death by giving him a mind-numbingly tedious blow-by-blow account of every feature. If Ethan had heard once about the supercharged V8 engine, he'd heard it a hundred times. And for the record, the man *was* a total, gold-plated prat. A pretentious arse who was currently necking glass after glass of expensive wine that Ethan could ill-afford and which he hoped might choke the man.

As usual it had been Francine's idea to invite the Paxtons for dinner and as usual she had spent as much on food and wine as a small country would allocate for its defence budget. If he were to suggest she cut back and shopped at Lidl or Aldi, the shock would probably kill her.

And as usual during one of these horrendous evenings, whilst Francine was giving herself a nervous breakdown in the kitchen assembling plates of damned-near-raw guilt-free, dolphin-friendly, sustainable tuna and falafel, it was Ethan's job to make polite conversation with two people he couldn't abide. Frankly, he'd swap roles with Francine any time. What's more, he'd cook the bloody tuna properly while he was about it!

He had never been able to make up his mind which of the Paxtons he disliked the most – Adam with his excruciating pretensions or Christine with her brazen insincerity.

Since moving in next door, Christine had become Francine's new best friend, but what kind of friend came on to her best friend's husband? She had done it more times than he cared to remember and it went without saying he had never once taken Christine up on any of the offers she had made.

Point taken that he was in no position to take the moral high ground, but even he knew better than to play around on his own doorstep. Quite apart from that, he wasn't so desperate that he would go to bed with a woman he so thoroughly despised.

Once or twice he had wondered if he was being set up. He wouldn't put it past Francine to ask Christine to act as bait to test whether he was being faithful to her or not. However, something in the way Christine's eyes were always making contact with his and the way she frequently and blatantly pressed a part of her body against his, made him think she was acting off her own bat. On one occasion he had actually considered telling Francine just how phoney her so-called best friend was but when he thought of the potential fall-out he decided to keep his mouth shut. There was also the matter of Katie Paxton being Valentina's best friend. They were out together tonight, at a party. God only knew what they would be getting up to.

From the day she was born, Ethan had done his best to protect his daughter and to arm her with sufficient common sense to deal with the big bad world, but he suspected she thought she knew the world far better than he did. It didn't seem that long ago when she had idolized him, when she had only to look at him and he felt a great tender love for her. But somewhere along the line that had gone. Now, when she bothered to let her gaze fall upon him, she looked at him with withering disdain. It was not a happy admission, but the sad truth was, she was too much her mother's daughter. Not to mention Francine's mother's spoiled granddaughter. It was all in the genes and Ethan knew when he was fighting a losing battle. He knew and accepted he was no match for them. Put those three generations of women together and they were an unassailable force. The government should stop messing about; they should bring home the troops from Afghanistan and deploy Francine, Shirley and Valentina to sort out the rebel forces. Within twenty-four hours those hardened fighters would be throwing down their rocket launchers and begging for mercy. World peace would be assured.

Ethan put his wine glass to his lips and took a mouthful, vaguely conscious that the soundtrack of Adam banging on about, well, essentially Adam with a bit more Adam tossed in, was not showing any sign of fading out.

He had always suspected that Adam's one-upmanship stemmed from the simple fact that The Lilacs was bigger than his own house. As a consequence Adam's every action and word suggested that he had to out-car, out-earn, out-gizmo or out-holiday Ethan. It was laughable. Ethan wasn't in the business of needing to out-do anyone. He didn't give a damn who earned the most, although almost certainly given the current state of things, it was Adam who was easily out in front, because lucky old Adam seemed to be totally unaffected by the financial crisis.

Whereas thanks to those bankers – or something that rhymed with it – and their ilk in the States who'd kicked the whole thing off with their bloody sub-prime mortgages, and thanks to the thieving bastards here who'd run the banks with as much sense as a bunch of alcoholics running an off-licence and had then walked away with sodding great bonuses – and get this: those crooks had walked away with the government's blessing – so yes, thanks to the lot of them, Ethan was up the proverbial creek without a boat, never mind a paddle! It was mad. Bloody mad. What, he wanted to know, had happened to good old-fashioned accountability? But hadn't it been ever thus? Those in power were seldom held to account. Seldom did they pay for the consequences of their power-hungry actions. No, the consequences were left to the likes of Ethan to cope with whilst those dishonourable twats in Westminster got off scot-free.

But lucky old Adam was riding high on the crest of the wave. Apparently he'd never been busier. He was an actuary, which had to be one of the dullest jobs going. Let's face it: anyone who compiled and analysed statistics in order to calculate insurance risks and premiums for a living was never going to be that interesting a guy. So let Adam think he was the mutt's nuts. Let him gloat over his new Range Rover if it was that important to him, if it made him feel more of a man. The only thing that Ethan cared about was survival. Oh, and being happy. If he could just know a moment's genuine happiness now and then, that would do for him.

He took another mouthful of wine, then put his glass down. As tempting as it was to drink himself into oblivion whenever he was unfortunate enough to be in the company of his neighbours, Ethan's golden rule was to do the opposite, to keep his alcohol intake deliberately low. He feared an excess of wine would loosen his tongue and he would blurt out what he really thought of them.

'I still think you should have gone to the police, Ethan.'

Ethan raised his eyes from his plate of half-eaten food – the tuna may have come from a sustainable and dolphin-friendly source but it was playing merry hell with his stomach. He doubted he'd be able to force much more down, which would annoy the hell out of Francine – *Well, thank you very much!*

I slave away in the kitchen for hours on end only for you not to touch any of it!

God, what he'd give to escape the boredom. Except of course he wouldn't. People always said things like, 'I'd give anything for a nice cup of tea,' or 'I'd do anything for a bit of peace and quiet,' but no one ever meant it. Challenge someone to hand over their house and all their worldly possessions in exchange for a cup of tea and just see what reaction you got. Nobody ever meant what they said. It was all meaningless nonsense. Just like this evening. He breathed in and out very deeply. He felt like he was trapped in a vacuum, suffocating.

'Ethan?'

Oh, God, somebody half a century ago had said something to him, hadn't they? He mentally shook himself into a semi-conscious state and tried to look alert. Tried to remember who it was who had spoken. But the task was beyond him. 'I'm sorry,' he said to no one in particular, 'I was miles away.'

'I'm not surprised,' said Christine. 'You're probably still in shock from your awful ordeal last night.' She smiled at him through the candlelight across the table. 'But Francine's right; you should have gone to the police.'

He automatically put a hand to his ear, the lobe of which was covered with a dressing. 'I'd hardly describe it as an ordeal,' he replied.

'Oh, listen to him! He's so brave.'

Adam laughed loudly. 'Come off it, Christine, I'd hardly call it brave being rescued by a woman!'

'Honestly, Adam, you're so mean to poor Ethan. Ignore him, Ethan. I for one am very grateful that woman helped you. And I bet you are too, aren't you, Francine?'

'Of course.'

Ethan felt the full force of his wife's deadly gaze homing in on his plate. She was probably thinking she'd cut both his ears off if he didn't hurry up and finish eating the fruits of her labour. He noticed that everyone else's plate was empty, knives and forks neatly placed. He forced another mouthful down, then made his apologies. 'I'm sorry,' he said. 'I don't seem to have much of an appetite this evening.'

'Perhaps some exercise would help,' Francine said with the sort of acerbic edge that made caustic sarcasm pass for cute and cuddly. 'You can take the plates out to the kitchen. But don't put them in the dishwasher; it's the best china. Put them to soak in the sink and you can wash them later.' She pointedly handed him her plate.

There, that would teach him for not eating up like a good boy.

'Here, let me help.' Christine had leapt from her chair before Ethan was even on his feet.

Great, he thought. Just what he needed: a farcical Benny Hill-style chase round the domestic appliances.

In the kitchen, Ethan busied himself with filling the sink with hot water. But there was no ignoring Christine. Her hands were on his shoulders. 'You feel so tense, Ethan. Is there anything I can do to help you?'

'You could pass me that plate from over there, please.'

She laughed. 'I wasn't thinking of that kind of help. I was thinking more along the lines of something a lot more fun. Something to put a smile on that serious face of yours tonight.'

'Um ... nothing springs to mind.'

Another laugh. She moved her hands down his back, then round to his chest. She sighed and rested her head against his shoulder. He smelt her cloying perfume and felt her nails digging into his flesh. He stopped what he was doing. Enough. He shrugged her off and turned round. 'Look, Christine, I really think you should stop this.'

She tilted her head back in the classic you-can-kiss-me-if-you-like position, lips parted, the lids of her heavily made up eyes slightly lowered. 'You don't mean that,' she said softly. I've seen the way you look at me. I know you want me; it's just that you're scared of Francine finding out. But I promise you she won't. I'll be the soul of discretion.'

'Stop it, Christine.'

'You know as well as I do there's always been something special between us.'

'You're wrong,' he said firmly. 'In fact you couldn't be more wrong. Now, please, go back and join the others.'

She stared at him, her eyes wide now. Very slowly she straightened her back, tipped her chin up. 'You're making a big mistake.'

'Not as big as the one you're trying to force me to make.'

Her expression hardened and she stepped away from him. 'Don't you believe it.'

'I'll take my chances.'

It was while they were having coffee in the sitting room and Adam was sharing with them how his mother's will had finally been sorted – she had died more than ten months ago – and that he and Christine were now faced with the awesomely thorny dilemma of where to invest their newfound dosh: a second home in Spain on one of those upmarket golf complexes or a place nearer to home. *Abroad!* Ethan wanted to shout. *Iraq! Afghanistan! Somewhere where there's a strong likelihood of you both being blown to smithereens!* Surely there had to be a golf complex in at least one war-torn country in the world?

Then as if she needed to get in on the act, Francine said, 'Guess what! We're having the dining room redecorated.' Even to Ethan's ears this sounded pretty small potatoes compared to a villa on an upmarket golf complex, with or without the gunfire. But redecorating was news to him. He wisely kept his mouth shut.

'Really?' responded Christine, who amazingly hadn't broken stride since their exchange in the kitchen. 'What are you having done?'

'I've found this amazing decorator. She's a specialist painter and is going to—' Francine broke off and put down her cup and saucer. 'I'll show you exactly what she's going to do.'

Disappearing out of the room, she reappeared within seconds with a magazine in her hands. 'Look,' she said, showing it to Christine and Adam. 'This is what I'm having done.'

Ethan couldn't stop himself. 'Don't you mean, what *we're* having done?'

Francine gave him a cool look. 'Darling, since when have you been interested in how the house is decorated?'

Since you became hell-bent on spending more than I earn, he wanted to say. But again he kept his mouth shut. It wasn't the time or place to have yet another argument over money. The world could stop spinning, but here at The Lilacs one had to pretend that all was well. They had a position and reputation to uphold, after all. 'Can I see?' he said, reaching for the magazine. His eyes nearly popped out of their sockets. Holy hell, how much was that going to cost him?

In bed later, his hands folded behind his head as he lay on his back, watching Francine at her dressing table removing her jewellery and putting it carefully away in their original velvet boxes, he said, 'When did you decide to change the dining room?'

She shrugged. 'I'd been thinking of doing it for a while, then I saw that article in the magazine. You'll love it when it's done.'

'And how much will it cost?'

'Oh, don't start. I knew this was how you'd react so that's why I kept quiet about it.'

'You don't think I have a right to know?'

'I was waiting until the moment was right.'

'And that was tonight, in front of Adam and Christine?'

She snapped the last of the jewellery boxes shut and stood up. 'No, it just slipped out. I wanted to wait until I'd received the quote before I told you.'

'So we're not committed at this stage?'

She eyed him warningly. 'Don't even think about it.'

'Oh, go ahead, why don't you? Bankrupt us completely.'

She shot him one last look and then flounced out of the bedroom to her dressing room and bathroom.

He stared up at the ceiling. *Flounce all you like, Francine, but it won't keep us afloat when HMS Recession takes us down with all hands.*

He squeezed his eyes shut as the acid in his stomach made another assault on his insides. He waited for the pain to subside. What the hell would Francine do if everything tanked? If he lost the lot?

It was the wrong line of thought to pursue. His stomach burned ever more fiercely. He dragged himself out of bed and went to his bathroom. He opened the cabinet and stared at the array of medicine. He picked the bottle that contained the strongest and fastest-acting remedy and measured out the recommended dosage. Replacing the bottle in the cabinet, he stared at himself in the mirror, in particular the dressing on his ear. Tomorrow he'd change it, as he'd been instructed. He hadn't wanted to go to A and E but when he'd driven away from the station, the flow of blood had shown no sign of stopping and so reluctantly he'd made a detour. He had been lucky in that he was seen relatively quickly – it had been too early in the evening for the drunken louts to roll in – and a young junior doctor had sewn his ear up with a couple of stitches. 'You did the right thing in coming in,' the doctor had joked. 'I need all the practice I can get when it comes to needlework. And tell you what, we'll do a tetanus shot while we're about it, to be on the safe side.' He had driven home thinking about the woman who had saved him from having more than his ear cut: the Dragon Slayer.

He wondered now, as he got back into bed, if she had received the flowers he had sent. He shouldn't really have spent so much money on them, but he wanted to show her that he was grateful for what she had done. He had thought about putting his email address or mobile number on the card so that she would ring him and thereby give him the opportunity to thank her again verbally. But he had decided against it.

It would give her the wrong idea. And she really wasn't his sort – woolly hats and clompy boots were definitely not his thing. He liked something more feminine. Something curvy and sensual.

Apart from anything else, he wanted to stick to his New Year's resolution. That slip down in London was to be his last. From now on, there would be no more women to alleviate the boredom and frustration of his passionless marriage. From now on, there would be no energy wasted in covering his extra-marital tracks. He had made his bed and as disastrous as it was, he had to lie in it. Better to immerse himself in saving his business from going into freefall than to waste time and energy on anything so risky.

He'd just turned out his bedside light when Francine reappeared. Straight away he saw that she was dressed for sex – short, transparent black negligee, the hem of which was edged with velvet, hair brushed and perfume freshly applied. Sex had always been her answer to any disagreement between them. It was her way of winning him over. There had been a time when it had worked, but now there was only one thought going through his head. 'Is that new?' he asked, staring hard at the negligee as she got into bed beside him.

'I've had for it ages, silly.' Her voice was light and playful.

He didn't believe her.

She pushed the duvet back and slid on top of him. He used to be able to do sex to order, any time, any place. Now he couldn't.

It soon became apparent to Francine that her efforts were in vain. She rolled off him with a sulky pout. 'I suppose you're still cross with me,' she said.

No, thought, Ethan, I'm cross with myself. I have been for years.

Chapter Nine

The last week had flown by and once again Maggie was back at The Lilacs.

As was that woman who was going to do the decorating work in the dining room. She was downstairs with Mrs Edwards, being instructed on the dos and don'ts of life at The Lilacs. Turning up late was definitely a no-no.

Maggie knew all about that. She had arrived twenty-five minutes late this morning. It had snowed in the night and there'd been chaos on the icy roads, cars skidding about all over the place. More snow was on the cards for later tonight. The weather people on the telly and radio kept talking about the Arctic temperatures that they were in for, but Maggie had news for them: even with global flipping warming, it was nowhere near as cold here as it was in the Arctic. Maggie hated it when people exaggerated. Or when they couldn't see sense when it was staring them in the face.

Take Mr Blobby for example. *Oh, please, somebody take him!* He had admitted at breakfast this morning that the new DVD player he'd got so cheaply – the one that had gone on the blink within two days – had come from a bloke at the pub and Maggie wasn't to tell anyone. How dumb would you have to be to buy a cheap DVD player from a bloke in the pub? As dumb as Mr Blobby, she supposed.

Mrs Edwards had given Maggie one of her foul looks earlier when she'd finally made it through the snow to The Lilacs. Which was a miracle in itself. With the amount of Botox Mrs Edwards was having pumped into her face, the woman was lucky she could pull any kind of a face. Perhaps Maggie should suggest that she go to Poland with The Sisters of Fun.

The big news last Saturday night when Maggie had been at the bingo with Mum and her friends was Mo announcing that she was treating herself to a face-lift and a tummy tuck. She'd found a clinic in Poland on the internet and wanted the rest of the gang to go with her and have something done as well. She was probably thinking safety in numbers.

For the rest of the night the discussion had been about what work they'd have done. Peggy had joked that in her case it would take more than a tummy tuck to sort out her jelly-belly, but Betty, the more cautious of the group, asked Mo if she had done her research about the clinic. What about the risks? What if something went wrong? Betty had taken the words right out of Maggie's mouth. Mo said she'd sooner trust a Polish doctor with a knife in his hand than a slapdash, half-asleep doctor here. But as Peggy pointed out, doctors doing private work here and coining it in weren't the ones who were overworked and half-asleep. But there was no telling Mo when she got an idea into her head. Ever since she had a Polish plumber to fit her new bathroom – and a lot more besides according to Mum – she reckoned Polish men were the bee's knees, the best at everything.

Maggie had been invited to join them on the trip. She wouldn't know where to start with improving her body. Or maybe she did. Maybe what she needed was a new mind. The wobbly bits of her size twelve body were the least of her concerns. It was what was going on inside her head that was causing all the trouble. Anyway, she wouldn't be going, she didn't fancy waking up in a foreign country with a new face, a face she didn't recognize.

As Maggie began removing the cushions from the sofas in the sitting room so she could give them a deep clean with the vacuum cleaner, she listened to Mrs Edwards lecturing the decorator. It was the usual lecture she gave anyone who came to work for her, the one about only using the loo off the utility room and how any hot drinks consumed had to be made and drunk in the utility room. The same went for anything eaten. The kitchen was out of bounds for the workers. Maggie could be trusted to clean it but not to use it. The lower orders had to know their place, was the general idea.

An hour later and Mrs Edwards had left the house for one of her exhausting sessions at her spa. Listening to the front door closing, Maggie thought that if there was a god, he would do the decent thing and arrange it so that the horrible woman got stuck in a whopping great snowdrift somewhere.

It was eleven o'clock: time for elevenses. With the coast clear, Maggie went to put the kettle on – not in the utility room, but in the kitchen. It was her one and only act of defiance. She then went to introduce herself to the decorator and to see if she wanted a drink.

In the time it took for the kettle to boil and for her to make two mugs of instant coffee, Maggie decided she liked Ella. Probably because Ella was more than happy to go along with her act of defiance in the kitchen. That and the fact that she got a packet of chocolate Hob Nobs out of one of her bags and shared them with Maggie.

'I've had any number of clients who have banned me from using their kitchens,' Ella was saying now as they both leaned against the breakfast bar and dunked their biscuits in their coffee. 'I never take it personally. One woman insisted that I ate my lunch in the garden. Or if it was raining, the garage. She didn't want to see me eating.'

'Blimey, what did she think you were, a dog? Or was she one of those anorexic types or something? If you ask me, there are some strange people about.'

'You're not kidding.'

'Do you think it's the money that makes them act so hoity-toity?'

'Sometimes, yes.'

'I'll tell you now, Mr Edwards isn't like that. He's a nice

regular bloke. No airs and graces about him. So what are you doing to the dining room? If you don't mind me saying, it doesn't look like it needs redecorating. It was only done last year.'

After Maggie listened to Ella's answer, she came to the conclusion that it sounded a bit batty. Not that she said that. But she'd prefer plain cream walls any day. It was how she'd like her house to be. All cream and no fuss. As it was she had to suffer the awful stripy job-lot wallpaper Mr Blobby had got at a bargain price from a mate five years ago. The whole house was decorated with it. The stripes made her think of prison bars. As if she needed to be reminded that she was living in a prison.

To Maggie's disappointment, Ella said she wouldn't get as far as painting anything that day. She had to get the preparatory work done, which meant covering everything with dust sheets, sanding where necessary and then setting up her laptop to project what she needed to draw on the walls. By the time Maggie had finished her work and was putting away the vacuum cleaner in the utility room along with the mop and bucket, Ella had drawn what looked like a very large chessboard on the four walls. She explained that she had to divide the walls up into segments. On one of the walls was what looked like the rough outline of a Walt Disney castle. Just as Maggie had thought, it was all a bit batty.

'How long will it take you to do?' Maggie asked, shoving an arm through the sleeve of her coat.

'A couple of months, probably. I have to fit it in around the other jobs I've got on the go at the moment.'

It sounded expensive work to Maggie. She hoped Mr Edwards had his chequebook ready. 'I'll be off, then,' she said to Ella.

'Take care in the snow,' Ella said, glancing out of the window; the light was already fading. 'It'll probably be freezing again by now.'

'Thanks. You mind how you go as well. Will you be here this day next week?'

'Hopefully. It all depends how my other jobs work out.'

As Maggie slowly negotiated the roads, which had indeed frozen again, she found herself looking forward to returning to The Lilacs; she was curious to see what Ella would have done by next week. She liked the way Ella spoke – she had a nice voice. Not a la-di-dah sort of voice, but a calm one. If you had to hear bad news, you'd want a voice like Ella's to break it to you. She couldn't imagine Ella getting angry. And she had lovely skin. Very natural looking. No need for her to go to a clinic in Poland, that was for sure. Her dark brown hair done in two long plaits and her clothes – big and baggy – created a look that Maggie imagined passed for arty. But those long, dangly sleeves would drive Maggie crazy – they'd be forever getting in the way.

It was going to be nice having Ella around for a few weeks. She'd be a much-needed breath of fresh air at The Lilacs.

Chapter Ten

Five days into her new job at The Lilacs, the clickety-click of *I'm-the-boss-and-don't-you-forget-it* acted as a perfect early warning system for Ella. She didn't need to be warned to look busy and hard at work – there would be no chance of catching her slacking – but anything that tipped her off to Mrs Edwards' presence was a good thing.

The clickety-click of heels emerging from the kitchen came to a stop. 'Ah, there you are.'

Where else did Mrs Edwards expect to find her? Lolling on the sofa gorging herself from a super-sized tub of Häagen Dazs ice-cream whilst watching Jeremy Kyle? From her position halfway up the stepladders, Ella carefully turned round and looked down at Mrs Edwards, adopting a politely interested expression.

'I'm going out now,' Mrs Edwards said. 'I should be back before it's time for you to leave.' The message was implicit; under no circumstances was Ella to consider knocking off early. The point made, Mrs Edwards stared hard at the area of wall that Ella was working on; she was still at the sketching stage. 'You haven't done much, have you?'

And the Oscar for Best Hard-Faced Bitch goes to Mrs Edwards!

'This is the most important stage,' Ella replied. 'Rush this and the whole thing will fall apart.'

Mrs Edwards didn't look convinced. She then cast her disapproving gaze over Ella's clothes – shabby old jeans, shabby old Timberland boots, shabby old pullover over shabby old shirt, and hair tied up in a loose knot on top of her head. Ella would be the first to admit that she was not exactly dressed for Ascot, but while she was working, shabby did the job just fine.

In contrast, Mrs Edwards was dressed as if she was on her way to Ascot, kitted out in a natty black and turquoise suit that had probably cost her a surfeit of arms and legs. The titchy-witchy little skirt and jacket didn't look like they would protect her against the freezing temperature outside. Did she not listen to the weather forecasters? Or look out of the window before choosing what to wear? She was smothered in some pretty serious-looking jewellery – if it was the real deal, it looked as if it might solve the global economic crisis in one fell swoop. Certainly it would do away with the need for any quantitative easing.

'When will you actually get some paint on the walls?' she asked Ella.

Had Michelangelo been asked the same thing when working on the Sistine Chapel? Or Giotto with his frescos in the Scrovegni Chapel in Padua? Maybe they had. Maybe the boss was always the boss no matter what the commission, or who the artist. *Oi, amico, when are you going to get down to painting the walls, never mind all this sketching lark?* Ella was hardly in the same league, but a little respect, please. A hint of some manners. Would it kill Mrs Edwards to be nice?

'As I say, it's important not to rush this stage,' Ella explained. 'It could be disastrous if I don't get the composition right at this point. You wouldn't thank me for a botched job, would you?' This wasn't strictly true – she could fudge over a mistake with the greatest of ease. What *was* true was that she was methodical and always wanted to do the very best job for a client. It was why she had so many repeat customers; they liked what she did and came back again and again.

'No I wouldn't,' replied Mrs Edwards stiffly. 'A botched job is certainly not what I'm paying you to do.'

Glad we got that sorted, Ella thought as she returned her

attention to the wall and listened to the welcome sound of retreating heels. Minutes later, after she'd heard the front door
being shut, she repositioned the stepladders further along the
wall. She then slipped a pair of headphones on and scrolled
through the playlist on her iPhone. With The Killers' *Day and
Age* album selected, she climbed back up the stepladders and
got herself settled.

She always worked best when she was alone. Completely
alone. At times she had no choice but to adapt and work with
a team, as she was currently doing at Belmont Hall. Recently
bought by a young single man, Belmont Hall was a stonk-
ing great house that the new owner wanted to bring into the
twenty-first century. To do the job, he had employed an army
of builders, plumbers, electricians, plasterers, joiners and
decorators – including Ella. Tomorrow she would be there to
make a start on applying the final coat of eggshell paint to the
kitchen units Phil had finished installing last week.

Phil had called round last night to ask if she would be able
to make it tomorrow and when he'd spotted the large vase
of flowers in the sitting room, he had raised an eyebrow and
asked if there was someone new in her life. She had explained
about her act of heroism and also mentioned the mystery of
how the sender of the flowers had known where to send them.
Phil had immediately solved the mystery. 'Your number plate,'
he'd said. 'The man must have got that and done a search for
your address on the internet. Don't ask me how exactly.' She
had been shocked and furious that such a thing was possible.
She had been so cross she had thrown the flowers away. Well,
they *were* past their best.

Was it irrational of her to feel that the man had had a nerve
to invade her privacy in such a way? If there was one type of
man she didn't like, it was a pushy man.

That was one of the things she had liked most about
Lawrence: the refreshing absence of pushiness in his character. Of course, towards the end of their relationship, when she
was near breaking point and a hair's breadth from pushing

Alexis out of a very high window, she had longed to shout at him to stand up to his bloody awful daughter.

In her ears now was the song 'I Can't Stay'. Funny how music could say it all for you. Three small words that packed the punch like nothing else could.

She climbed up onto the next step of the ladders and began sketching in more detail to the higher area of the wall. She had sectioned off each of the four walls with a grid of twelve-inch squares. On this wall alone she still had ten squares yet to complete. Then there was one remaining wall to make a start on. Despite the awfulness of the client, Ella was enjoying the task she had been set. It wasn't the largest mural she had been asked to paint and it was by no means the most distasteful, but the cherry on the icing of the cake was that it was going to pay exceptionally well. She had pitched her quotation on the side of hopeful fantasy, inasmuch as she had bumped it up according to what she had suspected she could get away with, based on the size of the house and the car parked out on the drive. She felt no guilt in what she had done, not when she would have to put up with Mrs Edwards for the duration of the job.

She wondered how Maggie, the woman who cleaned here, put up with her employer. Perhaps she had acquired a very thick skin. Unfortunately, Mrs Edwards wasn't the only person at The Lilacs with whom she had to contend. Yesterday Ella had had the bad luck to meet the daughter of the household: Valentina.

Ella's first impression was that the obnoxious girl was going all out to notch up a perfect ten in the Yeah-Whatever-I-Don't-Give-a-Shit World Championship event. Home from school, her face as sour as a lemon, she had mooched about the dining room, twirling her long blonde hair around a finger while she inspected the work Ella had done so far. After rudely fiddling with Ella's laptop and then pointing out that there were errors in parts of the sketching – well, of course there were; it was a work in rough progress! – she had asked what qualifications Ella had for the job. Ella had wanted to take a freshly sharpened pencil and shove it right up one of the girl's nostrils. But having graduated from Mayfield with a first-class honours degree in anger management, she had gritted her teeth and politely refrained from such a violent act.

To have a wife and progeny who both excelled in such flagrant bad manners and such arrogant condescension, it made Ella wonder what kind of man Mr Edwards was. Was he worse? Was he even more of a monster? Or a total wimp under the thumb of his wife? Maggie seemed to think he was a decent man. A 'regular bloke' was how she had described him. But what kind of regular bloke had a family like this?

She tried to recall him from the photograph she had seen on the sideboard during her first visit here. Since that day the dining room had been emptied so there was no chance of having another look at it, and from the bits of the house she had seen to date, there didn't seem to be any other family photographs around. So she was dependent on her memory, which sadly was letting her down. All she could recall was that a pink shirt had been involved and that she had thought him absurdly good looking. A wolf in sheep's clothing, perhaps? But shame on him for producing a child like Valentina.

A similar thought had often passed through her mind during her relationship with Lawrence and it still amazed her that he hadn't seen what a piece of work Alexis was. In Ella's opinion, based on all the family and child psychology books she had read in the hope she could understand Alexis and therefore help the situation, his mistake had been to indulge her by constantly giving in to her whims and tantrums and excusing her behaviour on the grounds that she had lost her mother at so young an age. Not once had he ever admonished her – not when Ella caught Alexis pouring the contents of her favourite bottle of perfume, a present from Lawrence, down the sink, and not even when Ella found a photograph album hidden under Alexis's bed. Opening the album Ella had seen that she had been systematically cut out from all of the photographs of the recent holiday they had taken in Cornwall. Imagining Alexis sitting upstairs in her bedroom snipping away with calculating intent had sent a chill through Ella. Had it not been for her love for both Lawrence and Toby she may well have made a run for it there and then. With hindsight she should have done. But this was only a year into family life at Mayfield; it was merely the start and Ella had foolishly believed she would win Alexis round.

Onto his fifth cup of coffee of the morning, Ethan was not in a good mood. He'd come to the conclusion that there were simply too many irritations in life that one had to suffer. At present his top five irritations ran as follows:

1. *Annoying neighbours.* Adam and Christine Paxton spoke for themselves.

2. *Bad weather.* Again, self-explanatory. Snow was all right when it was fresh and powdery and when it was the stuff of an Alpine resort and was topped off with a clear blue sky. But he could do without snow that hung around in dirty and treacherous icy lumps just waiting to catch out the unwary. He'd narrowly missed skidding into a bollard this morning on his way to the dentist. Which brought him neatly to his next gripe.

3. *Dentists.* Why did they have to be so damned smug and annoyingly jolly? When Ethan had lain back in the chair earlier this morning, his mouth wide open, his eyes closed and feeling as vulnerable as a puppy left on the roadside, the dentist had said, 'Ooh, lookie, lookie, and what do we have here?' He had sounded as if he'd just produced a shiny coin from behind a small child's ear. *What do we have here?* proved to be the need for an ancient filling to be redone. Half an hour later Ethan had emerged with a partially numb mouth and a vicious assault made on his wallet.

4. *In-laws.* Dear sweet God in heaven – where to start? How did he end up with such a pair? A more destructive and toxically poisonous duo you could not meet. But it explained

a lot about Francine. Chips and blocks. Say no more. Actually, there was a hell of a lot more he could say on the subject, but now wasn't the time. Tomorrow he had an evening of their company to look forward to. Oh joy of joys!

5. *Computers*. And here we have it, his total, one hundred per cent *bête noire* of the moment. The damned things were fine when they were working as they were supposed to, but turn your back on them for no more than a nanosecond and they'd plot and connive to drive you stark raving bonkers. Just as it had happened to him this morning. The system in the office had gone into meltdown while he'd been at the dentist. It meant that nothing could be done. Not in the usual manner, anyway. Orders were now having to be processed the old-fashioned way – pen, paper, calculator. Cock-ups would be guaranteed. And cock-ups he could do without. They were too costly. Getting an order wrong never went down well with a customer. Especially if the customer was already screwing you on the deal and would seize any opportunity they got to squeeze a further reduction on the price.

For most of the time Ethan could kid himself that he was up to speed with the latest technology, but computers were sly buggers and when they crashed, they crashed and there wasn't a damned thing a mere mortal like him could do about it. That was why he paid Warren so handsomely. Warren was a freelance techie consultant and he had promised to be with them within two hours. At twenty-four years old, there wasn't anything Warren didn't know about computers and it was he who had helped Ethan to track down the Dragon Slayer. 'No problem,' he had said when Ethan had phoned him. Less than an hour later he was calling Ethan back with the address. Ethan hadn't asked if it was strictly legal how Warren had obtained the information – he suspected Warren may have accessed the DVLA records somehow – but what harm had been done?

*

When Warren telephoned to say that he was going to be delayed by an hour, Ethan decided to go home and use the computer in his office there. Better still, he would have the house to himself, as Francine would be out at another of her Ladies Who Lunch dos. He didn't know how she did it, but she had an inexhaustible supply of lunches to attend. He just hoped today's get-together wasn't one of those lavish charity events with an auction that would compel her to bid for an extravagant luxury item they had no need for. 'That's the point of it,' she said the last time she came home having made the winning bid for a pair of tickets for dinner at a recently opened restaurant trying to make a name for itself. 'Luxury means indulgence.'

It also meant expensive, which was exactly what that dinner had turned out to be. When the credit card statement rolled in he discovered that Francine had paid nearly three hundred pounds for the privilege of dining at a restaurant that closed barely six months later due to substandard food and a dearth of punters over the threshold. He knew why she did it – made excessive bids for something they didn't need. It was a need to flaunt her position in the pecking order of Ladies Who Lunch. She needed to be valued as the Queen Bee, the one the others looked up to. No point in being a drone, in her book. Not when she was married to one.

And with that depressing thought uppermost in his mind and an antacid tablet in his mouth, he slowly drove the icy five-mile journey home. He hoped to God that Francine drove carefully wherever she was; the last thing he needed was a garage bill for her Beamer.

The moment he saw the car on the drive he realized he wouldn't have the house to himself. He'd forgotten about the wretched woman painting the dining room. However, he hadn't forgotten the astronomical price she was charging for her work. Unlikely that he would when it would drag him yet another step nearer financial ruin.

Feeling cheated – he'd been looking forward to some time

on his own – he put his key in the lock of the front door. He'd just turned the key when he hesitated. He looked over his shoulder, back at the other car. The Toyota Rav. The dark blue Toyota Rav. He then registered the number plate.

The weird thing about his brain was that he might struggle to remember the name of a woman with whom he'd just had sex, but it was wired to process and retain numbers in a flash. He wasn't one of those mathematical genius types who could multiply two sets of seven-figure numbers in his head, divide the answer by a prime number, square it and shove it through the wash to the power of ten, blah di blah, but give him a balance sheet to tot up and he could do it in his sleep. Memorizing numbers was also second nature to him; he knew all his credit card numbers off pat and give him a telephone number to remember and he could do so without having to write it down. It had been a party trick of his when he'd been at school. And it still came in handy now and then.

A slow smile covered his face. So, he thought, as he let himself in, we meet again. What were the chances of that happening? And in such circumstances.

He walked through the house, loosening his scarf, unbuttoning his coat, heading straight for the dining room, all set to surprise the Dragon Slayer. But when he reached the doorway, it was he who was surprised. He leaned against the doorframe, folded his arms across his chest and settled in to watch the show. His day had suddenly got a whole lot better. This was definitely worth coming home for.

Chapter Eleven

There was something so free and joyous about the way she was dancing. Lost in her own world, or the world she was tuned into through the small headphones in her ears, her body was moving with a sinuous looseness.

Despite the baggy and unattractive clothes she was wearing, her every movement was extraordinarily fluid. Sensual even. There was absolutely nothing overtly erotic in what she was doing; it wasn't sexual at all. And yet ... and yet there was something intensely tantalizing and intimate in the way that she appeared to be dancing entirely for her own pleasure and delight.

As she slowly spun round, graceful and loose-limbed, her eyes closed, a deeply contented smile on her face, her arms above her head, Ethan felt strangely moved by what he could only describe as the sheer radiance of her. She didn't look like she had a care in the world. How he envied her. He also found himself wondering what it would feel like to have those long, graceful limbs wrapped around him.

Lost in the moment and feeling that time had been oddly suspended, a sense of discomfort crept over him. He felt he had no right to be watching her. What she was doing was too intimate for his eyes. For the eyes of a man she didn't know. He pushed away from the wall and stood up straight. He really shouldn't be here. Which he knew was ludicrous – this was his house, after all – but the unpalatable truth was, he felt like a no-good peeping Tom.

He took a step back. His plan was to sneak away as if he

had never been there. But no sooner had he taken a second step than she stopped spinning and opened her eyes. It was a moment of excruciating embarrassment for them both, although it was clearly she who was the more embarrassed of the two of them.

Her face no longer radiating inner contentment, but pink with mortification, she whipped off the headphones and stared at him. '*You!*' she said.

'Me,' he said, realizing that she was doubly wrong-footed.

'You,' she repeated.

He smiled. 'Yes, I think we've established it's me. I'm sorry I interrupted you. You dance beautifully.'

If it was possible, her face glowed a deeper shade of pink. She didn't say anything.

He stepped into the room. 'What were you listening to?'

'Coldplay,' she murmured.

'Really?' He couldn't have been more surprised. 'Not a band I normally associate with happy music,' he said.

'"Viva La Vida". It always makes me want to dance.'

'Then you should listen to it all the time. I've never seen anyone look so happy whilst listening to a piece of music.' He stepped further into the room and looked about him. 'How are you getting on?'

Appearing to regain some of her composure, she said, 'It's going well. And just in case you were wondering, I don't spend all my time dancing the minute your wife's back is turned.'

He caught the sharp, defensive tone in her voice. The sharpness reminded him of the night they'd met. Amused, he said, 'I wasn't suggesting you did.' Just to rattle her, to see what her reaction would be, he added, 'You don't come cheap, do you?' He saw her bristle.

'I should hope not,' she said. 'I'm very good at what I do.'

'That's reassuring to know.' He went over to take a closer look at the wall where the stepladders were positioned. Previously he hadn't really been interested in the work being carried out, but now it was different. Now he was very interested.

'How's your ear?' she asked from behind him.

'I beg your pardon?' he said.

'I said how's your ear?'

He turned and gave her one of his full- strength smiles. The smile he was known for. The smile guaranteed to provoke the required response. He did it deliberately; he wanted to see how she would respond. 'It was a joke,' he said, touching his ear lightly. 'A poor joke, I grant you. Thank you for asking; it's fine. I had the stitches taken out yesterday.'

'So you took my advice.'

He registered the point she had scored. And the fact that she had completely ignored his smile. 'When it's good advice,' he said, 'I always take it. I haven't once spoken on my mobile in the dark since that night. How about you?'

'How about me, what?'

'Do you take good advice when it's offered?'

She gave his question some thought, then shook her head. 'Not often.'

'You know, somehow that doesn't surprise me.' He took off his coat, slipped it over his arm. 'I came home to do some work. Do you mind?'

She raised an eyebrow. 'Why would I mind? It's your house.'

'I wouldn't like to cramp your style. You might want to dance again.' He was rewarded with another satisfyingly crimson blush.

'Please, can you forget you ever saw that?'

'I'm afraid not. That's going to be the highlight of my week.'

'Don't tease me. I don't take kindly to it. Oh, and something else I don't take kindly to is strange men hunting me down on the internet.'

'Ah, so you did get the flowers. But how else was I to thank my very own Dragon Slayer?'

'You thanked me perfectly well the night I helped you,' she said crisply.

74

He wanted to laugh out loud at her. How wonderfully prim and standoffish she sounded. He couldn't help but tease her some more. Just a little. 'Didn't you like the flowers?'

'The flowers were lovely,' she said after a brief hesitation. 'What I didn't approve of was the means by which they were sent. As I said, a strange man poking about on the internet trying to track me down makes me feel uncomfortable.'

'It's a regular thing with you? You've had other men do this?'

She frowned. 'You're the first and hopefully the last.'

'Perhaps you would have preferred chocolates? Maybe that was where I went wrong.'

She gave him a look that could have detonated a bomb.

'I'm joking,' he said. 'And I'm sorry I overstepped the mark by wanting to thank you properly. I promise I won't do it again.' He gave the room one last look and said, 'Right then, I'll leave you to it.'

Ella waited until she was sure he had really gone and then she silently screamed at the same time as going through the motions of banging her head against the wall but not actually making contact. Oh, the shame! The total humiliation! To have been caught doing her 'Viva La Vida' dance! She would not have felt more embarrassed or vulnerably exposed had the wretched man caught her in the shower, videoed her and put it on YouTube. Well, that was the last time she would loosen the tension out of her aching shoulders by dancing in a house she believed she had to herself.

How long had he been watching her? She shuddered from the top of her head to the tip of her toes. How she had managed to get through their conversation just now she didn't know. What must he think of her?

He seemed very sure of himself and not at all shocked to see her. Perhaps that was because he'd had the advantage over her as – apart from witnessing her making an idiot of herself – he must have seen her car on the drive. Being such a busybody expert when it came to number plates, he had to have recognized it. There was also her quotation and invoice to factor in. Her name, as small as it was, was written there at the bottom of the page. Had he known all along that she was here working in his house? Or had his wife kept the paperwork from him? No. He'd made that comment about her not being cheap. Too right, buddy!

The coincidence of her now working for him was uncanny. Just goes to show, you never know what's around the corner. But at least now she had figured out why there had been something familiar about him that night in the station car park. That very day she had seen a photograph of him. She was pretty sure the man in the photograph hadn't been wearing glasses. That must have been what had thrown her. One thing she hadn't got wrong was that he was a looker. It hadn't been so evident that night, what with the dark and the blood pouring from his ear, but it was all too apparent today. But he needed to crank down the charm; it was wasted on her.

She held to her original view, though – a man as attractive as he was had to be a whole lot of trouble. He was probably very used to getting his own way. In his favour, however, he didn't have the same rude and condescending manner as his wife. And he did seem genuine in his desire to thank her, so maybe she had been a little quick to condemn him for the way he'd tracked her down to send her the flowers. Perhaps she should apologize for appearing so ungrateful. Unless she had got it very wrong, he would be the one who would pick up the tab for her work here, which meant there was no point in biting the hand that feedeth.

With a series of emails sent, received and dealt with Ethan rummaged around in the in-tray on his desk, the one for household expenses. He soon found what he was looking for.

He hadn't noticed it before, but sure enough, in small print at the bottom of the quotation and the invoice was the name

Ella Moore. All he'd previously taken note of was the hair-raising cost of the work to be done, the amount requested up front, and the company name – Finishing Touches. He could remember thinking it wasn't a bad name. Short and catchy. Business names were important. His own – Lamont Devereux – had come to him as a result of an old hand in the industry telling him to go for something that sounded classy and double-barrelled, a cut above the competition. After a lot of thought, he'd taken his grandmother's surname, Lamont, and added Devereux to it after hearing the name on the radio. The two together sounded perfect to him.

But it was extraordinary that he had missed the name Ella Moore on the paperwork and therefore hadn't made the connection with his Dragon Slayer. Warren had, of course, supplied him with the name, but Ethan hadn't really thought much of it; to him she was the Dragon Slayer.

He leaned back in his chair, took off his glasses and rubbed his eyes. In his mind, he replayed the way she had been dancing, so openly and so expressively liberated. He could never dance like that. He had three left feet, never mind two. There again, it would be worth trying just to see the look of horror on Francine's face.

He smiled. The Dragon Slayer's face had been something else when she had realized she wasn't alone. He couldn't remember ever seeing anyone so embarrassed. But how quickly her mood had changed when she recognized him. As if a switch had been flicked, she had become a very different woman. Quite the snappy terrier. But then people usually did go on the attack when they felt their defences had been breached. It was only natural. Funny though, he hadn't expected her to be so cross over the flowers he'd sent. That had been a surprise. No, more than that, it had been a disappointment.

He put his glasses back on and glanced at his watch. It was gone two o'clock and he hadn't had any lunch. Time to remedy that.

*

'Lunch?' Ella repeated from the top of the stepladders.

'Or have you eaten already?' he asked.

'No, I haven't.'

'Come and join me, then. I wouldn't feel happy eating on my own in the kitchen knowing you were slaving away in here.'

'We slaves don't normally eat with the boss. It isn't the done thing.'

'That's okay, because I'm not the boss here. My wife will confirm that for you. Come on, come and eat something with me. I'm sure you must be hungry.'

Ella *was* hungry and as they sat in the kitchen with two plates of cheese and Branston pickle sandwiches in front of them, she tucked in gratefully. She had left in a hurry that morning and hadn't had time to throw anything into her bag to eat. They had both eschewed the pâté, the bags of spinach salad and ready prepared crudités, the pots of hummus, tara-masalata and soured cream dip in favour of something more filling. 'You can't beat a cheese and pickle butty,' he had said as he'd buttered the bread. She was inclined to agree with him.

'This is very kind of you,' she said.

He waved her words away with a flick of his hand. 'I'd hardly call this being kind. Kind was what you did for me the other week. Brave, too. Are you always so impetuous?'

'Depends on the situation. But yes, more often than not, I am.'

'And would I be right in thinking that you're a bit of a free spirit?'

'Are you accusing me of being a hippie?'

He smiled. 'I wouldn't dare accuse you of anything.'

'Now you're making me out to be some kind of ogre.'

'You did rather bite my head off earlier.'

'I'm sorry about that. And I meant what I said; the flowers were beautiful.'

'But you guard your privacy jealously, is that it?'

She shrugged. 'Maybe I went a little over the top with you. I'm sorry.'

He raised his hand again. She noted the absence of a wedding ring. 'That's two sorrys now,' he said, 'and more than enough. Would you like a cup of tea or coffee to finish up with?'

'Tea would be lovely, thank you.' She watched him fill the kettle and wondered if he had any idea how his wife treated the 'staff'. Or the ill-feeling she fostered.

He plugged the kettle in and with his back to her, he said, 'Is there a Mr Dragon Slayer at home, along with a host of junior slayers?'

'No,' she said.

'Milk?'

'Please.'

He had just opened the fridge when Ella saw a woman appear at the French doors. The woman gave a cursory knock on the glass, then opened the door. As an icy draught swirled into the kitchen, a muttered, 'Oh hell,' came from over by the fridge.

'Ooh, sorry, Ethan, I didn't realize you had company.' The woman gave Ella a long hard stare. She seemed to be out of the same over-dressed mould as Mrs Edwards.

'That's all right,' he said, although from his expression Ella didn't think he meant it. 'If it was Francine you wanted, she's not here.'

'No, actually it was you I wanted to talk to. I saw your car on the drive and grabbed my chance.'

Another look in Ella's direction and Ella got the message loud and clear. She slipped off the bar stool and took her empty plate over to the sink. 'I'll get back to work now, Mr Edwards. Thank you for lunch.'

'There's no need to rush off,' he said. 'Let me introduce you. This is Christine Paxton from next door. Christine, this is Ella Moore; she's the specialist painter Francine found for the dining room.' Christine Paxton nodded but made no move to shake Ella's hand.

Ella smiled sweetly. 'Good to meet you,' she lied. 'I'll leave you to it.' This she said to Mr Edwards.

She was barely out of the kitchen when she heard the woman say, 'You gave her lunch? Good heavens, Ethan. Whatever would Francine think?'

Chapter Twelve

Christine Paxton had wanted Ethan from the very first day she and Adam and Katie had moved into Lilac Avenue. She had taken one look at him and thought, *He's mine.*

She knew from Francine that she was not the first woman to think the same. She also knew from the confidences Francine had shared with her that some years ago Ethan had strayed. He'd had an affair, which Francine had found out about and in her own words, she had made him pay. But Francine was a fool to think she could keep a husband in the way she believed she could. Sooner or later Ethan would leave her. Christine just hoped it was sooner rather than later.

What wouldn't she give to swap boring old Adam for Ethan? Financially Adam was a good husband and he had the level of ambition she admired in a man but as for the rest, he bored her to tears. He was letting himself go, turning into a revoltingly middle-aged man. He was too heavy. Too out of shape. Too self-important. Just too plain old gross. Of course, in bed with him, she had the perfect antidote to his repulsiveness – she simply closed her eyes and imagined that it was Ethan making love to her. From the word go, fantasy sex with Ethan was always mind-blowingly explosive. Adam remarked only recently how much more fun their sex-life had become. He had been full of himself, naturally taking the credit for the upturn in their bedroom activities. Poor deluded fool! Little did he know that it had nothing whatsoever to do with him.

The only problem with fantasy sex was that it made her want Ethan all the more. When she was near him, she could barely keep her hands off his body. In her mind, she knew every inch of his delectable body, knew how to please him, and he knew how to please her. The other night when she had been massaging his shoulders, her desire for him had reached an all-time high. Perhaps that was why she had reacted the way she did when he had rejected her so brutally.

That was why she had gone next door this afternoon. She had seen her error, realizing that she couldn't force the situation. She had to let Ethan come to her. Given the hold Francine had over him, it was understandable that he was trying to do the right thing. When she had noticed his car on the drive, knowing that Francine was out for the day, she had seized her opportunity to speak to Ethan on his own. She had wanted to apologize, to blame her behaviour that night on the amount of wine she had drunk during dinner.

But then she had witnessed the cosy little scene going on in the kitchen between Ethan and that woman, Ella Moore. A scene that didn't fool her. An innocent lunch? Not this side of reality. Nobody employed someone to work in their home and then offered them lunch. You only did that when you had an ulterior motive. But surely Ethan wasn't attracted to a woman like that?

Christine shuddered at the thought of the woman's tatty paint-splattered jeans, the baggy jumper and her awful boots. She looked down at her beautiful Christian Louboutin shoes and shuddered again. And as for the woman's hair, why, even Amy Winehouse and Helena Bonham Carter combined couldn't have as bad a hair day as that!

The more Christine thought about it, the more she began to see that it really wasn't possible that Ethan would be attracted to such a dreadful-looking woman. It was much more likely that Ella, as with so many before, had made a move on Ethan and had talked him into providing her with lunch, and Ethan being his normally good-natured self had been left with no choice but to be polite and do as she had asked.

Christine had seen women making a play for Ethan many

times. Just a few weeks ago when she and Adam had thrown a Boxing Day party, there had been any number of women flirting with him. She had watched them carefully, observing how they had spent the evening stripping him with their eyes. As well as watching those women Christine had watched for Ethan's reaction. He had caught her eye at one point and then quickly glanced away. Had he done that because he had been tempted and knew he'd been caught out?

Yet whatever temptation came his way, she had never seen him behave other than with impeccable correctness. It was the nature of his fidelity – barring that slip from way back – that was part of the attraction for Christine. She wanted to be the one for whom he finally weakened. She wanted to be the one for whom he would forsake all else and all others.

Francine would never speak to her again, of course, but no matter; it would be a small price to pay. And anyway, their friendship wasn't important to Christine. It was merely a means to an end. Being close to Francine enabled her to be close to Ethan.

The truth was, she despised Francine. She was stupid to think she could treat Ethan the way she did and expect to keep him. More fool her.

But what of Ella Moore? Was she a threat to Christine's plan? She better hadn't be. As much as she had just rationalized the scene she had earlier interrupted at The Lilacs, the picture of the two of them sitting at the breakfast bar, all cosy and intimate, ripped through Christine. She had never once felt jealous of Francine, but she suddenly felt scorched by its white heat. In the year and a half she had known Ethan, why hadn't he invited her to join him for lunch?

From the sitting room came the sound of Maggie starting up the vacuum cleaner. The noise reminded Christine that she needed to tell Maggie that she hadn't cleaned the landing properly last week. There was dust on the skirting boards. Plus she had been too idle to put Katie's clothes away, had left them at the end of the bed.

People joked that you couldn't get the staff these days. But it was true. And it was no joke. Maggie would have to buck her ideas up or she would have to find some other mug to work for.

Accused of not doing her job properly! Friggin' unbelievable!

Maggie would like to see Mrs Paxton do any better. She probably wouldn't know how to take the cap off the polish, let alone empty the Dyson. If she didn't need the money, Maggie would tell Mrs Paxton just where she could stick her lousy job. But needs must.

It was the end of the day and as she drove home, money was very much on Maggie's mind. She had decided to open a building society account in her name and pay a small amount of her wages into it every week. It was to be *her* money. Mr Blobby wouldn't know anything about it. It would be her very own secret fund. Something for a rainy day. She didn't know why she had never thought of doing it before. It gave her a warm glow inside whenever she thought about it.

A warm glow was just what she needed. The heater in her car had packed up and the weather was freezing again. She had spoken briefly with Ella as she had been about to set off from the Paxtons'. Ella had also just finished work at The Lilacs and was putting her things in her car. Mr Edwards had come out as they'd started talking and had helped with the rest of Ella's things. It wasn't everyone who would be so helpful. But then he was nice like that. Very considerate. Mr Edwards had warned them both to take care on the roads, that more snow was on its way. Maggie was heartily sick of this cold weather. She wished winter would hurry up and be done with itself.

When she arrived home, before she had even got her coat off, Mr Blobby was on at her complaining that there weren't any sausages in the fridge for his tea. Hanging up her coat in the under-stairs cupboard, she said, 'Thursday is when I do sausages for you.'

He looked at her as though she had grown an extra head. 'It's Thursday, Mags,' he said, doing that stupid rolling of his eyes thing, 'which means it's bangers and mash day. So why aren't there any in the fridge?'

'It's Wednesday, that's why. I'm going shopping after work tomorrow. As I always do.'

'But it's Thursday.'

'Dave,' she said tiredly, 'it's definitely Wednesday. Which means it's faggots and mash day.'

'You're losing it, Mags.'

Losing it, was she? She'd show him who was losing it. She picked up the newspaper from the kitchen table where it had been left open at the sports pages. She patiently showed him the date, wishing that she could break out from the straitjacket of what she was and was not allowed to cook. Foreign muck was definitely off the menu and heaven help her if she ever wanted to try something new.

He grunted. 'Okay, so I got ahead of meself. It's an easy mistake to make.'

The next morning most of the country woke to find it was snowed in. London was claiming to be the worst hit, but it was no picnic in Kings Melford. For the first time ever Maggie couldn't get to work. Nor could Dave or Dean. Along with their neighbours they tried shovelling their way out of the road, but the snow was coming down so fast they were forced to give up. Dave was not happy. Staring out of the window, he said, 'I s'ppose now I'll have to go without my bangers tonight.'

'You could try walking down to the corner shop for some,' she said.

He ignored her, pointed the remote control at the telly and got himself comfortable on the sofa. 'Put the kettle on for a brew if you're going that way.'

Maggie wasn't. She had other ideas. She wanted to go across the road to check on Mrs Oates at number twenty-six.

She wanted to make sure the old lady was all right. You never knew with this weather; people could freeze to death in their own home.

Mrs Oates often told Maggie to call her Mary, but Maggie couldn't do it. The most informal she could manage was to call her Mrs O. Getting on a bit – she was nearly in her eighties – her husband had died three years ago and she didn't get out too much these days. They'd never had children so there was no family close by to keep an eye on things. Every other week Maggie took her to the supermarket and in return Mrs Oates made her one of her fruitcakes. No guesses for who stuffed most of it down his great fat gob!

'Can I tell you a secret?' Mrs Oates said after she'd put the kettle on and had dug around in the ancient biscuit barrel.

'You can tell me anything you like,' Maggie said.

'You promise you won't laugh or think I'm being a daft old woman?'

'There's nothing daft about you, Mrs O. So come on, don't keep me in suspense; tell me what the big secret is.'

'I've been asked out,' the old lady said, 'on a *date*.' Her eyes were suddenly as big as saucers.

Maggie tried not to laugh.

'You're laughing! You said you wouldn't.'

'I'm not laughing,' Maggie lied. 'Honestly. No, really I'm not.'

Then they both got an attack of the funnies and started to giggle like a couple of silly children.

'His name is Jack Potts,' Mrs Oates confessed when they'd got the better of their laughter and the tea was made and poured, 'and he's a widower. I met him at the doctor's surgery last week. He held the door open for me, said I was to mind the step. He has beautiful manners. He's asked to take me for afternoon tea at The Courtyard Café in Crantsford. What do you think? Should I go?'

'Abso-bloomin-lutely, Mrs O! Go and have some fun.'

Mrs Oates smiled. 'You know, I think I might just do that.'

Maggie wished she could do the same. Only not with an old widower. A gorgeous, fit young bloke who would treat her to tea and scones would be right up her alley.

Chapter Thirteen

The following week at Belmont Hall Ella had issued the edict that not a speck of dust was to be stirred anywhere near the kitchen. She was applying the final coat of paint to the cupboard doors and both Malcolm the electrician and Karl the plumber had worked with her before and knew better than to ignore her instructions. Belmont Hall being as large as it was, it wasn't difficult for them to make themselves useful in another, more distant part of the house.

The one person who wasn't taking the hint to leave Ella in peace was the client: Hal Moran. For reasons known only to himself he had moved into the house last Friday, despite the perishing cold and building work chaos. His move had coincided with the coldest weekend in years, following two days of blizzard-like conditions. As with many others last week Ella had been snowed in and hadn't been able to get to work, which hadn't pleased Mrs Edwards.

How Hal Moran had coped over the weekend without any heating or hot water she didn't know, but she hoped for all their sakes Karl would have the heating up and running by the end of the day. She had come prepared this morning, dressed in so many layers of clothing, including a hat, scarf and fingerless mittens, she could be mistaken for an intrepid Antarctic explorer.

There were no creature comforts at Belmont Hall – no furniture or carpets, not even a proper bed. Just lots of walls taken back to the brickwork and carefully removed floorboards (they were original and would be re-laid at a later date), and pipes and wiring exposed. If all went to plan, at least by tomorrow the kitchen would be fully operational. To his credit, Hal Moran didn't appear at all fazed by the mess or lack of facilities and had created what he called his base camp in the main bedroom upstairs, where he had installed a camp bed and Primus stove. A regular boy scout. And like a small boy wanting proudly to show off his stamp collection, he had shown Ella where he was camping out.

She had been amazed at what else he had in the room. Never mind the spirit of Baden Powell living on, it was like NASA and mission control in there. There was a seriously impressive-looking Bang and Olufsen hi-fi system on the window seat with speakers strategically placed around the room, but taking up most of the space was a horseshoe arrangement of desks, on which sat a bank of computers, all humming and flickering with activity. 'Work,' he had said when she had asked what they were doing. He hadn't expanded. In fact he had looked and sounded vaguely embarrassed. But then he did a lot of that. He and Belmont Hall seemed a strange match. She knew from local gossip that the Hall had been on the market for a cool three and a half million and after ten months of little interest the price had dropped to two and a half million. Whichever way you viewed it, Hal Moran, who couldn't be much older than twenty-eight, had to be pretty much loaded to afford such a price tag. And that was before the cost of all the alterations was factored in.

She couldn't help but be curious as to what he did for a living. Now that she had seen his room upstairs, she wondered whether it was something to do with computers – software perhaps. She didn't mean it unkindly, but he was classic geek material. Always dressed in the same way, jeans, shirt, pullover and black and white Converse trainers, there was a boyish innocence to his quietly unassuming manner and with his slight build and fine sandy hair, the fringe of which he constantly had to push out of his eyes, he looked as though he should still be living at home with his parents studying for his A-levels.

Up until today she had had the minimum of contact with him, but ever since she had arrived here this morning, he had been like a shadow, hovering over her as she set about her work and twice had offered to make her coffee on his Primus stove upstairs. There was, she had to admit, something endearing about him. Although she was finding him a little less endearing right now. She wanted to get on, but with him watching her every move and wanting to chat she felt hampered. She didn't work at her best with an audience. Somehow she had to very politely get rid of him. 'Mr Moran,' she said, 'I'd hate to think I was keeping you from your work.'

'Please, it's Hal. And you're not keeping me from anything special. You must have incredible patience.'

You're not kidding, she thought. She stood up and moved her kneepad along so she could work on the adjacent door. 'What makes you think that?' she asked, dipping her brush into the pot of pale grey matt paint. The units were predominantly pale grey with a stronger shade used for the central aisle unit. With black slate floor tiles, black granite worktops and stainless steel and chrome accessories and all the statement toys a man could want in a kitchen, it was going to look very state of the art.

'I'm sure I wouldn't be any good at it,' he said.

'That's a good thing as far as I'm concerned,' she said with a small laugh. 'The fewer people out there in competition with me, the better. Better that you stick to what you do. What exactly is your line of work?' she asked, seizing the convenient segue and determined to satisfy her curiosity.

'Nothing terribly earth shattering,' he said.

'I'm sure you're being modest.'

'I assure you I'm not.'

She reloaded her paintbrush and waited for him to go on.

He did. 'Unless you're into it, I guarantee your eyes will glaze over,' he said. 'Have you heard of a computer game called The Four Zoas?'

'Sorry,' she said, 'I'm a complete philistine when it comes

to anything like that. What sort of game is it?'

'It's based on William Blake's poem, 'Vala', or 'The Four Zoas'. The four zoas being Urthona, Urizen, Luvah and Tharmas. Yeah, I'm boring you, aren't I? I can see your eyes glazing over already.'

'Not at all. Tell me more.'

'The poem was split into what Blake called the Nine Nights, and based on that I created a series of nine computer games. I had to take a few artistic licences here and there, play down the sexual content and play up the themes of jealousy, imprisonment, the nature of intelligence and renovation, and ultimately man's limitations. I started work on it when I was at university.'

'Sounds impressive. And presumably the series was a hit?'

He nodded. 'A biggish hit.'

'How biggish?'

He pushed his hands into the pockets of his jeans. 'All around the world.'

She smiled. 'I was right when I said you were being modest, wasn't I? I'm sorry I've never heard of the game, though.'

'That's okay. If it's not your thing, it's not your thing.'

'Are you working on something now?'

'I'm tinkering. Playing with a few ideas.'

Five minutes later Hal was called away by Malcolm, the electrician; he needed Hal to make a decision on something upstairs. Thinking that Hal was one of the nicest and most interesting clients she had worked for Ella got back to her painting. It was a refreshing change to work for someone like him. Too often she encountered the weird or the outright offensive. On one occasion she had been cornered in a house by a particularly loathsome man who had got it into his head that a weekend away in the Lake District with him was the best offer she was ever likely to receive. As she had pointed out to him, his wife might have other ideas. Another client had requested she kiss him when she arrived for work each morning. Men! What were they like?

The sound of her mobile ringing from the other side of the kitchen had her standing up. Stiff-kneed, she hobbled over to her bag. Caller ID informed her who it was and she answered the phone warily.

Very warily. It was Alexis.

Chapter Fourteen

In a long history of desperate attempts to bring about family accord at Mayfield, Ella had once sought professional advice.

It had actually been Lawrence's idea and one she had wholeheartedly resisted, seeing it as an admission of failure. Failure was not in her lexicon. But in the end, after yet another 'incident' Ella felt she had no choice.

The 'incident' involved an attack of histrionics on Alexis's part as a result of her being kept awake by what she described as the disgusting noises coming from her father's bedroom – it was never Lawrence and Ella's bedroom, only her father's. They had always tried to keep the volume of their lovemaking down, rather than full-blown headboard-banging-against-the-wall ecstatic abandon, but despite their best efforts Alexis had burst in on them one night. 'Stop it! Stop it!' she had screamed. For the next half-hour she had been beside herself with tearful rage, hysterically beseeching her father never to do anything so disgustingly horrible again. Embarrassed by all things of a sexual nature in front of his children, Lawrence had had no way of handling his daughter. There followed several sex-free months and then finally Ella accepted that they had a problem that was beyond her capabilities to resolve and so she relented and telephoned the number Lawrence had so thoughtfully given her.

The so-called family expert was a chubby, balding, spectacled man with a manner so earnest it made Ella want to punch him. The first session was for Lawrence and Ella, followed by a lone session for Ella, and then a week later it was a family session to include Toby and Alexis. Ella would have preferred all the meetings on her own so she could let off steam and rid herself of her choking anger and frustration, but it was not to be.

As close as she was to her own family, she hadn't uttered a single word to them about the trouble she had taken on. Her pride wouldn't allow her to admit to her family or friends that she wasn't able to cope. How could she when she had chosen to ignore their advice and warnings? The bottom line was that she wasn't very good at accepting she was fallible. Not even with those she loved.

So she was stuck with confiding in the chubby expert. It had, however, been difficult to take him seriously and during that first joint session with Lawrence she had caught his eye and had known that he too was struggling. She had felt a wave of relief at this; if Lawrence was complicit in distrusting the man, it lessened her own misgivings. In the car afterwards as they drove to a nearby pub for a much-needed drink – much needed on her part at any rate – they had reflected on what had been said. Lawrence had been of the opinion that nothing would change overnight, that they would have to be patient. Which was exactly what he had been telling her ever since she had moved in with him. Slowly, slowly was his answer to everything. Any slower, she had wanted to shout, and nothing would ever change: they would be stuck in this bloody awful nightmare for ever with Little Miss Malevolence calling the shots.

'And just how loudly do you feel like shouting?' Chubby had asked her the following week when she had confessed this frustration. Louder than you'll ever know, she had thought. 'On a scale of one to ten, how loudly would you like to voice your unhappiness?' he had pressed.

'Off the scale,' she had admitted. 'To the point of shattering every glass, mirror and window in the house.'

Chubby had made a note of this. 'You want to destroy what you have?' he had asked, his tone implausibly neutral.

'No, I merely want to change things,' she had said. 'For the better.'

'For the better,' he had repeated ponderously, 'as *you* see it?'

'You think it's beneficial to live in the past?' Ella had retorted hotly, letting loose a tiny burst of steam. 'You think it's beneficial for Alexis to have kept all her mother's old clothes? To wear them sometimes?'

'It's not important what *I* think. Tell me about Alexis. Is she a pretty girl?'

'Very.'

'Clever?'

'Very.'

'And her father loves her very much?'

'Of course.'

'And he loves you very much?'

'I certainly hope so.'

'You're not sure?'

'I ... I was sure. Before ...' Her voice had trailed off at that point. Chubby had stared at her blankly through his glasses; one of the lenses was so badly smeared with grease she had doubted he could see out of it.

'When did you begin to doubt his love for you?' he had asked.

'I would have thought that was perfectly obvious,' she had fired back, thoroughly irritated that he should ask such an obvious question.

'Are you irritated that I've asked such an obvious question?'

'I'm not irritated,' she had lied.

He had made another note on his pad. 'Let's talk some more about Alexis. Would you say she's a high achiever?'

'Yes. She does consistently well at school. You name it, she's good at it. Class work. Sport. Music. She's a gifted all-rounder. Naturally Lawrence is very ... naturally *we're* both very proud of her.'

'Naturally,' he echoed. 'So you'd say she has great potential?'

'Potential for what?'

'To do or be anything she wants.'

'I can't see her failing to get her own way in anything she wants to do, so if that amounts to the same thing, then yes, she has great potential.'

'Have you never wanted a child of your own?'

'Yes. But ...'

'But what?'

'Lawrence didn't want another. And anyway, he'd had a vasectomy.'

'Was that a disappointment to you?'

'Not really. All things considered, we had enough problems with Alexis without complicating matters further.'

'How old are you, Ella?'

The swerve of his question had taken her by surprise. That and the use of her Christian name. 'I'm thirty-four.'

'At an age when most women who haven't yet had a child are conscious of time passing them by.'

'I'm not scared of getting older,' she had said stiffly, wondering where the hell Chubby was going with this line of thought.

'It's not uncommon for mothers of very attractive and high-achieving daughters to feel threatened by them. To resent them even.'

The penny had then dropped. As had Ella's jaw. 'You're saying I'm jealous of Alexis? That I resent her?'

'Aren't you? Don't you?'

'But I'm not her mother.'

'No, you're her stepmother.'

'Not really. Not officially. I'm not married to her father; don't forget that.'

'Is there a reason you and Lawrence are not married, that you're not the second Mrs Seymour?'

'We didn't want to rush things.'

'Lawrence hasn't asked you to marry him?'

'Not in so many words.'

'That probably adds to your uncertainty, doesn't it? And your jealousy of Alexis.'

'But I'm not jealous of her! What have I got to be jealous about?'

Chubby didn't answer straight away. Instead he removed his glasses, polished both the lenses on a small black cloth from his jacket pocket and carefully put them back on. The smear was now gone. Then finally, when Ella had thought she couldn't take the strain of his silence a moment longer, he said, 'Have you ever considered the possibility that you're both in competition for Lawrence's love and that the way you see it, currently Alexis is out in front in the race to win his affections. She appears to be able to do no wrong in his eyes. Isn't that so?'

'You've certainly got that last bit right. As for the rest, I've never been jealous of anyone in my entire life. Least of all a conniving, stroppy little cow like Alexis. I have no qualms about growing older and I certainly have no qualms about my own abilities. I've never felt threatened by anyone.' *Pssssh ...* went a long burst of steam.

Those were the last words Ella exchanged with Chubby. She drove home to Mayfield and informed Lawrence that as far as she was concerned the sessions weren't helping and she wouldn't be attending any more. The following week, Lawrence took Alexis and Toby for their group session. When they returned Toby was carrying four boxes of take-away pizzas and Alexis was wearing a look of triumphant delight on her face.

For the next week Alexis's behaviour was exemplary in front of her father. Behind his back, when it was just her and Ella, she was up to all her old tricks. The new cashmere scarf Lawrence had bought Ella for her birthday suddenly developed a gaping hole. The book Ella had just bought found its way into the kitchen sink full of greasy water. Ella's favourite bone china mug got dropped. Her Filofax with all her appointments went missing. Important work-related telephone messages were lost from the answerphone.

It was business as usual. And since Ella had burnt her bridges by refusing any more help from Chubby, she had no choice but to take whatever Alexis threw at her. She could hardly complain about the girl when deep down she knew she had behaved no better than a child herself.

The unedifying truth was, she had been jealous of Alexis. She had been pitifully green with envy that Lawrence's love for his daughter made her feel isolated and excluded at times. Just as Alexis wanted him all to herself, so had Ella. They had been rivals in love in the worst possible way. Ella hated Chubby for forcing her to acknowledge this appalling truth about herself.

But now, out of the blue, Alexis – her nemesis – had phoned Ella to say that she had to see her. The girl had refused to say what it was about, and thinking that this was yet another example of Alexis playing the drama queen, Ella had been disinclined to play along. But then Alexis's voice had adopted an almost desperate tone. '*Please*,' she had said, 'it's important. There's no one else I can talk to.'

'How about your father?' Ella had responded with considerable feeling.

'*No!*'

'What about Toby?'

'I can't bother him.'

'Then it can't be that important.'

Again, the pleading voice. 'Please, Ella. *Please* do this for me.'

As so many times before, Ella had relented. Now she was taking an extended lunch break from work at Belmont Hall and was on her way to Crantsford to pick Alexis up from school.

*

There was no doubt about it, the moment Alexis got into the car and uttered the words, 'Thank you, Ella,' it was clear something was wrong with her.

'I haven't done anything to be thanked for other than give up my lunch break,' Ella replied. 'What's wrong?'

Her face set like stone, Alexis said, 'You have to take me to a chemist. I had unprotected sex last night and I'm worried I could be pregnant. I need the morning-after pill.'

'Right,' Ella said calmly.

'And no lectures,' Alexis said in a bored voice. 'I was at a party and got drunk. I didn't know what I was doing. Blah, blah.'

'Where exactly do I come into this? You could walk into any chemist here in Crantsford and sort out the problem yourself.'

'Don't be stupid, Ella. It has to be a chemist miles from here. Somewhere nobody knows me. Somewhere nobody knows Dad.'

'Alexis,' she said slowly, 'don't ever accuse me of being stupid. It wasn't me who got drunk and had unprotected sex.'

Alexis reached for the door handle. 'Oh well, if that's how you feel, don't bother. I'll just have to find a way myself. Or perhaps I'll take the risk and hope I'm not pregnant.'

'Oh, stop being so dramatic! Put your seat belt on and tell me where you want to go.'

Twenty minutes later when Ella had parked outside a small, anonymous chemist that Alexis approved of, the girl refused to get out of the car. Her hands twisted into bone-white, tight fists on her lap, she said, 'Will you go in and get the pill for me?'

It would have been so easy to say something about taking responsibility for oneself and facing the consequences of one's actions, but Ella didn't. Forgiveness, she reminded herself; that was the way forward. 'If that's what you want,' she said, 'I'll be back in a few minutes.'

But it wasn't as straightforward as they had thought it would be. When Ella approached the counter of the small shop and made her request, the woman behind the counter called for the pharmacist. The pharmacist emerged from a back room and in a discreet voice suggested that Ella might like to move to a more private area of the shop. This done, she said, 'When did you actually have unprotected sex? How many hours ago?'

Ella hadn't been expecting this. She had assumed she could simply hand over some money and take the pill and run. 'It's not for me,' she said. 'It's … it's for a friend of mine.'

'Then your friend will have to come in and run through some questions with me.'

'Can't I answer the questions on behalf of my friend?'

'Sorry, it doesn't work like that. What's more your friend will have to take the pill in front of me.'

Ella thanked the woman and went back out to the car.

'Have you got it?' Alexis asked. The relief in her voice was pitiful.

Ella explained the situation. 'Do you want to go inside on your own? Or do you want me to come with you?'

'Come with me,' Alexis said. She suddenly looked like a very anxious child.

Dressed in her school uniform, there was no mistaking that Ella's 'friend' was of school age, but the pharmacist didn't bat an eyelid. She presented Alexis with a page of questions to answer, helpfully suggested she might like to use condoms in the future, and then finally handed over the pill with a paper cup of water.

Mission accomplished, they returned to the car. 'Well,' said Ella. 'I think we both deserve some lunch now, don't you?'

'You're not going to use that as an opportunity to lecture me, are you? Just kill me now if that's what you plan on doing.'

The anxious child had been replaced with the monster Ella knew of old. It was almost a relief; she knew where she stood with Alexis the Monster. 'If you've got any sense, you don't need anyone to lecture you on what you've gone through. Just make sure you insist that the boy uses a condom another time. Come on, let's find something to eat.'

At Alexis's request they stopped at a chip shop and bought two bags of chips drenched with vinegar and dusted with salt. They also bought two polystyrene cups of tea. Ella drove the short distance to the outskirts of the town and parked in a lay-by. For a full five minutes they sat in silence as cars and lorries thundered by and the steady whirr of the car heater filled the space between them.

In the end it was Alexis who broke the silence. 'Thank you,' she said quietly.

Ella chewed on a chip and chose her response with care. 'I'm glad you came to me for help, Alexis, but I'm sure your father would have handled things just as well as I did.'

Alexis shook her head vehemently. 'Dad still thinks I play with Barbie dolls.'

'I hardly think that's true,' she replied recalling one such doll of Alexis's with its head and limbs ripped off.

'You know what I mean, though. And you know what he's like about sex. He can't talk about it.'

Ella couldn't stop herself. 'I have a strong recollection of what you used to be like on the subject. You certainly had plenty to say about it back then.'

Alexis turned and looked at her. 'I was a kid back then.'

As opposed to what now? Ella wondered. An experienced sixteen-year-old girl with a morning-after pill hurtling through her system?

'And anyway,' Alexis continued, 'sex is for the young. You old folk should know when to do the decent thing and give it up.'

'Newsflash, Alexis! Sex is wasted on the young. What's more, I have no intention of giving it up for a long while yet.'

'Have you got a new boyfriend?'

Ella laughed bitterly. 'No I haven't, but I hear your father has had a string of new women in his life since I left.'

Alexis rolled her eyes. 'Tell me about it! Each one gets worse than the one before. He's making a fool of himself. I've tried telling him but he won't listen.'

'Funnily enough, I can just picture you doing that,' Ella said.

Alexis said nothing. She finished the last of her chips, screwed the greasy paper into a ball, then after discarding it onto the floor at her feet, she reached for her polystyrene cup of tea. She took a sip. Then another. 'Do you hate me very much, Ella?' she asked.

Ella thought of her New Year's resolution. 'I wouldn't be here if I did,' she said.

'But you did hate me, didn't you?'

'No comment.'

'It's okay, you can be honest with me. I hated you from the moment Dad first mentioned you. Then I hated you some more when he first brought you to the house.'

'And let me guess, that hatred kept on growing all of its own accord.'

'Something like that.'

'Do you still hate me?'

'I don't know really. I sort of miss you.'

'You miss having someone to fight with, I suspect.'

Alexis gave a short laugh. 'Maybe. But I'll tell you this: as much as I hated you, you're nowhere near as bad as the women Dad's now bringing home.'

And you have only yourself to blame for that dear girl, Ella thought. 'Right,' she said decisively, 'time to get you back to school.'

'Bad idea, questions will be asked. Better if I skive off for the rest of the day and get Dad to write a note saying I wasn't feeling well. Can you take me home?'

During the drive back to Crantsford, Ella reflected on the change in Alexis. Only a few weeks ago when Ella had dropped Toby off at Mayfield, Alexis had seemed her usual manipulative self but today she was different. There was a raw and refreshing honesty to her. Was it possible that the two of them had turned a corner? An important corner?

But so what if they had? What could come of it now that she and Lawrence were no longer together? It was interesting though; now that Ella wasn't a threat to Alexis, the girl's attitude had changed. In a moment of crisis she had viewed Ella as a potential ally and not the enemy.

And what precisely would Chubby have to say on the matter? Quite a lot, probably.

Chapter Fifteen

A week later than planned, due to the snow that had brought the country to its frozen knees, Ethan was chez Shirley and Alan Connolly and being subjected to an entire evening of their stultifying company. Did he really deserve such punishment? Was he really so bad a man? He didn't think so. And wasn't he practically a reformed character these days? Apart from that slip up at the start of the year he hadn't put a foot wrong. He was practically a living saint!

Okay, that was pushing it, but, to quote a certain golfer, it had not crossed his mind to transgress.

Okay, that was pushing it, too. He'd had plenty of thoughts just lately that were of a transgressive nature, all of which surprised and amused him, but as conceptual transgressions went, they were perfectly harmless because nothing was ever going to come of them.

Suddenly aware that a response was expected from him, Ethan looked up from the Inland Revenue papers he was in the process of signing for his accountant – his accountant who just happened to be his father-in-law. This was no chance arrangement; it was a shitstorm of an arrangement that Francine had insisted upon when their marriage had been redefined in the aftermath of his misdemeanour. Francine had frequently told him it was her insurance policy. It was her way of making sure that she kept Ethan and the lifestyle to which she wanted to remain accustomed. In short, it meant he couldn't pull a fast one.

'Did I miss something?' Ethan asked.

It was his daughter who answered him. 'You're so, like, out of it, Dad! Haven't you, like, heard a word we were saying?'

He tapped the papers with his pen. 'I was giving my all to these. You know what a stickler your grandfather is for making sure everything's just as it should be.' Which was a polite way of saying, *You know what a bastard crook your grandfather is and I wouldn't trust him as far as I could throw his sorry arse!*

'We were discussing the possibility of going over to Abersoch,' Francine said. 'Daddy says the Selbys are about to put their house on the market, but if we get in early we could cut out the need for either party to go through an agent. And you know I've always thought the Selbys' place could be made into a truly special holiday home. Wouldn't you like a beautiful beach house to escape to, darling?'

Ethan couldn't believe what he was hearing. If anyone should know that this was the worst idea in the history of bad ideas, then it was Dearest Daddy. The man knew better than anyone how dangerously close to the wind the business was currently sailing. He risked a glance in Alan's direction. The steely-eyed look he was met with said, Want to take me on, son? Actually he did. He really did.

'As great an opportunity as that sounds,' Ethan said, pushing back his chair and getting to his feet, 'I'm sorry to be the bearer of bad news, but now really isn't a good time to be splashing out on a holiday home.' He wanted to shove the papers he'd just signed in his wife's face. *Get a load of that tax bill!* he wanted to shout. With a tax bill like that they would be lucky to have enough left in the kitty to buy a beach towel in Abersoch, never mind a beach house!

And what was the big deal about Abersoch? Just because Mummy and Daddy had been going there since for ever and reckoned there was nowhere better, it didn't mean the rest of them had to suffer the bloody place as well. God, he was angry! In direct response to his sudden fury, a searing pain took hold of his insides. He went over to the worktop where he'd left a file of papers. As the pain continued to scorch its way deep into the pit of his stomach he pretended to flick through the file. With his back to everyone else – he could hear them muttering amongst themselves – he squeezed his eyes shut and willed the pain to stop. At last it did. But not before he'd thought that perhaps the answer to all his problems would be to drop down dead. Right now. This very minute, chez Shirley and Alan in their brand new kitchen, his head smashing against the floor, splattering blood everywhere. It would be satisfying to think that the stain of his blood would be there for ever more, an indelible record: Here died Ethan Edwards.

When he opened his eyes, he found that he was alone with Dearest Daddy. Oh, shit, what now? What patronising knuckle-rapping session was he in for now? Whatever it was, the old devil could think again. He wasn't going to give an inch on this one. 'Alan,' he said, determined to head him off at the pass. 'You of all people know that I don't have the money for a second home. It's so far out of the question as to be laughable. No accountant in his right mind would sanction such a risky financial step.'

Alan nodded. 'You're absolutely right. Which is why I asked the girls to leave us so we could have a little chat, man to man. There was really no need for you to go jumping off at the deep end so dramatically.'

As cringingly awful as it was, Dearest Daddy really did refer to his old crone of a wife as a girl. 'I'd hardly call stating the obvious as being dramatic,' Ethan said, fighting to keep his temper.

'No matter,' Alan said dismissively. 'The important thing now, now that we're alone, is that you listen to me. Of course you can't afford to buy another property given the current economic situation, but there's no reason to alarm Francine with all that. As you well know, I've always believed the reason Shirley and I have had such a good marriage is because I've kept anything from her that I considered to be counterproductive to her wellbeing. I've told you before, women have a propensity to worry far more than we men and in my opinion it's the job of a good husband to keep his wife happy and worry-free. Which is why I've never allowed Shirley to worry about money; that's my responsibility. Just as it's your responsibility to keep my daughter happy. You once made her very unhappy and I'll never countenance that situation occurring again. So this is what I suggest you do: you borrow the money from me to buy the Selbys' house and pay me back when things have picked up again.'

And there endeth the first lesson according to Dearest Daddy.

'What if I don't want to borrow the money from you?' Ethan said. 'Or anyone else, for the simple reason I don't want the millstone of a second home hanging round my neck?'

Alan cleared his throat and narrowed his steely blue eyes into what he probably thought was a ruthlessly tough gaze. It didn't intimidate Ethan. Quite the reverse; it made him want to put a fluffy white cat in his hands and imagine him saying, *So Mr Bond, we finally meet*. But while Alan didn't intimidate him, Ethan knew it was a mistake to underestimate the man. For the greater part of his working career Alan Connolly had been a senior partner in a prestigious firm of accountants in Manchester and at the age of seventy-one he was the archetypal old warhorse and loved nothing better than to boast of the poor fools he had ground underfoot on his way up the ladder.

Still affecting his tough-man gaze, he said, 'Ethan, all I've ever wanted is for my only daughter to be happy. My only granddaughter as well. And having a holiday home near us in Abersoch would make them both very happy. Now why don't you come to your senses and accept my offer. You know, given the circumstances, I do think you could show a little more gratitude to what this family has done for you, and what we're prepared to go on doing for you.'

And there endeth the second lesson according to the Gospel

of Dearest Daddy. A not-so-subtle prod and a poke at Ethan's past sin. The sin that would never be forgiven or forgotten. The sin that would be the thorn in Ethan's side for as long as he was married to Francine.

Was it any wonder he sought refuge in sex with other women?

Was it any wonder he probably had an ulcer the size of the Grand Canyon burning a hole in his stomach?

Chapter Sixteen

There had been a right old kerfuffle earlier when Mrs Edwards had been firing off orders about what needed doing in her absence, but with the old witch now safely out of the way, Maggie suggested that it was time for elevenses.

'I know I shouldn't speak out of turn,' Maggie said as she carried two mugs of coffee through to the dining room and Ella removed her earphones – she was always listening to something – 'but anyone would think Mrs Edwards was going away for a month the way she was carrying on. Did you see how much luggage she had? It was enough for a trip round the world, never mind a couple of days in Abersoch. Not that I've ever been on a trip around the world, or am ever likely to, so what do I know? Come to that, I've never even been to Abersoch. Have you travelled much, Ella?' She cradled the hot mug in her hands and thought of all those thrown-away holiday brochures. Dave had said he wasn't going anywhere foreign where they didn't speak a proper lingo, so she could get that nonsense out of her head!

'Not so much recently,' Ella replied, 'but yes, a number of years ago I did. I lived in Italy for a while.'

'What was that like? Were the men ... you know ... were the Italian men as ...' She stopped herself short, suddenly embarrassed. Italian men in the stories she read were always dynamite in bed. Romantic, too.

Ella laughed. 'You mean, are they obsessed with sex and do they devote all their energies to trying to live up to their stallion reputation?'

'Something like that,' Maggie said, blushing into her coffee.

'More or less. And if they're not doing it, they're talking about doing it. And if they're not talking about doing it, they're imagining doing it. Sex is a full-time occupation for them. It's a wonder they get any work done.'

Maggie smiled. 'I expect you had your fair share of romances, then?'

'One or two.'

'What made you leave?'

'A man. An English man.'

Maggie couldn't think why anyone would want to leave a country where the men sounded a lot more exciting than anything cold, wet, miserable Britain had to offer. Certainly a sexy Italian lover who wanted to make mad passionate love to her had the edge on anything she had experienced with Dave of late. A once-a-fortnight prod and a poke was the best that he could manage. But if she was honest, she was grateful it wasn't anything more.

Worried that she was asking too many personal questions, she went over to the wall that Ella had started painting. The room now smelt of paint, but not the ordinary kind of decorating paint; this was a different kind of smell. But then Ella was a different kind of decorator.

Maggie would be the first to say that she knew about as much about art as she knew about travel, but she liked what Ella had done so far. There was a strange dreamy feel to it. Almost magical. She felt that if she was to stare hard enough at the hills and forest that were slowly appearing on the wall, she might get sucked into the picture and disappear into another world. A better world.

She thought about the awful wallpaper she had at home and wondered what Dave would have to say if she announced she wanted a mural on one of their walls. Odds on he would accuse her of having another of her funny turns. Maybe he would be right. She seemed to be having a lot of funny turns these days. Even her mum had commented on the fact that she seemed to be constantly away with the fairies. Perhaps she was reading too much and losing herself in the stories like she was now imagining she could lose herself in Ella's painting. But how good it would be to do exactly that, to run free amongst the trees and flowers, to have no one making any demands upon her, to wake up every morning happy. She reluctantly turned away from the wall. 'I hope you didn't think I was being nosy just now,' she said.

Ella smiled back at her. 'Not at all. The truth is, I gave up my life in Italy to be with a man I thought I was going to spend the rest of my life with. Unfortunately it didn't pan out that way.'

'I'm sorry.'

'I am as well. But hey, life goes on. How about you? Are you married?'

'Yes. And as you just said, but hey, life goes on.'

A moment passed between them, during which Maggie felt strongly tempted to tell this woman, a woman she hardly knew, her secret thoughts. But why would Ella, so clever and confident, be interested in anything going on in her life? 'Right,' she said, feeling cross with herself, 'I'd better leave you to get on. Sorry if I wittered on.'

'You didn't,' Ella said. 'And it makes a change for me having a woman to talk to. Often when I'm on a job the atmosphere is more like that of a building site and I'm surrounded by men trying to outdo each other, wanting to shock or embarrass me with their filthy jokes.'

'It makes a change for me having someone nice to talk to, as well,' Maggie admitted shyly. She extended her hand. 'Finished with your mug?'

At four o'clock Maggie left The Lilacs with an armful of the Edwards' clothes for the dry cleaners and Ella had the house to herself. A not altogether happy woman, thought Ella absently as she stood back to scrutinize her work. Something in the way Maggie spoke suggested that she wanted more from life.

But that could describe almost the entire population. When it came right down to it, who was one hundred per cent happy with their lot?

She rolled her head from side to side, trying to ease the tension in her neck and shoulders. She then slipped on her headphones and scrolled through the menu on her iPhone for a rousing piece of music to get her through the next few hours. She had decided to take advantage of no one being around and work late – Mrs Edwards had said her husband was away on business and her daughter was going into Manchester after school for some concert or other with the girl from next door.

As Handel's *Messiah* started up in her headphones, one thing she wasn't going to risk was releasing the tension in her shoulders by dancing again. It was almost two weeks since she had been caught doing her 'Viva La Vida' dance and she still cringed at the memory. She wondered if Mr Edwards had shared the joke with his wife. Though she couldn't really picture them sharing any kind of joke with each other. It was difficult to imagine Mrs Edwards having a sense of humour. But then who was Ella to judge? She was hardly Miss Congeniality these days, was she?

Her main preoccupation currently was Alexis. Ever since she had helped the girl she had been worried about her. She had tried ringing Alexis's mobile several times, but there had been no response. She had actually considered speaking to Lawrence, convinced that he should know what Alexis had been up to. But then each time she had got as far as reaching for the phone, she had warned herself to back off. Mayfield and all its goings-on had nothing to do with her anymore. Hadn't she learned anything from those seven years with Lawrence? Nothing she had said or done had made a blind bit of difference. Like it or not, she couldn't change anything. Change had to come from within. If the redecorating work at Mayfield was anything to go by, it looked as if Lawrence and Alexis might have made a much-needed start.

During the really frustrating and difficult times with Lawrence there had been one question Ella had repeatedly asked herself but had always been too scared to answer. It was this: *It's all very well staying in a relationship in the hope that it will change, but what if it never changes?* The question had buzzed around inside her head like an angry wasp until finally she had answered it and followed the only course of action open to her: she had walked away. But it was so galling to think that Lawrence and Alexis might now have realized the error of their ways and instigated some tentative changes to their lives.

Yet whatever heartache had gone before, Ella wished Alexis would answer her calls. She was anxious about the girl. What if there was a chance in a million of an adverse reaction to the morning-after pill and it had happened to Alexis and had made her dangerously ill? The worst of it was, Lawrence would blame Ella; he would never forgive her for endangering the life of his precious daughter.

Then the calm voice of reason cut into her panicky thoughts. Toby would have got in touch if anything serious had happened to his sister. Of course he would have.

Ethan had managed to wind things up a lot faster than expected with the buyer and instead of staying the night as originally planned he had decided to head for home. With Francine away in Abersoch with her parents and Valentina with Katie in Manchester and the pair of them staying the night with a friend, he would be happily home alone. He would cook himself something that he wanted to eat, and what was more, he would eat it in the sitting room whilst watching something he wanted to watch. He would not be reduced to watching a tedious soap or some hideous old hag going under the knife and God knew what else to appear ten years younger. Was it him, or did the women all end up looking like transvestites? And why did Francine and Valentina enjoy watching such trash? Was it to make themselves feel better about their own perfect bodies? But was there such a thing as a perfect body? He had seen many a naked female body in his time and he could write the book on the number of variations out there. Beauty was internal, that much he knew.

He turned into Lilac Avenue, passed the Paxtons' house – a blaze of lights on – then onto his own house. The sight of the dark blue Rav parked on the drive made him pause. He no longer thought of its owner as the anonymous Dragon Slayer. She was now Ella, very real, and very much flesh and blood and in his thoughts. He wondered whether he would catch her dancing again. He hoped so. He could do with a boost to the memory that was still causing him to have the occasional and enjoyable mental transgression.

He let himself in and walked quietly through the house towards the dining room. But he was out of luck; history was not going to repeat itself. Ella was halfway up a pair of stepladders, headphones in place, brush in hand, her brow drawn, her lips parted and the pink tip of her tongue showing. Breathing in the smell of linseed oil, he didn't think he had ever seen such concentration before; he felt compelled to watch her.

But he was to be denied the pleasure. She turned her head a fraction of an inch and caught sight of him. She visibly started and put a hand to her chest.

'Sorry,' he said as she removed her headphones. 'I seem to have a habit of catching you unawares. You realize what time it is, don't you?'

She pushed the cuff back on her sweater sleeve. 'Oh,' she said, 'it's even later than I thought. I'll pack up my things and get going.'

'No hurry. Not on my account, anyway.'

She looked at him hesitantly. 'You want me to carry on working?'

He smiled and shook his head. 'No. I meant that by all means pack up your things, but there's no need to hurry off. Why don't you stay and have a drink with me?'

She gave him another hesitant look. This time there was a hint of a frown. A frown of cynical disapproval. 'What time is your daughter due back?' she asked.

'She's not. She's staying the night with a friend over in— Ah, I see, you think I'm offering you more than a drink?'

She looked away, embarrassed. 'Of course I wasn't.'

'As a matter of fact, I am,' he said, unable to resist teasing her.

He watched her pull a dirty bit of rag out of a pocket and wipe her paintbrush on it. Her lips were tightly pursed and she was looking anywhere but at him. Her obvious discomfort suddenly made him realize what a colossal prat he was being. 'I'm sorry,' he said, 'what I meant, when I wasn't trying to prove what a jerk I can be, was that if you have nothing better to do, I'd be happy to provide you with something to eat, seeing as it's so late.'

She slipped the paintbrush behind her ear, stuffed the bit of rag back into her jeans pocket. 'I don't know why, but I meet a lot of jerks in my line of work. If they did what they did in the normal workplace, they'd be had up for sexual harassment.'

'It wouldn't be anything fancy.'

'And I'm sure I've never done anything to encourage it.'

'Some pasta maybe.'

'So I really hope we can be clear on the ground rules of my working here for you.'

'How does spaghetti carbonara sound? With a perfectly chilled glass of Chardonnay?'

She looked directly at him, her eyes wide. 'You are listening to me, aren't you?'

He nodded. 'I have no intention of harassing you, sexually or otherwise. I'm merely offering you supper in exchange for some intelligent conversation.'

'What makes you think you'll get that from me?'

He cast his gaze at the four walls around them. 'Because you're capable of doing something as unusual as this.'

'Sorry to disappoint you, but any half-decent art student could do it.'

He laughed. 'Steady, or you'll be talking yourself out of your fee.' He wandered over to the wall behind her, the one that she was working on. 'You know, it's growing on me. I like it more than I thought I would. I have no idea what made my wife want it so badly, other than some actress I've never heard of having something similar, but there's something ... I can't quite put my finger on it, but there's an engagingly innocent quality to it. Dreamlike, perhaps.'

'That's because it's Utopia in context.'

'That's it exactly. An ideal state.' He shrugged. 'A sadly unattainable state.'

'It's what the human spirit craves, a perfect world. We all dream of it.'

He turned and looked at her. 'There, that's the first intelligent conversation I've had all day. No, strike that, the first intelligent conversation I've had all week. Will you stay for some supper? With absolutely no hidden agenda attached. You have my word.'

She had shopped for tea, she had cooked tea, she had eaten tea, she had washed up after tea. What a life she led! And just like any other evening, with not a word of thanks, Dave and Dean had gone off happy as a couple of Larries to The Crown for a drink. Father and son. Chips and blocks. Peas and pods. Bloody ungrateful sods!

Still, two could play at that game. Maggie could go out too. She would go and see Mrs Oates and hear the latest news about her 'gentleman friend' as the old lady referred to him.

She was crossing the road to number twenty-six when she saw that there was a car directly outside Mrs Oates's house. She knew from Mrs Oates that Jack Potts drove an immaculate dark green Vauxhall Corsa, so the car wasn't his. 'He keeps it very nice,' Mrs Oates had said proudly of his Corsa. 'Spotless. You can practically see your face in the paintwork.'

Maggie had a mental picture of Jack Potts in his shirtsleeves carefully polishing the car inside and out before taking Mrs Oates anywhere in it. It was a stupid thought because it was winter and no man of Jack Potts' age should be out in the cold dressed only in a shirt. Well, he'd have his trousers on, of course. Socks and shoes, too. Just no pullover. Although according to Mrs Oates, he wasn't a fan of pullovers; he was more of a cardie man.

The car outside number twenty-six was a BMW, a black convertible with fancy alloy wheels. There were two large exhaust pipes and in the light cast from the street lamps, Maggie could see the windows were tinted and the paintwork polished to a high sheen. It looked like it was someone's pride and joy. Whoever its owner was, Maggie didn't think they were visiting Mrs Oates. It was probably for the house next door.

She rang the doorbell. A few minutes passed, then the door opened and a stranger stared back at Maggie.

A very handsome stranger.

He was tall and slim and dressed in pale blue jeans with a close-fitting white shirt. The jeans were tight – very tight – and the neck of his shirt was unbuttoned to reveal a V-shaped area of chest. A smooth hairless chest. His hair was dark and short and, and ... and he smelled amazing. Like nothing she had ever smelled before. It made her want to close her eyes and drift away on it.

But with her eyes firmly open, she saw his lips move and she clocked that he was smiling at her. Friggin' Moses in a basket ... what a smile!

'Yes,' he said.

'Um ...' That was when she noticed his eyes. Piercing blue eyes. Lovely, dazzling, heart-melting blue eyes. The kind of eyes that could melt icebergs in seconds flat.

He leaned forward. The closeness of him nearly made her pass out.

'Yes?' he repeated. 'Can I help you?'

Yes please, she wanted to say. Oh, yes please.

'Is it Mary you want?' he asked. He was still smiling at her and his voice was surprisingly calm, given that he probably thought he was dealing with the local neighbourhood nutter.

She nodded dumbly.

'You'd better come inside, then. She's just in the middle of thrashing my uncle and me at a game of Scrabble.'

Christine looked out of the bedroom window and couldn't believe what she was seeing. A dark blue Toyota Rav was driving down the avenue. A dark blue Rav that had no right being in the avenue at this time of night.

Furious jealousy ripped through her. How could Ethan do this to her? How could he betray her for a woman like Ella Moore?

Chapter Seventeen

With Ella gone, Ethan poured himself another glass of wine and went and stood in the dining room. But it wasn't the painting on the wall that he was interested in, it was the lingering feel of the woman who was responsible for changing the room that he wanted to explore.

When it came to women his track record gave a very clear indication that Ella Moore was not the kind of woman to whom he would be attracted. She simply didn't fit the profile. Her clothes were wrong (not feminine enough) and her body was wrong (too tall). But there was definitely something about her that he liked. He couldn't quite put his finger on what it was, but he certainly enjoyed her company.

Without exception all the women he had taken to bed had had one thing in common; they were knowing women, they understood the rules and how to play the game of extramarital sex. The golden rule being that one night of sex did not a relationship make. Only once had he made the mistake of getting too involved with a woman and committing himself to a full-blown affair. And just look at the trouble that had caused.

Invariably the women with whom he had slept in the past had been what he would call 'willing' but subtly so. The women he had assiduously avoided were the ones who blatantly threw themselves at him; he couldn't think of a bigger turn-off than a woman like Christine Paxton. Admittedly he hadn't known Ella long enough to have completely figured her out yet, but he doubted she had ever thrown herself at a man. She was probably the type who didn't rush into relationships lightly.

He had to acknowledge that she intrigued him, or more precisely, he was intrigued by his reaction to her. As the evening wore on he had realized something important; he was experiencing a refreshing and satisfying sense of ease in her company and enjoying being himself with her. So often he hid behind a wall of pretence with people by hitting the charm button, but with Ella he didn't have to pretend to be someone other than who he was. It made him realize what a conceited and shallow smart arse he must have originally come across as being to her.

What surprised him most about Ella was that he was beginning to view her as a potential friend. A friend in whom he could confide. He didn't make friends easily – it was a trust issue, he supposed. Too often he had been the focus of envy in his life, because on the face of it he had everything going for him: a successful business and a beautiful and adoring wife. What a joke that was. People had no idea what his life was really like or the strain he was under to keep the show going.

For a crazy moment during the evening he had imagined being totally honest with Ella, telling her that life chez The Lilacs was nothing but a shabby lie. But he'd kept quiet, understanding all too clearly just how he would appear: a chancer spinning the old line about his wife not understanding him.

He took a sip of his wine and moved in closer to the part of the wall that Ella was currently working on. He remembered the expression of intense concentration on her face when he had caught her unawares earlier that evening. He truly admired her ability to focus her thoughts so deeply. Perhaps that was one of the things that he found so intriguing about her – her capacity to be so thoroughly absorbed in what she was doing.

He would be lying if he said he hadn't experienced more than a moment's curiosity during the evening as to what sex might be like with her, but he had suppressed the impulse and relaxed into satisfying his curiosity in a very different way by discovering more about her while at the same time trying to put her at ease. He now knew that she had never been married and that for seven years she had been in a long-term relationship with a widower with two children and that it hadn't worked out, not for her at any rate.

He also knew that she had an eclectic taste in music, that she had lived in Italy and loved Italian food (lucky move when he'd suggested pasta!), she couldn't abide reality or makeover shows on the television whether it was for houses or women (something they had in common), she hated ostentatious pretention of any sort (another thing they had in common) and she dreamed of one day buying a small place in Italy to do up. Her expectations of life, she had admitted, were pretty straightforward and modest: a roof over her head, enough to eat and a supply of good books to read whilst listening to an equally good supply of music would be enough for her. 'No desire for a husband, then?' he had enquired.

'Probably not,' she had replied.

If only Francine had such modest expectations.

In his experience women had far higher expectations than men. It was the woman who laid down the law when it came to anything to do with the home. It was her domain and therefore she was the one who dictated what was required and how and when it would be obtained. Net result, the husband had to get out there and graft for it. The one thing you could rely upon with a woman was that no matter what you gave her, it was never enough. The goal posts were constantly being moved.

It was the same with sex; women had any number of expectations and they changed as often as the wind changed direction. One minute they wanted candles and romantic music and Mr Darcy, and the next they were demanding to be tied to the bed by a grunting caveman. And heaven forbid that a man failed in his duty to bring a woman to an earth-shattering orgasm. For some time now Francine had been complaining that their sex life had stalled. She had even quoted Adam, who had apparently boasted to her that sex with Christine had never been better in the last year. Presumably Francine thought that comparing him with Adam-the-Super-Stud would in some macho egotistical stand-off way fire him up. It was just another example of the mind games women played; they were always planning their next move or analysing their last.

Of course Francine wasn't the only woman to find fault in his prowess of late. There was that woman down in London, then last August a woman had got alarmingly angry with him when he failed to climax; she had taken it as a personal slight, a questioning of her desirability. Another had taken it as a challenge and had kept him in bed for hours as she tried every trick she knew to make him come. When she finally admitted defeat, she had casually asked him if he had ever considered the possibility that maybe he was gay.

Expectations. Oh, yes, he knew all about them. He knew, too, that sex for him had changed from being a way of making him feel whole and alive, to making him feel sick of heart and yet more of a failure. The instinct was there all right, but that was all. It had become no more than a basic urge to scratch an itch. He couldn't remember the last time he had experienced a genuine connection with a woman.

Maggie held out her empty glass and allowed Jack Potts's nephew to refill it with sparkling white wine. Jack and Mrs Oates were on the medium sweet sherry – a little of what you fancy as Jack called it with a wink – and Daryl was drinking some non-alcoholic lager. 'Designated driver,' he said with a smile in her direction as he poured the lager slowly and carefully into a glass and not directly down his throat as Dave and Dean did. 'I pulled the short straw.'

'Hark at him,' laughed Jack. 'Anyone would think I forced him to drive. I said I'd drive but he wouldn't hear of it.'

Maggie didn't think she would be able to take much more

of Daryl smiling at her. He was beyond gorgeous. He was all-out hot. He was *dee*-licious. Her dream man. He made every single one of those men she had read and fantasized about seem as desirable as Gordon Brown. He was the real thing, all six-feet-plus sexy muscle-toned inches of him. And here he was, in Mrs Oates's front room, sexy bum perched on the arm of the sofa where his uncle and Mrs Oates were sitting like a pair of cosy lovebirds.

Even his name was ringtone perfect.

Daryl Delaney.

Could there be a more perfect name in the world? The more she said it inside her head, the more she wanted to say it. She was reacting like a total idiot, but she didn't care. If this was what it felt like to lose your head, then count her in!

How glad she was that she had decided to pop over the road and ended up gatecrashing her neighbour's impromptu party. Apparently Jack had wanted Mrs Oates to meet his nephew and had asked if he could call in with him this evening. They hadn't arrived empty-handed, so Mrs Oates had told Maggie; they had brought her chocolates, flowers and a bottle or two picked up from the off-licence to oil the wheels of the evening. No wonder Mrs Oates looked so happy. What woman wouldn't have a smile on her face a mile wide when treated so well?

'Are you always so quiet and thoughtful?'

Maggie looked up. Daryl had moved from the far arm of the sofa – home to the lovebirds – and was now lowering himself onto the arm of the chair she was sitting in. At such close range his presence and the mouth-watering smell of him were almost too much to bear. If he leaned in any closer she would either faint or burst into flames. Maybe both. Surely he should come with a government health warning? Surely there were laws passed to protect innocent bystanders from the threat of such a heady overload of sinfully irresistible testosterone? She forced her brain to connect with her tongue so she could answer him and after the connection had seemingly taken the long and scenic route, she found herself saying, 'That's me, Mrs Quiet and Thoughtful.'

He smiled. 'Better that than someone who doesn't engage their brain with their mouth. I hate people who do that. What were you thinking of?'

'Oh, nothing important. Just idle daydreaming. I do it all the time.'

'Nothing wrong in dreaming,' he said.

'Wouldn't that depend on what the dream is?'

'Definitely. So what do you dream of, mostly?'

She blushed and took a gulp of her sparkling wine. No way was she going to say out loud what she spent her time dreaming about, least of all admit that from now on he was going to feature heavily in her fantasies. *Sorry, Miguel, but you and your dusty ranch are history now!*

'Shall I tell you what I dream of?' he said. He had the loveliest of accents. A soft Yorkshire accent. Well, that's what she thought it was.

She took her life into her hands and risked glancing back up into his face. His dazzling blue eyes were fixed on hers. A shiver went down her spine. 'Go on,' she murmured.

'You promise you won't laugh?'

'I'll try not to,' she said lightly, recalling Mrs Oates saying the same to her not so long ago.

'I dream that one day—'

You'll meet a woman called Maggie and fall madly in love with her and whisk her away from the loveless and boring life she leads, she wanted to suggest.

'—I'll,' he continued. But he got no further. From somewhere about his perfect body came the unmistakable trill of a mobile. 'Sorry,' he said as he got to his feet and pulled the mobile from his pocket. After the briefest of looks at the phone, with an apologetic shrug of his shoulders he said, 'Sorry, but I'd better take this. I'll go outside.' As he hurried from the room with his uncle looking on disapprovingly, he spoke into the phone. 'Hello, love, of course you're not disturbing me. I told you to ring me any time you wanted.'

'Mobile phones should be banned, in my opinion,' Jack said. 'They always end up spoiling a good conversation.'

Maggie couldn't agree more. 'I think it's time I was going,' she said.

Chapter Eighteen

There was no getting away from it; Ella had made a spectacular fool of herself last night.

She should never have agreed to have dinner with Ethan.

And she most certainly should not have accused him of wanting more than dinner with her. What had got into her? She had dealt with men like Ethan Edwards many times before; there had been no need to react in such a ludicrously over the top fashion. Even if he was an instinctive womanizer, it didn't mean she had to go around playing the sexual harassment card.

So what if she suspected he had been toying with her?

So what if she suspected he was the type of man who didn't take his marriage vows too seriously?

So what if she could picture him standing in front of the altar the day of his marriage with his fingers crossed behind his back when he promised to love, honour and do whatever else it was that men and women promised each other when they planned to spend the rest of their lives together? But did anyone know what they were doing in such a moment? And what, for the love of God, had Ethan seen in Mrs Edwards? Or had she been a sweet and innocent little thing back then? A fragrant nosegay of loving adoration who worshipped the ground upon which he walked?

Relationships – they were the weirdest things. Ella didn't think she would ever fathom them out or comprehend what drove two people to be attracted to each other. Or what kept them together. Could a promise to love someone for ever really hold firm? Ella wasn't so sure it could. Love was capricious. It oscillated according to the conditions and pressures put upon a relationship.

Realizing she had distracted herself from the original train of her thoughts, she marshalled them back into line. Back to Ethan Edwards, and the real cause of her anger. At home in bed last night when she had been replaying the evening in her head, she had experienced a feeling she wholeheartedly wished she hadn't. But the feeling had been real. And very dangerous. She had felt her body betray her with the first unmistakable stirrings of attraction to Ethan. To make matters worse, she had then dreamed of him. And not any old dream: this had been a sexually explicit dream the like of which she had never had before. When she had woken from it she didn't know what shocked her more – the fact that her subconscious had conjured such a thing or that she immediately wanted to go back to sleep in the hope of the dream repeating itself.

Now, at eight thirty in the morning as she pulled onto the drive at The Lilacs, she promised herself that whatever madness she had experienced last night, it stopped as of now. She would not give a charming womanizer – let's call him what he was – the satisfaction of knowing he had provoked any kind of reaction in her. Absolutely not. Give a seasoned campaigner like him an inch and he would take more than a mile. He would take the length and breadth of every available liberty.

Fully resolved, fully prepped, she rang the doorbell. Ethan had said he would wait to let her in before leaving for work. She wished that he had simply handed over a spare key to her last night; it would be easier all round. The thought immediately made her crosser still. What was the matter with her? Could she no longer trust herself in his company without fearing she would do something silly? Earth to Ella Moore: *Get a grip!*

There was no response, so she rang the bell again.

Oh my God! she thought when the door finally opened. He's done this deliberately.

Oh, hell, thought Ethan, when he opened the door. She's going to think I've done this deliberately.

Fresh out of the shower and clutching a hastily grabbed towel around his waist, he said, 'I'm sorry; I overslept. I forgot to set the alarm on my mobile. I can't remember the last time I did that. Come to think of it, I can't remember the last time I slept so soundly.'

He was talking too much. Gabbling like an idiot. And not convincing her from the look on her face as she stepped inside – her eyes were fixed on the lower reaches of him, on his feet where a cold draught was now nipping at his bare, wet toes. 'Make yourself at home,' he said, closing the door and retreating to the stairs. 'You'll find what you need in all the obvious places in the kitchen if you want to make yourself a drink.'

Upstairs he gave himself the fastest shave on record, then threw on the first clothes to hand. As he buttoned his shirt, he wondered why he had been so concerned that she would think badly of him. What was the big deal? *Shock, horror – call the police: man caught opening front door in nothing but a towel!* That would really make the front pages.

He went downstairs. There was no sign of Ella in the kitchen, or of a boiling kettle. He went through to the dining room and found her there. She had taken off her coat, hat and scarf and was squeezing a small tube of paint onto a palette. 'Everything okay?' he asked.

'Fine,' she said without looking up from the palette.

'You didn't make yourself a drink,' he said. Oh, great, nothing like stating the obvious.

'No,' she said.

Nothing like a monosyllabic response either. 'Would you like me to make you one?'

'No, thank you.'

That was progress. From monosyllabic reply to a mighty three words in one easy step. 'Sorry about before,' he said.

Except he wasn't. He had a perfect right to answer the door wearing whatever he so chose. Next time he might greet her dressed in a gorilla suit whilst playing a banjo. See what she made of that!

Nothing back. Which only reinforced the desire in him to squeeze something more out of her. Not unlike the way she was now squeezing the remains of a manky-looking tube of violet paint onto her palette. Why the coldness towards him? What had changed since last night? Last night she had been warm and interesting; now she was cold and indifferent. If he wanted that kind of treatment, he could join his wife in Abersoch. 'Right,' he said. 'I'll leave you to get on.' He turned to go. But he couldn't resist one more try. All he wanted was a small reaction from her. A small smile, for instance. Would that be too much to ask for? He turned back. 'I enjoyed your company last night,' he said. 'You brightened up my evening.'

At last she raised her gaze from what she was doing so intently. For a split second her face was unmasked and she seemed at a loss as to what to say. 'Thank you,' she said eventually. 'I enjoyed myself too.'

And that, he thought as he left the house and drove to work, was what he had wanted to hear from her. He wanted to know that she had found his company as pleasant as he had found hers. He had wanted to know that the evening hadn't been one-sided. He wondered whether he could possibly engineer a repeat performance tonight. He didn't see why not. The thought instantly cheered him.

But then he remembered that Valentina would be around. Having his daughter play gooseberry would hardly be conducive to what he had in mind. Although it was difficult to pin down exactly what it was he had in mind when it came to Ella. Okay, there were those interesting thoughts he'd had about her, but when he was actually with Ella, sex wasn't uppermost in his thoughts.

*

Next door, as she followed Mrs Paxton's instructions to the letter and polished the Aga, Maggie couldn't stop thinking of sex.

Sex on a tropical beach.

Sex on a windswept moor.

Sex on a bed of feathers.

Sex on a rug in front of a log fire.

Sex in a hay barn.

Sex on a four-poster bed.

Sex in an olive grove.

Sex in a hot tub.

God, she'd settle for sex in the back of a car! It would have to be a very shiny black car and the man in question would have to be Daryl Delaney.

Daryl Delaney.

Just thinking his name made her body zing. She couldn't recall ever feeling this way before. Dave had never made her want to rip his clothes off and lick him all over.

She gulped. Where had that thought come from? She rubbed extra hard at the chrome rail on the Aga and tried not to think of the pathetic uselessness of having a severe case of the lusts for a man like Daryl Delaney. He probably had a mile-long queue of attractive girls and women who fancied him. What would he see in someone as unattractive as her? She was thirty-six years old, she cleaned other people's houses for a living, she couldn't remember the last time she had been to the hairdresser, let alone treated herself to some decent new clothes, and she just happened to be married.

And let's face it, a bloke like him had to have a knockout-looking girlfriend.

Hello love, he'd said when he had answered his mobile last night. Hardly the way you'd greet a friend, was it?

Whoever he had been talking to, she was a lucky woman.

But then there were plenty of women who were lucky, women who didn't have a clue just how well off they were. Take Mrs Paxton and Mrs Edwards – they had it all: big fancy houses, flash cars and a life of luxury. They never had to lift a finger or worry about how the next bill would be paid. But two more mean-spirited, miserable bitches you couldn't meet.

Some people would probably say that Maggie was lucky, too. She was married with a son who wasn't in any trouble, she had a roof over her head, was in good health, and had a job, so yes, she was better off than many. So why then did she feel she could walk away from it all? Why couldn't she be happy? Why couldn't she feel satisfied with her life? Why did she spend all her time dreaming of something better?

'I'm not paying you to daydream.'

Maggie nearly jumped out of her skin at the sound of Mrs Paxton's voice. How had the evil woman crept up on her so silently? 'Sorry,' she said, 'I was miles away.'

Mrs Paxton stared coldly at her. 'And that's exactly where you'll find yourself if you don't watch it. I've told you before that your work is below standard. I shan't warn you again; I shall simply find a better, more reliable cleaner. Have I made myself clear?'

As clear as the shine on this bloody Aga I've just spent the last twenty minutes cleaning, thought Maggie. 'Yes,' she said.

'You should have told her where to stick her bloody standards. I've told yer before, Mags, yer shouldn't let people walk all over yer. Bring us another beer if yer passing the kitchen. My throat's as dry as a cat's bum.'

Why Maggie had shared with Dave what Mrs Paxton had said, she didn't know. He was hardly likely to offer any real sympathy. Only bluster. Since she was actually going to the kitchen to do the washing up, she got him another beer from the fridge. She was probably making more work for herself, but she couldn't resist giving the can a shake. With a bit of luck it would spray all over his fat, idle body and the sofa would be spared. She went back into the lounge where he was channel-hopping and gave him the beer. He took it without a word or a glance.

On an impulse she decided the washing up could wait. She was in the hall putting on her coat when she heard Dave yelling. 'Oi, Mags, get us a cloth, will yer?'

'Just going over the road to see Mrs Oates,' she called out as if she hadn't heard him. How was that for not letting people walk all over her?

Mrs Oates admitted to having had a slightly sore head that morning. 'I shouldn't have had so much sherry last night,' she said after she had made a pot of tea. 'It was a shame you didn't stay longer. Daryl told us some wonderful stories about his work. He's an entertainer, you know. A singer. He had me in tucks. Jack simply can't understand why he isn't married; he's thirty-nine and seems very eligible to me. You don't suppose he's gay, do you?'

Gay? The gorgeous Daryl Delaney, *gay?* Never! Not possible! Not in a million years!

Maggie had come over in the hope of learning more about Jack Potts's nephew only now to discover he was beyond even her wildest dreams. 'I don't think he is,' she said. 'He doesn't seem the type to me.'

But the seeds of doubt had been sown. A man who looked and smelt as good as he did, a man who obviously took such good care of himself ... did that mean he couldn't be straight? He had been very nice to her, had actually shown some interest in her. Did that also mean he couldn't be straight?

'He did seem to be wearing jeans that were very tight,' Mrs Oates said. 'I think that's a sign, isn't it? Don't they all do that?'

'Not necessarily.'

'Not that I have anything against gays,' Mrs Oates said. 'Nothing at all. I'm not prejudiced; please don't think I am. Ever since Rock Hudson and Liberace I've had an open mind about homosexuals.'

They were in the front room, the scene of last night's little get-together. Maggie drank her tea on the sofa with Mrs Oates and stared longingly at the arm of the chair where Daryl had sat next to her. She was tempted to go over and sniff the chair, to see if any trace of the man remained.

'Now be honest with me, dear,' Mrs Oates said. 'What did you think of Jack?'

'I thought he was just as you'd described him. He was very nice. And he's clearly very sweet on you.'

Mrs Oates smiled. 'You know, I think he is.'

'And are you sweet on him?'

The smile widened. 'I could be tempted.'

'Then be tempted, Mrs O. Have some fun.'

'You don't think I'm being a silly old fool?'

'Would it be so wrong if you were?'

'I've never been very good at being foolish. I've always been so sensible. Mr Oates and I courted for five years before we got engaged and then we waited another three years before we married. Cautious and sensible. That's how I've always been.'

'Then maybe it's high time you went a little crazy and threw some caution to the wind.'

And Maggie really wasn't talking about herself. No, she was thinking only of Mrs Oates.

Chapter Nineteen

Ella decided not to work late that evening at The Lilacs. It had nothing to do with worrying about being alone with her client again and all to do with being exhausted. She had just started packing up her things when she heard the front door open. Damn, she thought.

But it was only Valentina, home from school. The girl put her head round the door of the dining room and declared that the whole house stank of paint. 'It's, like, proper minging,' she said in her carefully dumbed-down voice, wrinkling her nose.

Valentina might not have any manners, but Ella did. She smiled politely and said, 'How was the concert last night?'

Valentina stared at her. 'Like, what is this? Interrogation City?'

'Your father mentioned it to me and I was just wondering if you'd had a good time.'

'Well, *duh*, it was a gag fest.'

Not having a clue whether that meant it had been good or bad, Ella finished packing up her things.

When she arrived home after stopping off at the supermarket, she saw a car parked on the road outside her house. The sight of the car filled her with foreboding.

She was right to be concerned. She had scarcely switched off the engine and pushed open the door when a very angry man was accosting her. 'What the hell did you think you were doing?' he demanded.

'Nice to see you again, too, Lawrence. Just passing, were you?'

'Don't you dare patronize me!'

He was fuming. Thoroughly steamed up. 'Please don't yell at me on my drive,' she said quietly. 'If you have something to get off your chest, come inside and do it.'

He didn't offer to help carry any of the bags of shopping into the house and she didn't ask him to help. She had never seen him so furious. She tried to defuse his anger by offering him a drink.

He wasn't having it. He plainly hadn't come here to be calmed down. He'd come for a showdown. 'What gave you the right to think you could withhold something so important from me?' he seethed, the height and breadth of him filling the space between them. 'Come on, just tell me! What the hell did you think you were doing?'

'I assume you're referring to Alexis,' she said calmly.

'Of course I am! Why else would I be here?'

'Why else indeed? Certainly not to enquire after my health or exchange a few pleasantries.'

'What's that supposed to mean?'

'Oh, forget it. Forget I ever existed. But what am I saying? You've managed to do that already, haven't you? I'm just surprised you remembered where I now live. Jogging your memory must have been quite a stretch for you.'

'I don't recall you ever being so bitter before.'

'That's because you never really knew me. Now please, I've had a long day and I'm tired, so can we get to the point of your visit? You want to know why I helped Alexis and why I didn't rush to tell you about it, is that it?'

'Precisely that. You had no right to do what you did. She's barely of a legal age to have sex. A few months earlier and it would have been rape!'

'It was no such thing and you know that. I helped Alexis because she asked me to. She didn't have anyone else to whom she could turn.'

135

'That's simply not true. She has me. I've always been there for her. Nothing is more important to me than her well-being.'

'Do you really want me to comment on that?'

For a moment he looked confused. He recovered himself quickly. 'There's nothing you could say that would make me believe I haven't done the best job as a father.'

'Then you have to ask yourself why she didn't turn to you when she needed help. And why you feel so angry that she didn't.'

He looked like she'd slapped him. 'I ... I don't know. I ...' his voice trailed off.

'You might also like to mull over why you're so angry with me,' Ella continued.

'That's easy. You should never have hidden something so important from me. It was unforgivable what you did. Worse still, it had nothing to do with you.'

'Oh, get down from your high horse and face facts. You're furious with Alexis and because you can't show her how angry you are, the only person you can take it out on is me. I put up with a lot from you before, Lawrence; now I won't. Now I'll be as blunt and as honest as I should have been when we were together. I should have told you years ago exactly what I thought.'

'Which is what, exactly?'

'That you and Alexis have put each other on a pedestal and neither one of you can admit that you're not perfect. Alexis couldn't tell you she'd messed up for the simple reason she knows you think she's perfect, and the fact that she's having unsafe sex at her age would be a huge disappointment to you. Your relationship goes dangerously deeper than the normal father and daughter relationship. Her having sex is practically a betrayal of your love for her.'

In the silence that followed as they stood face to face, the bags of shopping still at her feet, Ella watched the man she had loved so much slowly crumple before her. His whole body seemed to collapse like a deflated balloon. He turned away from her, pushed a hand through his hair, then slowly swung round. His eyes were dark and full of pain. She felt a wave of intense sadness for him.

'I've screwed up, haven't I?' he murmured. 'All the time I thought I was being a good father. What's worse, you warned me. You told me I was indulging her too much but I didn't listen.' He slumped into the nearest chair. He bent his head and covered his face with his hands.

His obvious distress softened her heart and Ella went to him. She put a hand on his shoulder. She could feel a tremor running through him. 'Lawrence, I know Alexis means the world to you, but you have to start treating her as a normal daughter. As a normal, fallible human being.'

'I was trying to be all things to her. She had lost her mother. I thought—' He started to cry.

Ella increased the pressure of her hand on his shoulder. 'I know,' she said gently. 'You thought you were doing the right thing. It's what any good parent needs to believe.'

'But you've just said I haven't been a good parent.'

'I didn't say that. In some ways you've been an excellent father, but in other ways—' She stopped herself from going any further. It seemed unnecessarily cruel.

He uncovered his face and looked up, his expression bleak. 'Go on,' he said, 'finish what you were going to say.'

'You know yourself what you've done; you don't need me to spell it out. Now why don't you accept that drink I offered a few minutes ago?'

He nodded.

'Coffee or something stronger?'

'Coffee,' he answered. Then: 'May I ... may I use the toilet, please?'

'Of course. Back out into the hall, first door on the left.'

While he was gone, Ella unpacked the shopping, put it away and made a pot of coffee. She had everything organized when he finally reappeared. He must have washed his face, judging from the splashes of water on his shirt. He looked much more his customary composed self. He lowered himself into the chair where he'd sat earlier. 'I'm sorry,' he said when she put a mug of coffee in front of him. 'Sorry I went off the deep end with you.'

'That's okay. What are ex-girlfriends for, if not to sound off at?'

He winced. 'You were more than a girlfriend, Ella.'

'Really? It didn't feel that way at times.'

'Then I'm sorry for that, too.'

'All water under the bridge,' she said. 'No point in dwelling on it.' She took a sip of her coffee. 'How did you find out about Alexis?'

'I …' He rubbed at his eyes. 'I read her diary.'

'You did *what*?'

'I know, I know. I crossed a line.'

'And you had the cheek to say what I did was unforgivable. What made you do it?'

'I knew something was wrong with her and no matter how I tried to get her to open up, she kept saying I was imagining things, that there wasn't anything wrong. But I knew. I knew there was something she was keeping from me. I was worried it might be drugs. It's every parent's worst nightmare. I had to find out what it was. Isn't that what any good parent would do?'

Ella scratched her head. 'I don't know. There are all sorts of trust issues at stake here. Does Alexis know what you've done?'

He shifted awkwardly in his seat. 'No. I read what she had written and came straight here.'

'Are you going to tell her?'

'Should I?'

'You really want my opinion?'

He nodded. 'I'm out of my depth, Ella. I don't know what to do. It seems a bit late now to give her the safe sex talk and preach about the dangers of alcohol. I'm no good at that sort of thing. I thought school would have it covered.'

Ella recalled the first occasion and all the subsequent times when she had proposed the idea that one of them, if not both of them, should have that particular discussion with Alexis. She recalled too how Lawrence had repeatedly asserted that Alexis was too young, that she wasn't ready yet. With nothing to be gained in reminding him of this, Ella said, 'I think you should leave well alone. If Alexis ever finds out that you read her diary, she'll never trust you again.'

'I don't think she trusts me anyway. Otherwise she would have come to me for help.'

'As I said, there are all sorts of trust issues at stake here. But really, when you get down to it, how many daughters would ask their father to help them to get the morning-after pill?'

'I'm glad she came to you. Thank you for being there for her.'

'I really didn't have much choice. I must admit, though, I was surprised she asked me to help.'

'I think she misses you.'

Ella smiled. 'She said as much to me. I suggested she missed having someone to argue with.'

'Don't do yourself down. You did a great job in the circumstances.'

'Pity you didn't tell me that at the time.'

He sighed. 'Oh, Ella, how did it all go so badly wrong between us?'

'I'm going to stick my neck out and say I think you know the answer to that one too.'

Chapter Twenty

Two hours after she had performed the winner's dance Maggie still couldn't believe that she had scooped the jackpot of five thousand pounds.

If it hadn't been for Peggy keeping an eye on her bingo card, she would have missed it. She had been busy daydreaming again – fantasizing that Daryl, with the lights definitely switched off, was slowly undressing her – and then suddenly Peggy was yelling in her ear. 'You've won! You've bleedin' won!' Mo had then held up the card and waved it frantically in the air, shrieking her head off at the same time.

Stunned and embarrassed as she was forced to perform the winner's dance, Maggie had remembered the last time she had won something; it had been a jar of pickled onions six months past its sell-by date in a raffle at the British Legion.

To celebrate her big win she and the Sisters of Fun were having supper at the Taj Mahal, Maggie's treat. At the rate Lou and her friends were going they'd soon have the money spent. Not on curry and poppadoms, but on new clothes and a makeover for her.

'You should come to Poland with us, chuck,' Mo was now saying.

'Yes,' chimed in Lou. 'You could get those bags under your eyes done.'

'Thanks a bunch, Mum!'

'Don't be so touchy. A slice off here and there and a bit added elsewhere and who knows, it might put some zip back into things between you and Dave.'

Maggie snapped her head round and looked at her mother. 'Why do you say that?'

Her mother shrugged. 'Stands to reason, doesn't it? Things get stale. You've got to pep things up after a while.'

The others all agreed.

'But why?' asked Maggie. 'If a marriage has gone stale, isn't it better to leave it and try something fresh? And why should it be me who has to change? Why shouldn't it be Dave who has something sliced off? He's got plenty going spare, after all.'

Everyone stared at her.

'Are you saying what I think you're saying?' Lou said.

With more wine inside her than usual, Maggie did that rare thing – she squared up to Lou. 'I don't know, Mum. What is it you think I'm saying?'

'Whatever it is,' Mo said brightly, while breaking a piece off the last of the poppadoms, 'it's going to have to wait; here's our main course. How about another bottle of wine, girls? Same again?'

With the arrival of their food and after the scramble of everyone helping themselves from the stainless steel dishes, Maggie's spirits sank. Even Mo doing her famous impersonation of Tom Jones ringing her up and asking her out did nothing to lift her mood.

'Question is,' said Peggy, pointing her fork at Mo, 'now that Tom's gone grey, do you still fancy him?'

'Are you kidding? Whatever the colour of his hair, you know I'm fully dysfunctional when it comes to The Tom. And get that bit of spinach out of your mouth, Peggy; it looks like you've lost a tooth.'

The talk then turned to one of their favourite subjects, their Top Ten of Sex Gods. When they'd exhausted that – George Clooney coming out on top as usual – Betty made a second visit to the ladies. When she was back at the table she confessed to having trouble with her waterworks – she was always having to go to the loo.

Peggy sympathized. 'Let's face it, girls, it's the future for us all. It won't be long before we'll have to rename ourselves The Tena Ladies.'

'Or how about The Four Tenas?' laughed Mo.

She was onto her fifth glass of wine – or was it her sixth? – when Maggie heard someone say, 'I don't love him, you know. I can't remember when I did. I don't know if I ever did.'

The table went quiet.

Everyone stopped what they were doing and were staring. They were staring at *her*.

She groaned. Oh, God, the 'someone' was her. How had it happened? The answer, of course, lay in the glass in her hand. She took another gulp from it, hoping that it would turn into a huge pool of water and she could dive into it and disappear.

She groaned again. How drunk was she that she thought she could disappear into a glass of wine? She suddenly felt dizzy. And a little sick. Actually, a lot sick. She really shouldn't have drunk so much. Pushing back her chair, she got to her feet. 'I need the loo,' she said. Her head spun even more now that she was upright. She almost sat down again, but the need for the toilet was greater than her need to sit down. She stumbled to the door marked with a woman in a stupid bonnet and crinoline dress and pulled on the handle. It wouldn't open. She yanked on the handle again. 'Bloody stupid door,' she muttered.

'Perhaps I could help,' said a voice. A voice she was sure this time wasn't hers. It was definitely a man's voice. She turned round and realized that she was more hammered than she'd thought. Because only being tits-up drunk would conjure such a sight.

Just inches from her was Daryl-bootilicious-Delaney. The man of countless fantasies. The man who smelled like paradise. Oh, for being drunk! Cos when you were trashed anything was possible. When you were as drunk as a skunk and imagining things – like the man of your dreams was looking at you with an amused look on his face – you could do and say all the things you couldn't normally do or say. She raised an imaginary glass. 'Here's to being off my head,' she said, wobbling back against the door. 'And here's to you and you know what, as Mo would say, I'm fully dysfunctional about you.' She laughed, suddenly feeling like she was having the best time ever, even if the ground and walls did seem to be moving a bit too much for her liking. 'And may I also say,' she went on, as she steadied herself against the door, 'you've never looked more lickable? Who-*aaa!*'

The next thing she knew, she was flat on her back and her head was hurting. She could feel something cold beneath her. Something cold and hard. With her head turned to one side she saw that she was lying on the floor. She hoped it was clean, that whoever was responsible for keeping it clean did a proper job.

A few feet away she could see a pale green paper towel and a half-used roll of toilet paper. If she closed an eye and squinted the other, she could look right through the cardboard tube, just as she'd done as a child when pretending she was staring at the stars through a telescope.

Toilet paper, she thought. Did that mean she was lying on the floor of a toilet? Why? She looked up, straight into the face of Daryl Delaney. That was strange. What was he doing here? What was the ever-so-sexy Daryl Delaney doing here?

She was dreaming; that was what was going on. She was dreaming that she was lying on a toilet floor and he was here with her. Okay, it wasn't the normal kind of daydream she had about him, but it would have to do. He was looking at her in a very odd way, though. She tried to think why he might be looking at her like that, then she got it: he was worried. He leaned in closer to her and she got a powerful sexy waft of him. Could you smell things in your dreams? Well, she could in this dream. She could do anything she wanted. Maybe she could reach out and hug him, wrap her arms around his oh-so-lovely shoulders. The only thing wrong with the dream was that her head was killing her. Why couldn't she have a perfect dream? Why did everything have to be spoiled for her? It would be just her luck that any minute the lovely Daryl would change into Mr Blobby and her dream would become a nightmare.

'Are you okay?'

The voice sounded like it was coming from a long way away, or as if she was listening to it on the phone with a bad line. She forced herself to smile. 'I'm fine,' she said.

He frowned. 'Really?'

'Never better.'

'I somehow doubt that. You took a helluva tumble. Your head whacked the floor sommat bad. Do you think you can sit up?'

'I can tap dance if you like.'

He smiled. 'Maybe another time.'

He placed his hands under her and she felt herself being lifted. Please don't let him turn into Mr Blobby, she silently wished as she felt her body being pressed against his. How warm and strong he felt. Just how she had imagined.

She was sitting upright and deciding whether she had the energy to stand when she realized something bad: she was going to be sick.

And she was. Disgustingly so. All over the man of her dreams.

'You've got some explaining to do!' said Lou the next morning.

Maggie held the phone from her ear. 'There's no need to shout, Mum,' she whimpered.

Alone in the house, she was feeling very sorry for herself. Dave and Dean had left for work two hours ago, leaving her to call in sick to the people she normally cleaned for today; she had lied about having a stomach bug. A stomach bug was so much more respectable than the truth. Thank goodness they'd been okay about it. Thank goodness it wasn't Mrs Paxton or Mrs Edwards.

Now all she had to do was cope with Lou giving her an ear bashing. Nursing both a monumental hangover and a large and painful lump on the back of her head, she drifted in and out of Lou's rant, the bones of it being Lou had never been so embarrassed in all her life ... a daughter of hers rat-arsed ... in public ... collapsing in a toilet ... announcing to everyone that she didn't love her husband ... didn't she stop to think that she should be putting more into her marriage? ... And who, just who the hell was the good-looking man in the too-tight jeans covered in sick? ... Where the hell had he come from? ... And was he responsible for making her think she didn't love Dave? ... Although what the hell he saw in her, she didn't know ... the man in the jeans, not Dave.

When at last Lou shut up, Maggie said, 'I'm sorry, I'm going to have to go. There's someone at the door.'

'I didn't hear the doorbell.'

'It was a very quiet ring. Whoever it is probably knows I'm not feeling well, what with having such a nasty bump on my head.'

'To say nothing of a hangover. But that's what you get for drinking too much.'

'You make it sound like I do it all the time. I've never done anything like that before. Never.'

'And just you make sure you don't get into the habit of it. I suppose I can trust you to keep your marriage together and not go cheating on Dave until I get back from Poland?'

'I'm going to have to go, Mum,' she said. 'Whoever's at the door is ringing again.'

'I still can't hear them.'

'Bye, Mum. Enjoy Poland. Don't get too much changed, will you? I'd like to recognize you when you get back.'

'Maybe I won't come back.'

'And wouldn't that be a dream come true?' Maggie muttered under her breath.

'What's that?'

'Nothing, Mum. Bye.'

She made herself a cup of tea, took it through to the lounge, switched on the gas fire and covered herself with the blanket she had brought down from upstairs. Her stomach had settled and she no longer felt so queasy, but her head was still pounding. She cradled the hot mug carefully in her hands, closed her eyes and listened to the soothing hiss from the gas fire.

The pain was so bad in her head she wondered if she should have gone to A and E last night in case she had congestion.

Was that what she meant?

No, she meant confusion.

No, that still didn't sound right. She *was* confused but that wasn't the word she was searching for.

Concussion! That was it. Was she suffering from concussion? She didn't know. All she knew was that she felt awful. What must Daryl have thought of her? She was actually sick on him. Oh, nice going, Maggie Storm.

And what was it about Maggie Storm that first attracted you to her, Daryl?

Oh, that's easy. It was when she threw up all over me. What man could resist such ladylike charm?

She couldn't really remember exactly what happened after she'd been sick, because that was when Lou and Peggy came into the ladies'. It was all a nightmarish blur after that. She could remember being helped outside for some fresh air and then put into a taxi and taken home. There had been no sign of Dave or Dean. She had no idea what happened to Daryl. Maybe he'd been there at the Taj Mahal with a girlfriend, or on a date. A first date perhaps. She pictured the scene: Daryl going off to the gents – presumably that was where he was heading when he found her – and then arriving back with a partially digested chicken tikka masala down him, not to mention more than a bottle of white wine. That must have made for a very impressive first date.

Once again, let's hear it for Maggie Storm. Nice going, Maggie!

The only good thing about last night was her jackpot win. And no way was she going to let on to Dave that she had won so much money. It was going straight into her secret building society account. She would have to prime Mum to keep quiet about it, but she could do that by lying to her; she could pretend that she was putting the money aside to treat the family to something nice one day. A surprise.

She didn't know how long she had been asleep, but the door-bell woke her. She decided to ignore it – she wasn't fit for company – but then she thought of Mrs Oates. What if the old lady needed help with something?

She pushed the blanket away and went out to the hall, opened the door and her jaw dropped. There in front of her was the last person she expected to see, or wanted to see; it was Daryl.

'Hiya. I wondered whether you might like these when you're feeling a bit … a bit less poorly,' he said, obviously assuming the worst as to how she would be feeling today. He held out a large box of chocolates.

'Chocolates,' she said, dazed. 'But how did you know which house was mine?'

He tilted his head towards the other side of the road. 'I asked Mary. Do you mind?'

'No. I'm just … just surprised that you should go to so much trouble. I mean … I was sick all over you. Did I spoil your evening?'

He smiled. 'I'd say you added to it.'

She swallowed. In her totally wrecked state, she really wasn't strong enough to cope with one of his smiles. 'I can't think how or why,' she said.

'I think what did it for me was when you mentioned there was something lickable about me.'

She put a hand to her mouth. 'I never did!'

His smile got bigger. It made her wilt. 'I'm very interested in seeing how you tap dance,' he said.

What was he talking about? 'But I can't tap dance,' she said. 'I've never tap danced in my life.'

'That's not the impression you gave me last night.'

'Oh,' she said flatly. 'I think I may have said a lot of things last night I didn't mean to say.'

'That's a shame. How's your head?'

'Painful,' she said.

'I'm not surprised; you hit the deck hard. If I'd had my wits about me I might have caught you.'

'How did I fall? I have no memory of it.'

'You leaned against the door that only moments earlier you had been trying to pull open. The trick was in pushing it. As you soon found out.'

'Oh,' she said again. 'Did I at least look funny?'

'You did, actually. It was like the famous Del Boy scene from *Only Fools and Horses* – you know the one, when he leans against the bar.'

She risked a sickly smile back at him. But then they seemed to run out of things to say.

'Well,' he said, 'I'll leave these with you.' He handed her the chocolates. 'I hope you feel better soon.'

Then he was gone, walking fast towards his car. He unlocked it, looked over his shoulder back towards her where she was still standing and slid inside. He started up the engine, waved at her through the driver's window and took off down the road.

Take me with you! she wanted to call after him. *Wherever you're going, take me with you.*

Suddenly aware of the biting cold, she closed the door. Two things struck her as she went through to the lounge. The first was that there was a scrap of paper attached to the lid of the box of chocolates. A phone number was written on it, followed by three words: *Call me, please.*

The second thing was that she was still wearing her night-dress and her shamefully old dressing gown.

There really was no end to her talent for making a good impression, was there?

Chapter Twenty-one

'Have you chosen?'

Ella looked up from the menu she had been staring at for the last five minutes but not a word of which she had taken in. She had been too uptight, too busy trying to decide if she had done the right thing in coming here. For all the amount of thought she had expended she hadn't reached a conclusion. 'Not yet,' she said. 'How about you? Seen anything you fancy?'

'You know me; it'll be my usual predictable choice.'

Ella knew exactly what that meant: prawns of some sort followed by a steak. Lawrence could dissect a menu in a blink of an eye when seeking out his preferred meal of choice. Sure enough, when she returned her attention to her menu, she spotted his starter and main course. Knowing also how he liked to get the tiresome job of ordering over and done with as fast as possible, she quickly opted for avocado with crabmeat and Dover sole to follow. 'A double helping of healthy fish,' she announced. 'That's what I'll have.'

Right on cue, a waitress who looked to be about the same age as Alexis approached their table. She smiled brightly at them. Lawrence gave her their order and then showed her the page from the wine menu he'd been studying. 'A bottle of the Torretta Trebbiano,' he said, 'it'll go well with your fish, Ella.'

'What about your steak?'

'Don't worry about me, I'll be fine.'

Ella had always thought it was to his credit that in spite of being so knowledgeable about wine, he wasn't precious about it, nor did he ever patronize the less well-informed by expecting too much of, say, a teenage waitress who probably wouldn't know an alcopop from a Riesling.

The job done, he sat back in his chair then leaned forward as if thinking better of the distance between them. 'I'm really glad you agreed to have dinner,' he said. 'It means a lot to me.'

Nearly a month had passed since Lawrence had shown up on her drive spoiling for a fight. A series of phone calls had followed – mostly Alexis-related – the consequence of which was that a truce had been put in place between them. Now here they were, civilized face to civilized face over a white-clothed table in Crantsford having dinner. Just like old times.

Except it wasn't old times, Ella reminded herself. These were new times. She had moved on. So had he, if the number of women who had been and gone since their break-up was anything to go by. But she had to concede it wasn't too awful being here with him. In fact, now that she was beginning to relax, it felt rather nice. It was good to see Lawrence again, like this, especially as he seemed genuinely pleased she was here with him. She realized that with all the bitter disappointment she had gone through, she had suppressed the memory of just how attractive he was, how she had always loved the quiet strength of him. 'You look very smart,' she said. 'New jacket?'

'I bought it today. Alexis insisted I brushed myself up for the evening.'

Still Alexis calling the shots, was Ella's first thought. Then she wondered why Alexis would be so keen for her father to 'brush himself up' for the evening. 'Do we have her blessing for tonight, then?' she asked.

He smiled shyly, his soft hazel eyes looking at her intently. 'It would appear so.'

That shy look of his ... she had forgotten how powerfully engaging it was and how susceptible she was to it. She found herself remembering how she'd felt when they'd first met and how happy they'd once been.

Ethan was having a monster of a bad evening. He was in York crawling up the backside of one of his most lucrative clients: Tony Clarkson. As schmoozing exercises went, it was on a par with the joy of pushing needles into his eyeballs.

Tony had always been an important client for him and never more so than now. Two clients had been in touch this week to say they wouldn't be ordering from him again – they couldn't go on; they were closing down. One had been forty-five per cent down on his takings compared to this time last year. The other wouldn't even admit how bad things were, only that he was getting out before he lost everything.

But with a chain of more than twenty stores throughout the country, Tony still appeared to be doing well. And so long as he was, Ethan would do whatever it took to keep the man's business. He would crawl on his belly through landmines. He would even listen to Tony's continuous stream of lewd talk and sexual boastings. If the man was to be believed there wasn't a woman in the north of England whom he hadn't bedded. Married to wife number two, who was twenty years his junior, and with two grown-up sons and an ex-wife to support, he was the epitome of the aging, self-made man who couldn't keep it in his pants. There was a strong suspicion of Silvio Berlusconi hair dye about him; it was much too dark for a man of his age. He wasn't very tall either and wore stacked heels. All in all, he was a complete tosser.

'So tell me, how's that great little wife of yours?' he asked, pushing aside his finished plate of cheese.

'She's well,' Ethan replied, trying not to wince at how Francine would react to being so described.

Tony summoned their waitress, a girl of Eastern European origins, who so far had had to cope with Tony checking out every inch of her body, even touching it at one point – a hand around her waist – as well as fending off a barrage of unoriginal and throat-clenchingly embarrassing questions such as, 'What's a beautiful girl like you doing working here?' And: 'What time do you finish work? Maybe we could go for a drink later?' The girl was undeniably pretty, but she was also young enough to be Tony's granddaughter.

To the girl now, Tony said, 'When you're ready, love, we'll have a couple of brandies.' He tried to get her to make eye contact with him but she kept her head down and made herself scarce. 'I dunno, Ethan,' Tony said wearily, 'am I losing it, or what? Or are the girls playing harder to get these days?'

'It's the recession,' Ethan joked. 'It's hitting people in different ways.'

Tony laughed loudly, his head flipping back, his rubbery mouth wide open, revealing gaps in his teeth as well as a smattering of gold fillings. He really was the most repulsive man. More so for his ego being pumped up with all the red wine he'd knocked back. He stopped laughing abruptly and leaned forward, elbows on the table. 'I've always envied you, Ethan.'

Here we go, thought Ethan. 'Why's that?' he said.

'You've got it all. A good business, a classy wife who loves you and a great kid.'

'All of which you have, too,' Ethan said smoothly.

'To buggery I have! I have a wife who doesn't let me touch her and two kids who are too bloody idle to pick up the phone, never mind come and see me. Anyone would think they were ashamed of me. And after everything I've given them. The best schools, holidays, cars the moment they turned seventeen – and not any old cars. *Porsches* I bought them. Bloody hell, when I was seventeen d'you think I had a Porsche?' He shook his head vigorously. 'When I was fifteen I was doing a milk round, up at four every morning. I had my first market stall when I was seventeen. D'you know, I've even bought the ungrateful buggers flats down in London? They've never wanted for nowt. I've bank-rolled them to the hilt.' He shook his head again. 'I dunno, you wonder sometimes why you do it. What's the point in it all? I've been slogging away like a dog all my life, and for what? God, I swear I could kill for a cigar. Worst thing this country ever did was to ban smoking in restaurants.'

'But you're extremely successful at what you do,' Ethan said, after their waitress had brought them their brandies and quickly escaped. 'Your business continues to go from strength to strength.' God in heaven, in his booze-fuelled state the disgusting man wasn't about to confess that he was on the verge of skid row, was he?

Tony fixed him with a dead straight look, or it would have been if he hadn't been having trouble focusing. 'There's more to life than bloody business, Ethan. Sure I'm minted and surviving the recession better than most, but I want more. I want excitement. I want to walk on the wild side.' He leaned forward, his voice low. 'You ever experimented with drugs?'

Ethan was shocked. 'No,' he said, an awful image flashing through his head of Tony suggesting they go somewhere quiet and shoot up.

'Me neither,' Tony said with a sigh. 'My drug of choice is sex. And lots of it. If you're prepared to pay for it, there's plenty of it out there. But then why am I telling you this? You don't need to pay for sex when you have your Francine to keep you happy. First time I ever met your good lady at that bash I threw all those years ago, I thought, now that's one hot classy lady Ethan's got himself. Bet she works well between the sheets.' He raised a hand. 'Sorry. Inappropriate talk from me. Forget I ever said that.'

'No problem,' said Ethan tightly. 'We're old friends; you can say whatever you like to me.'

They were the last to leave the restaurant, the staff politely eager to be rid of them. By way of apology Ethan had wanted to leave an extra big tip for their waitress, but unsure how the poor girl might view the money – payment for being pawed – he had thought better of it.

After he had settled an unsteady Tony into the back of a taxi, he stood alone in the dark on the pavement. He welcomed the cold night air and stood for a moment breathing in its sharpness, as if cleansing himself of the grubby evening he had just endured. He felt soiled by it.

It was gone midnight when he reached his hotel. Ideally he would have preferred to drive home after dinner, but knowing the amount of alcohol that he would be expected to consume in the name of keeping Tony company, he had done the safe thing and booked himself a room.

He took off his coat and jacket, hung them in the wardrobe and caught his reflection in the mirror. He looked tired. As well he might; it had been a long day and to compound matters his stomach felt like it was on fire. Too much rich food. Too much alcohol. Maybe even too much coffee. He'd noticed a pattern recently. At the start of a meal he felt okay, but often by the end of it, or soon after, he felt worse. If he had more time, he'd look into it. Or even go and see a doctor. He knew what a doctor would say, though. That he should ease his foot off the pedal, slow things down a bit. Fat chance of that ever happening. He'd had wall-to-wall problems these last few weeks, including a major cock-up at one of the factories in China which had necessitated him flying over to sort the mess out.

But the tiredness he was experiencing wasn't just down to work. He was tired in his spirit. Being with Tony always had a depressing effect on him. Except tonight had depressed him more than usual. Was Tony his future? Given time, would he turn into a version of Tony Clarkson? A repugnant old man still thinking he could cut it when it came to charming obscenely young girls?

He would sooner take a vow of celibacy than end his days like that.

He remembered the occasion to which Tony had referred when he'd first met Francine; it had been a day at York races. Tony had laid on a lavish do, private stand, first-class lunch, and champagne flowing like water. Francine had played her part well, laughing at Tony's jokes, even flirting with him a little, batting her eyelashes, touching his arm – Tony had been between wives then so had been more than receptive to her attentions. Fair play to Francine – she had known exactly what was at stake. That was back in the days when everything was going well for them. When they were happy and still knew how to have fun together.

He really hadn't wilfully thrown his marriage away. Who did that? Who wouldn't rather be happily married and in love? No one in their right mind deliberately took the option to be unhappily married. Just as he hadn't deliberately chosen to fall out of love with Francine. There'd been many a time when he'd wanted nothing more than to turn back the clock and recapture what they'd once had.

When they'd first met, at a club in Manchester, he had taken one look at Francine and promised himself he wouldn't leave without her phone number. Easily the best-looking and best-dressed girl there, she had embodied everything he liked in a woman – eye-catching, feminine and sexually aware. He'd watched her chatting and laughing with her friends and had known that she knew he was watching her, that she was enjoying the attention. He'd taken his time before going over and casually asking her if he could buy her a drink. 'I thought you were one of those boring shy types who was never going to ask,' she'd teased him. Two hours later and he was driving her home to Prestbury in his new car – a black Porsche, which he knew impressed her. That it was second-hand with over eighty thousand miles on the clock he had kept to himself. Her hand was on his leg the whole way, her fingers moving in slow provocative circles. 'You want to go to bed with me, don't you?' she said after she'd instructed him to turn into a driveway that led to an imposing house.

He'd liked that about her, her cool directness. 'Yes,' he said simply, switching the engine off. 'And you want me to take you to bed, don't you?'

'Oh yes. Right from the second I laid eyes on you.'

'What do you suggest we do about it?'

'I suggest you come inside.'

He looked up at the large house; security lights had flashed on. 'And meet your parents?'

She smiled and worked her fingers further up his thigh. 'They're away on holiday.' She pressed her hand against the hardness of him. 'It'll be just you and me.'

'Perfect.'

And it was from that day on.

They married a year later and honeymooned in Barbados. It was the best ten days of his life, ten days of pure unadulterated pleasure. He was the happiest of men and not once did he imagine that anything would change between them. They had it all. A truly charmed life. They were the envy of all who knew them.

Perhaps that was the mistake he'd made, to believe that nothing could go wrong. He should have been on his guard, alert to the slightest thing that could threaten their happiness. Or more importantly, alert to the undeniable fact that people changed and relationships had to be continuously recalibrated.

He sighed heavily. It was all very well accepting that he'd messed up, but it didn't alter anything. The past was the past and now was now.

He stripped off the rest of his clothes, hung them up and lay on the bed. He was suddenly overwhelmed with the need to clear his head of the questions that had been bothering him so much lately.

Where was he going with his life?

Where did he want it to go?

What was so wrong with the one he currently had?

And how much longer could he go on walking through life in slow-motion?

Tony had spoken of wanting excitement, of wanting to walk on the wild side. That wasn't what Ethan wanted. He wanted the opposite – a sense of peace. He wanted to wake up in the morning and ... well, yes, as trite as it sounded, he wanted to wake up and smell the roses.

But the treadmill he was on didn't allow for that. He had no time for such self-indulgence. Despite his adamant opposition to the idea, Francine had gone ahead and made an offer on the house in Abersoch. *Daddy Dearest* was stumping up the readies, with the understanding that Ethan would pay back the loan when the economy picked up.

At least the new house was proving to be a distracting hobby for Francine and seemed to keep her happy, and therefore out of his way. She had all but lost interest in the dining room project and was showing signs of impatience that the work still wasn't finished. Regardless of that, she had mentioned once or twice that if the wretched woman – Francine's words, not his – could pull her finger out and show some commitment, maybe they would ask her to do some work on the new house.

Ironically the transformation of the dining room was now of more interest to Ethan. After a difficult day's work, he enjoyed being in there on his own with a glass of wine while losing himself in the landscape Ella was creating. The feeling of make-believe had a soothing effect on him and at times he felt happily lost in it. The style of painting reminded him of an old-fashioned storybook he'd had as a small boy. It had been a favourite of his and one that he had treasured; his father had given it to him. He rarely thought of his childhood – it was too loaded – and so anything that reminded him of it was usually a no-go area, but Ella's depiction of a fairytale-like landscape was making him think of things he hadn't thought of in a long while.

Disappointingly, due to various work commitments and going to China he had hardly seen anything of Ella in the last few weeks. Too often he found himself wondering how she was, where she was or what she was doing. The bottom line was that he missed her, which was absurd. He really didn't know her well enough to miss her. Logic told him that the little time he had spent in her company was having a wholly disproportionate effect on him, but somehow she had got under his skin in a way no other woman had. There really was no logic to it.

He wished he had someone with whom he could share his feelings, but there was no one. Paradoxically, the only person with whom he felt he could be entirely honest was Ella. Just as paradoxical, his wanting to confide in her seemed infinitely more dangerous than merely wanting to have sex. For him, confiding in her would be a far greater act of intimacy.

A man like Tony wouldn't ever understand that. Tony didn't want a woman to talk to; a woman to him served only one purpose. It pained Ethan but he knew that most people would see no difference between him and Tony; they would both be condemned for the same crime – of being incapable of fidelity.

In his defence, if such a thing was possible, Ethan had always been discreet. He had never bragged about the number of women he'd slept with and over the years he had steadfastly gone to great lengths to maintain the image of a happily married man. It was an image that Tony, in common with everyone else, believed to be entirely true.

Question was, how much longer did he want to go on living the lie?

He turned his head to look at the digital clock on the bedside table. It was half past twelve. He wondered what Ella was doing. Probably sleeping the untroubled sleep of the innocent.

Lawrence was tracing circles on the table with his long fingers, something he had often done when he was nervous. Ella had always thought he had hands that should have stroked the keys of a piano. She recalled how they used to slide up and down her back in bed.

'It's late,' she said. 'I ought to be going.'

'No, not yet,' he said. 'There's something I want to say and it's taken me all evening to work up the courage to find the right words.'

They were sitting in the kitchen at Mayfield. Lawrence had invited her back for coffee after dinner. That had been nearly two hours ago. Alexis was upstairs in bed and the house was very quiet. In the portentous silence, Ella waited anxiously.

'Mayfield hasn't felt the same without you,' he said. 'Things have changed here. You can see that for yourself. Why don't we try again, Ella? Why don't we give ourselves a second chance and see if we can get it right this time?'

Chapter Twenty-two

It was laughable. Buying a house in Abersoch? Oh, really. Couldn't Francine have come up with something better?

No sooner had she and Adam mentioned that they were thinking of buying a holiday home than Francine was trying to outdo them. A house in miserable old Abersoch – or a *beach house*, as Francine kept referring to the pebble-dashed monstrosity Christine had checked out on the internet – was so very yesterday.

The place to be was Sandbanks down in Poole. That was where she and Adam were now hoping to invest. It was so much more stylish and upmarket than boring old Abersoch. A better class of neighbour, more importantly. A really smart apartment was what they were on the lookout for. It would cost, but it would be the perfect investment.

Just to rub Francine's pert nose – pert was being kind; pointy was nearer the mark – into the shabbiness of her precious beach house, Christine reached for her bag and the magazine she had brought with her. It was Dorset's equivalent to *Cheshire Life* and it was full of stunning properties for sale. She opened the magazine at a page she had earlier earmarked. 'I brought this with me to show you, Francine,' she said. 'I wondered whether you'd like to see what we've got lined up to view at the weekend.'

They were at the Spa, wrapped in fluffy white towelling robes and reclining on a pair of wicker loungers, both of them having been exfoliated, waxed and massaged. They were taking a break before being manicured. On the glass table between them was a jug of high-energy vegetable juice, the predominant ingredient of which Christine suspected was grass cuttings. At the price the Spa was charging, it had better not be. It had a disgusting taste, but it seemed to do the trick – it both energized her and stopped her from being hungry.

Francine held out her hand for the magazine. 'I still think you're crazy to buy down there. It's such a long way, especially if you only want to go for the weekend. Abersoch is so much more convenient.'

'Oh, you know perfectly well what Adam is like once he gets an idea into his head: it's all or nothing with him. What do you think of the apartment with the circular white kitchen?' She watched Francine's face closely for a giveaway reaction. Of course, what with all the Botox, Francine wasn't really capable of frowning these days. Thank God Christine didn't have a thin, wrinkle-prone face like Francine. Luckily nature had saved her from that fate and had rewarded her with her mother's excellent genes and wide cheekbones. As a result she was blessedly wrinkle-free and would remain so for some years yet.

'For the price it's a little on the small side, isn't it?' Francine said. 'It's only two bedrooms.'

And so out of your price range, it's making you as green as this juice, thought Christine. She tried not to smirk. Her objective achieved, she turned to look through the glass window to the pool area. Katie and Valentina were in there and to Christine's annoyance, Katie wasn't swimming; she was lolling around in the jacuzzi gossiping with Valentina. Valentina could afford to loll and gossip, but Katie could not: she was overweight and needed to do something about it.

It didn't matter how many times Christine nagged her daughter, the silly girl just went on snacking on crisps and chocolate and fizzy drinks. God only knew what she ate when she wasn't at home. Pizza with a side order of chips and teenage angst, most likely. It was nothing short of a miracle that her skin was as good as it was. She lacked any real staying power, that was the trouble; she would start a carefully selected diet that Christine had chosen for her and two days later she would be packing away the carbs. She claimed her hunger was stress induced, that the school put too much pressure on them. Pressure! She didn't know the meaning of the word.

Christine had never been entirely convinced of the appropriateness of Katie's friendship with Valentina. The thought always lurked in her mind that Valentina used Katie, that Katie was there to play the part of slightly less attractive friend to Valentina's shining star. And Valentina really was a shining star. She had legs like a Russian tennis player, a perfectly flat stomach and breasts that gave every promise of passing the pencil test for several decades. In contrast, Katie had what could kindly be described as a comely figure. Her breasts were much bigger than Valentina's and already sagged. It was just as well she was book-smart, because her looks were never going to get her far.

There was nothing new in having an ugly friend to bolster one's own ego, and to be fair, Katie wasn't ugly; she was just erring on the plain side. The girl didn't help herself, though. 'Get on the treadmill!' Christine often wanted to yell at her when they came here together. 'Shake off some of those excess pounds that are dragging you down!' She only had to mention the word salad and Katie would be sulking rattily and accusing her of trying to make her anorexic.

Adam said she was too hard on her, that their daughter couldn't help the genes with which she had been born – in other words *his* deficient genes, including the lardy-bum one. But Christine disagreed. Being born with dud genes meant that you had to work harder to keep yourself looking good. And anyway, she wasn't doing anything that Christine's own mother hadn't done to her. A shame Adam's mother hadn't been more instructive with him. Had she taught him to moderate what he ate and drank then maybe he would have a body more like Ethan's.

Aah, Ethan ...

Her vigilance regarding the daily comings and goings at The Lilacs had so far not proved conclusively whether things had progressed any further between Ethan and Ella Moore, but then from what Francine had said, Ethan had been away a fair bit recently. There had been no sightings of his car arriving home early in the afternoon and nor had she spotted Ella's car sneaking out of the avenue late at night again. It was always possible they were meeting elsewhere, at Ella's place perhaps.

But Christine was determined not to torture herself by imagining what Ethan may or may not be up to. Instead she was forcing herself to stick to her original plan of wait and see. Only when she was absolutely convinced the moment was right would she make her move.

Lawrence had told her that Mayfield wasn't the same without her. He'd said that she belonged there.

Being told what she was or what she wasn't didn't always go down well with Ella, and a slither of irritation had made its presence felt when Lawrence had uttered those words. She knew the sentiment behind them was well-meant, but she couldn't deny that it had made her feel slightly uncomfortable.

That conversation had taken place three days ago and she was no nearer to giving Lawrence an answer than she had been when they had been sitting round his kitchen table in the early hours of the morning. He had expected so much of her, there and then, an instant decision. How could he think she could put everything behind her so easily?

'I need time to think about it,' she had said. At once his face had been crestfallen. Presumably he had been so focused on gearing himself up to deliver his speech to her, he hadn't considered a negative or even an ambiguous response. 'I'm not saying no,' she had added. 'I just don't know how I feel about what you've asked.'

'I understand,' he had replied.

Now, in her workshop as she started applying a layer of decorative gold leaf to the Louis XV-style chair she was working on for a client, she very much doubted that he did. He had sent her flowers the next day with a note saying: *Take all the time you want.*

Was she being overly sensitive when she imagined a nudge of impatience behind his note? Again, she had felt a slither of annoyance. Who was he to dictate or give permission as to how long she should take to consider something as crucially important as her future?

Or was she merely being difficult, acting no better than a contrary child who, after pestering for weeks and weeks for a much-wanted toy, when finally given it, tosses it aside ungratefully.

Was she being ungrateful? Wasn't this exactly what she had wanted? But now it had been offered to her, with an apparent cast-iron guarantee that Lawrence and Alexis had changed, why did she feel so jittery and unsure?

She tried to shake the doubts from her head by reminding herself how much Lawrence had meant to her. She also thought of their shared dreams, that of one day buying a place in Tuscany with land so that Lawrence could fulfil his own particular dream, that of creating a vineyard.

As she dwelt on that recollection and pictured the two of them in the sun in Italy, Ella began to feel less jittery. And just a little surer. Could they really do it? Could they recapture what they had lost and share their dreams again?

The ringing of the telephone made her start – not good when handling such expensive and delicate material. She carefully replaced the sheet of gold leaf she had just removed from its protective sheets of paper and went to her workbench, where amongst the clutter of paints, rags, art books and drawings was a phone.

'Hello, Toby,' she said when she heard his upbeat voice at the other end of the line. 'Long time no hear.'

'Yeah, sorry about that. I've been busy.'

'Studying hard, I hope.'

He laughed. 'Let's say hard enough and leave it at that. Look, I've just heard the news about you and Dad and wanted to say how brilliant it is.'

Ella hesitated. 'Er … what news exactly have you heard?'

'That you and Dad are back together.'

'Your father told you that?'

'No, it was Alexis. She called me a few minutes ago.'

'And she *actually* said Lawrence and I were back together?'

'Her exact words. Why? Isn't it true? Oh shit, don't tell me it's another of my screwed up sister's psycho mind games!'

'Alexis has jumped the gun a bit,' she said. 'Your father and I are indeed getting on better now and he has asked me to move back in with him, but—'

'But you're not sure? You haven't decided? Is that it?'

'Correct.'

'Anything I can say to help persuade you?'

'Toby,' she sighed, 'if only it were that easy.'

'It could be.'

She caught the hopefulness in his taut voice and wanted to hug him hard. Knowing how happy it would make Toby, she was almost tempted to ignore her qualms. But she knew as well as the next life-battered survivor that it was the preserve of the young to believe uncompromisingly that life could be so simple. Sadly, age and experience taught one otherwise.

Chapter Twenty-three

A week later another bouquet of flowers arrived, just as Ella was leaving for work.

She was reversing out of her drive and running late – a new client had kept her on the phone wanting to discuss in detail the cracked glaze finish she wanted for a dressing table – and somewhat ungraciously she snatched the flowers out of the woman's hands and tossed them on the passenger seat beside her. She didn't bother to read the note, interpreting this latest gesture from Lawrence as further hassling her into a decision.

She arrived at The Lilacs more than thirty minutes late and Mrs Edwards greeted her with a face like granite. 'I thought I made it clear that you had to be here by nine-twenty, that I was going out for the day and that Maggie wouldn't be around to let you in as she was collecting the dry-cleaning.'

'I'm sorry,' Ella said. 'I got held up with a phone call.'

'That's none of my concern. My concern is you getting here on time and finishing the job I'm paying you to do.'

Don't you mean the job your husband is paying me to do? Ella had wanted to snipe back. 'I'm sorry I've inconvenienced you. I'll work longer this evening to make up the lost time,' she said with so much polite obsequiousness she felt nauseous. 'Perhaps,' she went on, deciding to chance it, 'if you were to give me a key it would make things easier for you.'

'A key?' the other woman said in much the same manner Lady Bracknell would refer to a handbag. 'A key?' she repeated, presumably in case her outrage was lost on Ella.

'It's what a lot of my clients do,' Ella said. 'It saves situations like this. I'm quite trustworthy. I assure you any key in my possession would be safe.'

'It's out of the question. I can't have any old Tom, Dick or Harry coming and going when the mood takes them. Now, I really must get on. I'm late enough as it is.'

Her parting words were to instruct Ella to let Maggie in when she arrived. As if Ella was too stupid to think of doing that herself.

When Maggie did arrive, Ella saw at once that she looked different. Her normally mousy shoulder-length hair wasn't tied back in its customary ponytail – it had been restyled into something shorter that was sleek and shiny and swung jauntily whenever she turned her head. But it wasn't just the more flattering hairstyle that was different; there was a cheery lightness about her. It was a few weeks since their paths had last crossed at The Lilacs, but something had evidently happened to Maggie in the intervening time. This wasn't the care-worn Maggie Ella had come to know. This was a happy, young-looking Maggie.

'You look very chipper,' Ella said when they were having their usual illicit cup of coffee in the kitchen.

'I feel chipper,' Maggie answered with a smile that brightened her face even more.

'Oh? Any special reason why?'

After the briefest of hesitations Maggie said, 'I've had a win on the bingo since I last saw you. I won the jackpot.'

'Hey, that's brilliant! Congratulations. Any idea what you're going to spend it on?'

'I've bought some new clothes and had my hair done, but I'm saving the rest.'

'Good for you. Nice hair by the way.'

'Do you mean that?' Maggie patted the side of her head self-consciously. 'I only had it done yesterday and it still feels odd to me.' She gave her head a little shake and her glossy hair shimmered in the weak February sunlight coming in through the window.

'Don't take this the wrong way, but it makes you look much younger.'

Maggie beamed. She actually *beamed*. Ella didn't think she'd ever seen such a transformation in a person. It was as if she was lit up from within. 'You're not just saying that?' Maggie said.

'No. You look great. Honestly.'

They sipped their coffee and lapsed into silence. Then Maggie said, 'Can I ask you something? It's ... it's about a friend of mine.'

'Of course.'

'What would you do if ... if a really good-looking bloke who you hardly know turns up on your doorstep with chocolates and a note asking you to ring him?'

Ella laughed. 'Depends how good-looking he was. Are we talking up there with the Cloonster?'

'Oh, way better than George Clooney.'

'Wow! Then it would be very wrong for your friend not to do as he asked, wouldn't it?' Ella said with a smile.

'But ... um ... what if that friend was ... was married?'

Uh-oh, thought Ella. Steady as you go. 'Ah, that does rather muddy the waters, doesn't it?' she said. 'It would also depend on the state of your ... your friend's marriage. Is she happy?'

'Um ... not really.'

'Well, if she was seriously considering calling the man, she needs to be very clear in her mind why she's doing it. Would she, for instance, be lonely and just want to see what it feels like to talk to someone who seems nice? Or does she ... does she fancy him?'

Maggie's gaze was no longer meeting Ella's; she was staring resolutely at the rim of her mug. 'A bit of both, I think,' she said quietly.

'I suppose the correct advice to give your friend would be

for her to try and figure out why she isn't happy in her marriage before she gets involved with anyone else.'

The look of disappointment on Maggie's face was so acute, Ella wished she hadn't sounded like an agony aunt delivering boringly sensible advice. Whoever wanted to hear the voice of common sense when the heart was involved? 'Does the man, whom your friend hardly knows, realize that she's married?' she asked, trying to soften the damage she had inflicted.

'It's not really come up in conversation, but he must know that she is.'

'Then you ... your friend has to wonder what his motives are. Marriage wreckers aren't nice people on the whole. Your friend needs to be careful.'

'He doesn't seem like a marriage wrecker. According to my friend,' Maggie added hastily.

Ella drained the last of her coffee and went to the sink. She washed her mug and took Maggie's from her and washed that too. 'I don't suppose I've been very helpful, have I?' she said as Maggie started to dry the mugs. The other woman looked lost in thought. 'Maybe you could help me,' Ella said more brightly, wanting to reinstate Maggie's good mood by sharing something with her. 'Remember the man I told you about, the one I gave up my life for in Italy?'

'Yes,' Maggie said, 'the bloke it didn't work out with.'

'That's right. He wants me to get back together with him.'

'What's brought that on?'

'Good question. And if I knew the answer, I'd be surer of my response. He says he's changed, that he now sees the mistakes he made, but ...' Her voice trailed off as she gazed out at the garden and the hideous water feature. A couple of crows were perched on the top.

'But you don't believe him?' Maggie prompted. 'Is that it?'

'Leopards and spots, I guess,' Ella said, as she watched one of the crows fly off, followed soon after by the other. 'I need hard evidence that he's changed. And his daughter.'

'Life's full of choices, isn't it?' Maggie said faintly.

'And none of them easy to make,' Ella said with a smile. 'Right then, I'd better get on. I'm already in Mrs Edwards' bad books for being late this morning.'

Maggie had surprised herself. She hadn't come to work this morning intending to confide in Ella, but all of a sudden she'd felt fit to burst if she didn't talk to someone. No way could she talk to Lou, who was now back from Poland and in hiding until the scars and bruises had healed, but then she'd never discussed anything important with her. And anyway, after the way Lou had reacted to her drunken confession about Dave, she was the last person Maggie could talk to without bringing on a huge ruckus. She had thought of talking to Mrs Oates, but had decided against it. It was sad, really, when she thought about it, because apart from Mrs Oates she didn't have any proper friends of her own.

Sharing the little that she had with Ella had felt good. Whether or not Ella suspected Maggie was talking about herself and not a friend didn't bother her. Nor was she worried that Ella would tell anyone what she'd said; she wasn't the sort to do that, she wasn't a blabbermouth. But there had been so much more Maggie had wanted to say. She had wanted to say that ever since Daryl had turned up on her doorstep, she had felt like she was floating ten inches off the ground. She had wanted to say that nothing seemed to bother her, that she felt as if she was filled with a glowing warmth.

Was this what it felt like to be on drugs? Mo had got hold of some anti-depressant pills off the internet last year and she'd said they'd made her feel dreamy and lightheaded and all fuzzy at the edges. But Maggie didn't feel fuzzy. She felt as if she was experiencing everything in sharp focus, more intensely.

Every romantic song she heard on the radio seemed to have been written especially for her; every cheesy line described her feelings for Daryl. She had taken to singing along, but only when she was alone. She had lost weight, too. She had no appetite; her stomach wasn't so much all of a flutter with an attack of the butterflies as trashed by a flock of starlings. She had also started to read her horoscope, something she had never done before. No matter what paper or magazine she read, love and change were always in the air for her.

Everything reminded her of Daryl. If she saw a black car, she thought of him. Pale denim made her think of him. The smell of aftershave – not even his brand – made her think of him. If it was raining she imagined them sheltering from a storm together, his jacket held over their heads. If it was windy, she pictured him holding her tight so she didn't get swept away.

And she couldn't stop smiling. Dave had caught her smiling last night when he was stuffing his face full of Daryl's chocolates – she'd told him Mrs Oates had given them to her as a thank you present for some help Maggie had done for her around the house. 'What's up with you?' he'd said as if it was the biggest crime going to smile. It went without saying that he didn't think much of her new hairstyle. 'What was wrong with the old style?' he'd wanted to know.

'This is the new me,' she'd told him.

A roll of his eyes said what he thought of that. But she didn't care. She hadn't changed her hair for his benefit anyway.

So was this what love did to a person?

Was she in love?

Or was she off her trolley?

But whatever was happening to her, should she ring Daryl? Should she take that next step? What if she did and then it all went wrong? She didn't want to do anything that might make her miserable again. Wasn't it better to carry on as she was, knowing that Daryl cared enough to bring her chocolates, that he had wanted her to call him? Why not leave it at that? She had experienced so very little real happiness in her life, why throw away what she had now? And – and this was a big *and* – if she didn't make that phone call, she wouldn't have done anything wrong. There would be nothing to feel guilty about.

But ... a small voice whispered inside her head, *ringing Daryl might make you feel even happier. Wouldn't you like to feel even happier? And would it really be so wrong?*

As she vacuumed, dusted, scrubbed and polished her way round The Lilacs, Maggie alternated between the two voices inside her head. It wasn't until she was pulling on her coat and saying goodbye to Ella that she reached a decision. Or rather, it was Ella who helped her reach a decision.

'Maggie,' Ella said from the top of her stepladders, 'I've been thinking about ... about your friend. I think she should definitely ring the man who gave her the chocolates. It would be rude not to thank him properly, wouldn't it?'

'Do you really think so?'

'Yes, I do.'

When she was in her car, Maggie hunted through her bag for the piece of paper with Daryl's phone number. She held it in her hand and thought about what Ella had said. Ella had known all along that Maggie wasn't talking about a friend, hadn't she?

She took out her mobile, held her breath and with fingers that had suddenly turned into bananas she fumbled to tap in the number. She hesitated when she had entered the last digit. It wasn't too late to back out.

She swallowed, took a deep breath and pressed the 'call' key.

Seconds passed and then the ringing tone started.

She remembered the call he had answered that evening at Mrs Oates's – *Hello, love ...*

Who was 'love'?

The ringing tone continued.

And continued.

Four was her lucky number. She would let it ring four more times, then she would hang up.

One.

Two.

Three.

Four.

Five. Well, maybe five was her new lucky number.

'Hello.'

No! He'd answered.

'Hello?' he repeated.

Where was her voice when she needed it? She cleared her throat, tried to force something out of it. 'Hello,' she managed.

'Is that who I think it is?'

She swallowed. 'That depends on who you think it is. Who do you think it is?'

'I think it's someone I've been waiting to hear from. I'd given up hope. Just to be sure, are you that person? I'd hate to have the wrong conversation with the wrong person. Or do I mean the right conversation with the wrong person?'

'It's me, Maggie.'

'Hiya, Maggie. You okay? You sound upset?'

'I'm fine, it's just ... it's just that I shouldn't be ringing you.'

'There's a law against it?'

'I'm married.'

'And being married means you can't talk on the phone to other folk? That must make life difficult for you.'

'You know what I mean.'

He paused. 'Yes, I do and I'm sorry for being glib. It's because I'm nervous.'

'You? Why are you nervous?'

'Because that's how you make me feel.'

'Me? Why do I make you nervous?'

'I'm frightened of saying the wrong thing and scaring you off. When can I see you?'

Maggie swallowed again. 'Why do you want to see me?'

'I would have thought that was obvious.'

'Not to me it isn't.'

'It's because I like you. I like it when you smile. I've thought a lot about the way you smile. Are you smiling now?'

'Not really.'

'That's a shame. You couldn't manage a small one for me, could you?'

'I've heard about men like you. They ring up those special telephone numbers and get women to do and say all sorts of things over the phone.'

He laughed. 'I promise you, I'm not that kind of a man. Look, and I don't want to push you, but I really would like to see you. When can we meet? During the day would be best for me.'

'I ... I don't know. I've never done anything like this before. I don't know if I can do it.'

'All we'll be doing is having a drink together, Maggie. You can manage that, can't you? We'll be two friends having a coffee together. Nothing to it.'

When she didn't say anything, he said, 'I'm sorry, I'm being glib again and that's not fair of me. It's just that I can't stop thinking about you.'

'Please don't say that.'

'Why not?'

'Because I think I might pass out.'

He laughed. 'That would be the second time in as many weeks. Is it something you do a lot of?'

'It's never happened to me before I met you. I could see you next week during my afternoon off.'

'Where?'

'Um ... at the library in Kings Melford.'

'Okay. What day and what time?'

'Wednesday, twelve o'clock.'

'I'll be there. Meanwhile take care. And no more passing out. Okay?'

'I'll do my best.'

'Maggie?'

'Yes.'

'Can you give me one last smile before we say goodbye?'

She smiled. She couldn't help herself. 'Goodbye, Daryl.'

'You are smiling, aren't you? You're not selling me short?'
'I'm smiling, I promise you, you daft bugger.'
And for the rest of the day she couldn't stop doing it.

Chapter Twenty-four

At half past two Ella stopped work for lunch.

Lunch today consisted of a Cup-a-Soup and an apple. Her soup made, back in the dining room, mug in hand, she heard the sound of the front door opening. She thought of the give-away sign that she'd used the kitchen – steam rising from a recently boiled kettle – and hoped that it wasn't Mrs Edwards home unexpectedly early.

'Only me!' called out a voice, followed by approaching footsteps. Not Mrs Edwards, thank goodness, but Ethan Edwards. He stood in the doorway. 'Mm ...' he said, sniffing the air, 'something smells good. And it's not paint.'

'Chicken and leek soup,' she said. 'From a packet. Nothing very exciting.'

'Sometimes the simplest things in life are the most exciting and enjoyable.' He took off his coat, hooked it over his arm. 'I haven't seen you in a while. How are you?'

'I'm fine, thank you. I've made a start on the final wall.'

'So I see.'

He came into the room and stood so close to her she couldn't help but be suddenly acutely aware of his presence. He was wearing jeans and a cashmere sweater the colour of warm butterscotch; it had the effect of enhancing the darkness of his brown eyes. She'd never noticed the colour of them before. She couldn't think why. Normally it was one of the first things she spotted in a person.

As he studied her work, she took the opportunity to study him. For some reason he seemed taller than she remembered and his face appeared more open and frank. Maybe that was because he wasn't wearing glasses today. He had a strong jaw and high cheekbones with a broad forehead that was emphasized by well-defined brows. His body was well-defined too: broad chest, wide shoulders and slim hips with long legs. There was no getting away from it: he was absurdly handsome and carried an excess of dangerously potent masculinity.

From the murkiest reaches of her mind where it had lain untouched for some weeks, the memory of the shocking dream she'd had of Ethan stirred itself. She fought it, but it was no good: like an unravelling spool of film, the memory unwound itself and the explicit detail of the dream was evoked in all its shameful and sexual glory and she succumbed to the unedifying truth that Ethan affected her in a way that went against every moral fibre of her being. She hated the fact that he was capable of exposing such a weakness in her.

'Are you pleased with it?' he asked.

She hurriedly rearranged her thoughts as he continued to study her work. 'I am,' she said, 'but the important question is, are you and Mrs Edwards pleased with it?'

He moved further along the wall to inspect another section, a distant view of a tumbledown watermill complete with pool of improbably clear water. 'I wouldn't dream of speaking for my wife, but I like what you've done. I have to be honest with you; I didn't think I would. Originally I thought it might end up looking a bit naff.'

'I've had more effusive comments made about my work, but I'll try and take what you've said as a compliment.' Remembering the mug of hot soup in her hands, she raised it to her lips and took a sip.

'Sorry,' he said, glancing briefly at her. 'I could have put it better, couldn't I?'

She shrugged, a gesture that went unnoticed by him as once more he'd returned his attention to the wall. 'The client's allowed to say whatever he or she wants,' she said.

'In that case, can I ask you something that I've wanted to ask for some time now?'

'If it involves any radical criticism regarding the work I've done so far, I may withdraw the last remark.'

He finally turned and looked at her properly. 'It's nothing to do with your work. It's something of a personal nature.'

On her guard, she said, 'Do I have the right to refuse an answer?'

'Of course. I've never forced anyone to do anything they didn't want to do.'

No, thought Ella, but you've probably persuaded a lot of people into doing things they might not otherwise have wanted to do. 'Go on,' she said, her tone measured.

'I'd like to get to know you better,' he said.

She'd heard some lines in her time, but that was a new one. 'Why?' she asked.

His gaze strengthened its hold on her. The penetrating intensity to it made her feel exposed and defenceless. She took another sip of her soup and armed herself with an unruffled look.

'I like being with you,' he said. 'You make me feel different about things.' He let out his breath in one long sigh and rubbed at the back of his neck. 'And I don't even really know what I mean by that. All I know is that ever since we met, I've wanted to get to know you.'

'You're married,' she said bluntly.

'Yes, I'm married. No argument there.'

'Which for me precludes what you're suggesting.'

'But do you know what exactly it is that I'm suggesting?'

'You want an affair,' she said tersely. 'Okay, you've dressed it up to sound like something else, something almost respectable, but the bottom line is you want to have a bit on the side. I want you to know that you could not have insulted me more.'

He shook his head. 'You're wrong. You couldn't be more wrong. I want someone I can talk to. I ... Oh hell, this is going to sound weird, but I want a friend. Is that so very wrong?'

'Then ring up the speaking clock,' Ella snapped. 'She'll talk to you all you want. She'll give you all the time in the world.'

A mischievous smile twitched at the corners of his mouth. 'I don't think she would be as interesting as you.'

'You mean she would be impervious to your charm and wouldn't give in.'

'Give in to what exactly?'

'Going to bed with you, of course.'

He tilted his head to one side. 'Have I so much as hinted at any point during this or any of our previous conversations that I wanted to go to bed with you? Maybe it's you who's obsessed with the idea of going to bed with me.'

She laughed bitterly. 'Don't kid yourself. You're not that hot.' *God help her for lying!*

'I don't recall saying I was.'

'No, men like you don't need to.'

'You've met a lot of men like me, have you?'

'You're a type.'

'Really? Go on – I'm intrigued. Tell me more.'

She put her mug of soup down on the workbench next to her. 'Okay,' she said, 'this is you in a nutshell.' She tapped her right forefinger against her left, ticking off her first point. 'Firstly, you grew up believing that the world revolved around you – your mother's probably to blame for that; she spoilt you and encouraged you to think you were the original blue-eyed boy.' She tapped her middle finger. 'Secondly, from there you progressed to having an over-inflated sense of entitlement; if you wanted something it was yours for the taking. And thirdly,' she tapped her ring finger, 'you've yet to grow out of this belief. How am I doing? Do you recognize yourself?'

He shifted his coat, which was still hooked over his arm. 'You couldn't be more wrong,' he said slowly. 'Along with countless others over the years who have made misguided assumptions about me. I know you'll find this hard to believe, but I'd very much like to share the real me with you.'

'But why? You hardly know me. I'm as good as a stranger to you.'

'I suspect that's part of the attraction.'

'Oh, please, save me the mysterious stranger routine. Let's not even go there. Instead, let's remind ourselves of your wife. Would I be right in assuming that you're not entirely faithful to her?'

'I don't know why you'd think that.'

'Let's just call it a well-educated guess.'

'Whether I am or not, is my faithfulness at all relevant to what I'm proposing between us?'

Ella snorted. 'I'd say so. But for the sake of clarity – after all, you did just say you wanted to share the real you with me – let's go with the theory that affairs are not uncommon for you.'

'I wouldn't call them affairs as such.'

'One-night stands, then. Does that cover it?'

He nodded. 'More or less.'

'And your wife knows what you get up to?'

'Absolutely not.'

Ella stared at him. She was shocked how cool and barefaced he was. 'Why do you do it?' she asked, exasperated. 'Because you can and it gives your ego a hit? Is that it?'

'It's a means of escape,' he replied, his voice low, his eyes not quite so squarely on her now.

'That's either the most pathetic thing I've ever heard, or the saddest.'

'To be fair, it's both of those things.'

His answer took her by surprise. 'Then why don't you change?'

'That's exactly what I'm trying to do.'

'Coming on to me isn't the best way of going about it.'

'I hate to keep correcting you, but I haven't come on to you. I've merely asked to get to know you better so that we could be friends.'

'But you must have real friends you can talk to.'

'I don't.'

Ella was about to say that that was either the second saddest or second most pathetic thing she had heard, when she thought about her own situation. Apart from her family, who did she talk to these days when she was really up against it? During her relationship with Lawrence she had been so hell-bent on proving she could make it work between them she had unintentionally isolated herself from her old friends. They, meanwhile, had moved on and had married and started families of their own. When she had at last emerged, bloodied and weary with defeat from the battle at Mayfield, her old friends had been too busy for her. The few who had had time for her became a painful reminder that all along they had been right and she had been wrong. They had never said as much, but it was there all the time, pushing the gap between them wider still. For a while she had pretended not to care, but then she'd realized that genuine friendship couldn't be sustained on pretence and falsehood and it seemed better to drift apart completely. It was more honest that way.

And was that what Ethan Edwards was being with her: unreservedly and brutally honest? He had owned up to his extra-marital activities, hadn't he, and frankly with a wife like his, who would blame him for looking elsewhere?

But that wasn't the point, she warned herself. Given the effect he had on her, getting involved, just as a friend, could lead to all sorts of problems. Why put herself through the trouble?

She looked at him once more and saw that he was waiting for her to say something. She cleared her throat. 'So let's get this straight. You don't want to get me into bed, you just want to talk to me.'

'Correct. I want to spend time with you. I want to—'

'There's a lot about your "wants" in all of this,' she interrupted him. 'What about me? What do I get out of it? Other than being a cheap therapist for you?'

'I'd like to think the friendship would be mutual, that you

might enjoy my company. I'm no expert, but I have a suspicion that that's how this friendship thing works.'

'I don't know,' she said doubtfully. 'Would your wife know about this friendship of ours?'

'No,' he said without hesitating.

'A friendship your wife doesn't know about. Doesn't that have a dangerously iffy sound to it to you?'

'I know what you're saying, but why don't we try it?'

'But try what exactly? What do you have in mind? Because I'll tell you now, I'm not doing anything that would give your wife cause to think we were having an affair. She doesn't strike me as being the understanding sort.'

'Certainly we would have to be careful.'

Ella couldn't figure him out. He seemed so convincingly sincere, so very serious about what he was proposing, as though it was a perfectly normal arrangement. 'Couldn't you just find yourself a pal at the golf club or something?' she tried. 'It would be a lot easier.'

'I don't play golf.'

'What about your neighbour next door, the husband of that woman I met?'

'I'd sooner impale myself on a pitchfork.'

She winced at the image. 'Okay, so he's not a front-runner. But there must be someone.'

'There isn't. Besides, it's not a normal friendship I'm looking for. It's something special.'

'And there you go again!'

'There I go again, what?'

'You throw a line out like that and still expect me to believe that it's a platonic friendship you want.'

'As before you've misinterpreted what I said. If you don't mind me saying, you do seem to have a one-track mind.'

She looked at him, aghast. 'You've got a nerve!'

'Not at all,' he laughed. 'Here I am trying to be friends with you on a purely companionable level and you keep tossing sex into the mix. But if *you* could stop coming on to *me* for a moment, perhaps you could give me your answer.'

She suddenly felt like laughing, too. The conversation really was just too peculiar. 'What was the question?' she asked, keeping her face deadpan.

'Will you be my friend?' he asked, his expression suddenly imbued with such a devastating look of beguiling and soulful appeal, her stomach lurched and she felt weak.

Uh-oh, she warned herself for the second time that day.

Say no, her head advised. Tell him categorically, unequivocally *NO!*

But since when had she taken anyone's advice, least of all her own?

Chapter Twenty-five

That evening, no sooner had Ella dealt with the many messages left on her answerphone and was contemplating a hot, relaxing bath, there was a ring at the doorbell. She hoped whoever it was wouldn't keep her for long. She had the beginnings of a headache and was in no mood for anyone trying to sell her something she neither needed nor wanted. Recently she had been inundated with so-called handy men with thick Irish accents pestering to retile her roof or tarmac her minuscule drive. She had begun to reach a state of paranoia, thinking she was being singled out because she was a woman on her own, but Phil from next door had said that the entire neighbourhood had been targeted.

As she went to answer the door, the word paranoia resonated with her. Had she been paranoid during that bizarre conversation with Ethan this afternoon, imagining that he was after only one thing? But surely any woman in her shoes would have had the same reaction?

Her mood not improved by another long and insistent ring, she yanked open the door. 'Lawrence!' she exclaimed in surprise. 'What are you doing here?'

Ignoring her question and barging in over the threshold, he said, 'I thought you were never going to come to the door. It's turned into a foul night; the rain's lashing down.' He shrugged off his coat, giving her a taste of how bad it was out there by showering her with water. He hung the dripping coat on the newel post at the bottom of the stairs and turning to face her, he smiled happily and kissed her cheek. 'I've brought a bottle of wine,' he said. 'Shall I open it?'

His sense of entitlement riled her. Funny how she had accused Ethan of that earlier, only for him to flatly deny he had anything of the sort. Funny, too, that there in the murkiest reaches of that treacherous mind of hers, there was a perverse echo of disappointment that it wasn't Ethan offering to share a bottle of wine with her.

'I haven't eaten yet,' she replied. 'I've only been home a short while. I don't think I'm going to be very good company. I have a headache.'

'In that case, my timing couldn't be better. You need someone to kick back with.'

Someone to kick, more like it, she thought, annoyed that Lawrence wasn't picking up on her mood. But no change there; in common with most men he never had been very good at doing that. Even when she had been fuming over something Alexis had done, he had carried on blithely unaware that she was near to self-destruction.

Lawrence had already eaten so she knocked together one of her favourite in-a-hurry suppers – spaghetti and tinned sardines – knowing what he would say about it.

'I've never understood how you could eat that,' he said reprovingly while he poured two glasses of wine and helped himself to some Stilton from the selection of cheese she had banged down on the table in front of him. 'You got the flowers, then,' he remarked, going over to look at them where they lay on the worktop, still in their cellophane wrapping. They were wilting, having spent the day in her car.

'Yes,' she said. 'Thank you.' She didn't know what else to say.

The spaghetti cooked, she sat opposite Lawrence and tucked in with exaggerated gusto. She then wondered why she was behaving so grudgingly. What was the matter with her? Why wasn't she pleased to see Lawrence?

*

'You could at least look pleased to see me.'

'Of course I'm pleased to see you,' Maggie lied as her mother-in-law lit up another cigarette. On the sofa beside Brenda was Evil Sid. Evil Sid was the ugliest dog that had ever barked or cocked its leg. He was a fat, two-year-old stinking pug who was so obese he could barely walk: Brenda carried him around most of the time. Panting and wheezing noisily – he probably had a forty-a-day habit from inhaling Brenda's second-hand smoke – Evil Sid bared his teeth at Maggie and growled. Doubtless he hadn't forgotten his last visit here at Christmas when Maggie, after discovering he'd weed on the landing carpet, had secretly whispered in his ear that it was a lie that a dog was for life.

'You don't *look* pleased to see me,' Brenda said. Her voice was raspy and her breath as wheezy as Evil Sid's. 'You look a right mardy madam.'

'I'm tired, that's all,' Maggie said. 'I've had a hard day.'

'A hard day! Don't make me laugh. In my day, a hard day meant just that. Cleaning's not difficult. Any fool can do it. Except for you. You should be ashamed of the state of my room. I swear if I had a mind to, I could write my name in the dust on the top of the wardrobe.'

What the hell was the old bat doing checking the top of the wardrobe? 'If I'd known you were coming,' Maggie said calmly, 'I'd have given the spare room a thorough clean.'

'I bet you would've! Anything to cover up how slapdash you are. I showed our Dave the dust and I told him, I said, that's what you get for letting your wife get away with murder.'

Never had the mention of murder seemed more tempting. 'Shall I make you a cup of tea?' Maggie asked, mentally stirring in two large spoonfuls of rat poison in place of sugar, at the same time reminding herself of her New Year's resolution, that she wasn't to lose it. But then she'd also promised to stand up for herself, hadn't she? Easier said than done with Brenda.

'I thought you'd never ask; I'm proper gasping. And make

sure you put enough milk in. You're always too stingy with it. And don't go fobbing me off with any of that semi-skimmed rubbish. I want full-fat milk. You have got some, haven't you?'

'I'll get some in the morning.'

Brenda sucked hard on her cigarette, her eyes narrowing to slits, her sunken, wrinkled cheeks flattening against what was left of her rotting teeth in her revoltingly gummy mouth. 'That corner shop will be open, won't it?' she said.

The choice between getting soaked in the rain or sticking around to be insulted non-stop wasn't a difficult one to make.

Maggie flung on her coat in the hall and grabbed her umbrella. She mouthed to Dave, who was on the phone, that she was going out for some milk for Brenda and banged the door after her. The pelting rain was bouncing off the pavement and within no time Maggie's legs were sopping wet and her shoes were letting in water. But she didn't care. Anything had to be better than breathing in the same poisonous air as Brenda.

After her brilliantly happy day – speaking to Daryl and arranging to see him – she had arrived home to find the hall jammed with bulging suitcases. 'Mum's come to stay,' Dave had told her. 'The roof's leaking at her place and I said she could stay with us until the council's got it fixed.'

There had been no point in asking how long that would take, or why Brenda couldn't stay with Dave's brother and his wife – they did, after all, have the bigger house, as they never failed to remind Maggie and Dave. Boasting came as naturally to them as being a total cow came to Brenda Storm.

It was a long walk through the estate to the shop and she passed few other people mad enough to be out on such a night. Mr Patel greeted her politely with one of his friendly smiles – no matter what the weather was, or what was going on in the world, Mr Patel was always polite and cheerful.

There was only one carton of full-fat milk left in the chilled cabinet and Maggie paid for it gratefully. To return empty-handed would set Brenda off for the rest of the night. She was halfway home when her mobile beeped with a text message. What now? Dave texting more demands from Brenda?

But it wasn't Dave; it was Daryl. And what he'd written made her forget all about Brenda and Evil Sid. She walked the rest of the distance home with an enormous grin on her face.

Ethan was tempted to get in his car and go and see Ella. But if he did, questions would be asked. Francine would want to know where he was going and since he didn't have a convincing reason for why he suddenly needed to dash off somewhere at this time of night, he had to stay put.

He read through the email he'd been writing – confirmation on a batch of colour swatches that had arrived that morning from China – and hit send. He then grabbed the remote control and turned up the volume on the CD player on the other side of his study, and leant back in his chair. Nick Drake's album *Five Leaves Left* had always been a favourite of his. Not the cheeriest of CDs, admittedly, but with its stripped-back purity, it had plenty of depth, truth and bittersweet torment, and sometimes that was what was required. And lyrics like, 'Time has told me you're a rare, rare find, a troubled cure for a troubled mind' couldn't be more poignant or apposite for him right now.

Ella was a cure for his troubled mind, he was sure of it. When he thought of her now, especially after what she had agreed to today, he felt a surge of happiness. His proposition hadn't really come out as he'd hoped, but given the circumstances it was never going to come out well. That she had granted him his wish filled him with an optimism he couldn't explain. It was astonishing that such a small thing could have such an effect on him.

Her only caveat was that there would be no crossing of any lines. He had given her his word that that wouldn't happen. It was a promise he fully intended to keep. He didn't want to do anything that would jeopardize the fragile balance of what he had put in place. He didn't think he could bear it if he lost her good opinion of him.

Or more accurately, the good opinion he hoped one day she would have of him.

Chapter Twenty-six

It had been the same at Christmas when Brenda had come to stay: the complaints, jibes and criticisms were never ending.

Nothing Maggie did was ever right or good enough. The meals she cooked were too salty, not salty enough, too bland, too overcooked, too undercooked, served too early or too late. 'Do you really expect me to eat at this time of night?' Brenda had said yesterday after Maggie had arrived home at seven o'clock from her last cleaning job and started cooking. 'If you're ever hungry, you can always ask Dave to make you something,' Maggie had said as she attacked a potato with the peeler, gouging out a sprouting eye with great feeling.

'I wouldn't dream of asking our Dave to cook when he's been at work all day,' Brenda had replied, outraged. 'You've only got to look at him to see how exhausted he is.'

Maggie's job counted for nothing in Brenda's eyes. It didn't matter that Dave was always home by five forty-five every day and did nothing but read the paper whilst waiting for Maggie to come home and get the tea ready, and that after he'd eaten he was off out to the pub, leaving Maggie to tidy up.

Sometimes she daydreamed of ending the complaints and criticisms once and for all. The frying pan that she so often imagined taking to Dave's head she now pictured using to knock Brenda into next week, along with Evil Sid. The foul mutt had decided it was too much effort to waddle to the back door and had started treating any leg of furniture as a convenient place to cock his chubby leg.

All that kept Maggie going was the thought of seeing Daryl

today. She still couldn't believe that he wanted to see her. Nor could she believe that she'd said yes. Whenever she began to panic about what she was doing, she calmed herself with the promise that they were only meeting for a chat over a cup of coffee. There was no law against that, was there? And it didn't mean anything that Daryl had sent a text saying he couldn't wait for it to be Wednesday, that he couldn't stop thinking about her. He was just being friendly. And she was being just as friendly by sending a message back saying that she couldn't stop thinking of him either.

Meanwhile, she had breakfast to cook. Dave and Dean were cock-a-hoop because Brenda had insisted they couldn't go to work on nothing but toast as they normally did and so Maggie was having to serve up a daily diet of a heart attack on a plate. According to Brenda, Mr Storm – that was how Brenda always referred to her dead husband – had never left the house with anything less than a full English inside him. So no surprise then that he had died aged only fifty-five of a massive heart attack ten years ago and had weighed over twenty stone when his coffin had thudded into the ground. But try telling Brenda that. Try telling Brenda, who consumed nothing but nicotine for her breakfast, that she had killed her husband just as if she had taken a knife and stuck it in his heart.

'What's this?' Dave asked when Maggie put the killer plates of greasy food on the table.

'Your breakfast,' she said.

Dave humphed. 'Not much bacon.' Picking up his fork in his beefy hand, he prodded at the two rashers of bacon on the plate. 'Where's the rest?'

'It's all we had left,' Maggie replied, carefully fighting the urge to pick up the plate and hurl it against the wall. 'Your mum wanted a couple of rashers for Sid.'

'You'll have to get some more on your way home from work,' Brenda said. 'And while you're about it you can get me some more fags, I'm down to my last two packets.'

'Hey, Mum, where's the brown sauce?'

Maggie gripped the handle of the frying pan as she carried it to the sink. 'Sorry, Dean, we're out of that, too,' she said, her back to the table.

'Our Dave, I've said it before and I'll say it again: I don't know how you put up with it. Does nothing get done properly in this house?'

'Yer know me, Mum. I don't like to make a fuss.'

Oh, don't you? thought Maggie. She ran the hot tap and scrubbed at the frying pan. Then she thought, to hell with it! She switched off the tap and tossed the sponge into the sink. 'I'm going to have to go,' she said, 'or I'll be late.'

'What? You're just going to leave the washing up? Well, I've never heard the like.'

Maggie swallowed. She counted to three and turned round. 'If you've got a spare minute during the day, maybe you could do it for me, Brenda.'

Brenda ground her cigarette out savagely in the overflowing ashtray on the table. 'Now I've heard everything! Me a guest in your house and you expect me to wash up because you can't be bothered. You beggar belief sometimes, Maggie.'

Don't I just, Maggie thought.

With her only job of the day finished, and the owner of the house at work, Maggie used the downstairs toilet to change out of her work clothes and put on a set of brand new clothes – black trousers, a silvery-grey roll-neck sweater and a pair of black boots. They had a much higher heel than she normally wore. Then she carefully brushed her hair, having spent the last hour working with large velcro rollers in it – she'd done her best to copy what the hairdresser had done when she'd had it cut. Lastly she tried out the new make-up she had bought. Usually she used no more than a dab of mascara or lipgloss, but today she was using some foundation and blusher. She put it on sparingly, terrified she would end up looking slutty or, worse, like her mother, who favoured the trowel method and always wore too much.

When she'd finished, she stood back from the mirror, turned sideways and then swung her head round trying to catch her reflection unawares. She did this several times and then stared long and hard at herself. Better, she decided. Yes, definitely better. But not too different. She didn't want to look different. She wanted to look like she had made an effort but hadn't tried too hard. Her reflection told her that she was basically the same old Maggie, but inside she felt a hint of a new Maggie, a confident Maggie.

She arrived at the library with five minutes to spare and as the automatic doors swished behind her, she took a deep breath to calm her stomach, which was tying itself into a bundle of very tight knots. *I'm doing nothing wrong*, she reminded herself as she skulked past the counter where one of the librarians was sorting through a pile of returned books. There was no need to skulk, she told herself. She came to the library every week. She wasn't doing anything to be ashamed of. All she was doing was meeting a friend for a chat. Nothing more. She imagined herself as the new and improved Maggie. The confident Maggie who was going to take life by the scruff of the neck and have some fun for once.

She moved along the aisles of books and was about to take a familiar sharp right at Crime and Thrillers for Romance when a familiar voice made her let out a startled cry. 'Look at you all dressed up! I almost didn't recognize you, chuck.'

'Mo,' she said, when she'd recovered. Then: 'It is you, Mo, isn't it?'

Hidden behind sunglasses and a pink baseball cap, the peak of which was pulled down low over her forehead, Mo said, 'Yes, it's me all right.' She raised the peak of the cap and removed her sunglasses carefully. Maggie winced. Mo looked like she'd gone ten rounds in the boxing ring with someone a lot bigger than she was. The skin around her eyes was bruised and puffy and the rest of her face didn't look much better. All shades of faded bruising, the skin was so tight and shiny

Maggie's eyes watered. 'I've just been to have the stitches out,' Mo said, indicating her eyes. She lifted the hair above her right ear. 'Look, you can see where the staples are still in place.'

Where earlier Maggie's stomach had been knotted with nerves, it now felt sloppy and queasy. 'How's Mum doing?' she asked, wondering if she looked as awful as Mo. 'She's told me I can't see her until the bruising and swelling's gone down.'

'Oh, she's doin' nicely. You should have come with us. We had a right old laugh. Peggy got stuck in the loo on the plane coming back; she couldn't unlock the door. God, it was a laugh. I've gotta say, you look well, chuck. Like I said earlier, I almost didn't recognize you. Is that foundation you're wearing? I've never seen you with foundation on before.'

'Um … no, it's … it's concealer. I've got some kind of rash.'

Mo leaned in and peered closely at Maggie's face. 'A miracle concealer in that case. I can't see nowt but a perfect complexion. You must tell me the make – I could do with something good to use while I wait for my face to settle down. And that's a great new hairdo you've got, I swear you look ten years younger than when I last saw you.'

'Thank you,' Maggie said, wishing she could say the same of Mo. She glanced anxiously around the library: Daryl would be here soon, if he hadn't arrived already. The last thing she needed was Mo tittle-tattling to Lou that she'd seen Maggie all dressed up and covered in slap, and guess who else just happened to be in the library at the same time? That bloke in the tight jeans! The adding of two and two and coming up with a whole lot of trouble made Maggie say, 'Sorry I can't chat for longer, but I'm due at my next job in half an hour.' Her secret afternoon off would no longer be secret if Mo went blabbing to Mum.

'You're never going cleaning in those clothes, are you? They're as smart as paint.'

'What, these old things?' Maggie said dismissively. 'They're ancient. Bye, then. Say hi to Mum when you see her next.'

'I'll walk out with you,' Mo said, putting her sunglasses back on. 'I've got what I came in for.' She waved a leaflet at Maggie. 'It's about the country and western night in the town hall next month. You should come with us, chuck. It'll be fun. A right laugh.'

A right laugh indeed, thought Maggie as she was forced to leave the library with Mo, at the same time keeping a worried lookout for Daryl. This is what you get for playing with fire, for sneaking around and pretending you're doing nothing wrong, she thought wretchedly. Her earlier confidence now in tatters, she was suddenly near to tears at the thought of what Daryl had talked her into doing. How could she have agreed? How could she have thought she could get away with it? What had made her think she deserved any fun anyway? As Brenda would say, who did she think she was?

The thought of Brenda and her spiteful tongue brought Maggie up short. The new confident Maggie wouldn't stand by and let a woman like Brenda push her around. Nor would she let a lazy-arsed husband and son get away with what they did. No, the confident Maggie would tell them where to go. Not only that, she would do as she pleased for a change and to hell with the consequences!

They were passing the Oxfam shop when Maggie made her decision. 'I'm sorry, Mo,' she said. 'I've just realized I've left my umbrella in the library.'

Mo looked up at the clear blue sky, then at Maggie. 'You thought it was going to rain today, chuck?'

'You know me – always better safe than sorry. I'll see you. Bye.' And before she lost her nerve, she dashed back the way she'd just come.

The library doors swished behind her and she checked her watch. She was now fifteen minutes late. Her heart beating overtime, she scanned the aisles, tables and chairs. There was no sign of Daryl. He must have given up waiting for her.

Or he'd been delayed.

She hung onto this hope. Along with the hope that he'd call her on her mobile to say he'd be late, that he was on his way.

She waited a further ten minutes.

And then another ten minutes.

All the while checking her mobile. Even stupidly shaking it at one point in case it wasn't working properly.

At last she had to admit she'd been stood up. Worse still, Daryl had probably never had any intention of meeting her. Why would he? A man as good-looking as he was could have any woman he wanted. She'd made a proper fool of herself. She should never have been taken in by him.

It was just like that time at school when she'd fancied Eddie Landers something rotten. He was one of the most popular boys in the school and somehow he'd found out how she felt about him. When he asked her to go to the May bank holiday fair with him she couldn't believe her luck. He told her to wait for him by the hot dog stall, except he hadn't turned up and back at school she discovered everyone had been in on the joke, that he had never intended to go with her. They all knew that she'd waited more than two hours for him. She had never eaten another hot dog since.

Chapter Twenty-seven

As her relationship with Lawrence proved only too well, once Ella decided upon a course of action she clung to it with all the single-mindedness of a very tenacious barnacle. Doubts and second thoughts were anathema to her.

However, in the days since she had agreed to Ethan Edwards' strange request, she had had real doubts about what she had done. It was the most natural and uncomplicated thing in the world at the age of seven to agree to be someone's friend, but signing up to be the friend of a forty-something man who wasn't happy in his marriage was altogether a different matter. And that was without factoring in her own rather questionable feelings about him. So to say she had misgivings was a huge understatement.

She hadn't seen or heard anything from Ethan since that unexpected conversation and with each day that passed she wondered if he had regretted what he had shared with her. Perhaps, given that they hardly knew each other, he now saw that his openness about his extra-marital activities was an admission too far. Who was to say she wouldn't go running to his ghastly wife just to make trouble? There was also the possibility that he had been playing some kind of ego-boosting game with her; reel her in, then toss her aside when he had acquired the desired response.

She sighed with irritation. How many times had she played this same loop inside her head? It was beginning to annoy her. Part of that annoyance was knowing that she had allowed a situation to get the better of her, and wasn't that something she had vowed would never happen again? Staying in control of her life – that was the promise she'd made to herself.

She climbed down from the stepladder to reposition it, then climbed back up to the top step. She was once again at The Lilacs and on the home straight; she had only a third of the last wall to do now. As was usually the case, she had the house to herself. Mrs Edwards had let her in this morning and informed her that she and her daughter would be away for the next couple of days in Abersoch and that Mr Edwards would let her in tomorrow morning.

Ethan wasn't the only one to be conspicuous by his absence; Lawrence had also gone quiet on her. Following the evening when he had shown up with wine – and as it turned out, a good deal of expectation – he had backed off. She had hurt his pride by refusing to go to bed with him. 'Can't blame a man for trying,' he had said ruefully when he had made his move and she had declined and said she didn't want to take that step until she was absolutely clear in her mind that they were doing the right thing. 'Of course,' he'd said. 'I'm sorry. It's just that I feel so sure about you returning to Mayfield, it's difficult for me to imagine you don't feel the same way.'

'I need more time, Lawrence,' she had said. 'You hurt me so much before. I can't go through that again.'

'I promise you that will never happen again.'

But Ella knew that promises meant nothing – they were easy to make and just as easy to break. They were mere words. Nothing more.

Lawrence had been pulling on his coat to leave when he had asked her if she had met someone else. Was that why she had doubts? She could tell from the way he blurted out the question that he immediately regretted it. She had assured him there was no one else for him to worry about.

What he would make of her arranged friendship with Ethan Edwards was anybody's guess.

*

Maggie was having one of those days when she wanted to yell and scream every known obscenity.

Road rage, queue rage, supermarket-trolley rage, kept-hanging-on-the-phone rage, stubbed-toe rage, car-won't-start rage, can't-find-something rage – put them all together and it didn't come close to what she was feeling.

Earthquakes, nuclear bangs, erupting volcanoes, NASA rockets taking off – put them all together and they wouldn't have half the explosive energy she was trying to keep a lid on.

One more offensive criticism from Brenda.

One more roll of the eyes from Dave.

One more request for a clean shirt from Dean.

One more growl from Evil Sid.

Just one, and she wouldn't be responsible for the mayhem that would follow. They would cop the lot of her anger. Every seething ounce of it. What's more, they would cop Daryl Delaney's share. Oh, yes! They could have that smooth-talking bastard's share of her anger.

It was twenty-four hours since Daryl had humiliated her and there had been no word from him. Not a word of apology. Nothing. It had all been a massive joke to him. He was probably having a good laugh at how easily he had conned her. What a mug she'd been. A pathetic idiot who, for a stupid moment, had believed she was special. That was what hurt the most; he had made her think that she was special and deserved something better than the life she had. How could she have been so gullible, such a gormless moron?

Because she'd been desperate to believe in the dream she'd thought he was offering her, that was why. She had thought her life could change like one of those women she was always reading about. She wouldn't be filling her head with any more of those books! From now on she would read different ones. Books about murder. The gorier the better. Or how about true-life crime? No, better still, she would write her own true-life crime. She would write the story of a woman who was pushed too far, a woman who wiped out her family along with the man who had made fun of her. That was how serial killers were made – cruelly teased at some time in their lives, they turned into monsters and became obsessed with revenge.

From what she knew of prison life, she reckoned it would be better than the life she had now. She would sign up for all the education classes. She would learn to speak another language. She would study books, too. Clever books, like the ones she had seen at the library but had never felt brave enough to tackle. Knowing her luck, she would be handed a mop and bucket on her first day and told to clean the place; there would be no learning for her!

She got up from where she'd been kneeling on the cold tiled floor. She wished Doctor Whitworth, a GP from the local health centre, would at least rinse the bath out after she washed her dog in it. She was sick of dealing with the disgusting mess; hairs, mud and God only knew what else.

She went downstairs for a fresh cleaning cloth. She was at the bottom of the stairs when her mobile rang in her pocket. She answered it on the third ring, not checking caller ID. If she had, she might not have answered it.

'Maggie, it's me, Daryl.'

She caught her breath.

'Maggie?'

She didn't reply.

'Maggie? Can you hear me?'

'Yes,' she said finally, the one small word almost choking her. She closed her eyes and pictured a volcano erupting, hot molten lava spewing into the sky.

'Oh, thank God for that. Look, I expect you're pretty pissed off with me, aren't you?'

She pictured the lava, fiery red and orange, burning and destroying everything it touched.

'I'm so sorry about yesterday,' Daryl said. 'But ... but something awful happened and—'

'Yes,' she said, her voice frighteningly calm, 'you're right, something awful did happen. You made a fool of me. You had no intention of meeting me, did you?'

'Maggie, please don't think that. You couldn't be more wrong. I was really looking forward to seeing you. It was all I could think of. And then—'

'So why didn't you come?' she interrupted. 'And why didn't you let me know?'

There was a silence at the other end of the phone. He was stalling, trying to come up with a convincing excuse. As if he'd not had time enough to do that. 'All you had to do was ring or text me,' she said. 'Why didn't you?'

The silence continued in her ear, then there was a sound she couldn't make sense of. Then she got it; it was the sound of stifled laughter. He was laughing at her. He was bloody sniggering his great big bloody head off at her! She was about to shout back at him exactly what she thought about him when she hesitated. He wasn't laughing, he was … he was crying. Daryl was *crying*. 'Daryl!' she said. 'What is it? What's wrong?'

It was a while before he could get the words out. 'My best friend …' She heard him take a deep breath. She sat down where she was on the stairs. 'Sorry,' he said. He sniffed loudly and tried again. 'My best mate's wife died yesterday. We all knew it was going to happen sooner or later – she had been on dialysis for ages – but it's still been a helluva shock.'

Maggie felt awful, regretting every bad thought she'd had about him in the last twenty-four hours. She wished she could unsay what she'd just said. 'Daryl, I'm so sorry.'

'Cerys was like a sister to me,' he went on. 'I've known her almost as long as I've known Matt. I can't believe she's dead.'

'How's your friend coping?'

'He's numb. And knackered. He's got three kiddies to bring up on his own.'

'The poor man.'

They both fell silent. Then Maggie said, 'I'm sorry I was cross with you just now.'

'It's okay, I understand. You thought I'd stood you up and, you had every right to be angry.'

'Is there anything I can do to help?' She didn't have a clue what she could do, but she wanted to do something, *anything*, to make Daryl feel better.

'Are you busy later today?' he asked.

'I finish work at six,' she said.

'Can we meet? I might not be the best of company right now, but being with you, if only for an hour or two, will give me something else to think about. It'll take my mind off how shitty everything feels right now.'

Ethan had had an anxious day.

First off he'd had a nerve-racking meeting at the bank to get through and then he'd received a call from his agent in China saying that an investigative journalist had been snooping around some of the factories in the area and had unearthed evidence of widespread child labour.

Ethan had always insisted that the factories he dealt with were one hundred per cent ethically sound and most importantly they were not to employ children. The factory owners were under no illusions with him: if children were found to be employed he would cease trading with them. He'd made good his threat last year with one particular set-up when he'd discovered girls as young as ten were being used for cutting and hemming, and regardless of the inevitable problems that had followed his decision, he wouldn't hesitate to do it again. On Ethan's behalf, the agent on the ground had made enquiries of his own at the factories and had finally, despite how late it was there, reported back that Ethan had nothing to worry about.

With a profound sense of relief, he finished work early and drove home. He had been waiting for this moment ever since Sunday when Francine had announced that she was going to

Abersoch with her parents for two days. Never had Abersoch sounded so good to him, especially as Francine had decided to incur the wrath of Valentina's headmistress and take Valentina out of school to go with her.

A whole two days to himself was most appealing. It could even stretch into more if Francine decided to stay on for the coming weekend. He could only hope.

Knowing from Francine that Ella was at the house today, he hoped that she would still be there and that he would be able to persuade her to take a break and chat for a while, or better still, take the rest of the day off. If she was determined to carry on working, so be it: he would talk to her while she painted. He quite liked the thought of that, of watching the look of intense concentration on her face.

When he turned into Lilac Avenue and approached the house, he could see at least one of his hopes had not been in vain. He parked alongside Ella's car, gathered up his things and let himself in.

Such was the buoyancy of his mood it was difficult not to greet her with a kiss. Just a small kiss, his mouth light against her cheek. A perfectly friendly greeting. The kind of innocent kiss no one would think twice about. A kiss between friends.

He didn't, of course. Instead he took up his usual stance in the doorway of the dining room, a shoulder pressed against the frame. 'Hi,' he said casually. Or as casually as he could. Not having spoken to her since their last encounter here, he was suddenly apprehensive how she might regard him.

She wasn't plugged into her iPhone as she usually was and so must have heard him come into the house. 'Hi,' she said back at him. 'What do you think?' She indicated the wall she was working on. 'I've made good progress today.'

His first thought was of disappointment. The room would soon be finished. Soon there would be no reason for her to come here. The thought so depressed him, all he could say was, 'It's great. Yes,' he repeated, 'it's great.'

She gave him a penetrating sideways glance. 'You don't sound convinced.'

For the first time in her presence he felt ridiculously tongue-tied. Perhaps even a little shy. Actually, he realized, it was the first time in any woman's presence that he'd felt tongue-tied or shy. For what felt like for ever, they stood in a tense, awkward silence, as if they were both strenuously trying to act normally, as if they really were friends and not *trying* to be friends. And because he couldn't think of a single clever thing to say, he resorted to the old standby of: 'Would you like a drink?'

'Tea would be nice. Thank you.'

'Any particular sort? Earl Grey? Peppermint? Ordinary?'

'A cup of *extra*ordinary tea would be nice.'

He caught the hint of a teasing smile playing at the corners of her mouth and he relaxed. He went to her, removed the paintbrush and palette from her hands and placed them carefully on the workbench. 'Come with me,' he said. 'I'm not going to risk leaving you here on your own. You might start laughing at me behind my back.'

'Why would I do that?'

'You know why.'

'Do I?'

'You're making me edgy.'

'Really?'

'Yes, now stop asking so many questions.'

'Don't you ever say please?'

'*Please*. And yes, I'm well aware that that was another question you slipped in.'

In the kitchen he invited her to sit on one of the stools at the breakfast bar while he filled the kettle and plugged it in. He then removed his tie and suit jacket – specially worn for the benefit of his bank manager – and undid the top button of his shirt.

'You are going to stop at that, aren't you?' she asked.

He raised an eyebrow, knowing she was teasing him again. 'You've seen me in a lot less.'

'True.'

'And in case you were wondering, that wasn't deliberate on my part. You really had caught me on the hop that morning.'

'No worries. It often comes with the territory. One client who'd given me a key to let myself in with forgot to tell me he would be coming home a day earlier than expected and when I breezed into his bedroom to carry on where I'd left off the day before, he was not alone in bed. Nor was he asleep.'

'Interesting work.'

'Never a dull moment. How about your work?'

He made the drinks, having made the executive decision of giving her ordinary tea and coffee for himself, and said, 'It has its moments. Currently I'm flying on a wing and a prayer to keep things together while the economy levels out.'

'Do you think you'll survive?'

'I sincerely hope so.' He fetched a carton of milk from the fridge. 'Recently a dangerous thought has started popping into my head. I keep thinking, what the hell? Let it all go. Let the recession do its worst.'

'How would that go down, domestically?'

He laughed bitterly. 'You mean how would my wife cope? God only knows. What I do know is that whatever was in the kitty would be hers and I'd be out on my ear with nothing.'

'Surely that's not true.'

'Trust me, it is.'

'Well, would that matter so much? You just said that sometimes you think, oh what the hell, let it all go.'

'Fine words. The reality is I'm responsible for keeping the show going. It's not just about Francine and me; there's Valentina's future to consider. Not forgetting the people who work for me. I couldn't let them down. Sorry, I can't remember – do you take sugar?'

She shook her head and he passed her the mug of tea.

'Thank you,' she said. 'Far be it from me to judge, seeing as I've never been married, but it doesn't sound like you have the most harmonious of marriages.'

'Now you're being obtuse. You must have figured out for yourself that there's nothing harmonious about my marriage. If there was, would I have admitted to you the other day that I've been unfaithful to Francine?'

'I've been wondering why you confessed that to me. It was quite a risk.'

'Meaning you might let it slip to my wife?'

'Something like that, yes.'

'Is it the kind of thing you would let slip?'

She shook her head again.

'I thought not. I'm usually a pretty good judge of character. Biscuit?'

'No, thank you.'

He sat down opposite her.

'Stop staring,' she said when a few moments had passed.

'I wasn't aware I was.'

'You do it a lot. Stop it at once or I'll go back to work.'

He smiled. 'Don't do that. Not yet, anyway.'

Another moment passed.

'Am I allowed to ask you a question?' she said.

'I hadn't noticed you *not* asking any questions. Go on.'

'I'm intrigued by something you just said. You said you were responsible for keeping the show going. Is that how you see yourself? Solely responsible for keeping the world spinning on its axis? Your business, this house, your family.'

He considered her question. 'Are you about to imply that I have an over-inflated sense of my own importance?'

'If I thought that, I would have asked if you were ever tempted to wear your underpants over your trousers. No, I'm just curious.' She took a sip of her tea and became thoughtful, no longer looking at him, but off into the distance at the garden through the French windows. That was when he was struck by how perfectly heart-shaped her face was, and how long and delicate her lashes were. She wasn't wearing any make-up and her skin was bright and clear. He noticed too the colour of her eyes; they were a soft shade of blue, verging almost on grey. Large and expressive, they contained a remarkable depth of sincerity and intelligence. At once he understood that here was the reason he had been compelled to trust and confide in her. It was her genuineness that he had been attracted to; it had been there right from the start.

'What exactly are you curious about?' he said, rousing himself.

She swung her thoughtful gaze back to his. 'You strike me as a man who is going through the motions of his life. It's as if you think you don't have any say or any choice in what you do.'

'Why do you say that?'

She shrugged. 'The last time we spoke, you said that you have sex with other women as a way to escape. What are you escaping from? Is it the fact that everything you do is born out of a sense of duty?'

'Isn't that what everyone does?'

'To a degree, but with you I sense something else. Something that goes deeper.'

The frankness of her observation caught him unawares and he didn't know how to respond. He left his coffee and moved away from the breakfast bar, went and stood by the French windows. Unsettled, he pushed his hands into his trouser pockets. But wasn't this what he'd wanted, the chance to talk openly and honestly with her? Why then did it feel too painful all of a sudden to take that step?

'I'm sorry,' she said from behind him. 'I didn't mean to annoy you.'

He turned round. 'You haven't. I'm just so used to meaningless and superficial conversations, your perceptiveness threw me off balance.'

'That wasn't my intention.' She slipped off the barstool. 'I'll take my tea and get back to work now.'

'If it won't disturb you, can I watch?'

She frowned. 'Haven't you got anything better to do?'

'I enjoy watching you paint.'

She laughed. 'Nobody's ever said that to me before.'

'Then, if nothing else, I'm glad to be original. I'd hate you to think I was derivative in any way.'

Chapter Twenty-eight

The seemingly never-ending tussle between winter and spring was at long last over. Spring had definitely won and was making its welcome mark.

While she waited for her toast to pop up in the toaster, Ella stood at the window and watched a grey squirrel scuttle along the fence in the early morning sunshine. It leapt from the fence into the bushes below, then scampered across the lawn, weaving a path through the clumps of sunlit daffodils before disappearing behind her workshop where the garden sloped down towards a wooded area and the railway line.

Ella had always liked the month of March; it held so much hope and promise. Invariably the hope was misguided, as often when the first much-longed for daffodils burst into life, hurricane-strength winds arrived to lay waste to the fragile unfurling flowers. But even if it was illusory, Ella would always be seduced by the hope and the general sense of wellbeing spring instilled in her. It was perhaps because of this feeling, in an upbeat moment when anything felt possible and everything had potential, that she had agreed to Ethan's latest request – a request she had flatly refused when he'd first suggested it.

Against all the odds, their so-called arrangement had turned into something that was actually very like a *real* friendship. Increasingly she genuinely looked forward to seeing him; their conversations were always interesting, sometimes serious, sometimes sparked with humour, and sometimes surprisingly revealing.

Much to her amazement she had found herself confiding in him, in considerable detail, about her relationship with Lawrence, in particular the reasons why it hadn't worked. In turn he had told her how his father had died when he was ten years old and how dramatically his childhood had changed from then on. The family, which consisted of him, his sister and his mother, went from being reasonably affluent to having nothing. It turned out his father had borrowed money to keep his engineering business afloat, but when he died, the creditors descended and took what they were owed.

Ethan's mother had been twenty-seven years younger than her husband, and – this was Ella reading between the lines – with no real practical skills or intention of going out to work to keep a roof over their heads, she had put to use her two best assets, her youth and good looks, to find a new husband and provider. She proved to be a bad picker of men and she flitted from one disastrous relationship to another, regularly uprooting Ethan and his younger sister as one relationship ended and another started. At the age of fourteen Ethan had all but given up on school, attending the minimum number of days to keep the truant officer happy. At his mother's insistence that he took on the responsibility of supporting the family, he juggled four part-time jobs: a paper round first thing in the morning, helping on a market stall at the weekend along with gardening work, and stacking shelves in the supermarket five evenings a week. At the end of every week he handed over his wages to his mother.

It was at this part of Ethan's story that Valentina had arrived home from school, thereby denying Ella the chance to ask the question that had been on the tip of her tongue: why the hell hadn't his mother gone out to work to support the family herself?

Ella's previous assertion that Ethan had been a spoilt mummy's boy who imagined the world revolved around him had clearly been wrong. No wonder he had such a strong sense of duty and responsibility when it had been drummed into him from a very young age. It made her question what else she had got wrong. It also made her consider something she had thought before: that what Ethan needed most was a friendly ear, a confidante.

Which, as unlikely as it was, was what she had become to Maggie.

In the month that had passed since Maggie had asked Ella for her advice, supposedly about her married friend who had been asked out by a good looking man, Maggie's transformation had continued. She was much more confident, had lost weight and was tangibly happier.

Over coffee one morning at The Lilacs, she had confessed to what Ella had known all along: that Maggie had wanted advice for herself and not for a friend. 'Really?' Ella had said, her face serious. But then she had laughed and Maggie had laughed, too.

'I know it's wrong what I'm doing,' Maggie had said, 'but ... but I've never felt happier. I suppose you think I'm awful, don't you?'

Ella had been quick to assure Maggie that she thought no such thing. 'Life isn't the straightforward thing we start out thinking it is,' she had said.

'But do you mind me talking to you about it? Only I don't have anyone else I can talk to,' Maggie had further confessed. 'And you're a good listener. You really are.'

Taken aback, yet flattered, Ella had given Maggie her mobile number and said she could call for a chat any time she wanted.

Lawrence had often remarked that she was a good listener and certainly Ethan had said much the same, so maybe it was true. She had never really seen herself in that role before.

Up until now all contact between Ella and Ethan had taken place at The Lilacs, although recently he had begun emailing her. Usually late at night. She pictured him in his office, sitting at his desk while his wife was upstairs in bed. It wasn't an image she was entirely happy with – sneaky and clandestine were the words that sprang to mind – but nothing, absolutely nothing of a questionable nature had passed between them.

Other than the occasional innuendo or teasing expression on Ethan's face.

Other than the fact that Mrs Edwards was in ignorance of their friendship.

But friendship was what it was. An innocent and platonic friendship, at that. True to his word, Ethan had not once crossed any lines and the longer that went on for, the more at ease Ella felt in his company, and the more she looked forward to their conversations and exchanges of emails. She had dealt with the flashes of physical desire she had previously experienced for him by filing them under *Not Appropriate*, subheaded, *Don't Be So Ridiculous!* and consequently this had helped to strengthen the newly established equilibrium of their friendship. Just occasionally an inappropriate feeling would surface from her subconscious in the form of a dream, but now that she was one hundred per cent convinced that he only wanted her as a friend, she was able to dismiss her unmanageable dream-life as irrelevant.

Last week she had finished work on the dining room and after Mrs Edwards had deigned to admit that she was happy with the work Ella had done, she had asked her to revamp the master bedroom. Thinking it might be better to distance herself from The Lilacs, Ella had politely declined the job, using the excuse that she had a lot on her plate for the next few months. Naturally Mrs Edwards was not the kind of woman to take no for an answer and pursued the matter, dangling what she presumed was a tempting carrot of further work on the new house in Abersoch. Ella needed work as much as the next self-employed person, but she was aware that her acceptance of the job would mean more expense for Ethan, something she knew he could do without. But then two days ago Ethan had urged her to take the job on. 'How else will I get to talk to you when you won't let me come to your house?' he had emailed her. That was when she had taken a deep breath and replied, 'Maybe I could change my mind about that.'

The thought of not seeing Ethan again had made her realize that she didn't want to do without his presence in her life, and performing a complete U-turn, she had said he could visit her at Tickle Cottage. With spring filling her heart with positive and carefree thoughts, she had told herself no harm would come of it.

So today, Saturday, while his wife and daughter were shopping in Manchester for the day, Ethan was coming for lunch. She hoped she hadn't made a mistake, that her judgement hadn't become skewed in her wish to maintain their friendship.

Friendship was also what she had persuaded Lawrence to accept for the time being. His disappointment that she felt unable to commit to more had been all too evident in his dejected expression, but he'd had to accept it was that or nothing. She had rather expected his pride to dictate his reaction and for him to say that he wasn't prepared to wait for her to make up her mind, but his quiet acceptance that she would not be rushed came as a relief. There had been no more flowers, but dinner had become a regular event. She had noticed during these evenings out that at times the conversation between them had a tendency to be one-sided – he did all the talking while she listened.

In contrast, or maybe it was merely symptomatic of two people getting to know each other, Ethan displayed markedly more interest in her thoughts and opinions. He was particularly interested in the matter of Lawrence wanting her to move back to Mayfield and how she was going to reach a decision. It was good having someone objective to discuss things with; she hadn't dared breathe a word of what was going on to her family.

Currently Lawrence was preoccupied with problems at work, but he was also worried that Alexis was, in his own words, 'going off the rails'. Apparently she had arrived home last Saturday with a small tattoo of a butterfly on her wrist, and he was terrified that this was just the beginning of the end.

Tomorrow was Lawrence's birthday and Ella had been invited to join in with the celebrations at Mayfield. His parents – Keith and Jan – would be there, along with Deirdre, his widowed mother-in-law. Toby was also going to be home for the weekend. It would be an interesting get-together as Ella hadn't seen Deirdre or Lawrence's parents since her break-up with Lawrence.

No sooner had Ethan set foot over the threshold of Tickle Cottage than the telephone rang. While Ella went to deal with it he took the opportunity to investigate his surroundings.

He liked the house. It was compact but without feeling small or cramped. Just as he'd known it would be, Ella's taste in furniture and décor was excellent; nothing jarred on the eye. He prowled the sitting room, taking in the cluttered bookshelves, the arty bits and bobs, the pictures on the walls, and the framed photographs, including one of Ella with her arms around a young anxious-looking boy. Presumably the lad was the son of her ex.

The more Ethan heard about Lawrence, the more he disliked the man. Not that he had said as much to Ella, but in his opinion she would be mad to go back to him. Ethan was honest enough to admit, if only to himself, that his opinion was based on nothing more substantial or rational than selfish jealousy. He simply didn't like the idea of Ella being with another man, least of all a man who would monopolize her and put a stop to her spending any time with him.

He continued to investigate the room. Everywhere he looked he discerned evidence of Ella's artistic talent. It was there in the gold stencilling on the walls around the archway that led to the kitchen and dining area, the built-in cupboards either side of the fireplace with a pale cream distressed finish, and the matching coffee table. Everything had been done with a light touch and he found that he liked it; the room felt welcoming and comfortably lived in. There was also the appetizing smell of lunch cooking that added to the intimate ambience. He felt very much at home.

He frequently felt like a stranger in his own home. The Lilacs – in the hands of his wife – was cold and impersonal; it was too reminiscent of a show house with everything perfectly positioned. Ella's house, with its amusing name, was most assuredly a home; there was a living, beating heart here at the centre of it. A heart of warmth. Not one of stone.

Still talking on the telephone the other side of the archway, Ella shot him a look of apology. She mouthed the word 'client' and he smiled and gave her a don't-worry-I've-got-all-the-time-in-the-world shrug. He watched her write something down, heard her trying to bring the conversation to an end and wondered if anything in his recent behaviour had given him away. The thing was, he couldn't stop thinking about her. Uppermost in his mind was the increasing desire to go to bed with her. He still hadn't entirely figured out why he was so attracted to her but whatever it was, he didn't want it to stop. He knew that she didn't harbour the same feelings about him and knew also that one wrong move on his part and she would stop any contact between them, but he was fast discovering that denial was not without its appeal; it increased his desire for her in a way he had never experienced before.

'Sorry about that,' she said, her phone conversation now finished.

'That's all right,' he said lightly. 'It gave me the opportunity to snoop and pry behind your back.'

She raised an eyebrow. 'Did you find anything interesting?'

He wanted to say that he found everything about her interesting, but pointed to the photograph of her with her arms around the young boy. 'Your ex's son?'

She nodded. 'Toby was twelve when the photograph was taken; he's nineteen now and looks very different. Lunch is ready if you want to come through to the kitchen.'

He followed her. 'Anything I can do?'

'No, everything's ready. Just sit down and make yourself at home. You could pour the wine if you want. It's already open.'

He did as instructed, at the same time observing Ella out of the corner of his eye as she moved silently from cooker to table and back again. 'You okay?' he said after neither of them had spoken for a few minutes. 'You seem tense.'

'Honeyed lamb with apricots,' she said, putting a large, hot dish on the table in front of him.

'You've either recently become selectively deaf or you regret me coming here.'

Her hands inside the oven gloves, she brought them together abruptly with a muffled clap and puffed at some loose strands of hair that were dangling in front of her nose. Not so much tense as extremely agitated, he thought.

'Look, I'll level with you,' she said. 'I was looking forward to you coming, but now that you're here I'm not entirely convinced it was such a good idea. After all, this situation could be badly misconstrued. If your wife knew you were here, she would rightly have something to say about it.'

He took the oven gloves from her and went and hung them on the hook he'd seen her take them from. 'My advice is to forget all about my wife.'

Her expression flickered and tensed. 'You might be able to, but I can't.'

'But we're not doing anything wrong. We're two friends simply having lunch together.'

'And naturally you informed your wife of that earlier?'

He frowned and breathed a measured sigh. 'Don't spoil it, Ella. I like being with you. I enjoy your company. If I thought Francine would understand the innocent nature of our friendship, I would explain it to her, but since she wouldn't understand, let's leave her out of it, shall we?'

She homed in on his gaze like a heat-seeking missile. He tried not to flinch and therefore betray the lie of what he'd just said. There was nothing innocent about some of his thoughts regarding Ella.

'I have a question,' he said, some time later when she seemed more relaxed and was serving him a second helping of lamb. 'What do you think it is that we look for from love? Is it comfort and security, or a freeing sense of wild excitement?'

She stopped what she was doing and considered his question. 'Is that a general question, or are you asking specifically what it is *I* want from love?'

'You can answer it any way you like.'

'I'd say, in general, it's a bit of both. At the start of any new relationship we like the excitement it provides, so yes, there's an element of wildness to our emotions.'

He nodded. 'But then it changes?'

She continued serving him. 'It has to,' she said. 'Our bodies aren't programmed to remain in a permanent state of adrenalin-pumping, hormonally-charged passion.'

'So it then settles into something more mundane?'

'Hopefully not. Hopefully it settles into something more profound and satisfying, something that will stay the course.'

'And would you say love strengthens or weakens us?'

'It makes us vulnerable,' she said without hesitation. 'Horribly vulnerable. It makes us behave in ways we would never imagine possible. It brings out our every insecurity: jealousy, possessiveness, doubt, resentment. All the things we tell ourselves we'll never fall foul of.'

Ethan sipped his wine thoughtfully and considered his response with care. 'That sounds like the voice of experience. Was that what happened with you and Lawrence?'

'Yes,' she said tonelessly.

'But that doesn't sound like love. Not by your definition, anyway. You just said that it should become more profound and satisfying.'

Her face adopted an expression of serious perplexity. 'Sometimes what one says is not exactly what one actually means.'

'I don't think you ever make that mistake. Strikes me that you always speak and think with great clarity.'

'Have another potato and be quiet,' she said, her expression softening.

'No thank you,' he said.

'Does that mean you're not going to be quiet?'

He laughed. 'Not a chance in hell. I enjoy talking to you too much ever to do that.'

Her gaze fell from his face to where his hand now lay. Without being conscious of what he'd done, he had reached out across the table and covered her hand with his. Very slowly, very reluctantly he removed his hand. It was, he realized, the first time he had properly touched her.

Chapter Twenty-nine

Maggie was having the best Saturday afternoon ever. She'd just had the best sex of her life, and not once but twice. *Twice!* Honest to God, what was she like? She laughed out loud and pulled the duvet up over her head to smother the noise of her laughter. And just think, Jack Potts had thought that Daryl was gay! She had news for Jack! The reason he hadn't been married before was simple: he'd been on the road so much with his work, he'd never had time to meet the right woman. He'd only decided recently to make a proper home for himself here in Kings Melford when his uncle had moved to the area. Daryl had told her that the two of them had always been close; Jack had been like a dad to him ever since his parents had both died when he'd been young.

From the other side of the partition she could hear the sound of Daryl singing 'The Great Pretender'. He had a wonderful voice. The kind of sexy voice that could strip the clothes off a nun. When Mrs Oates had said that Daryl was an entertainer, that was only half the story. Daryl could sing just about any song asked of him, but his speciality was his act as a Freddie Mercury impersonator. He performed all over the country in clubs and pubs. He had shown her his costumes. He even had a red cloak with white fur trim and a crown. He kept his costumes and props in a cleverly built-in cupboard at the other end of his boat. Give him any song to sing – not just a Queen song – and he could sing it beautifully; he was mad talented. He'd told her that he'd sung at his best mate's wife's funeral and there hadn't been a dry eye in the church when he'd sat down. He'd sung one of Cerys's favourites, 'This Could Be Heaven'. Maggie wished she'd been there to hear him. She would have been so proud.

When Daryl had said that he lived on a boat moored on the canal she had imagined something small and poky and very leaky, but *Bohemian Rhapsody* was amazing. It was a narrowboat that went on and on, and had almost everything a normal house had – a shower and loo, a neat little kitchen with a proper sink, a proper oven and hob and a proper fridge. There was even a washing machine and dryer, and a telly with satellite. Best of all there was a solid fuel stove that kept the saloon dead cosy. See, she even knew that the lounge bit of the boat was called a saloon. She had learnt so much since getting to know Daryl.

The sound of 'The Great Pretender' had grown louder. She pulled the duvet down from her face and looked up to see Daryl standing in the small doorway. He was butt naked and carrying a tray. He stopped singing. 'Cheese on toast and two mugs of tea m'lady,' he announced. 'And your tea is just how you like your men: hot and strong!'

She laughed and moved so he could get back in bed with her. 'I don't think there's a happier person in all the world,' she said, sitting up but covering herself with the duvet. It was okay for Daryl to show off his perfect body, but she wasn't so keen to show off hers.

'Wrong,' he said. 'I'm way, *way* happier.' He leaned in and kissed her, at the same time pulling the duvet away from her. 'Stop hiding yourself from me,' he said with a smile. 'Come on, eat your cheese on toast while it's still hot.'

She took the offered piece of toast hungrily. Good sex, she suddenly thought, forgetting all about her nakedness, made you hungry. 'I wish I knew what I've done to deserve you,' she said.

He passed a mug of tea to her. 'Why do you always put yourself down? Don't you think I'm the one who doesn't deserve someone as special as you?'

'But I'm not special. I'm ordinary.'

'You should look in the mirror more often. You're beautiful. I reckon you just haven't been told it enough times to see it, or believe it.'

'You're soft in the head, you are.'

He shrugged. 'Just speaking the truth. Are you sure you can't come and hear me sing tonight?'

'I can't, Daryl. I'd love to, but—'

'But your husband will notice you're not around,' he interrupted, 'because there's no tea on the table.'

The limited time she spent with Daryl, the last thing she wanted to do was waste it yakking on about Dave, but Daryl had dragged it out of her. He said he hated the idea of her being taken for granted so much.

'There is that,' she said, 'but tonight's different. I've been invited to a party.'

'A party? I don't like the sound of that. You might meet some other bloke.'

How could that be possible? she thought in amazement. Daryl jealous she might meet someone else? Who'd have believed it? 'I promise you I won't,' she said. 'It really isn't that kind of a party. There won't be any men there for a start.'

He still looked doubtful. 'What is it, a hen party? Coz let me tell you, I've performed at enough of those dos to know how dangerous they are.'

She blushed. 'It's an underwear party that a friend of my mum's giving.'

His face lit up. 'Oh aye? Tell me more.'

'I've never been to one before so I haven't got a clue what goes on.'

'You're such an innocent, Maggie,' he said with a laugh. 'But I look forward to seeing what you buy.'

She looked at him shyly over the top of her mug of tea. 'Do you have any preferences?'

'My preference is for you without anything on, but I've got

nothing against some wrapping. On the understanding that I get to unwrap you.'

They had long since finished lunch and Ethan was now insisting on washing up for Ella. From the mocking look in her eyes – a look that Ethan was coming to know well – she clearly thought this was highly amusing. 'You're worried I'm the kind of man who doesn't know which way is up,' he said, 'let alone know how to wash the dishes. Am I right?'

'Not entirely,' she replied. She was hovering hawk-like at his side, a tea towel in hand.

'Then show a man some trust and go and sit down. Try relaxing. You probably don't do enough of it.'

'And you do?'

'Touché.'

He'd washed all the plates when she looked up from drying one and said, 'This feels weird.'

'In what sense?'

'In the sense of I can't begin to imagine what your wife would make of what we're doing. I don't think I'd feel any guiltier if she was to catch us red-handed in bed together.'

'I thought we'd covered that; leave Francine out of this. Let me be happy for a while, is that really too much to ask?'

'It is when it's at the expense of someone else's happiness.'

He straightened his back, stared out of the window, down the length of Ella's garden. It was long and thin, bordered with trees and bushes on one side and a fence on the other. At the far end, against a backdrop of yellow daffodils, was a circular stone table with four wooden seats around it. To the right of the table was a large wooden shed; Ella had told him it was her workshop. 'Will you show me your workshop?' he asked.

'It's just my workshop. It's nothing special.'

'I'd still like to see it.'

'You're a strange man – you know that, don't you? And very slow at washing up.'

He laughed and passed her a glass to dry. 'Do you really think I'm strange?'

'You're certainly different from most men I know.'

'You know a lot of men?'

'Enough.'

'Then I'm glad I stand out from the crowd.'

'Oh, I think that's a given, and you know it all too well, so no fishing for compliments.'

'Perish the thought that you would give me one. But I don't think I like the idea of you accusing me of disingenuous behaviour.'

'I'm much too polite to accuse you of anything.'

'Now that, if you don't mind me saying, is clearly untrue. Why don't you have a dishwasher like any normal person?'

'Bored already with the novelty of such a humdrum task? I might have known it would be too onerous for you.'

He flicked a handful of soapy suds at her. 'But a dishwasher is such a practical thing to have and you're one of the most practical people I know.'

'Perhaps you haven't noticed, but I live alone. Washing up isn't that big a deal when it's only for one.'

'Would I be right in thinking you enjoy living alone?'

'I certainly enjoy the simplicity of it.'

'And of being in control of your life?'

'As much as I can be, yes.'

'I envy you.'

A moment passed before Ella spoke. 'If you hate your life the way it is so much, why not change it?'

'Do I detect irritation in your voice? Are you thinking I should change the record or shut up?'

'Mm ... maybe.'

He rinsed a large saucepan under the hot tap and placed it on the draining board. 'How long did it take you to square up to the truth of your relationship with Lawrence, that it wasn't working and that you should walk away from it?' When she didn't reply, he said, 'Sorry, was that below the belt?'

'No more than I deserved. But you're right. I procrastinated for too long.' Then in an obvious change-of-subject voice, she said, 'Tell me some more about your mother and sister. I'm curious why your mother didn't get a job to support the family, but expected you to do so.'

'I don't think it ever crossed her mind to work. If it did, she dismissed the thought at once.'

'Doesn't that make you angry?'

'Why? I assumed the mantle of breadwinner quite happily. School bored me and I simply saw what needed to be done and did it.'

'Your mother wouldn't get away with that kind of behaviour today. The appropriate authorities would come crashing down on her now.'

'You really think so? I'm not so sure. And really, was it such a bad thing what she did? I learned to be independent, to be reliant on my wits, to—'

'At what cost?' Ella interrupted him. 'What happened to your childhood?'

He pulled on the plug and watched the soapy water drain away. 'My childhood was fine, in my opinion.'

'But I bet you wanted more for Valentina when she was born. I guarantee you wanted the perfect childhood for her.'

He slowly dried his hands on the towel hanging on the hook next to the sink. 'Okay, I admit you're right. That's exactly what I thought. But can you honestly say from what you've seen of my daughter that giving her everything I never had has benefited her?'

'I'm sorry, I'm not in a position to comment. I hardly know the girl.'

'You know enough to know that she's her mother's child and that she's thoroughly spoilt. This is a girl who thinks it's child abuse if I refuse to buy her shoes that cost in excess of three hundred pounds. If I suggest she ought to consider a small part-time job, like babysitting, to learn the value of money, she's reaching for her mobile to call ChildLine.'

'I'm sure you're exaggerating.'

He looked at her closely. 'And I'm equally sure you know I'm not.'

'When did it all start to go wrong for you? It can't always have been so bad.'

'You're right,' he said, leaning back against the worktop. 'In the early years Francine and I were good together: we were both pulling in the same direction. There was actually a time when I truly thought I had it all – a business that was going from strength to strength and a wife who I loved and who believed in me and what I was trying to achieve.'

'So what changed?'

'I made a colossal error of judgement. I saw an opportunity to expand the business, to buy out two other companies that would give me a bigger share of the market as well as a better means of distribution. Sadly, I got it wrong and lost a lot of money. I very nearly lost everything, and I would have if it hadn't been for Francine's father stepping in and bailing me out, but on the proviso that from then on the business was put into Francine's name. It's a decision I've regretted ever since, yet at the time it was a lifeline and I grabbed it with both hands.'

'Then what happened?'

'Then I made everything a thousand times worse. I'm not making excuses or justifying my behaviour, but let's merely say my ego was bruised and battered and I needed to readjust the balance.'

'Don't tell me, that involved another woman?'

'Quite a few actually. Nothing of any importance, but then, seven years ago I made the mistake of getting involved with a woman who, after several months, claimed she was pregnant.'

'Claimed?'

'That was what she said and I had no reason to doubt her.'

'And the consequences?'

'When I tried to explain that we'd both known all along that it was an affair we'd been having, not a lasting relationship, so therefore a baby was out of the question, she said she was in love with me and wanted to keep the child. She even talked about us getting married. When I said that was never going to happen, that I had no intention of leaving my wife – how could I when I was so beholden to her family for bailing me out? – things got nasty.'

'A bunny-boiler situation?'

'As good as. She began popping up when I was least expecting it, usually at work. Then late one night she came to the house and told Francine everything. To give Francine her due, she's an amazing actress and responded by saying she knew all about my philandering ways and that this woman wasn't the first to present herself on our doorstep making out she was pregnant.'

'Cool customer.'

'Dangerously cool. With everything out in the open, including my misdemeanour shared with her parents, she made me promise that nothing like that would ever happen again and said that if it did, she would take the business lock, stock and barrel – it was, after all, in her name. I then threw myself into the business, determined to do even better, I guess my pride was on the line again. Meanwhile, Valentina was being moulded by her mother and grandmother. I hardly featured in her life. I was merely the provider.'

'Just as you'd been as a child, dare I say?'

He shrugged. 'I never thought of it that way. I did what I had to do.'

'What became of the woman with whom you'd had the affair? Did she have the baby? Do you have another child somewhere?'

'No. She wrote a particularly hate-filled letter to me saying she hoped I was happy now because she'd had an abortion. She said I'd left her no choice but to murder our child.'

'You must have wondered more than once what the hell it was you'd seen in her in the first place.'

'I always put her reaction down to anger; it can alter a person beyond recognition. Besides, I'd hardly behaved well with her, had I?'

'True. Had Francine really known all along that you'd been unfaithful?'

He shook his head. 'No. She was devastated, but then not surprisingly that too quickly turned to anger. I think she's been furious with me ever since.'

'So why did she want to stay married to you? Why didn't she sling you out on your ear and take you to the cleaners while she was about it?'

'I've often wondered that myself. She said at the time that she loved me, that we made a good partnership, but sometimes it felt more like she wanted to stay married purely to punish me. And don't forget, we had Valentina, it wasn't just the two of us to consider. Francine would never want her to grow up with the stigma of coming from a broken home. Francine is very conscious of keeping up appearances; she doesn't want to be part of the divorced set. All her friends think we have the perfect marriage and that's a state of affairs she wants to maintain. As misguided as it sounds, she relishes the fact that her friends are jealous of us. It gives her extra status. Moreover, being one half of a perfect couple gives her a sense of identity. It feels cruel to take that away from her after everything else I've done.' He sighed and pushed himself away from the worktop. 'You know, you're the first person with whom I've ever discussed any of this.'

'Really?'

'Yes, really. I suppose your opinion of me has plummeted yet further, hasn't it?'

'Not particularly. But I am struck, as before, by your deep-seated sense of responsibility. Even if you're not directly to blame for a situation you see it as your duty to do the right thing or to put it right, don't you?'

He shrugged again. 'I'm to blame for most of what's wrong in my life, so maybe I do see myself as having to stick it out and hold things together.'

'Meaning your marriage?'

'Partly. But I'm not that altruistic; if I walk away and Francine gets the business, I'll have nothing.'

'Nothing except peace of mind.'

'Oh, I gave up on that years ago.'

An hour later, when they emerged from Ella's workshop and Ethan was saying that it was time he went, Ella heard the sound of a car door shutting. Within seconds, the gate at the side of the house opened and Lawrence stepped into the garden; he had recently got into the habit of using the back door rather than the front.

Oh hell, she thought as the two men eyed each other suspiciously.

Chapter Thirty

From the first day they had met, Brenda and Lou had rubbed each other up the wrong way. It had caused no end of problems over the years, which was why Maggie did her best to keep them apart as much as she could.

'I'll only keep my mouth shut for your sake, Maggie,' Lou would say when an unavoidable family get-together loomed. Just before Christmas, Lou had phoned Maggie and said, 'If that bitch opens her fat gob over the Christmas turkey and makes just one snidey remark or gives me one of her arsey looks, I'll whack her in the chops so hard her rotten teeth, what's left of them, will drop out!'

Brenda had never made any attempt to hide the fact that she believed she was class and that Lou was trash. Last year she had described Lou as looking like she had shopped at Tarts R Us for what she was wearing. Granted Mum had been decked out in a sparkly boob-tube and purple Lycra leggings with white PVC platform boots, but it had been a seventies night at the Legion and everyone had been dressed just as badly. Except for Brenda, who hadn't made any effort at all, other than to have her usual pensioner's rate Margaret Thatcher shampoo and set. 'At least I haven't got a mug on me like that ugly bum-faced dog of yours,' Lou had fired back. 'Mind you,' she'd gone on, 'they do say owners often resemble their mutts, don't they?'

Brenda had puffed extra hard on her cigarette and said, 'And they say daughters always turn out like their mothers. Which is why I warned our Dave not to get in the gutter and marry your daughter.'

'Don't you talk about my Maggie like that!' Lou had hissed. 'That girl's way too good for your lazy-arsed son!' She had then tipped her glass of peach schnapps over Brenda's stiff-as-cardboard hair.

When Brenda had screeched and threatened to have Lou arrested for assault, they were asked to leave the party. What stuck most in Maggie's mind from that night was the way her mother had defended her. It was probably one of the nicest things Lou had ever done for her.

So with the way things were between the two women, Maggie had asked her mother not to risk coming in for her this evening, but to wait outside in the car. Now as she got changed to go out, she wondered why her mother, when her opinion of Dave wasn't that good – lazy-arsed she had called him – had been so angry when Maggie had admitted last month that she didn't love him. What was more, the whole point of inviting Maggie to this underwear party tonight was, as Lou had said, to jazz things up in the bedroom with Dave. Why was Lou so keen to keep Maggie stuck in a marriage that was making her miserable?

According to Lou and the Sisters of Fun, if a woman decked herself out in some fancy frills and a bit of underwired padding, you grabbed a bloke's full attention and he was putty in your hands. 'It's easy to forget just how insecure a bloke can be,' Peggy had said. 'Play to his weaknesses and you'll get exactly what you want from him.'

Little did Mum and her friends know that the only reason Maggie had agreed to go to Mo's tonight was because anything she bought would be for Daryl's benefit and not Dave's. Though if today was anything to go by, 'jazzing things up' in the bedroom with Daryl wouldn't be necessary. She felt a small stab of guilt as she thought of what she and Daryl had got up to today. It had been their first time in bed together and what little guilt she felt wasn't enough to stop her wanting to do it all over again. And then some more. What that man could do to her body didn't bear thinking about! Well, it did – just not when she was around other people.

When she had left Daryl earlier that afternoon he had said he didn't want her to regret what they'd done. He'd said a lot of other things too, all of which had made her want to stay with him on his boat. When she was there with him, she felt as if she'd escaped everything bad in her life. When she was with Daryl, everything felt new and wonderful.

Dave had made no attempt to have sex with her in ages and that was the silver lining to the enormous black cloud that was having his mother sleeping in the room next door. The roof problem with Brenda's house had snowballed into a far greater problem; subsidence had been discovered and the council had officially declared the property, along with all the others in the street, unsafe. Alternative accommodation had been offered while the structural repairs were carried out, but Brenda had kicked up a right old to-do at the idea of being fobbed off with a shabby third-floor flat where she claimed she would be surrounded by whores and drug dealers. Instead she had extended her stay with Dave and Maggie until she could return home.

At half past seven, just after Maggie had finished the washing up and Dean had asked her to iron his best jeans for a snooker competition he was playing in that evening, Lou beeped her car horn on the road outside. Maggie hadn't said where she was going, only that she was having a night out with Mum and her friends. She could just imagine Brenda's disgusted reaction if she got a whiff of the truth.

Grabbing her jacket and handbag, Maggie poked her head round the lounge door. 'I'm off, then,' she said. Nobody said anything, they didn't even look at her. They were too busy watching *Britain's Got Talent*. Only Evil Sid looked at her. He gave Maggie a surly glare, then got back to the business of licking his bum.

*

There were fifteen very raucous women crammed into Mo's front room; it was buzzing with enough energy to power the national grid. Various items of furniture had been removed and all of Mo's kitchen and dining room chairs had been squeezed in to seat everyone. Maggie sat between her mother and Peggy while glasses of wine and sausage rolls and crisps were passed around. It was the first opportunity she'd had to see the results of the trip to Poland for the Sisters of Fun and Maggie wasn't sure it had been entirely successful. There was still something odd about the stretched tightness to their faces, especially around Mo's eyes. Perhaps it was early days.

'Bang goes my diet,' Lou said with a loud laugh as she helped herself to a sausage roll. Sipping her wine, Maggie had to fight the urge to fetch a dustpan and brush to tidy up the flaky pastry that was being carelessly scattered on the carpet.

When everyone had a drink, Mo got things underway and then handed over to a woman who was standing in the bay window surrounded by two shiny chrome racks of lingerie. 'Hi,' the woman said in an overly cheerful voice, 'my name is Kimberley and ladies, pucker up, we're in for an evening of fun!' Everyone laughed, but Maggie suspected that they were in such high spirits they would have laughed at the Ten o'clock News. When the laughter had died down, Maggie suddenly recognized Kimberley. Some years back the woman had worked in Superdrug. Then she had been a brunette; tonight she was a shaggy blonde with dark roots showing through, and her long nails were false and squared off like spades.

Five minutes into her spiel, which sounded suspiciously as if Kimberley had said it once too often, she was asking for volunteers to model the underwear. Lou nudged Maggie in the ribs. 'Go on, Maggie,' she said, 'give us all a laugh and strut your stuff.'

'Don't be daft, Mum.'

Kimberley's heavily made-up eyes homed in on Maggie. 'Are you volunteering, love?'

'No!' Maggie squeaked.

'You'd look a real tasty treat for your old man in one of these.' Kimberley held up a red lacy corset complete with suspenders.

Maggie shook her head, her face nearly as red as the corset.

'Come on, don't be shy. We're all friends here tonight. What's your name, love?'

'Her name's Maggie,' Lou called out.

Kimberley smiled. 'Well, Maggie, how about in black? Would you prefer that?' She checked one of the rails. 'Yes, here we go. And it's your size: medium. You're a twelve, aren't you?'

'And the rest!' Lou cackled.

Maggie nodded back at Kimberley. It was a mistake, as Kimberley took it as willingness to model for her. As did Lou and Peggy. The next thing they were standing up and pulling her to her feet. 'No!' Maggie squeaked again. 'I can't. Put me down.' But they weren't listening. Everyone in the room was egging Lou and Peggy on and before she knew it she was in Mo's dining room having her clothes stripped off.

'You've been dieting,' Lou accused her, and pinched at her waist. 'There's nothing of you!'

'Well, bugger me!' exclaimed Peggy. 'Your mum's right. What's your secret? How've you managed to lose so much weight when your mum and me are never off a diet and we can't so much as shift a friggin' ounce.'

'Please,' Maggie begged them, 'don't make me go out in that ... that thing.'

'That *thing*, as you call it,' Lou said sternly, 'is a basque and it may well save your marriage. Now c'mon, let's have done – get your bra off.'

'Why can't one of you try it on?'

'Don't be so poxy cruel! You know Peggy and I can't get near a size fourteen, never mind a twelve.'

'Ask Kimberley for the next size up, then.'

'I'm warning you, Maggie, don't make me smack you.'

'Mum, I'm thirty-six years old – you can't smack me!'

'Just watch me! Now do as you're told; everyone's waiting for you in there. You always were a one for causing a fuss.'

There was nothing for it but to give in and get it over and done with. When she was finally strapped into the black basque, Lou and Peggy led her back into Mo's front room; she was greeted with loud cheers and wolf whistles. Kimberley grabbed hold of her and dragged her to stand in the bay window – *thank God the curtains were drawn!* She shrank beneath the weight of so much attention. Never before had she felt so embarrassed. Never before had she felt so exposed and vulnerable. She felt as if she was as good as stark naked and that any moment everyone would start howling with laughter at her.

'You know what, ladies?' Kimberley said with a huge grin on her face. 'I reckon Maggie looks that bloody sexy I could be tempted myself if I wasn't so chuffing straight. What do you lot think?'

'She looks beautiful,' someone Maggie didn't know called out. 'Go on, give us a twirl!'

'Her fella's a lucky man!' shouted another.

'Yeah, wait till he cops a load of you in that. He won't be able to keep his hands off you. Even with that witch of a mother in the room next door!' Maggie knew that voice; she shot her mother a furious look.

'I'll have one of those basques if you've got it in a large,' said someone else.

'Me too.'

Kimberley winked at Maggie. 'You're the perfect model,' she whispered. 'You're doing my job for me. Will you try on something else? I've got this dead lovely negligee you'd look brilliant in.' She hunted through one of the racks, found what she was looking for and held up something that was the colour of strawberry ice-cream and as see-through as a net curtain. 'Just slip it over what you've got on already.'

Maggie was shaking her head and trying to back away

when she remembered one of her New Year's resolutions: to do something new. She also thought of what Daryl had said of her body that afternoon in bed, that he loved the curvy softness of it. He'd called her luscious. As luscious as a ripe peach, he'd said. If she had the courage to have an affair, surely she had the courage to model a negligee. And it *was* rather nice. Or did she mean sexy? She pictured herself wearing it for Daryl, lying casually on his bed, waiting for him to ... Her knees went weak at the thought. Oh, yes, she definitely meant sexy.

Whispering in her ear again, Kimberley said, 'I'll give you a good discount on anything you buy. Come on, kid, do this for me. I've had a crap couple of weeks and I need to meet my targets tonight or I'll be on skid row.'

'Okay,' Maggie said quietly. 'I'll do it.'

Really, it was amazing how far she had come in so few months. Who'd have thought it? What was next for her?

Chapter Thirty-one

It was Sunday afternoon and at Mayfield, Ella was feeling very much on the periphery of what was going on. It was an uncomfortable reminder of how she had often felt during the time she had lived here.

But being on the periphery – being the outsider – meant that today, unlike before when she had been too emotionally involved, she could observe Lawrence and his family as they applied themselves to the task of celebrating his birthday. And from what Ella could see, it seemed to be a considerable task for them, a strain even. There was a jarring false note of merriment to the proceedings. The smiles and light-hearted chat seemed forced and hollow, as if they were trying to convince Lawrence that he was having a good time. Maybe they were trying to convince themselves that *they* were having a good time. Yet it was clear to Ella that Lawrence, who had been drinking a lot more than he usually did, was a long way from enjoying himself. If she didn't know better, she would say that he was sulking. Was this perhaps whom Alexis took after? All those years with Lawrence, and Ella hadn't known that he could sulk so spectacularly.

She strongly suspected that his petulant mood had something to do with her, or more particularly with what had happened yesterday when he had unexpectedly turned up at her house. Conscious of the delicate nature of Ethan's presence in her home, she had overreacted – only realizing this too late – and had made things look worse than they were. Making no attempt to introduce him to Lawrence, she had hustled him off in the direction of his car – he had, after all, just said he ought to leave. Ethan had given her a look of amusement as she loudly explained she would be in touch with a quote for him regarding a job. Lawrence had looked on dubiously.

'Do you treat all of your clients so unceremoniously these days?' he had asked when Ethan had driven off.

'Only the ones who make a nuisance of themselves and call round on a Saturday afternoon when I'm busy,' she had replied breezily. He had looked less than convinced. When she had led him inside the house to the kitchen, she had had a moment of panic – the evidence of lunch for two would take some explaining. But then she had remembered Ethan's eagerness to wash up. Thank goodness he hadn't taken no for an answer!

However, a tidy kitchen of blameless rectitude had been of no interest to Lawrence and he had let rip with an extra-ordinary outburst – an irrational outburst that made adding two and two together and making five look like the work of a mathematical genius. 'You lied to me,' he accused her, his voice raised. 'I asked if you had met somebody else and you said you hadn't. Now I understand why you've been so reluctant to move back to Mayfield. What I don't understand is why. Why didn't you just tell me the truth? Or were you hedging your bets, seeing if this other man was a better pros-pect than me? How long were you going to string me along for?'

'Lawrence,' she had said with as much patience as she could muster, 'you couldn't be more wrong. That was a client. I promise you I'm not involved with him in the way you think. Now what brings you here? Is it something about tomorrow?'

'No,' he'd said tersely, 'and does there have to be a reason for me calling in, other than the desire to see you?'

She had tried to lighten her tone, but it hadn't been easy. 'Thank you, that's ... that's very nice of you.'

'Nice?' he'd repeated. 'Is that all I am to you?'

It was obvious that she couldn't say anything right to him and so she suggested he leave before they both said anything they would regret. He had agreed only too readily and left at once, his face tight, his shoulders hunched. Late that night, while she was getting ready for bed, he had called to apologize. 'I'm sorry,' he had said. 'I don't know what got into me, I was behaving like an idiot. It's just that I can't bear the thought of not being with you, of losing you for ever. Can you forgive me?'

'Of course.'

'You will still come tomorrow, won't you? Everyone's really looking forward to seeing you again. Especially me.'

'I'll be there.'

And so here she was, back at Mayfield in the somewhat prickly bosom of Lawrence's family. Deirdre – Abigail's mother – was in a particularly skittish mood, flitting manically from one subject to another as well as being in hot cahoots with Alexis, organizing drinks and lunch and generally bossing everyone about, including Lawrence. The woman was so artificially 'up' Ella wouldn't have been surprised if she was consuming something of a chemical nature every time she bustled out of the sitting room. She was also always about three sentences behind everyone else in the conversation.

Meanwhile, at the Prozac end of the spectrum, Keith and Jan were as laconic as ever and monopolizing Toby, wanting to know every minute detail of his life up in Durham. Ella could see Toby's patience and politeness stretching to breaking point.

As for Lawrence, whilst he had been contrite and apologetic on the telephone last night, now, with the benefit of an excess of red wine inside him, he had a distinctly belligerent and sarcastic manner. Earlier, to everyone else's bemusement, he had twice asked Ella if she had had any *clients* calling on her that morning before she'd left for Mayfield. He could not have weighted the word 'client' with any more cynicism if he had tried.

'Present time!' Alexis suddenly announced with a clap of her hands, jumping smartly to her feet. Sounding worryingly like an overly enthusiastic infant-school teacher, she whipped out of Lawrence's hands the book that he'd been reading for the last ten minutes while assiduously ignoring Ella and said, 'Come on, Dad, you can open my present first. I guarantee you'll love it.' She looked at Ella. 'You too.'

The poor girl could not have misjudged things more. The swirly patterned black and white wrapping paper dispensed with, Lawrence held up a hand-painted photograph frame. 'I decorated it myself,' Alexis said proudly, taking it from him to show everyone. 'Look, Ella, I even stencilled it like you once showed me. Do you remember teaching me how to do that?'

'Yes,' Ella said quietly. 'It's lovely. You've made a wonderful job of it.' What wasn't so lovely or wonderful was the expression on Lawrence's face as he stared at what the frame contained: a photograph of Lawrence and Ella. She remembered Toby taking the picture two Christmases ago. She remembered how she'd had to strain to make herself smile – Alexis had just been horribly rude to her, had once again very nearly reduced her to tears of angry frustration.

'Do you like it, Dad?' Alexis asked.

'The frame is beautiful, Alexis,' he replied flatly, his head lowered. 'But I think it would be greatly improved by a different photograph. One without Ella in it, for instance.'

The room went deathly quiet.

'Dad, you're joking, right?'

'Do I sound like I'm joking, Toby?' He raised his head and looked directly at Ella. 'I expect you'd rather be photographed with one of your *clients*, wouldn't you?'

'Please don't do this, Lawrence,' Ella murmured. 'It's not fair to everyone here.'

'You think it's fairer to let them go on pretending that you and I might get back together again, when all the time you had no intention of doing so? I don't even know why you're here.'

240

'I'm here because you invited me.'

'Yes, and what a fool you've made of me.'

The room was still deathly quiet. Ella didn't need to look at anyone to know that they were staring at her. She slowly stood up. 'I don't know what's got into you, Lawrence, but I can't think of a single reason why I should subject myself to your appalling rudeness a moment longer.' She glanced at Alexis and then Toby. 'I'm sorry, but I think it's better that I leave.'

His brow furrowed, Toby looked pained and confused. 'For God's sake, Dad, what the hell are you playing at? Apologize to Ella.'

'I'm not playing at anything,' Lawrence said. 'If anyone's guilty of that, it's Ella. Ask her about the man I caught her with yesterday.'

There was a stirring of embarrassed muttering amongst Deirdre and Keith and Jan, but it was Alexis who spoke up, her cheeks flushed with anger. 'Ella, how could you? How could you do that to us? I thought you cared. How could you spoil Dad's birthday like this? How could you—'

'I haven't done anything to you or your father,' Ella interrupted Alexis with a searing flash of indignation. 'What he imagines I've done is no more than the product of a ridiculously jealous mind.' She returned her attention to Lawrence. 'I hope you're happy. All afternoon you've been spoiling for a fight, intent on ruining your birthday, and now you have. Congratulations.'

'On the contrary,' he said coldly, 'I haven't ruined it one little bit; I've quite cheered myself up. Please don't let me keep you. You can see yourself out, can't you?'

Chapter Thirty-two

Sunday dinner had been delayed because Dean had had a late night and hadn't bothered to shift himself from his bed until gone two. 'Oh, let the poor love sleep – you're only young once,' Brenda had said when Maggie had gone marching upstairs to tell him dinner would be ready in an hour's time.

Just like Dave, Dean could do no wrong in Brenda's eyes. The fact that he'd stumbled in at three in the morning and had woken Maggie by being sick all over the bathroom floor did nothing to tarnish the halo he wore.

'I remember our Dave doing the same thing when he was that age,' Brenda said, now at the dinner table. 'What a lad you were,' she cooed, 'always being chased by the girls. What in the name of God did you do to this beef, Maggie? It's as tough as old boots!' She passed a piece of it to Evil Sid, who was slathering noisily on her lap. The honking smell coming from him was making Maggie's stomach turn.

'I don't think it did the meat any good being cooked to death while we waited for Dean to get up,' Maggie said as an image of Evil Sid in the oven on a low heat popped into her mind. 'Another Yorkshire pudding anyone?' she offered.

'Yeah, bung us a couple this way,' Dave said. 'And I'm that hungry, I'll risk some more of the beef as well.'

'More gravy and roasties over here,' Dean said, his mouth full. 'Say what you will, Gran, you can't fault Mum's roasties. They're the best.'

Brenda sniffed, looking very like she could find plenty to fault with them. But was Maggie hearing things? Had she just

242

had a compliment from a member of her family? She went out to the kitchen. After what Dean had said she could almost forgive him for the disgusting mess he had made last night on the bathroom floor. But how unfair was it that he was showing no sign of a hangover? She remembered how ill she had felt not so long ago after the night of her bingo win. Every now and then she thought of the money she had tucked away in her secret savings account and pictured herself using it to escape. A one-way train ticket would do, or better still, a one-way ticket for a flight that would take her thousands of miles away. It didn't even have to be somewhere hot and sunny. Cold, wet, windy, snowy, it didn't matter. Just anywhere she wouldn't have to set eyes on Brenda ever again.

With a plate of seconds rounded up and on her way back to the dining room, she heard her mobile buzzing from inside her handbag, hanging on the back of the kitchen door. She hurriedly put the plate down and rooted through her bag, hope zinging through her that it might be Daryl.

It was!

Buy anything nice last nite?XXXX he'd texted.

Her fingers moving at the speed of sound, she wrote: *This and that.XX* She slipped the mobile back inside her bag and returned to the dining room trying not to smile. She was about to sit down when she realized she was being stared at. 'What?' she said.

Dave shook his head. 'I dunno, Mags, you're all over the place these days. What've you done with the spuds and Yorkshires?'

Blushing from head to toe, she shot back to the kitchen, only to hear her mobile buzzing again.

When cn I c u nxt? Daryl had texted.

She didn't dare risk replying. Reluctantly she put her mobile on silent mode and retraced her steps with the plate of seconds and jug of gravy. 'Sorry,' she said, 'I'll be forgetting my own head next.'

'Perhaps you're menopausal,' Brenda said with a sneer as she lit up a cigarette.

'Menopausal?' Maggie repeated, stunned. 'How do you work that out? I'm only thirty-six.'

'It's either that or you're losing your marbles.'

'If I'm losing my marbles then I'm looking at the reason why,' she said cheerfully, staring straight at Brenda.

Brenda's jaw dropped. 'I beg your pardon?'

'You heard me, you miserable old cow.'

Well, that was what Maggie would have liked to have said, but instead she said, 'Sorry, I was distracted by a text from my secret and very sexy lover.'

No, she didn't say that either. 'I've got a lot of work things on my mind right now,' she lied.

Brenda snorted. 'Can't think what that could be. I mean, you're not exactly running the country, are you?'

No, just running around after you lot, day in, day out, thought Maggie. 'More of anything?' she said, passing the plate of seconds to Brenda and wondering if one of the roast potatoes was big enough to ram in the old witch's mouth to keep her quiet for the rest of the meal.

Brenda dragged heavily on her cigarette. 'You know I eat less than a sparrow. But I'll take some more of that dreadful beef for Sid.'

It was a relief an hour later – after Maggie's apple crumble had been criticized by Brenda for being too tart and the custard too lumpy – to disappear to the kitchen on her own to wash up. For once she was glad that Martians would land in the garden before anyone offered to help her. With her back to her handbag she resisted the temptation to check her mobile to see if Daryl had texted her again, by thinking what she would say in reply to the last one he'd sent. *When cn I c u nxt?* Tonight, if she had her way.

But how? How could she slip away without questions being asked? She had come in for enough flak last night when Lou had dropped her off. With her purchases hidden under her coat, she had sneaked upstairs to hide them and then poked her nose into the lounge where Brenda and Dave were watching the telly. 'Can I get anyone a drink?' Maggie had asked as if she hadn't been out at all.

'Dave has already made us a brew,' Brenda had said accusingly.

At bedtime, when they had crossed paths on the landing, Brenda had said, 'I don't know how our Dave puts up with you going out all the time. A decent wife wouldn't dream of leaving her husband on his own. You're asking for trouble. He's still a good catch and any number of women would give their back teeth to have him.'

They'd be welcome to him, Maggie thought now as she began drying the dishes. What was more they could keep their back teeth; they'd need them to grind on, especially when they realized that Brenda was part of the deal.

With the kitchen tidied and cleaned, Maggie finally allowed herself to check her mobile. Her heart gave a small lurch; there was another message from Daryl. *Jst taking Jack 2 c Mary, any chance u cn call in?*

The text had been sent forty-five minutes ago. She flew upstairs to look out of her bedroom window, her feet barely touching the stair carpet. He was there – his car was outside Mrs Oates's house! She looked at herself in the mirror above the dressing table. *Argh!* What a mess! How could she possibly see Daryl like this? She decided she would keep her jeans on, but ripped off her ancient top, swapped it for a closer fitting and more flattering one, and then grabbed her hairbrush and tried to work a miracle. She dashed some lipgloss on, squirted some perfume on her neck and took a deep breath.

Right, all she had to do was tell them downstairs that she was nipping across the road to Mrs Oates. She picked up the half-read book by the side of the bed and went downstairs. She didn't bother putting her head round the lounge door. 'I won't be long,' she called out from the hall. 'Just returning a book to Mrs Oates.'

'I don't believe it,' she heard Brenda say. 'She's going out again!'

'What a nice surprise, Maggie,' said Mrs Oates when she opened the door to her. 'Come on in. You'll never guess who else is here: Jack and his lovely nephew.'

'Oh, I don't want to intrude,' Maggie said, pretending to dither on the doorstep.

Mrs Oates smiled. 'Don't be silly, of course you're not intruding. I've just put the kettle on. Look who's here!' she said when she led the way into the front room.

Forever the gentleman, Jack rose from the sofa and beamed at her. 'Well, well, well, we meet again.' He shook her hand warmly. 'How are you, my dear?'

'I'm very well, thank you.'

'You remember my nephew, Daryl, don't you?'

Her heart crashing wildly about inside her ribcage, Maggie managed to say, 'Yes, I remember him.'

As if in slow motion, just like in a film, Daryl came towards her, his hand outstretched. When their hands made contact, she could have sworn a jolt of electricity passed between them. 'Hiya,' he said. 'It's great to see you again.'

'Nice to you see you again, too,' she said, forcing herself to breathe normally, at the same time hoping her face wouldn't give her away. Then she reluctantly let go of his hand and turned back to Mrs Oates. 'I only bobbed over to return the book you lent me, Mrs O,' she said.

Mrs Oates tutted. 'How many times have I told you, it's Mary. Now sit yourself down and I'll make us some tea.'

'I have a better idea, Mary,' Daryl said. 'Why don't you sit down with Jack while Maggie and I make the tea?'

'Champion idea,' Jack said, guiding Mrs Oates by the elbow to the sofa. She tried to protest but Jack was having none of it. 'Now, now, Mary, do as you're told and let the young'uns wait on us while we relax.'

Out in the kitchen, Daryl immediately caught Maggie in his arms. He held her so tightly he lifted her off the ground and when he kissed her he knocked what little breath she had clean out of her. Her head spinning, all she could think of as his hands slid over her body was how much she wanted to fling off her clothes and get into bed with him. 'I thought you weren't going to come,' he said when his lips briefly lost contact with hers and he buried his mouth into her neck.

'I came as soon as I read your last text. I—'

He silenced her with another kiss on the lips and just as one of his hands slipped under her top and she felt the warmth of his touch on her skin, she heard a gasp.

But it didn't come from her.

And it didn't come from Daryl.

Standing in the doorway of the kitchen was Mrs Oates, an expression of flustered shock on her face. 'Ginger nuts,' the old lady murmured. 'I ... I just came to say there are ginger nuts in the biscuit barrel.'

Since leaving Mayfield, Ella had spent the rest of the day taking out her fury on sanding down sixteen kitchen cupboard doors for Phil. But no matter how vigorously she rubbed at the wood, it didn't have the required effect of ridding her of the indignant anger fizzing through her. If anything, she felt even angrier than when she had driven home.

She simply couldn't believe how atrociously Lawrence had behaved. It was inconceivable that after knowing him for as long as she had, she had only now discovered that he was capable of such cruel and childish behaviour. It just went to prove you never really knew a person. The one positive aspect to come out of the day was that in revealing his true self to her this afternoon, Lawrence had done her a favour. The dilemma with which he had presented her was no more.

Really, she had had a very lucky escape. She had to be happy for that, at least.

Even so, it still hurt that he had been so rude to her in front of Alexis and Toby. Especially Toby. She had wondered if Toby would ring her, but so far there had been nothing from him. It was quite possible that he was angry with her too. If he believed what his father said, that she had been stringing him along while seeing another man, then he had every right to be cross with her. It upset her deeply that Toby might think badly of her. Which only served to fuel her anger at Lawrence.

With the kitchen cupboard doors finished and nothing else to do in her workshop, she switched off the lights, locked the door and went back inside the house. She washed her hands, poured herself a glass of wine, opened a bag of crisps – they would do for supper – and switched on her laptop which was on the kitchen table. Perhaps Toby had emailed her.

He hadn't.

But Ethan had.

Hi Ella,

You're probably rolling your eyes as you read this and thinking, 'Hasn't he got anything better to do than pester me?' Sadly, the truth is I haven't. But don't judge me too severely, not when it gives me so much pleasure to be in your company, or simply to email you. I like feeling connected to you, even if it is only through the ether. Right now I'm enjoying imagining your reaction to this email. My guess is that you're outwardly tutting but inwardly smiling. Is that presumptuous of me? If so, good! Hey, was that another tut? I thought so.

Anyway, seeing as I'm home alone, I thought I'd 'talk' to you – Francine and Valentina have gone to the cinema to watch some awful romcom. I have no idea whether it is actually awful, but I suspect it would have me snoring within minutes. Either that or walking out. Don't get me wrong, I have nothing against romance or love, but watching other people being unbearably happy only reinforces how unhappy …

Okay, I know better than to take that any further with you. You would only tell me to stop whingeing and do something about the mess I've made of my life. But you know, I admire the uncomplicated life you lead. I wish mine was equally uncomplicated.

Hey, you know what would be good? If this conversation wasn't one-sided. Do you have Skype? Do you instant message? If you do, tap in the following name and let's chat. That's if you're there, that's if you want to. I'll be home alone for the next hour or so.

Ella looked at the time the email had been sent: fifteen minutes ago. Should she do as he asked?

Oh, what the hell! Why not? In her current mood it would be good to talk to him.

She opened Skype and tapped in Ethan's contact details. '*Hi,*' she wrote, '*it's me, Ella.*' Within seconds she could see the pencil icon was bobbing back and forth in the top left-hand corner of the screen.

'*Hi yourself,*' he wrote back. '*How are you?*'

'*In a foul mood!*'

'*Why?*'

'*Long story.*'

'*I have time on my hands.*'

She gave him the bare bones of her day, and what had instigated it.

'*You're kidding?*' Ethan replied. '*He reacted like that because of me?*'

'*Yes.*'

'*I'm sorry.*'

'*Don't be. It wasn't your fault. The fault lies with Lawrence.*'

'*Would I be getting above myself to say you're better off without someone who behaves that way?*'

'Not at all. I'd reached the same conclusion.'

'To be fair to the guy, if I was in his shoes trying to win you back, I'd feel threatened by a potential rival. Whoops, I didn't mean to imply that I'm a potential rival, but you know what I'm saying.'

'But you'd listen to reason, wouldn't you?'

'Listen to reason? I'd do nothing of the sort; I'd be challenging the swine to a duel! Pistols at dawn! Breeches and flouncy blousons to the fore. Nothing less.'

Ella laughed. 'Thanks for cheering me up.'

There was a pause from Ethan's end. Then: 'That's what friends are for. You've cheered me up, too. By the way, thank you for lunch yesterday. I really enjoyed it. This is fun as well, isn't it?'

'What is?'

'Chatting like this. Or don't you think so?'

She started to type something, but hesitated. He was right; it was fun having someone to talk to like this. Someone with whom she could be honest. In so many ways he was the perfect companion. She just wished he wasn't married – that way she wouldn't keep feeling they were doing something wrong. It was why, she supposed, she had overreacted yesterday when Lawrence had come upon the two of them together in the garden. It was ridiculous that even in these wholly enlightened times it was still impossible for people to accept that a heterosexual man and woman could be friends, with nothing sexual going on between them. Lawrence's insanely jealous reaction proved that all too well.

She took a moment to think about this and quickly realized that she was guilty of being hypocritical, for hadn't she originally been suspicious of Ethan's motives? And let's not forget the embarrassing route some of her own thoughts had gone down. Mm ... another pot and another kettle for the lady?

A new message appeared on the screen from Ethan. 'You still there?'

'Yes. I was just thinking.'

'That sounds ominous. Anything you want to share?'

'I was thinking how much easier this would be if you weren't married.'

'We're only talking. We're not doing anything wrong.'

'I know that. So why does it feel so wrong?'

'Does it? It feels good to me.'

'That's because you're used to cheating on your wife.'

'Ouch …'

'I'm sorry. That was harsh, but unfortunately the truth often does hurt.'

There was a long, long pause while the pencil icon bobbed back and forth at the top of the screen. Finally Ethan's message came through.

'Okay, if it's the truth you want, how's this?

Yes, I've cheated on my wife many times in the past and used countless women in the process, and I'm not proud of that, but I want you to know that I'm not using you, Ella. I really like you. In fact, I like everything about you. The more time I spend with you, the more time I want to spend with you. You seem to be constantly on my mind. I can't remember the last time anyone had the same effect on me as you do.

But I respect and admire you, which is why I'm settling for friendship. I'd love nothing more than to make love with you, to explore every inch of your body, but since I know that's out of the question, and I don't want to compromise you, I'm happy with what we have. I promised myself at the start of the year, No More Women, and I'm sticking to that promise.

There, I've laid myself bare. Are you brave and honest enough to reciprocate, to do the same?'

Chapter Thirty-three

Ella stared at the screen in a state of shock. How on earth was she supposed to respond? Her mind racing, she started at the sound of the doorbell being rung. '*Sorry,*' she wrote, '*got to go. Someone's at the door.*' She doubted he would believe her.

Still flustered and shocked, and spilling tea from the cup that was wobbling in the saucer in her shaking hand, Mrs Oates said, 'I had no idea ... really ... no idea. Oh, Maggie, you be careful. You're playing with fire.'

Jack was equally shocked, but was taking a firmer line. 'Daryl,' he said sternly, his chest puffed out like a pigeon's, 'I'm a simple man, but I know what's right and I know what's wrong, and what you're doing is wrong. Maggie's a married woman. No good will come of the pair of you carrying on like this. No good at all. You've got to stop it.'

'I know you mean well, Uncle,' Daryl replied gruffly, 'but this is no one's business but Maggie's and mine.' He slipped his hand through Maggie's and squeezed it.

Her eyes swimming with tears, Maggie wished the ground would burst open and swallow her up. Being found out so explicitly in poor Mrs Oates's kitchen – how could they have been so reckless and thoughtless? – had brought home the horrible and disgraceful truth of what she had been doing. Cheating on her husband, sneaking around behind his back, fantasizing about another man ... how had she thought that what she was doing didn't matter? How could she have forgotten that she was a wife and mother and not some sex-mad slapper?

Her face burning with shame, she knew Jack was right; they had to stop it. She opened her mouth to speak but a tremble ran through her at the thought of never seeing Daryl again. Of never experiencing the joy of waiting for him to text her again. Of never kissing him again or feeling so alive and happy again. How could she give up all that when he was the only good thing in her life?

As if he knew what she was thinking, Daryl let go of her hand and put his arm around her shoulder. The reassuring strength of his touch calmed her.

'Maggie,' he said softly, bending in so close she almost forgot herself and turned to kiss him. Just in time she jerked her head away. 'Don't do or say anything hasty,' he said. 'This has got nothing to do with anyone else. We'll discuss it when we're alone.'

Jack cleared his throat noisily. 'I doubt Maggie's husband would agree with that sentiment.'

'You're not helping, Uncle Jack. Can't you see how upset Maggie is?'

'Aye, lad, then you'd best ask yourself why she's so upset. It's because at least one of you has a conscience.'

Maggie didn't want to be the cause of an argument between Daryl and his uncle. She didn't want to be the cause of anything. She just wanted to be the nobody she had always been. The Maggie no one ever looked twice at. The Maggie who always did what was expected of her. 'I'd better go home,' she said, unable to look anyone in the eye. She didn't think she would ever be able to talk to Mrs Oates again. From now on, the old lady would never trust her, she would always think of her as a liar and a cheat.

Daryl walked her to the front door. He put a hand on her arm. 'Call me tomorrow,' he said. 'Please,' he added. For the first time since Mrs Oates had discovered them in the kitchen, she met his gaze properly. She was shocked to see how upset he looked. His eyes, normally so blue, like the sky on a summer's day, were as dark as night. Her heart thudded and her own eyes brimmed with tears. 'Don't cry,' he said. 'It'll be okay. Everything will be all right, you'll see.'

'All I wanted was to be happy,' she said miserably.

'And all I wanted was to make you happy. I still do. I'm sorry for what my uncle said to you. He was out of order.'

'He was only speaking the truth.'

'But he doesn't understand how I feel about you. I don't think you understand that either.'

She blinked hard, fighting back another build-up of tears. 'I must go,' she murmured.

'Remember, call me first opportunity you get,' he said as she opened the door and stepped outside.

'I will,' she said, although she knew she wouldn't. As of tonight, the madness had to stop. Her life had to go back to how it had been before.

Chapter Thirty-four

The 'someone at the door' had turned out to be Toby and Alexis.

Having borrowed Lawrence's Volvo, it was the first time they had come to Tickle Cottage together; Toby had been many times on his own but Alexis only once, with her father. Now the pair of them were here, fully armed and gunning for Ella in a lethal two-pronged attack. Never had she felt so unable to defend herself or justify her actions. The folly of youth, she had to remind herself. Young people always saw things too simply; it was either black or it was white to them. They had no understanding of the myriad shades of grey in between.

They had come with the overly simplistic notion that they could make her change her mind. They had said Lawrence didn't know what they were up to, that it had been entirely their idea. It was because they cared, they explained. They cared about their father. And they cared about Ella. They wanted to see the two of them back together.

Scarcely drawing breath since they'd arrived, Alexis was off again. 'Dad needs you in his life, Ella. Since you moved out, he's been awful. You have to forgive him for what he said today. He didn't mean any of those things. He was upset. He was angry.'

'I know he was,' Ella said calmly. A calmness that was quite at odds with how agitated she felt. Alexis's wide-eyed, imploring appeals were wearing her down.

'He was also a bit pissed,' Toby joined in. 'It was the booze talking, not the real him. He was being a jerk. And not for the first time.'

'That's as maybe,' Ella said, 'but one thing you have to learn in life is that you can never un-say something. Once it's been said, it's there for ever.'

Alexis came to a stop on the other side of the room. For the last half an hour she had been prowling Ella's small sitting room, picking things up and putting them down, never in the same place. Ella's hands itched to reposition her things correctly. The girl's constant fiddling made her edgy. Alexis looked straight at Ella. 'Are you talking about *me* when you say that?' she asked in a quiet voice.

'Sorry?'

Still staring hard at her, Alexis frowned, her expression suddenly intense and somehow making her even more beautiful. With her pale, flawless complexion, her dark, spirited eyes and perfectly proportioned features, she was so obviously destined to grow into a stunningly attractive woman. Touched by the angels, her grandmother Deirdre always claimed. 'Are you saying that you could never forgive me for some of the things I've said to you?' she said.

The girl's directness was like a battering ram. 'Of course I've forgiven you, Alexis.'

Liar, a voice whispered inside her head. *You've merely shelved all the hurts. You've meticulously catalogued every single cruelly barbed taunt and accusation and carefully logged them into your memory so you can hold them against Alexis whenever you feel the need to blame her for Lawrence not loving you enough. Had he loved you enough he would have reined his daughter in. He would have saved the relationship. He could have done it. But he loved his daughter more ...*

'Of course I've forgiven you,' Ella repeated. Even to her ears she sounded less than convincing.

'Let's not get sidetracked,' Toby said with a flash of impatience. It was such a male thing to say: the authoritative voice of detached logic and reason. He leaned forwards in the armchair he was wedged into – it was much too small for his large frame and made him seem like a lumbering giant in a doll's house. 'Don't be cross with me, Ella,' he said, 'but is there any truth in what Dad said? Is there somebody else?'

'No!' Ella retorted. *Liar,* the voice whispered inside her head again. *If he wasn't married there could well be somebody else.* The voice of her subconscious so startled her, she blurted out, 'Really, Toby, I'm shocked that you would ask me such a thing. And anyway, I'm allowed to have men friends if I want to. There's no law against it.'

He looked stung by the severity of her reply, almost recoiled from it.

'Sorry,' she said less heatedly. 'What I meant was, I'm not seeing anyone else on the sly and the man your father saw me with is a client.'

'What was he doing here if he's only a client?' butted in Alexis, who was now fiddling with a Victorian glass paper-weight, a birthday present from Ella's parents last year. It had replaced the one Alexis had dropped. *The one Alexis had deliberately smashed last year.* Oh, the hurts were still there; they still had the power to wound, still resonated with all their original painful intensity.

'He came to discuss the job I'm doing for him,' Ella said. The lie was as smooth as the paperweight now being care-lessly passed from one hand to the other; Ella couldn't take her eyes off it. Was it paranoid of her to imagine that Alexis was doing it intentionally, giving Ella a message: *If you don't do as we ask, you leave us no alternative but to trash your little house.*

Definitely paranoid.

'Put that down, Alexis,' Toby snapped irritably. 'You know what a clumsy idiot you can be.'

Thank God for Toby-the-mind-reader!

'Ella,' he said. 'I'm sorry I asked you that. It's just that the thought that you might be seeing someone else is driving Dad round the bend with jealousy. I know it seems a bit late for him finally to come to his senses and realize just what you mean to him, but can't you give him another chance? How about you stay cross with him for a few days, to teach him a lesson, and then forgive him? Would that be so very difficult?'

'It's not a matter of wanting to teach him a lesson, it's more a matter of whether we still love each other.'

'But you did. I know you did. What's changed?'

His expression was so solemn, so heart-wrenchingly poignant, Ella had to glance away. Everything's changed, she thought. But then she forced herself to look back at Toby and all at once she saw him not as the tall, athletic young man he was, but as the young, anxious boy he had once been. The fragile, gentle-mannered boy she had promised herself she would always take care of, the boy she had sworn to protect so that he would never know another moment's hurt if it was within her power.

Alexis, having done what her brother had asked, now came and plonked herself on the sofa beside Ella. She bent down to her canvas shoulder bag at her feet and after a few seconds of rummaging, she pulled something out. Ella recognized the wrapping paper as the same that had been used for the present the girl had given her father that afternoon.

'This is for you, Ella,' she said. 'It matches the one I gave Dad. I wanted to thank you for ... you know, for helping me when I asked you to. You wouldn't have done that unless you really cared about me.' She slid an embarrassed glance over to Toby, then back to Ella. 'It's okay, I told him all about it.' She pressed the package into Ella's hands. 'Open it,' she said. 'I hope you like it.'

Ella carefully removed the wrapping paper to reveal a decorated picture frame just like the one Alexis had given her father. There was a photograph in it, a classic family shot of a classic two-point-two family – Lawrence and Ella, Toby and Alexis. The only person not smiling in the group was Alexis. Ella recalled that the moment when the photograph had been taken by Lawrence's father in the garden at Mayfield, Alexis had sulkily complained that she couldn't smile because the sun was in her eyes.

Right now Ella had tears in hers. Alexis and Toby had come here with one objective: they loved their father; they wanted him to be happy. And they truly believed Ella could make him happy. It was as simple as that.

What if they were right? What if she could make Lawrence happy and in turn be happy herself?

Chapter Thirty-five

It was Good Friday and Abersoch and the surrounding area was packed for the Easter weekend. You couldn't move for four-by-fours with their personalized number plates and trailer loads of jet-skis and boats jamming up the roads. When the vehicles did make it down to the slipway on the beach, tempers became frayed as flustered wives in oversized sunglasses and designer flip-flops failed hopelessly to understand the yelled instructions from their irate husbands on how to help get the boat from the trailer and into the water. And all with an audience of the self-satisfied who had already managed the task. Or those, like Ethan, who had no boat or jet-ski to flaunt, who were just hoping to get some peace and quiet.

No chance of that, he thought as he hammered home the last of the poles for the brightly coloured windbreaker to protect his wife and daughter from the ravages of the non-existent wind. It was always a tricky balance for Francine – whether to be protected from the elements, or to be seen. This, after all, was Abersoch, aka Cheshire-on-Sea, where the Cheshire Navy dropped anchor. So far Ethan had spotted five other couples he vaguely knew – parents from Valentina's school, Valentina's orthodontist and his wife, and two couples he couldn't name, just recognized their faces from somewhere.

The sale on Pine Tree Cottage had gone through three weeks ago and this was their first proper family stay in the house. The thundering juggernaut of Francine's spending showed no sign of slowing down; it was gathering speed if anything. She'd spent a fortune on furniture and what she called 'basic essentials' as well as finding an architect to revamp the property. God only knew where she thought the money would come from to pay for the alterations.

If that wasn't bad enough, he had his in-laws just two hundred yards down the road to contend with and the Paxtons were arriving in the afternoon. Francine had proposed a jolly fish and chip supper party for that evening. Funny how she would no more eat fish and chips at home than she would stick a fork in her eye, but here she found it quite acceptable, even *de rigueur*. He supposed she thought it quaint in the manner of Marie Antoinette slumming it as a peasant in the grounds of Versailles. *Oh, what a lark it is to eat the food of the common man!* It was no coincidence that the chippy Francine bestowed her custom upon was owned by a refugee from Chester and had been featured in *Cheshire Life* after winning an award for serving the best fish and chips in the area. As far as Ethan could see, the owner was getting away with murderous prices that no right-thinking local would pay – they had more sense and took their custom elsewhere.

His windbreaker duties completed, he lay back on his deckchair. It was one of the traditional affairs, made of wood and stripy canvas, the sort of deckchair he'd grown up with. Its design might be traditional, to the point of reminding him of many a finger-crushing tussle as a child, but it was hardwood from a sustainable source and the canvas was made of unbleached cotton. Which gave the shop where Francine had bought them the right to charge nearly ninety quid a pop. Ninety cheeky quid for a deckchair! The world had truly gone mad.

'Ethan, I've left my magazine in the car.'

And you want me to do *what* about that? He thought. When he didn't stir, Francine's voice took on a wheedling tone, the tone she imagined would win him round to do her bidding. 'Would you fetch it for me, *please*? I must have left it on my seat.'

He considered passing her the car keys, but thought better

261

of it. Better to have a few legitimate minutes wandering around on his own than sit here pretending he wasn't bored witless.

'Anything else I can get anyone while I'm on my feet?' he asked. 'Valentina? Anything you've forgotten? Or how about an ice-cream?'

Francine looked at him as if he'd just suggested he bury her in the sand. 'Do you know how many calories there are in an ice-cream?'

'I'll take that as a no, then,' he said. 'Valentina? You counting the calories?'

There was no reply from his daughter. She was too busy adjusting her bikini whilst watching a bare-chested, shaggy-haired, stubble-chinned lad ambling by in shorts that came down well below his knees. He resembled that nerdy guy from *Scooby-Doo*. Just a bit better built. Was that Valentina's idea of a good catch? The catch of the day?

So it was okay to consume a squillion calories of overpriced fish and chips from a trendy chippy, Ethan mused as he made his way along the beach and through the sand dunes to where he had left the car.

The car park was full now. Which didn't surprise him. The weather forecasters had predicted a 'scorcher' of an Easter weekend, and for once they had got it right and the world and his wife had made a beeline for the nearest beaches. It would be a nightmare when it came to leaving; the roads would be clogged to hell and back.

Some inconsiderate idiot had parked his gaudily painted camper van so close to Ethan's car that he had the devil's own job to open the passenger door. After much wriggling he managed to reach inside for Francine's magazine – a glossy home improvement mag – and locked the car again.

He was making his way towards the sand dunes when he slowed his step. Why hurry back? He went over to the kiosk and bought a double ninety-nine with a flake in it, then sought out a quiet spot in the sun-warmed sand dunes and sat on a large tussock of grass on the raised area behind the beach huts. He kicked off his deck shoes and relished the moment. In the distance the sea glittered in the bright sunshine and the tangy smell of salt filled the air. He had always enjoyed being by the sea. He liked the space, the sense of freedom the sea offered. He liked the expanse of limitless sky, too.

He was enjoying the quiet seclusion of the sand dunes. Save for the seagulls wheeling in the cloudless sky above him, he was entirely alone. It felt good. Not for the first time of late, he wondered what it would be like simply to disappear. To start a new life somewhere else, to assume a new identity. How difficult would it be?

Too difficult, probably. He thought of that couple who faked the husband's death in a canoeing accident. He couldn't do something like that; he couldn't ignore or turn his back on his responsibilities. Ella had got that right about him.

He hadn't seen anything of Ella since the day he'd spent the afternoon at Tickle Cottage. Two days later he had flown to Pakistan to check out a factory that he hoped would supply him with a new line of throws and cushions he wanted to add to his winter collection. But the trip had proved to be a waste of time as, after a terrorist attack on a nearby hotel, he'd decided the risks of doing business there were too great. To make matters worse, on his return home he'd been hit with a vicious stomach bug and had been stuck in bed for the best part of a week. He should have dragged himself out of bed to the doctor, but he'd felt too ill; he'd lost more than a stone in weight. He had surfaced in the nick of time to attend a trade show in Harrogate.

It had crossed his mind to invite Ella to go with him – all above board, separate rooms, separate hotels if she'd wanted – but he hadn't had the nerve to put the idea to her. Besides, trade fairs were time-consuming affairs and their time together would have been minimal. When he got back from Harrogate he had texted her, only to receive a message saying she was down in Canterbury doing some work for a long-standing client who had recently moved down there from Cheshire. He had texted her again: *I miss you.* She hadn't responded. He suspected he had said too much that evening when they had been chatting online. He knew it had been a gamble, but it had been one he had felt compelled to take. He had wanted her to know how important she had become to him.

Until Ella had pointed out what a deep-seated sense of responsibility he had, he had never really thought about it before. Maybe the reason for that was because there had never been time to do so. He had been too busy grafting, too busy trying to be the man his father had been, and the man he had promised he would be.

When he had been a small boy, Ethan had been devoted to his father, a man full of fun and laughter. Ethan had idolized him. He had called Ethan his protégé and through his young eyes, it seemed there wasn't anything his father couldn't do. He was Superman and Batman combined.

But, of course, his father wasn't a superhero, he was as fallible as the next man and proved it by dying and leaving his family flat broke.

Lung cancer killed him. A big smoker all his life, he had ignored what little advice he had been given. In those days smoking wasn't viewed as the ruthless killer it was today, but his father had been warned of the dangers and he had chosen not to take heed. Ethan had never smoked. He hadn't even tried it. Whenever anyone had offered him a cigarette as a teenager he had thought of his father lying in that hospital bed with his sunken, ashen face covered by an oxygen mask. He would think of his father's rattling, wheezy breath, his withered body. He would remember his father struggling to get the words out to tell him to take care of his mother and sister, the promise he had been desperate for Ethan to make.

So no, smoking had never been a temptation for him.

Perversely his mother had taken the habit up shortly after the funeral. 'It's to calm my nerves,' she had explained to Ethan. She had done a lot of things from then on supposedly to calm her nerves. 'I have to have a life,' she had shouted at

Ethan when he had argued with her about the latest man he had found her in bed with one morning when he was getting ready for school. 'Your father wouldn't have expected me to stay at home crying for him,' she'd said. She had also repeated what his father had made Ethan promise, that it was his job now to take care of the family.

Ethan had supported his mother and sister right up until he married Francine. Then things had changed. Francine was furious when she realized just how much money he was forking out. 'You have different priorities now,' she said. 'It's your mother and sister, or me.'

Officially he stopped the flow of money, but every now and then his mother would get in touch with a story of being down on her luck and he would give her what she needed. But then he discovered that both she and his sister had been stealing from him. His sister had been forging his signature on cheques. Fool that he was, he hadn't noticed that a cheque book had gone missing. They had all but cleared out his personal bank account. Francine had hit the roof and threatened to get the police involved. Whilst it was a massive blow to Ethan – after everything that he had done for them, how could his own family do that to him? – he had persuaded Francine not to go to the police. He didn't want to put his mother and sister through that. It just didn't seem right.

This had happened ten years ago and he hadn't seen or heard from them since. The last he knew was they had moved away. He didn't know where. Sometimes it bothered him, to think that his own flesh and blood was out there somewhere in the world and he didn't know where. It was crazy, but just occasionally he still felt responsible for them. He also wondered what his father would think about what had happened. Would he think Ethan had failed in some way, that he hadn't kept his promise?

His ice-cream finished, he reluctantly roused himself. Francine would be wanting her magazine. And heaven forbid that she should be kept waiting.

He stood up and had the weirdest feeling. Funnily enough, it was the second time he had experienced the sensation since arriving in Abersoch. It was a figment of his imagination, he knew. A case of wishful thinking. A case of wishing she was here with him and superimposing her features on another woman. But it was weird all the same. Because over there, way in the distance at the water's edge, was a woman who bore a more than passing resemblance to Ella. It was the way she carried herself.

Chapter Thirty-six

They were back from the beach.

Alexis, the silly girl, had refused to use any sun cream because she'd said the sun wasn't hot enough to burn her at this time of year, and she was now grumbling that her back and shoulders were hurting. From the look of her skin that was reddening fast, the worst was yet to come.

'Why don't you have a shower and then I'll rub on some after-sun for you?' Ella offered. As tempting as it was, there would be no told-you-so comment from Ella. Toby, however, had other ideas.

'You're such a whinge-bag, Alexis,' he said. 'Didn't Ella offer her sun cream to you?' He pressed a finger to his sister's shoulder. 'Ouch,' he said, blowing on his finger as if he'd burnt it on contact.

'Don't touch me!' Alexis shouted at him.

He grinned. 'Just pointing out the blindingly obvious to you: that you never listen to good advice. But then what's new?'

'Don't be cruel, Toby,' Ella said kindly. 'Leave your sister alone. She's in pain.'

'Who's a pain?'

The question was asked by Lawrence as he came down the pine tread staircase that led straight into the open-plan sitting area and kitchen.

'Toby is,' Alexis said, taking a swipe at her brother and then dodging out of his reach and passing her father on the stairs. 'I'm going for a shower,' she added. 'And what's more,

I'm going to use Toby's share of the hot water!'

'Family accord, you can't beat it,' Toby said as Alexis clattered noisily upstairs. 'What are we eating tonight, Dad?'

'How about fish and chips? Jonty and Fiona said there's a great new chip shop in the village.'

'Suits me.'

'Ella, is that all right with you?' Lawrence asked. He was so very solicitous these days. So very anxious to please her.

'Can't think of anything I'd like better,' she replied.

'Excellent. That's decided then.' He looked relieved, as if he had successfully jumped through another hoop. Ella wanted to tell him to relax, to stop worrying on her behalf. It was as if he was in a constant state of apology. But then as he had said, after the débâcle of his birthday, he had a lot to be sorry for.

At Toby's suggestion, Lawrence and Ella went for a drink before going on to the chip shop. It was the first time since arriving in Abersoch that they had spent any time alone together.

While Lawrence went inside to get their drinks, Ella grabbed the last free table on the terrace at the front of the pub that overlooked the main road through the village. It was still surprisingly warm and it felt good to be able to sit outside and soak up the last of the evening's sunshine. Making the most of the weather is what we British do best, she thought. We snatch what few opportunities of sunshine we get and throw ourselves full tilt at them. Which was certainly what everyone else on the crowded terrace was doing, judging by the sun-tanned faces and raucous laughter and chatter. And why not? Why not grab the chance of happiness when they could? Wasn't that what she was doing?

After Toby and Alexis had begged her to forgive their father, and she had promised to think about what they had said, Lawrence had sent her the most wildly extravagant bouquet of flowers. It was so large not only had the poor delivery woman struggled comically to carry it, but Ella had had trouble getting it through the doorway of her house.

I'm in abject pain at what I said to you, Lawrence had written on the card, in his own hand. *I'm mortified beyond belief. Is there anything I can do to make amends? Name it and I'll do it.*

Stop sending me flowers! she had wanted to write back to him. She hadn't, of course. She had phoned him that evening and suggested they meet for dinner the following evening so they could talk. She could hear the tense note in his voice at her words, the fragile hope that he hadn't blown it, that there was still a chance of forgiveness. It was there in his drawn face when they sat opposite each other in the restaurant and in the faltering attempts at conversation he kept stumbling over. Only someone with a heart of stone would have been unmoved by his obvious distress and unable to witness his pain a second longer, she had leaned across the table and placed a hand on his wrist.

'Lawrence,' she had said, 'it's all right, you don't have to go on torturing yourself. I haven't agreed to come here tonight to make you feel any worse than you do already. I know you're sorry for what you did and so long as you promise never to treat me so cruelly again, let's pretend it never happened.'

He had briefly closed his eyes and when he opened them, he looked at her properly for the first time since they had sat down. 'I don't deserve you,' he said.

She smiled. 'No, you don't. So be nice to me.' Her voice was light, in contrast to the pained thickness of his.

Reaching across the table for her hands, he held them within his. 'Maybe I was having some kind of mid-life crisis during this last year – it's the only explanation I can offer for my behaviour. But I do love you, Ella. I love you with all my heart and don't want to be without you ever again. I'm just sorry it's taken me so long to realize that.'

Filled with a rush of great tender love for him, she squeezed his hands. 'I'm glad you got there in the end,' she said quietly.

Now here they were on holiday together, and so far it was proving to be a lot more enjoyable than any previous holiday. The difference being Alexis. The girl had undergone a seismic shift in her attitude towards Ella and that had changed everything. If only Alexis had come to terms with her father falling in love with Ella seven years ago, how much happier they would all have been. But old habits die hard and every so often Ella would hesitate over a particular look or a certain remark made by Alexis and she would wait with bated breath for a barbed follow through. Those occasional flashes of doubt and anxiety had so far proved to be unwarranted; Alexis really was a changed girl.

Ella still hadn't taken the step of moving back to Mayfield, nor had she stayed the night, but then her work commitments had dictated that to a degree. As well as working down in Canterbury for a week, she had taken the opportunity to visit her parents in Suffolk and then drive on to her sister's new house in Lincoln where her husband, Andy, had recently been relocated. Ella had stayed longer than she'd originally planned after Catherine asked her to put some finishing touches to the kitchen they'd just had decorated. She had enjoyed her time with her sister and had plucked up the courage to tell her about the latest turn of events with Lawrence. Catherine's reaction had been predictably lukewarm, but then she had suddenly smiled and said she had news of her own: she and Andy had just found out that she was pregnant. Ella was the first to know. The announcement very conveniently put Ella's news very much on the backburner.

It was during her stay in Lincoln that Lawrence phoned to say that his old friends, Jonty and Fiona, had offered him the use of their holiday home in Abersoch for the Easter weekend. He had then invited Ella to join him and the children. It seemed a good idea to her to spend some time together on neutral ground, away from Mayfield and all its divisive associations. Things had been going so well that she wondered if it wouldn't be a bad idea for Lawrence to sell Mayfield and for them to start somewhere new together. How would Alexis feel about that, though?

For the first time since their break-up, Ella and Lawrence had slept together last night. Lying in his embrace had felt comfortably familiar yet at the same time strangely unfamiliar, and there had been an initial moment of awkwardness between them. Paper-thin walls and a comedy creaking bed had soon had them laughing and had put paid to making love. It hadn't felt important, though. The intimacy of being in each other's arms had been enough. It had undone all the harm that had gone before. Frustratingly, she hadn't been able to sleep straight away, her brain refusing to settle. It was as if her body needed time to reacquaint itself with the constantly shifting rhythm of Lawrence as he slept. She had forgotten how much he moved in his sleep.

She had woken this morning to find his side of the bed empty. Minutes later he reappeared with a breakfast tray – toast and coffee. He slid back into bed and kissed her on the forehead. 'How do you feel about breakfast in bed every morning?'

'*Every* morning?'

'Okay, then,' he said with a smile, 'as often as is practically possible.'

That was the thing about romance, Ella thought now as an open-top Porsche drove by with loud music playing. It had to be fitted in around the routine of everyday life. Being such a practical person, she had no problem with that. Her expectations had always been grounded very solidly in the real world. She had no time for gushing Hallmark sentiment; it embarrassed her. A very long time ago she'd had a boyfriend who had written poetry for her. Very bad poetry. Worse still, he had wanted to read it aloud to her. On one occasion she had instigated sex to shut him up. It was a mistake; from then on he imagined all he had to do to set the mood for sex was to read a few verses of his toe-curlingly awful poetry. Perhaps a less pragmatic woman would find it touching that a man would do that for her, but she wasn't that woman. As Ethan had said, she was one of the most practical women he knew.

The last contact she'd had with Ethan was a text message saying he missed her. With things by then resolved with Lawrence she had deleted the text and not replied. Ever since that online admission of Ethan's – that he would love nothing more than to make love with her, to explore every inch of her body – her attitude towards Ethan had changed. It had to.

True, there had been a moment when she had been flattered by his words, even a little thrilled, but then she had grown annoyed with him. She felt as if he had conned her. The cynic in her wondered if he had been playing a game with her right from the start – befriend her and then when her guard was down, make his move. She wanted to believe he was more honourable than that, that maybe he had genuinely wanted her as a friend but then his feelings had gradually changed.

But who was she to talk, when she had been guilty of having some very inappropriate feelings for him, too?

Whichever way she viewed the situation, she knew she couldn't possibly be friends with a married man who openly admitted that he wanted to have sex with her. It was asking for trouble. And she could do without that. If he contacted her again, she would have to make things clear. If he cared about her, he would understand. Part of her felt sorry for him that he didn't have anyone to confide in, but that was his problem. It couldn't be hers.

Her priorities had changed and uppermost in her mind was that she didn't want to do anything that would upset Lawrence. If she and Lawrence were going to make things work between them and have the shared future they'd so often dreamed of, they had to start afresh and be entirely honest with each other. Ella had been very clear on that point with Lawrence and it had led them to discuss the important reasons why their relationship had gone so wrong before. Hearing Lawrence acknowledge that he had been wholly at fault when it came to Alexis and that he would never allow that to happen again, Ella had been moved to tears. It was what she had been so desperate to hear for so very long. She knew then that they would be all right, that with a clean slate they could move on. And perhaps more importantly, Ella would be able to forgive Alexis.

Over by the main entrance into the pub, she saw Lawrence step out onto the terrace; he was scanning the tables looking for her. With the soft evening sun on him, she thought how well he looked and how attractive he looked in the dark blue polo shirt she had bought him today. She waved to him.

'Sorry I was so long,' he said when he had made his way to the table. 'You wouldn't believe the queue in there at the bar.'

She leaned across the table and kissed him on the mouth.

'What was that for?' he asked, a surprised look on his face. 'Not that I'm complaining.'

'Because you were gone for so long,' she said with a smile.

He smiled back at her, a warm loving smile. 'I could disappear again, if you like.'

'No need.'

He raised his glass. 'To us,' he said.

'To us,' she echoed.

The queue for the chip shop that Jonty and Fiona had recommended stretched out of the small single-fronted shop and onto the pavement. Ella and Lawrence joined the end of it. Lawrence was just calling Toby to say they would be some time yet, when Ella heard a voice that stopped her in her tracks. She slowly turned, convinced that she was imagining things.

But no, there he was and he looked just as stunned as she was. He shook his head and smiled. 'Wow, what are the chances of this?' he said.

Before Ella could reply, Lawrence ended his call and put his arm around her waist. 'Lawrence,' she said, as he drew her closer, 'you remember Mr Edwards, don't you?'

Uncertainty flickered across Lawrence's face, followed quickly by recognition. 'Ah yes, but I don't remember ever being properly introduced,' he said politely.

Ethan stuck out his hand. 'Ethan Edwards,' he said. 'And this,' he said, indicating the man at his side, 'is Adam Paxton, my neighbour from back in Kings Melford. He and his family are staying with us for the weekend.'

The man – paunchy and with a receding hairline – pumped hands with Lawrence, then Ella. 'Sorry,' he said to her, 'I didn't catch your name.'

'Ella Moore,' she answered, registering that he had to be the husband of the ghastly woman she had met in the kitchen at The Lilacs. She recalled Ethan saying he'd rather impale himself on a pitchfork than be friends with him.

'Ella is the creative genius who transformed our dining room so brilliantly,' Ethan said.

'Oh, *you're* the decorator I've heard so much about.'

Ella couldn't stop herself from correcting him. 'Specialist painter,' she said.

Adam Paxton laughed loudly. 'I suppose a fancy title bumps up the price a treat for the punters, doesn't it? But I have to tell you, you've obviously made a big impression on my wife, as she's got this idea into her head about tarting up our bedroom. I'm worried sick what godawful nightmare she's got in store for me.' He laughed loudly again. It was the kind of collusive laugh that was weighted with the assumption that they too were now all worried sick on his behalf.

Ella could see from Ethan's body language – he had some-how opened up a gap between him and Adam Paxton – that he didn't want to be associated with him in any way. 'How long are you staying here in Abersoch?' he asked.

'Until Monday,' Lawrence answered.

'In that case,' he directed his words at Lawrence, 'why don't you join us for a drink tomorrow evening?'

'That's extremely kind of you,' Ella said firmly – no way

was she going to agree to anything so hellish – 'but we're here with Lawrence's children.'

Now Ethan did look at her. 'Bring them along, too,' he said. His gaze dropped to her waist and Lawrence's arm.

'I'm all for a party,' joined in Adam Paxton, rubbing his hands together. 'How old are your kids, Lawrence?'

'Alexis is sixteen and Toby's nineteen, twenty next month.'

'Couldn't be better. Alexis will feel right at home with our two daughters and all I can say about Toby is that he'd better watch out. If you know what I mean,' he added with a wink.

Oh my God, thought Ella, the nauseating man actually winked. Any minute and he'd be nudging them in the ribs and saying, Do you get it? Do you get it?

Ethan was now staring determinedly across the road, his hands pushed deep into his trouser pockets. He could not have looked more uncomfortable. He also looked like he had lost quite a bit of weight, Ella thought with a small jolt of concern. There was a gauntness to his face and his trousers definitely appeared looser on him. She recalled him saying that now and then he suffered from stomach problems. Had those problems got worse? Had he seen a doctor? She hoped he had.

'What do you think, Ella?'

'Sorry,' she said, embarrassed that she had lost the thread of the conversation. 'What do I think of what?'

'I was asking what you think about accepting Ethan's invitation for drinks tomorrow. We don't have anything planned, do we?'

She switched her gaze from Lawrence to Ethan, who was now staring steadily at her. To refuse again would make her look unnecessarily rude. 'I don't see why not,' she said lightly. 'But only if it's not too much trouble for your wife.' He could not fail to catch her inference.

'No trouble at all,' he said equably. Shall we say around six thirty?'

Chapter Thirty-seven

Everyone had laughed at Peggy when last year she'd said, 'I had my heart broke over Ali the Turk, but now I've met Mr Wonderful.' Mr Wonderful – a carpet fitter from Runcorn – had buggered off two weeks later with her new telly and, weirdly, the contents of her freezer. She had laughed it off and said that when it came to love she had to be the most doomed woman alive. The upside, she'd said, was that Mr Wonderful would get what he deserved as some of the stuff he'd stolen from her freezer was years out of date and with any luck he'd die of food poisoning.

Maggie didn't think either Ali the Turk or Mr Wonderful had really broken Peggy's heart, not when she'd bounced back so cheerfully. But Maggie's heart *really* was broken. Life without Daryl was making her more miserable than she'd ever thought possible. She couldn't eat, sleep or think properly. She didn't know what she was doing half the time. Whenever she got into her car, she had to force herself to remember how to drive. Her concentration was so bad it was a wonder she hadn't had an accident.

Apart from Mrs Oates and Jack Potts, the only other person who knew about Daryl was Ella. A week after that awful evening at Mrs Oates's, she had bumped into Ella in the supermarket. When Ella had asked her how she was, she had fallen apart. She had cried and cried and Ella had tried to calm her down by taking her for a coffee. Maggie had blurted out the whole shameful story, and how she had refused to see or speak to Daryl ever again. Ella had been so kind to her, and each time Maggie had thought she was all cried out, fresh tears would roll down her cheeks.

The only advice Ella had given her was to accept that for now life would feel pretty shitty, but she had to believe that it would get better eventually. Ella had said she could call her any time she wanted. So far Maggie hadn't; she didn't want to make a nuisance of herself.

All she could think of was how much she wanted to see Daryl again, but she knew she couldn't, that it was wrong. She had made him swear that he wouldn't get in touch with her and whilst she was glad he had respected her wishes, she still longed for a text from him. Just something to let her know he was still thinking of her. But was he? Or had he already found someone to replace her, just as Peggy had done with Ali the Turk?

Nearly a month on and Maggie was still bursting into tears when she was on her own. Especially if something reminded her of Daryl. It seemed that every other record played on the radio was now a Queen or a Freddie Mercury song. She had been a proper mental wreck the other day in her car when 'This Could be Heaven' had come on the radio.

One thing was for sure: she wasn't in heaven, she was in hell. And hell of her own making. Why had she ever thought it was a good idea to get involved with Daryl? What had made her act so stupidly? Blethering on about being unhappy wasn't good enough. Plenty of people put up with boring marriages – but they didn't all go rushing off into the arms of someone else.

And Dave wasn't that bad, was he? He wasn't violent. He didn't shout at her. He didn't mistreat her. He just never thought about her. She was like a piece of furniture to him. Like a chair, which he would only think about if it was gone. Maybe only when he tried to sit on it and found himself on the floor. No, it was hardly his fault that he was dull and un-caring, that he was as sexy as a floor mop. None of it made it right for her to look elsewhere for romance and excitement.

She hadn't seen Mrs Oates since that evening and she didn't think she would ever be able to face the old lady again. Every time Maggie thought of Mrs Oates's shocked expression when she had found Maggie and Daryl kissing in her kitchen, she squeezed her eyes shut and shuddered. She hated the thought that someone as sweet, kind and honest as Mrs Oates knew that Maggie had been lying to her.

To try and put things right, if only in her head, she was doing everything she could to make her marriage work. Which was why, on Easter Saturday, she was now flogging herself to death whilst everyone else was having a good time in the garden.

What was it with men and barbecues? They banged on about how easy it was to do one, but what did they actually do? All Mr Blobby ever did – she really must stop calling him that – all Dave did was stand around with a beer in his hand, poking at the coals every now and then and yelling that there'd be nowt to eat unless someone brought the meat out, and where were the spuds, and what about the salad cream, the ketchup and brown sauce? Backwards and forwards Maggie had been going for the last hour, ferrying food, plates, salads, sauces, cutlery, glasses – you name it she'd taken it out to the garden. He'd be calling for the kitchen sink next!

To cap it all, Dave's brother and wife had come to spend the day with them. Or rather Vernon and Shelley had come to lord it over them. If Maggie had heard about their amazing new loft extension once, she'd heard it a hundred times. They'd also gone on and on about Shelley's new Mazda MX-5 and their recent holiday in Las Vegas. Oh, and the endless photographs, all shown to them on the stupid little screen on Vernon's new digital camera – Shelley on the slot machines, Shelley by the pool, Shelley wearing a pink tasselled cowboy hat, Shelley on their balcony, Shelley on the piss, Shelley all dolled up and posing by some fancy fountain at the front of some fancy hotel. There'd been video clips as well. All of them showing Shelley tanked up and pulling silly faces into the camera. Talk about the Shelley Show! If they hadn't heard Vernon's voice on the video telling Shelley to smile, they could have been forgiven for thinking he hadn't been on holiday with her.

As Maggie lugged another two six-packs of beer out to the table where everyone was sitting on the patio, she heard Vernon and Shelley talking about Babe. Babe was their latest accessory: a terrifying Rottweiler. She had been given to them in January by a friend who had gone to live in Spain. The dog was as big as a coal shed and as nasty-looking as a bucket of raw, chopped liver. Shelley was pleading in a silly wheedling voice to Brenda to let them fetch Babe from the car, where she was howling like something out of a horror film. 'She'll be as good as gold,' Shelley said. 'You'll not even know she's here.'

Then why bother getting her out of the car? thought Maggie. For once she was in agreement with Brenda, who had stamped on the idea of Babe getting anywhere near Evil Sid. Maggie had to admit that the idea of such a huge monster roaming the garden appalled her. Bad enough that Evil Sid was constantly crapping and peeing all over it, but let a dog that size use the place as a toilet and they'd be knee-deep in ... well, it didn't bear thinking about what they'd be knee-deep in.

When Vernon added his voice to Shelley's wheedling, Brenda, who had never been able to refuse either of her sons anything, lit another cigarette and gave in. 'Oh, go on, then,' she said with a mighty drag, 'but you be sure to keep an eye on her. You know how sensitive my Sid is.' Crouched on the lawn a short distance away from where they were sitting, Evil Sid was doing what he did best and with a look of intense concentration on his foul devil-like face. It was unbelievable just how much he could produce. But then maybe it wasn't so unbelievable what with the amount of titbits Brenda fed him.

'Burgers and sausages are ready!' Dave announced as Vernon went round to the front of the house. 'Got the plates ready, Mags?'

'On the table right next to you,' she said. 'More to drink, Shelley and Brenda?' she asked.

Shelley, who always had a darts player's thirst on her, held out her empty glass. 'I thought you'd never ask,' she said with a rattle of gold bracelets on her tanned wrist. Maggie had just filled it when Vernon reappeared. He was being dragged nearly off his feet by Babe, who was charging straight for Dave and the plate of sausages and burgers.

What happened next happened so fast and yet at the same time, so slowly.

One minute Vernon was yelling at Babe to 'stay' and the next he'd slipped on Evil Sid's fresh-off-the-production-line turd and was sliding across the lawn like he was water skiing. Maggie watched him try to dig his heels in the grass so he could get some kind of purchase, but despite his massive bulk he was no match for a slippery turd and Babe's brute strength. All he could do was hang onto the lead for dear life and shout, *Whoa!* Babe's response was to give a terrifying bark and throw herself at Dave, her front paws landing smack on his chest. The plate of meat went flying.

As did Dave.

As did the barbecue.

As did Vernon.

Evil Sid then joined in with the mayhem and made a dash for a sausage. But Babe wasn't having that and she growled ferociously, launched herself into the air off her powerful back legs, landed on top of Evil Sid, sank her teeth into his soft, fat body and began shaking him as if he was a toy.

The noise was terrible. And not just from Evil Sid. Everyone was screaming and yelling but not doing anything to help. Maggie grabbed the nearest object to hand – the shovel she used to clear up after Evil Sid – and crashed it down as hard as she could on whatever bit of Babe stayed still long enough for her to hit.

It turned out to be Babe's head.

The silence that followed was dreadful.

Chapter Thirty-eight

The evening was warm and balmy, the wine excellent, the smoked salmon canapés delicious, and the sea view stunning. Perfect ingredients for a perfect evening.

If only.

After a scant thirty minutes of being here at Pine Tree Cottage, the evening was shaping up to be the worst evening in the history of worst evenings. The clickety-click of *I'm-the-boss-and-don't-you-forget-it* heels had not been left behind in Cheshire. Quite the reverse. In her cream, peep-toe slingbacks, Francine Edwards could not make it more obvious that she considered consorting with the hired help while on holiday not the done thing. Instead of indulging in any of the usual drinks party chit-chat – the weather, the latest must-see film, the latest government shenanigans – as if to remind Ella of her place, she was sticking to the subject of Ella's work and pressing her to agree to help transform Pine Tree Cottage. She simply wouldn't leave the subject alone.

'Come on, Francine,' Ethan said at last, passing a glass platter of smoked salmon canapés round, 'let's discuss this another time. It's not fair to Ella to harangue her while she's here as our guest.'

His wife looked at him as though she might like to take the glass platter and make him wear it. 'I'd hardly describe discussing a commission of work as haranguing a person,' she said stiffly. 'I'd have thought in these difficult times Ella would be grateful for the work.' She snapped her head round. 'Wouldn't you, Ella? Wouldn't you be grateful?'

Ella forced a smile of utter sweetness to her lips. 'I'm very fortunate in that I have a pretty full diary for the months ahead. Over the years I've built up an extensive customer base of repeat clients and so long as they keep moving house or want to keep pace with the latest decorating trends, I'm in demand.' She intensified her smile. 'I'm very lucky.'

'Luck doesn't come into it,' said Lawrence, who until now had been noticeably quiet; his legs crossed, his left foot had been bouncing continuously since they'd been invited to take a seat on the terrace. She knew him well enough to know it wasn't a good sign. 'You've worked hard to build up a strong client base,' he continued, 'and an excellent reputation. We're all very proud of you. Isn't that right?' His question was directed at Toby and Alexis and whilst Ella could have hugged him for his loyal support, she didn't know what was more embarrassing – his clunky heavy-handedness or his children's dutifully nodded agreement.

'Goodness!' she said, her voice full of forced cheer. 'Let's change the subject, shall we?'

'No, let's not. I'd love to hear more.' This was from Christine, who kept staring at Ella venomously, and if she gave off any more false notes she would be in need of a sincerity tuner. Every time Ella risked a glance in her direction, she found she was on the receiving end of a stare of glacial condemnation. This was only the second time they had ever met, but for some reason that Ella couldn't fathom, Christine Paxton clearly disliked her. 'Adam and I appreciate just how in demand you are,' the woman said, 'but we'd love it if you could do some work for us. We want to give our bedroom a makeover. You could name your price.'

'Steady on,' chipped in her husband. 'Let's not get carried away.'

'Oh, darling, don't be silly.' Christine leaned in closer to him and stroked his arm in an overtly sexual way. 'You know we can afford it.'

Their daughter flicked her gaze heavenward, and who

283

could blame her? But the fool of a man grinned back at his wife. Putty and hands came to mind. 'Well, if it's what you really want,' he said.

'It is, darling.'

I'm going to be sick, thought Ella. Any minute now the manipulative woman would have her husband rolling onto his back so she could tickle his paunchy belly for him.

'Canapé anyone?' offered Ethan. From the expression on his face he too looked like he wanted to be sick. 'How about another beer, Toby?' he said genially. 'You look like you're running dry.'

'I'm fine, thanks,' Toby said. Poor Toby. How awful this must be for him.

'This is, like, way too boring,' Valentina said, jumping up from her chair. She was wearing a black strappy top and a frayed denim skirt that could not have been shorter without revealing the gusset of her knickers. 'Come on, Katie,' she said, 'let's leave them to it.'

'Hold on,' Ethan said with a frown. 'That's not very polite, Valentina. What about Alexis and Toby?'

Valentina shrugged uninterestedly. 'They can come too, if they want.'

Her supposed lack of interest did not fool Ella. Not a word had been exchanged between the four younger members of the party but Valentina had been far from slow in checking out Toby. In your dreams, thought Ella. He's way out of your league.

'And where exactly are you going?' asked Ethan.

'Hel-*lo*, Mr Lame, we're going where we went last night. Then later there's a beach party. You coming, or what?'

The question was directed at Alexis, but it was clearly aimed at Toby. Brother and sister exchanged a glance and then both stood up. A further glance was exchanged between Lawrence and Toby, and Ella recognized it as an unspoken instruction: *keep an eye on your sister.*

Still frowning, Ethan said, 'You know the rule: no alcohol. Not for you girls – you're under age.'

Adam Paxton laughed. 'Lighten up, Ethan, they'll be fine.' He delved into his back pocket and pulled out some money. 'Here you go, kids. Have fun.'

'No alcohol,' Ethan repeated sternly.

'Dad! Do you, like, have any idea just how totally uncool you're being?'

'I don't care how uncool I am. One whiff of booze on you when you get back and you're grounded,' he said firmly.

'Yeah, whatever.' She executed an eye roll that put any of Alexis's attempts not so much into the shade as on the dark side of the moon. 'Like you lot won't be all off your heads when we get back,' she said. 'How about some money from you, then, Dad?' She stuck out her hand.

The insolence of the girl had Ella wanting to slap some manners into her. What was it with teenage girls?

'So,' Adam said when it was just the so-called grown-ups left to battle it out, 'what's your line of work, David?'

'I'm a wine importer. And it's Lawrence. Not David.'

Adam slapped a hand against his forehead. 'Sorry. I'm useless with names. A wine importer. Bit of a dream job, that. You must give me your contact details; I could do with having a tame wine merchant on side.'

There was nothing tame about the tight expression on Lawrence's face, or the foot that was bouncing even faster now. He had to be wondering how the hell he'd ever got roped into such an awful evening. Ethan had a lot to answer for, Ella thought. Just what had got into him? What had he hoped to get out of throwing them all together like this?

Oh boy, thought Ethan, as he went in search of another bottle of wine in the kitchen. As ideas went, it was not one of his finest to invite Ella here for a drink. That would teach him for wanting to spend time with her.

It had been surreal bumping into Ella last night, but it had also felt as if it was fate. At least he now knew that he hadn't been imagining her presence here in Abersoch. As far-fetched as it sounded, he couldn't stop thinking that they were being kept together by a continuous flow of chance and coincidence. What other explanation was there for the way in which they had met and then their subsequent meeting, when he had arrived home and found her dancing in his dining room? Whenever he replayed the memory of watching her dance so joyously and so freely, something deep inside him craved to be as free.

He yanked the cork out of the bottle, gave it a sniff – wouldn't do to serve dud wine to Ella's boyfriend, would it? – and wondered what the hell Ella saw in him. He had public school written all over his condescending face. Probably in Latin. Okay, not Latin, because if it was, Ethan wouldn't be able to read it, would he? Latin hadn't been on offer at his school; there'd been no call for it. Why would there be when he and his classmates had been destined for factory work or signing on?

Way to go! There was nothing like a bit of chippy class warfare to bring out the best in a person, he thought wryly, reminding himself that Valentina was studying Latin at her posh expensive school. In his opinion, a GCSE in manners would be of more use to her.

'Good God, Ethan. What's taking you so long with that wine?'

It was Francine and she looked like thunder. 'As I've said to you countless times since last night, what on earth possessed you to invite them for a drink? It's not as if we're going to start socializing with them back at home, is it?'

'And as I told you countless times, I was just being friendly,' he said. 'It seemed the right thing to do.'

'In that case, why don't you put your friendliness to good use? If Christine pinches Ella and I don't get her to do the decorating work here, there'll be trouble. Big trouble.'

'What do you want me to do?'

'I want you to work on Ella. Make her change her mind.'

Trying not to smile, Ethan looked at her with an expression of disbelief, as if she had just asked him to split the atom. 'You really think I could?'

'I don't see why not. After all, you have a way with women, don't you?' Her tone dripped with acid. 'I know she's not your type, but try charming her. You could manage that, couldn't you?'

The strain of keeping his face straight was almost too much for Ethan. 'I'm not sure. I mean she's—'

'Oh, for heaven's sake. Why can't you do this one small thing for me? Why do you always have to make me fight you?'

'We're not fighting, are we?'

She pursed her glossed lips tightly shut, then opened them. 'Please don't try to be clever, Ethan. Get her on her own whilst I try talking to that boyfriend of hers. Though God knows what I can talk about with him.'

'Try wine,' he said. 'Give him the opportunity to show off his extensive knowledge. He strikes me as the type who would enjoy that.'

'Good idea. So what are you waiting for? Take that wine out to them. They'll be wondering what we're doing in here.'

'I expect they'll think we're sharing a romantic moment together.'

She looked at him hard. 'You've been in a very strange mood all day. Whatever is the matter with you?'

'Too much sea air, I shouldn't wonder.' Charged with his task, he took the opened bottle of wine outside and set about his assignment. Who was he to refuse an official diktat from Francine?

Christine was not happy. Not happy at all.

Things were not going to plan. She had only accepted Francine's invitation to come here in the hope she would be able to get Ethan on his own and show him how repentant she was for her behaviour earlier in the year, to explain that it was a horribly embarrassing mistake and could he possibly find it in his heart to forgive her? Yes, she'd had it all planned out so very neatly.

But then what did she find when she and Adam arrived? Ella Bloody Moore staying in Abersoch! What kind of co-incidence was that? None at all. Absolutely none whatsoever. How could it be a coincidence? Innocently bumping into each other in the queue at the chip shop ... she didn't think so. Did they really think anyone would believe a cock and bull story like that?

And just how blind was Francine to what was going on right under her nose? The woman really was a fool. Or was there a chance that Francine was playing her own game with Ethan? Did she suspect he was up to no good and was setting a trap for him? It was certainly a possibility, especially as Francine had always been a tough one to read, never more so than now with her Botoxed face.

It might explain why all of a sudden Francine was acting the perfect hostess and showing such interest in Ella's boyfriend – and annoyingly expecting her and Adam to join in with the conversation about wine – while leaving Ethan free to chat with Ella. Christine hadn't been able to believe her ears when just a few minutes ago she had heard Ethan ask Ella if she would like to see the view from the end of the garden. For pity's sake, he might just as well have stripped the clothes off her and carried her upstairs!

And as for this grotty house Francine and Ethan had bought, it was going to take more than a lick of paint to tart it up into something half-decent. She doubted it had had any work done to it in years; it was truly disgusting, nothing better than a naff chalet bungalow. Adam reckoned that Ethan would have to stump up as much as the asking price again to do everything that needed doing. Particularly with Francine's expensive tastes.

She took a long swig of her wine and watched the two

figures at the end of the garden. Now what were those two discussing so intently?

As if she couldn't guess.

'I'm sorry,' he said.

'So you keep saying.'

'But you don't believe me, do you?'

'I don't know what to believe about you, Ethan. This was a dreadful idea of yours.'

'You could have said no.'

'I tried to.'

'If you were so against it, why didn't you try harder?'

Ella mentally conceded that it was a good question. If she had said no, Lawrence might have had cause to wonder why she was being so rude – he might have thought back to when he'd first met Ethan at her house and wondered if there was more going on than she had admitted to, just as he'd suspected. 'It seemed easier to say yes,' she said finally. 'But what I don't like about the situation is that it makes me feel guilty.'

'What have you got to feel guilty about?'

'Please don't be disingenuous.'

He shoved his hands into his pockets and looked out at the sea shimmering benignly in the soft evening light. The surface of the water was very calm, very flat. None of which Ella felt right now. She felt disagreeably on edge. She wanted to increase the distance between the two of them but if she did, she knew Ethan would close the gap. Either that or risk talking in a voice that could be overheard.

'You mustn't ever do anything like this again,' she said. 'In fact, I don't want you getting in touch with me any more.'

He turned sharply. 'Why?'

'Because I'm back with Lawrence now. You may not understand the concept of loyalty to a partner, but I do. I don't want to do anything that might rock the boat with Lawrence, not after everything we've been through.'

'And having me as a friend would rock the boat?'

'Yes.'

There was a long silence. 'Are you back in love with Lawrence, then?' His tone was openly derisive.

'Why else would I agree to be with him?'

'Say the words.'

'What words?'

His dark eyes bore into hers. 'That you love Lawrence.'

'Of course I do.'

'Then why can't you say it? It's simple enough, surely?'

'I love him,' she said firmly. 'There. Satisfied?'

His gaze was still squarely on hers. 'Are *you* satisfied, Ella? That's what interests me. Does Lawrence really tick all the boxes for you? A short while ago he didn't pass muster at all. What's changed between the two of you?'

'Whatever changes have taken place between us, they're none of your business.'

'But you know how I feel about you, which means your happiness is very much my business. Just answer me this: when you're with Lawrence, does it feel like the sun is shining just for you? Does he incite passion in you? Does he make you want to tear off your clothes and—' he broke off to turn and look down at the beach below them, '—does he make you want to make love in the setting sun in a secluded bay?'

A hot spasm of indignation tore through Ella. 'You have absolutely no right to imply what you're implying.'

He looked back at her, his eyebrows raised in what she knew was mock innocence. 'What am I implying?'

'That Lawrence is ...' But she couldn't bring herself to say what he was trying to force out of her. 'You're suggesting that I could have more excitement with you,' she said.

A scarcely discernible smile appeared on his face. 'How do you feel about making love in the setting sun?'

She swallowed. 'And what would I be to you, other than another of your tawdry one-night stands?'

He took a step nearer to her. 'I promise you there would be nothing tawdry or dull about us making love in the sunset.'

She stepped away from him. 'You conceited bastard! And there was me worried for you earlier.'

'Really? Why?'

'Oh, forget it,' she said coldly. 'It's not important.'

'Ella, why are you so cross with me?'

'Because …' Ella's reply hit the buffers. She tried again. 'Because you don't listen.'

'Is that the only reason?'

'What other reason could there be?' She immediately regretted the question, fearing his response and what it might provoke her to say. 'Don't answer that,' she said as an intense throbbing in her temple warned her to end the conversation now. 'We should join the others or they'll be wondering what's keeping us so long.'

'No worries on that score. I'm under orders from Francine to twist your arm into taking on the project here. If you don't, there'll be hell to pay. And if you agree to do any work for the Paxtons in preference to us, my life won't be worth living.'

'None of which concerns me.'

She turned and walked resolutely back up the garden to rescue Lawrence.

Chapter Thirty-nine

They were all in shock. And no amount of tea could lessen it. Or change the fact that Maggie was being blamed. *Blamed!* She couldn't friggin' believe it!

It didn't matter how many times she said she was sorry, they treated her as a killer. A brutal killer of innocent dogs. Vernon and Shelley said she'd overreacted. Why couldn't she have just whacked Babe on the bum? they'd screamed at her. Why did she aim for the dog's head? They'd accused her of doing it deliberately. Apparently they'd always known she had a cruel and sadistic streak running through her. What was more, they'd always known that she'd had it in for them; she was jealous and this was her way of getting back at them. Every word of blame Shelley had shrieked at her had been loud enough to wake the dead. Not Babe, though.

They had clocked up nearly eight hours at the hospital and vet between them. Maggie had driven Vernon and Dave to A and E and Shelley, wailing like a banshee, had taken Brenda and the two dogs to the vet. Maggie had made Dean go with them, in case either or both of the two women lost it completely.

Dave hadn't only burned himself on the barbecue when he'd fallen back onto it, but he'd also broken his ankle in the chaos. Vernon had got off lightly with only a sprained wrist. That didn't stop him from making enough noise during the drive to the hospital to make everyone think he was at death's door.

In comparison Dave hadn't said a word in the car; he'd

been as white as a sheet. The doctor had wanted to keep him in overnight but Dave, woozy with painkillers, had said he'd never spent a night away from his own bed and he wasn't about to start now. Rather than let the offer of free bed and board go to waste, Maggie had wanted to check herself in and risk catching a killer dose of the MRSA bug rather than go home and face Shelley.

When Shelley had opened the door to them, she had looked murderous. An hour on, with Babe wrapped in a blanket in the back of their car – they were going to bury the dog in their garden – Shelley still looked like she might take the shovel Maggie had used earlier and bash her skull in with it.

'You killed my baby,' Shelley said while Maggie offered to put the kettle on again. The words were like a chant; she kept saying them over and over – *You killed my baby, you killed my baby, you killed my baby*.

Worried that if she apologized one more time it might come out wrong – like, 'I'm not sorry at all' – Maggie retreated to the kitchen, where she found Brenda bug-eyed and shaking with nicotine overload, having chain-smoked her way through the nightmare. On the floor in his basket were the remains of Evil Sid.

Well, they looked like his remains, since he had been so savagely chewed. He was properly goosed. The vet had stitched and bandaged him up as best he could and just as the doctor had wanted Dave to stop the night at the hospital, the vet had advised that Evil Sid would be better staying at the practice. Brenda had flatly refused to leave him and had brought him home. So far he'd done nothing but sleep, knocked out by the anaesthetic. What he would be like when he came to was anybody's guess. But at least he was alive. Not that this appeared to give Brenda any comfort.

'You could have killed poor Sid,' Brenda said as she lit another cigarette from the stub in her mouth, then ferociously ground out the stub in the overflowing ashtray on the table.

'But I didn't kill him,' Maggie said. 'I saved him.' Couldn't the old witch, just once in her life, thank Maggie for something?

'You've driven a wedge through this family,' Brenda wheezed. 'Shelley and Vernon will never speak to you again, you know that, don't you?'

And what a loss that will be, Maggie muttered silently to herself. 'What would you rather I'd done?' she said. 'Let Babe tear Sid apart?'

'There's no need to take that tone with me. All I'm saying is that you were lucky. If you'd missed and smashed Sid's skull like you did Babe's, I would have done the same to you. You'd better start praying that he pulls through.'

'Thanks a bunch.'

'I'm only being honest with you.'

Maggie's blood boiled. She'd had enough. Oh, so much more than enough. The unfairness of it all welled up inside her until a fury like no other she had ever experienced unleashed itself. 'And how about I be honest with you for a change, Brenda?' she said. 'How about I tell you what an ungrateful bitch you are? How about I tell you that I'm sick of you constantly finding fault with me, sick of you always putting me down. There's nothing I ever do that's right in your eyes, is there? Even when it comes to saving your precious Sid's life. You know what? I wish now I'd let Babe kill the bloody thing, because then I wouldn't ever have to clean up after yet another one of his shitty messes. What's more, I wish Babe had attacked you and bitten out your vicious tongue so I'd never have to listen to another spiteful word from you!'

Brenda stared at her through a thick haze of smoke, her eyes even more bug-like. She opened her mouth to speak, but no sound came out. She closed her mouth, then opened it again. And again. Up and down her jaw went: open and shut and open and shut. In the strange silence she looked like a gulping fish.

The silence seemed to last for as long as the last century and that was when Maggie realized she had actually said the words aloud. She had not said them inside her head as she so often did. No, the words had burst out of her mouth loud and all too clear. An icy chill ran up and down her spine. Oh, sweet Moses on a bike ... what had she done?

As if by an act of God, she was saved from dealing with whatever reaction Brenda had in store by Dave calling for her to help him upstairs to the loo.

It was no easy task. This was Mr Blobby, after all. Even with Dean's help, it was hopeless. Maggie said, 'It's no good, Dave: you're too heavy. You're going to have to try and shuffle your way up the stairs on your bum.'

'Yer've got to be joking!' he exploded. 'How d'yer expect me to do that when me arse is burnt to a crisp?'

From the doorway of the front room, his bulging Popeye arms folded across his massive chest, Vernon laughed. 'That'll teach yer to go shoving it in the hot coals!'

Brotherly love – there was nothing like it. Nor was there anything like exaggerating an injury. Yes, Dave had burnt his bum, but not badly and only an area the size of a digestive biscuit.

Then, as though suddenly surfacing from the shock of what Maggie had said in the kitchen, Brenda shuffled into the hallway. 'Do you know what that bitch had the nerve to say to me?' she wheezed.

'Not now, Brenda,' Maggie sighed tiredly. 'Can't you see we're trying to help Dave?'

Brenda ignored her and began repeating some of what Maggie had said. It sounded worse second time round.

Shelley had now appeared in the doorway behind Vernon. 'See!' she crowed, pointing a finger at Maggie. 'Didn't I say she had a sadistic streak to her?'

'But I didn't mean it,' Maggie lied. 'It's the ... it was shock that made me say it.'

'Shock?' cried Shelley, 'I'll tell you what shock is. Shock is watching a mad woman clubbing your poor, innocent dog to death like a defenceless baby seal!'

'I didn't mean to kill it. I was trying to save—'

'Please,' groaned Dave. 'Will someone—'

'So why did you just tell Brenda that you wished Sid had died as well?' Shelley ranted at Maggie, speaking over Dave, whose face was turning an ugly shade of red.

'Will you lot shut up and help me up the stairs!' he said. 'I'm soddin' desperate here.'

Shelley tutted. 'Don't tell me to shut up, our Dave. And if you'd done what I told you to do and extended this place you'd have a downstairs loo and wouldn't be in this mess. Even without an extension, you could have turned the under-stairs cupboard into a small cloakroom with one of those systems that chops everything up, and you'd—'

Maggie raised a hand and said, 'Do us all a favour and shut up, Shelley! Can't you see Dave's in pain?'

'Pain? I'll tell you what pain is. It's watching—'

'I said shut up!'

'Vernon, are you going to just stand there and let Maggie speak to me this way?'

'Please,' begged Dave, 'I'm not asking to be carried up bloody Everest, just helped to the top of these buggering stairs.'

'Come on, then, our Dave,' Vernon said. 'Let's get yer sorted before you let loose the python and jet spray the carpet like yer did on yer stag night.' In one easy move, despite his sprained wrist, he hoisted Dave over his enormous shoulder like a sack of potatoes. 'Anyone ever told yer that yer shouldn't have eaten all the pies? Joining a gym might be a good idea, too. Yer need to get yerself in shape like me or yer'll keel over from a heart attack one of these days, just like our dad.'

'Any more advice like that and I'll let loose the python on you,' Dave moaned.

They were at the top of the stairs when Maggie heard Vernon say, 'I'm gonna give yer some more advice, mate. Yer can't let Maggie get away with speaking to Mum the way she did. She was bang out of order. She wasn't too polite to my Shelley either. What's got into her?'

Maggie didn't hear Dave's reply as he'd disappeared inside the bathroom and shut the door. She turned away from the stairs, only to be confronted by Brenda and Shelley staring at her. Dean had made himself scarce. Maggie wished she could too. 'What?' she said.

'We're waiting for an apology,' Shelley said.

She'd come this far; no way was she going to back down, not when she had right on her side. 'Then you've got a very long wait,' she said, 'because I'm not apologizing to anyone. And if you're not happy with that, then I suggest you both leave.'

Shelley's eyes nearly popped out of their heavily made-up sockets. Brenda clutched at her wheezing chest.

'What's more,' Maggie continued – she was now an un-stoppable force, driven by years of never answering back, of putting up with insult after insult, of never being able to say exactly what she thought – 'the sooner you leave, the better. Good riddance to you both. And if anyone should apologize it's you two. You, Shelley, for bringing that dangerous mon-ster of a dog here, and you, Brenda, for not having a grateful bone in your body. I saved that foul-smelling mutt of yours, and yet you still can't bring yourself to thank me. How come you're not angry with Shelley and Vernon? That's what I want to know. How come I get all the blame? Is it because you hate me as much as I hate you? Is that it?'

Shelley gasped and put a protective arm around Brenda, who needed as much protection as … a killer Rottweiler. 'You can't speak to us like that,' Shelley pouted.

'Wrong. I just did.'

'We'll see what our Dave has to say about this,' Brenda joined in.

'If he knows what's good for him, he'll do as I say.'

'You're mad!' Shelley cried shrilly. 'Off your trolley!'

Maggie squared up to them both. 'You'd better believe I am. I'm on the edge, one step away from total lunacy, so watch out. A killer of dogs one day – who knows who or what I'll attack next?'

They backed away from her like two scalded cats.

'Come on,' she said. 'What are you both waiting for? Chop, chop! Up those stairs the pair of you.'

'Why?' asked Shelley.

'To do Brenda's packing, of course. It's your turn now to have the poisonous witch live with you. Let's see how long you last before you feel like wringing her scrawny old neck!'

Chapter Forty

When Ella realized that she was brushing her teeth so hard she was making her gums bleed, she looked at herself in the mirror above the basin and tried to think calming thoughts.

And came up with a sum total of nothing.

She could think of nothing but the disruptive effect Ethan had had on her this evening and the harm he could have caused to her relationship with Lawrence.

While they were walking home, her hand in Lawrence's, he had asked, with palpable restraint, what she and Ethan had been talking about at the end of the garden. She had repeated what Ethan had told her: that his wife had asked him to try and twist her arm to help decorate Pine Tree Cottage. Lawrence's response, other than a slight tightening of his grasp of her hand, was to comment on the dynamics between the Edwards and the Paxtons. 'A strange bunch,' he'd said. 'I got the feeling they don't really like one another very much.' She had agreed with him and changed the subject.

Now as she closed the door of the small en suite bathroom to the main bedroom, Lawrence looked up from the latest Sebastian Faulks novel he was reading and pulled back the duvet on her side of the bed. 'I was just thinking,' he said as she slipped in next to him. 'What are you going to do about those people?'

'Which people?' she asked, despite knowing exactly whom he meant.

'The Edwards and the Paxtons. Will you take on the work they want you to do for them?'

'I wasn't going to.'

'Could be worth your while, though. They've basically given you a licence to charge whatever you want.' He smiled. 'Opportunities like that don't come along too often, do they?'

She was shocked. 'I never had you down as being so mercenary or so devious.'

He continued to smile. 'They deserve it for putting us through such an awful evening.'

'I'm sorry I got us lumbered.'

'Hardly your fault. I'm glad, though, that Alexis didn't take a shine to Valentina. The thought of her being friends with such a rude, spoilt brat is too much.'

The irony of his words had Ella looking away from him. Until just recently, Alexis would have been worthy of such a description, if not worse, but thank goodness those days were gone. Now, compared to Valentina, she was a model teenage daughter.

When Ella and Lawrence had arrived back this evening, having excused themselves from Pine Tree Cottage as soon as they could politely do so, they had found Toby and Alexis on the sofa with takeaway pizzas, watching a DVD. They too had made their escape from Valentina and Katie as soon as they could. Proud of their discerning taste, Ella had hugged them both, prompting Alexis to ask if she was feeling all right. 'Better for being back here with you two,' she'd said, pinching a slice of pizza from the box on Alexis's lap – something she would never have dared to do not so long ago.

About an hour later she received a text on her mobile: it was from Ethan. *Sorry about tonight. I should have known better. Forgive me, please. X*

Yes, you should have known better, she'd thought as she immediately deleted the message.

And so should she, she thought now in bed with Lawrence. She should never have agreed to anything Ethan had asked of her.

As Lawrence went back to reading his book, she lay down and, staring up at the ceiling, began to sort through the catalogue of offences Ethan had committed. The list seemed pretty trifling when she thought about it, and she couldn't help but wonder if the greatest offence of all hadn't been the offence she had committed herself: that of giving in to him. And it wasn't difficult to figure out why she had done so. She had been charmed and flattered by his attention. She had enjoyed the attention of such an attractive and entertaining man; it had boosted her self-worth after it had taken such a humiliating battering at Mayfield.

But now she had no need of that.

Which meant she had no need of a man – a friend – like Ethan in her life.

'Lawrence,' she said, turning to look at him.

'Yes,' he replied distantly, his eyes still on the page he was reading.

'How would you feel if I moved back in with you at Mayfield?'

His full attention secured, he looked at her. 'Are you serious?'

'Yes. It feels right now.'

He smiled and dispatched the book to the bedside table. 'You have no idea how happy you've just made me.' He kissed her and as she kissed him back, she sank contentedly into the loving warmth of his embrace.

And to hell with paper-thin walls and a creaking bed. Tonight, she wanted to make love with Lawrence.

Chapter Forty-one

Whichever bright spark had come up with the idea that charity began at home hadn't met Maggie's family.

She'd spent the last two nights on her mother's sofa and felt wrecked; she had a crick in her neck and had scarcely slept. Lou had made it very clear that the arrangement was temporary and every opportunity she got, she banged on at Maggie that she had only herself to blame for the mess she was in. Lou's advice was to go home and pretend that nothing had happened. To tough it out.

How exactly was Maggie supposed to do that when no one wanted her back at home? Dave had shown his true colours when he'd finally made it downstairs after his brother had helped him to the loo. 'It's me or your mother,' Maggie had said when she had explained what had gone on. 'I've had enough. Either your mum goes or I do.' His response was to tell her to calm down and to stop being so hysterical. Vernon had muttered something about women always going off at the deep end at a certain time of the month.

'Dave, I am already calm, deadly calm,' she had said. 'You choose now: me or Brenda.'

That was when it must have dawned on Dave that she wasn't mucking about. 'Come off it, Mags,' he'd said. 'Yer can't say something like that. This is my mum we're talking about.'

Unbelievably, right on cue, Brenda had managed to wring a dribble of tears from her dried-out body at this point. What a piece of work she was! 'And me with poor Sid at death's door,' she'd snivelled. 'What kind of a woman have you married, our Dave?'

'A dog killer!' Shelley had leapt in. 'She's a dog killer! And she threatened us, Dave. She threatened to beat us to death with the bloodied shovel she used to murder Babe. She's sick in the bonce, that's what she is!'

Dave had shaken his head. 'Mags, what's got into yer? Yer're normally so, so easy-going and so—'

'So put upon,' she'd interrupted him. 'So taken for granted. So happy to be treated like dirt. Are they the words you're looking for?'

'Oh, here we go,' Vernon had chipped in with a roll of his eyes. 'A bloody woman complaining about her lot; who'd have thought it? She'll be saying next that yer don't listen to her, our Dave.'

'Chance would be a fine thing,' Maggie had fired back. 'So what's it to be, Dave? Have you decided?'

'I reckon Shelley's right,' he'd said. 'Yer're not well, Mags.'

'Is that your answer? To accuse me of having a screw loose?'

'More than one, in my opinion,' Vernon had sneered.

'Yer've got to admit, Mags, yer do sound a bit soft in the head. Yer've never once said a bad word about Mum before. P'rhaps it's clouting Babe the way yer did that's done sommat funny to yer. Y'know, the shock of it.'

'Maybe it's what's brought me to my senses.'

'Come on, Mags, yer don't mean that. Why don't yer make us all a brew and we'll sit down and—'

'If you want a brew, you can make it yourself!'

Thirty minutes later, with two bin liners of her belongings on the back seat of her car, she hurtled off down the road. The only place she could think to go was to her mother's.

Lou's welcome could not have been cooler. The reason for this was that she had company: his name was Gordon. They'd only met a fortnight ago but already he had moved in to her one-bedroomed flat, claiming the hook on the back of the bathroom door for his dressing gown and parking his manky old slippers by his side of Lou's bed. He seemed very at home.

Which was more than Maggie did. She was as welcome as swine flu.

Now, as Gordon – still dressed in his pyjamas and dressing gown at ten thirty in the morning – slurped his tea and dolloped marmalade onto his thickly buttered toast, Lou was advising Maggie on what she should do next. It didn't include the option of staying on indefinitely. 'You've made your point with Dave,' she said above the noise of Gordon chomping like a horse on his toast, 'now go home and make things right with him.'

'And how would you suggest I do that?'

'You say you were upset and didn't mean any of what you said.'

'But I did mean every word of it.'

'Then lie!' snapped Lou.

'Why should I lie? Why should I go on pretending?'

'Because that's what we all have to do in life. What makes you think you're any different from the rest of us? More to the point, you don't have the luxury of choice. You have nowhere else to stay, so you have to go home. And let's face it, it's not the first time you've tried a stunt like this, is it?'

While Maggie felt the sting of Lou's words, Gordon dabbed the air in her direction with the knife he'd just dipped into the pot of marmalade. An orange blob flew through the air and landed in the sugar bowl. 'Your mum's right,' he said. 'You've made your point with your old man. Now you need to swallow your pride and go home. I mean, it's hardly fair to your mum just to land on her out of the blue like this. She's got her own life to get on with.'

And you need to frig off! thought Maggie. 'I'm sorry to be such an inconvenience to you, Mum,' she said stiffly. 'I'll pack my things and leave you in peace.'

'That'll be best all round,' Gordon said. 'Any more tea in the pot, Lou?'

'Coming right up, pet.'

Maggie loaded her bin bags once more into her car and set off for work. She was in no state to make polite conversation with anyone, so it was good that the two families she cleaned for today were either on holiday or at work. Better that she was alone and could fret without interruption.

She didn't have a clue where she was going to spend the night, but it certainly wasn't going to be with Dave. There hadn't been a word from him since she'd left. The only message she had received was from Dean. For a fleeting moment, the mother in her had believed that he cared, that he was in touch to ask her to come home. But no, he'd texted to ask where his lucky T-shirt was, the one he liked to wear when he was in a snooker match. *Try looking in the washing basket*, she had texted back.

Daryl had been right; her family only missed her when she wasn't around to be at their beck and call.

Daryl. She had lost count how many times she had wanted to ring him, to turn to him for help. But she couldn't. She had deleted his number from her mobile. And even if she had his number, what would he think? That only when it suited her – when she was in trouble – did she contact him? He would have every right to tell her to get lost. She also had to accept that if he had really wanted to speak to her, he would have done so by now. He hadn't. But was that because he had respected her decision?

How she wished he hadn't.

She finished work at half past five and sat in her car. What should she do? Go home to Dave?

No!

But as Lou had asked, what was her long-term plan? Had

she left Dave for good? Was that what she had done? Or was she merely making a point as Gordon had implied?

And let's face it, it's not the first time you've tried a stunt like this, is it?

Lou had been referring to the time Maggie had run away as a child. She had been seven years old when she had packed her nightdress and toothbrush and a packet of custard creams into her schoolbag and walked to school as usual. When the bell had rung at the end of the day she had calmly walked away in a completely different direction from her normal route home.

It had been a warm summer's day and she had walked until she found herself in the middle of nowhere. Or what had felt like the middle of nowhere to a seven-year-old child. She'd squeezed through a gap in the hedge and wandered into a large field. Suddenly tired, she had sat down and opened the packet of biscuits she had taken from the kitchen cupboard at home. She had eaten nearly half of them when she lay back on the grass and fell asleep.

It was dark when she woke up. She had never seen such darkness before. There were no street lamps. No shop lights. No car headlights. And it wasn't warm any more. Clutching her knees to her chest for warmth, she had begun to worry about what she'd done.

Mum would be cross with her. Crosser than she usually was. Which was very, *very* cross. Mum had a shout on her louder than a fire engine siren when she wanted. Maggie didn't like it when people were angry; it made her want to squeeze her eyes shut and stick her fingers in her ears. Sometimes she hid under the bed. She had done that the other night. Mum and her new friend, Colin, had been rowing. They'd been rowing about Maggie. Mum had come in from work and found Maggie sitting on his lap as he brushed her hair while they watched the telly together. It had been nice because it made her think that maybe Colin really might become her new dad.

Her real dad had left when she was four years old. For ages

after she had thought he would come back to see her, but he hadn't. Mum had told her not to be so stupid – that her father was never coming back, that he was a useless waster. From then on she hoped that each new boyfriend her mother had would be like a proper dad to her.

Colin had been great; whenever he came to the house he always brought her sweets or a small toy. Often he would come when Mum was at work and he'd cook the tea. But last night, when Mum had come home and found Maggie sitting on Colin's lap, she had gone berserk. She'd sent Maggie to her room and shouted at Colin.

Later, when Colin had gone, Mum had started on Maggie. 'Why do you always have to spoil everything for me?' she'd yelled. Her cheeks were bright red and there were tears in her eyes, something Maggie had never seen before. Maggie hadn't known exactly why her mother was so cross, but upset that it was obviously something she'd done, she'd decided it might be better to run away, to let Mum have all the fun she wanted without her being in the way and spoiling it.

The sound of a dog barking made Maggie clutch her knees even tighter. Maybe it wasn't a dog. Maybe it was a wolf. A wild wolf that would eat her. She began to cry. She was cold and frightened now. She wanted to go home. She didn't want to be here in this big empty field; she wanted to go to sleep in her own bed. But Mum would be angry with her. She could hear Mum shouting at her in her head. She covered her ears with her hands and started to cry. It was the only way to stop the sound of Mum's angry shouting.

She fell asleep again and this time when she woke up, it was light. Her legs and arms were stiff and cold and she was hungry. She ate the rest of the biscuits and walked to the edge of the field. She hoped it was the way she had come. It wasn't. The gap in the hedge wasn't there, but there was a large metal gate. She climbed over it and followed a path.

Ahead of her she could see a house. She wondered if the person who owned it would let her use their toilet. She suddenly needed to go very badly. A big shaggy dog appeared from behind the house and seeing her it barked and rushed towards her. It was as big as a horse and she froze on the spot, terrified. And then she wet herself. The dog sniffed at her legs and the puddle on the ground. But still she couldn't move.

A door opened and a woman came out of the house. 'No need to be scared, lass,' she said. 'The dog's more likely to lick you to death than eat you.' She came towards Maggie. 'What you doin' round here so early in the morning, anyhow? Got lost on your way to school, did you?'

All Maggie could do was nod.

'Well, you look nithered to death! How about we get you cleaned up and then maybe you'd like something to eat?'

Maggie nodded again.

Inside the house, the woman said, 'Do you think we ought to ring your parents and let them know you're okay?'

'I don't have a dad,' Maggie blurted out.

'That's a shame. How about a mother? You have one of those?'

'Yes, but she'll be angry with me if I go home.' For a crazy moment Maggie imagined herself staying here with this woman and her dog that was still sniffing at her legs and shoes.

The woman smiled kindly. 'Being angry is all part and parcel of being a mother. Now then, let's get you sorted with a nice warm bath. By the way, what's your name?'

It was while Maggie was upstairs in the biggest bath she had ever seen, that the woman must have called the police. By the time she was wrapped in a towel and downstairs eating a bacon sandwich with the enormous dog sitting at her feet, a policewoman and Maggie's mum had arrived. Maggie had never seen her mum really cry before and she felt awful that she was the reason for making her so upset. Back at home Mum made Maggie promise that she would never do anything so silly again.

*

But all these years on and she had run away from home again.

Had she gone off at the deep end and overreacted? She replayed the scene in her mind and decided that she hadn't. Dave should have backed her up. He hadn't. He'd sided with his family.

But did she have any right to feel angry with him? After all, she had been seeing Daryl on the sly. Frankly, she didn't have a leg to stand on when it came to what was right and wrong. Yet she had tried. She had tried to put Daryl behind her, to make the best of a bad job with her marriage. She had thrown away the chance to be happy with Daryl only to be miserable with Dave and his rotten family.

Now she had nothing.

Or did she? Could she go to Daryl?

Only one way to find out.

She couldn't call him, but she could go and see him.

The nearer she got to where the *Bohemian Rhapsody* was moored on the canal, the more Maggie's hopes rose. She pictured Daryl's face when he saw her, pictured his arms around her, pictured him saying everything was going to be all right now.

Breathless with anticipation she spotted Daryl's car parked in its usual place. She left hers next to his and walked along the towpath. The light was beginning to fade and the canal was still and very quiet. A pair of swans gliding on the water peered at her – their toffee-nosed expressions reminded Maggie of Mrs Edwards and Mrs Paxton.

There was only one other boat permanently moored on this stretch of the canal and Maggie caught a glimpse of Daryl's neighbour inside his boat as he stood at the small sink washing up. She pressed further along the towpath, her excitement growing.

When she was almost level with Daryl's boat, she stopped to steady her breathing. The pair of snooty swans had kept pace with her and once more treated her to one of their high and mighty looks.

It was then that she heard the sound of laughter. A woman's laugh. It was coming from the *Bohemian Rhapsody*.

She moved closer to the nearest window, the window Maggie knew belonged to Daryl's bedroom. The curtains were drawn but there was a small gap; a soft light glowed through it. Not really knowing why she was doing it, she bent down and peered through the gap. Lying on Daryl's bed was a woman. And she didn't have any clothes on.

Maggie ran back to her car, tears streaming down her cheeks.

Wrong, wrong, wrong *again*, Maggie Storm!

How could she be so stupid? How could she have thought that Daryl wouldn't have moved on to someone new?

She had been as stupid as the seven-year-old runaway who had thought she could stay for ever with the kind woman and the big dog.

Chapter Forty-two

Originally Hal Moran had had very little idea as to how he wanted Belmont Hall to be decorated and had been quite happy to leave all the decisions to the interior decorator and Ella.

Recently, though, he had had a change of heart and wanted to be a lot more involved in the process, to the extent of having declined any further help from Lesley, the interior decorator. He'd confided in Ella that he found some of Lesley's ideas too over the top for his taste and had subsequently asked Ella to take charge, on the basis that his input would be given serious consideration. He'd also made it clear that he didn't want the place turned into a poser's palace, as he'd called it. He wanted to create a real home for himself – a home in which he could live comfortably without feeling he was rattling around in it. The challenge to do this with an eight-bedroom period country house with over a hundred acres of gardens and parkland complete with lake, once owned by a wealthy cotton manufacturer, was a tall order, but not impossible.

Ella had proposed they start work on his bedroom next – she felt sorry for Hal, still 'camping' on bare floorboards with no curtains and no proper bed to sleep on – but he had overruled her and asked for her to start work on the drawing room.

He had become one of her favourite clients, not just because he would be keeping her employed for many months to come and had therefore placed himself in the A-list category of long-term and lucrative customers. She would never take advantage of his goodwill, though, and nor would she over-charge him. Occasionally she did do this with a particularly obnoxious client, such as Mrs Edwards. She had, however, as she'd got to know Ethan, grown increasingly guilty about her inflated bill. But she felt no guilt now. Not after Abersoch and Ethan's stream of improper questions and insinuations. In her opinion she had earned every penny of that commission.

In her car now as she drove out through the electric gates of Belmont Hall, and using hands-free, she called Maggie on her mobile. Hal had asked if she knew of anyone trustworthy and reliable who would consider taking on the cleaning of the house for him. 'Actually, more than just cleaning,' he had explained. 'I want someone to take care of the place and to do all the things that I hate doing, like shopping and cooking.'

'You want a housekeeper?' Ella had clarified.

'That sounds a bit grand to me. I wouldn't want anyone to think I was getting above myself.'

She had smiled at that. Hal may well live in one of the grandest houses in the area, but he was the least grand person she knew.

Ella was on the verge of ending the call when finally Maggie answered. Or rather she thought it was Maggie – she couldn't be sure; the voice was so different, sort of muffled and barely audible. 'Maggie? Is that you? It's me, Ella.'

There was a long pause and then what Ella could only describe as a strangled sob. 'Maggie?' she tried again.

'I'm sorry, Ella. Now isn't a good time.'

'Why, what's wrong? What's happened?'

'It's ... it's—' another strangled sob. 'It's nothing.'

'It doesn't sound like nothing. Is there anything I can do to help?'

'I don't think there's anything anyone can do to help. I've ... I've been such a fool.'

A stab of apprehension pierced Ella. 'Is it something to do with that man you told me about?'

Silence from Maggie.

Ella took the silence as a yes and she began to feel uneasy. She had encouraged Maggie, hadn't she? She had told her life was short. She had said, 'Why not take a chance on being happy?'

'Where are you, Maggie? Can I come and see you?'

'I'm in my car and ... and I don't know what to do. My husband doesn't want me. And Daryl certainly doesn't.'

Ella took a deep breath. This was her doing. She was responsible. She owed it to Maggie to help all she could. 'Right,' she said. 'Here's what we'll do.'

Ethan wasn't exactly off his face, as Valentina would put it, but he was far from sober. It was Tony Clarkson's fault. If the man wasn't such a raging bore and a huge embarrassment to be seen with, Ethan wouldn't have felt the need to drink until the urge to ram a fist into Tony's leering, self-satisfied, ugly, bloated face had passed. As the evening turned to night, with each glass of wine that he downed, followed by two double whiskies, the brain-numbing boredom had lessened.

Tony had arrived in the office that afternoon and, after two hours of crunching the numbers, banging out percentages and convincing Tony he was getting preferential treatment because their relationship was special and would always be special, Ethan had accepted Tony's invitation to keep him company for the evening.

I'd rather perform open-heart surgery on myself, Ethan had thought. 'Great idea,' he had replied. Tony had gone on to say, 'And why not bring that lovely wife of yours along?' But Ethan had had more than enough of his 'lovely wife' in Abersoch over the Easter weekend. Moreover he didn't think Francine would thank him for asking her to be in the same room as a man she detested, even if he was one of Ethan's most important clients. He was showing an encouraging amount of interest in the new line of throws, cushions, tablecloths and matching napkins Ethan was trying out – a line he had invested in heavily. If it didn't work, he would be facing some serious losses.

So, gone midnight and he was drunk enough to have got through the evening and to see Tony safely installed in his hotel, but sober enough to know that he shouldn't risk driving home. He needed a taxi.

He wandered in the direction of where he thought there was a taxi rank, not far from where the local nightlife took place – a solitary nightclub called Secrets. He knew that Valentina and Katie had secretly frequented the place, despite being underage. He knew this because Warren, the techie consultant, was a regular visitor himself and had told Ethan he had spotted Valentina there with a group of girls on more than one occasion. Ethan had bunged Warren some money and asked him to keep an eye out for his daughter. He could have tried banning Valentina from going near the club, but what was the point? Anyway, according to Warren it was pretty safe and well run. Their eye for discerning underage girls was unquestionably not what it could be – didn't they have an ID policy? – but there again, by the time Valentina was fully decked out she looked much older than her fifteen years and could easily pass for eighteen.

He was in the back of a taxi and listening to Coldplay on the crackly radio when he suddenly had an idea. A genius idea. Why go straight home? He had the perfect excuse to stay out as long as he wanted: Francine knew of old that an evening spent with Tony never ended early.

He leaned forward to the driver and told him there had been a change of plan.

He instructed the taxi driver to park a short distance away; he didn't want his surprise ruined by the sound of an engine running and giving him away.

He walked along the kerb of the pavement, testing that he was able to walk in a straight line. There, not drunk at all, he told himself proudly as he mastered the kerb. Moments later he realized he'd been so intent on his purpose he'd overshot. He retraced his steps, this time extending his arms as if he was on a tightrope. When he'd found the right house, he slipped round the back and, adjusting his eyes to the darkness, reached over to release the catch on the gate. '*Ssh!*' He scolded the wooden gate when it creaked noisily in the deathly quiet of the night.

There were no lights on downstairs or upstairs. A window was open, though. As he took up his position on the terrace a security light flashed on and dazzled him to the point of blindness. When he'd recovered his sight, he smiled. Perfect. A spotlight to enhance his performance. How would she be able to resist?

She had known she wouldn't be able to sleep, so when she heard the creak of the gate, she was out of bed in an instant. Her heart banging against her ribs, she ventured over to the window she had left open, where light was flooding in through the curtains. Just as she was about to inch the curtains carefully apart so she could peer out without being seen, she heard the strangest thing: singing. There was someone singing out there.

She looked down into the brightly lit garden and got the surprise of her life.

Ethan was enjoying himself tremendously. Singing at the top of his voice and flinging his arms about him, he wondered why he had never thought of doing this before. What better way to declare his feelings than to sing and dance for Ella? Especially when he was singing one of her favourite songs.

Okay, he was a bit limited when it came to the lyrics, but what he lacked in lyrical know-how, he was making up for in volume and agility. He was giving it all he had. She deserved no less. He started to whirl around, then suddenly found himself losing his balance and falling.

The next thing he knew his head was making contact with something hard. Something very hard indeed.

This wasn't part of his genius plan.

Chapter Forty-three

'Mr Edwards, can you hear me?' It was the third time Maggie had asked the question. And the third time she had wondered what on earth had been going on between him and Ella. Finally he stirred, with a low groan.

'Thank goodness for that,' she said with relief.

'Is that you, my sweet darling Ella?' His voice was thick and slurred and he reeked of booze. This wasn't the neat-as-a-new-pin Mr Edwards she knew.

'Mr Edwards, it's me, Maggie.'

'I was singing for you, Ella. Did you like it? Did you like my dancing? I was dancing for you. Maggie? Who's Maggie?'

'Maggie Storm, your cleaner. Try opening your eyes, Mr Edwards.'

He did. Bleary-eyed, his focus came and went, then held fast. 'Maggie? What are you doing here?'

More to the point, she wanted to ask, what are you doing here? 'I'm staying here,' she said.

'With Ella? Where is she?'

'Ella isn't here. She's ... Well, never mind that. Come on, let's see if we can get you inside and I'll take a look at your head. You went down with a heck of a bang. That and the noise you were making before you fell must have woken up half the neighbourhood. Let's hope no one's called the police.' No sooner had she said the words than a window opened next door. 'Everything all right down there?' came a man's voice.

'Fine, thanks,' Maggie called back. She supposed it was

Ella's neighbour, Phil. Ella had said that she'd explained to him that a friend of hers would be staying for a while.

Initially Mr Edwards was like a dead weight as she tried to haul him to his feet, but then his body seemed to come to life, along with his brain, and he was upright and looking at her with embarrassment. 'I suppose you're wondering what the devil I'm doing here, aren't you?' he said.

'It's none of my business, Mr Edwards,' she said. She led him inside the house to the kitchen, sat him in a chair at the table and took a look at the back of his head. She winced. 'I was right; you've got yourself a nasty crack there. No, don't touch it,' she said as he moved his hand to feel the damage. He ignored her.

'I'm bleeding,' he murmured when he saw his hand. He sounded as surprised as a small boy who had just cut himself for the first time.

'No flies on you, Mr Edwards. Now I'm no expert, but I think you might need a few stitches.'

'I'd rather not.'

'Not even to be on the safe side?'

'But that would be the second time this year that I've had to go to A and E. It makes me look accident prone at best, a dangerous lunatic at worst. Can't you clean me up and stick a plaster on? I'm sure that would do.'

Maggie reluctantly did as he asked. And really, once she had cleaned away the blood, it didn't look so bad. 'You were lucky,' she said when she had closed the lid of the first-aid box that she had found in the bathroom upstairs. 'It could have been a lot worse.'

'Thank you,' he said. 'Thank you very much, Maggie.'

An awkward silence followed, during which she remembered she was wearing a nightdress and nothing else. It didn't feel at all right. But then nothing about the last twenty minutes had felt right. 'How about some coffee to—' she was going to say 'to sober you up', but thought it sounded too forward of her and said instead, 'to clear your head?'

318

'Oh God, is it so obvious that I'm horribly drunk?'

'Believe me, I've seen drunker men.'

It took her a while to find everything, but before too long they were both sitting at the table with two mugs of instant coffee.

'Obviously this is all rather embarrassing for me,' he said quietly.

'Obviously,' she repeated.

'Um … any chance we could keep it between ourselves? My wife doesn't need—' His voice trailed off.

'I won't breathe a word of it. But how will you explain the bump on your head to her?'

He shrugged. 'I'll say I was mugged. Again.'

'And what about Ella?'

'What about Ella?'

'It seems a shame she missed your performance out there on the patio. I'm sure she would have enjoyed it. Are you going to tell her what you did?'

'I don't know. Probably, when I've stopped feeling so foolish.'

Maggie smiled. 'You scared the living daylights out of me, you know.'

'I'm sorry about that. Obviously I didn't expect to find you here.'

'Obviously,' she repeated once more.

He took a sip of his coffee. 'Do you mind if I ask what you're doing here? Not that it's any of my business.'

'Long story. Basically I didn't have anywhere else to go and Ella's letting me stay until I get myself sorted.'

'I didn't know the two of you were such good friends. Where is she? Away with work?'

'She's moved back in with her fella.'

Mr Edwards put down his mug and stared across the room. 'That man's so dull he could give watching paint dry a run for its money,' he muttered.

'I wouldn't know about that,' Maggie said carefully. She

watched Mr Edwards pick up his mug and continued to watch him as he drank from it. He seemed to be thinking hard.

'I thought you were married, Maggie,' he said eventually.

'I am.'

He gave her a searching look. 'So why aren't you at home with Mr Storm?'

'I ... I suddenly didn't see any reason to stay.'

'I'm sorry to hear that. Have things been going wrong for a while between the two of you?'

'You could say that.'

'Can you put it right?'

'I don't know. I'm not sure that—'

'So you walked out with nowhere to go,' he interrupted. 'That was either very brave or very foolhardy.'

'I don't need anyone to tell me that I've been stupid,' she said defensively.

He raised a hand. 'Sorry,' he said. 'That came out wrong. Go on, I interrupted you.'

'Not much more to say,' she said with a small shrug. 'I left. I got in the car and left. As simple as that. I stayed with my mum for a couple of nights, but she's got some new fella living with her and I couldn't have been more unwelcome, so then I thought I could—' She stopped herself. Why was she telling Mr Edwards, of all people, this?

'And then what did you think you could do?' he pressed.

She sighed and told him what she had told Ella.

'That's rough,' he said when she had finished. 'But maybe it's worth getting in touch with Daryl properly. After all, he might only have taken up with somebody new because he needed a distraction, a way to move on. It's human nature.'

'That's what Ella said.'

He suddenly smiled and began to look much more his usual handsome self. The colour was back in his face too. 'Oh well,' he said. 'If Ella said it, it must be true.'

Having been so honest with him, Maggie saw no reason not to ask Mr Edwards a few questions. Fair exchange was no robbery and all that. 'So what's going on between you and Ella?' she asked bluntly.

'Nothing. Absolutely nothing.'

'Didn't look like nothing to me when you were singing and dancing your heart out in the garden,' she said with a smile.

He took a moment to reply, opened his mouth to speak, but then closed it. He reached for a tablemat and traced a finger round the edge of it. 'This stays strictly between us,' he said. 'Right?'

'Of course.'

'The truth is, there's nothing going on between Ella and me. And not for lack of trying on my part, but Ella is made of stronger stuff than you or I. She can resist temptation; it slides right off her as though she's made of Teflon.'

Maggie laughed. 'Maybe she just doesn't fancy you, Mr Edwards. Ever thought of that?'

He laughed too. 'Tell it how it is, why don't you?'

'I should have done that a long time ago.'

'You mean with Mr Storm?'

'Him and his rotten family. Every man Jack of them.'

'How many years have you been cleaning for my wife and me, Maggie?'

'Over four years.'

'You probably know more about us as a family than a lot of people,' he said, thoughtfully.

She nodded. 'It's part of the job. You clean a person's house, you discover all sorts of things about them. Not that I've ever gone snooping.'

'I wasn't suggesting that you had.' He finished his coffee. 'I ought to be going,' he said, getting to his feet. 'It's late.'

'You didn't drive here, did you?' she asked after she had looked at her watch: it was almost three o'clock. He may have sobered up since hitting his head, but he'd been pretty drunk before then. The thought of him behind the wheel didn't bear thinking about.

'No, I didn't drive; I came by taxi.'

'How will you get home? I doubt we'll be able to get a taxi at this time of night.'

'Oh,' he said. 'Good question. Good thing one of us is thinking.'

'You could stay here, I suppose, but I'm not sure how Ella would feel about that. I could drive you home, if you want.'

'Both of those options seem like a huge imposition.'

In the end, Maggie got dressed and drove him to The Lilacs. At his request, she stopped at the turning for Lilac Avenue and after he had thanked her for the hundredth time, she watched him walk away in the light from the street lamps, his shoulders hunched, his head down. Poor bugger, she thought, going home to that bitch of a wife. Whatever had he done to deserve her?

But fancy him having a thing for Ella! And for all Maggie saying that you get to know a family well by cleaning for them, she hadn't suspected a thing about Mr Edwards and Ella. She had to hand it to Ella; she played her cards close to her chest.

Driving back to Tickle Cottage, she wondered about what both Ella and Mr Edwards had said about Daryl. Were they right? Should she get in touch with him?

Chapter Forty-four

Ella was running late. She had promised to call in on Maggie after they had both finished work, but she had been so determined to complete the gilt finish to the cornice in the drawing room at Belmont Hall she had lost track of the time. It was only when Hal had come into the room and stood at the bottom of the scaffolding admiring her work and then remarked how late it was, that she remembered she was supposed to be meeting Maggie. She quickly packed up her things, left an apologetic message on Maggie's voicemail and drove home.

It was early days – she had only moved back to Mayfield two days ago – but mentally home was still Tickle Cottage. By no means had she moved in completely, and of course there was the enormous task of transferring the contents of her workshop to carry out yet, but *piano, piano* as the Italians would say.

Lat night Lawrence had queried her decision to let Maggie stay indefinitely in her house. His concern, he claimed, was based on Ella not really knowing the woman and who knew what trouble she might have brought upon herself? Ella suspected that Lawrence's attitude had a lot to do with class. In his eyes, Maggie was a cleaner and therefore could never be considered a friend or an equal. The closest he had ever got to the women who had cleaned for him over the years was to leave them a scribbled note of instructions on the kitchen worktop, along with their wages.

Ella had never been into all that class rubbish. There but for the grace of God go I, had always been her maxim. Her grandmother had worked as a scullery maid when she had been fourteen and had eventually risen to the rank of cook. She had stopped work when she married a boiler fitter and had her first child – Ella's mother – a year later.

But Lawrence was from a different background and so Ella didn't judge him too harshly for having a view that had been instilled in him since birth. He was solidly upper middle class, public school educated – Oundle – and politically to the right, but not so far right as to set any alarm bells ringing for Ella. It had been a constant source of amusement to her at the start of their relationship whenever he'd joked that he would soon cure her of her misguided inclination towards socialism, just as he had with Abigail. Her response had been to assure him that no such thing would happen and that, if anything, it was he who would be converted to her way of thinking.

The day Toby had moved up into the sixth form and announced that he wanted to be a member of the Labour Party, Lawrence could not have been more horrified. Toby might just as well have said he wanted to join a devil-worshipping sect. Lawrence had then accused Ella of having a hand in Toby's defection. She had laughed and told him not to be so daft. 'What else do you expect from your highly intelligent son? At his age it's the done thing to have left-wing tendencies.'

'But I didn't,' Lawrence had asserted.

Ella had laughed again and kissed him. He really did look so appalled. 'Don't worry,' she said. 'I'm sure you'll get over the shock before too long.'

It was whenever Lawrence found himself hopelessly out of his depth, and vulnerably confused as a consequence, that Ella felt that she loved him most. It was also when she felt at her strongest and most capable. It was that innate sense of wanting to make the world a better place for Lawrence, of wanting to make him happy, that first led her to believe that she could spend the rest of her life with him. She had never experienced those feelings for anyone else. It was a powerful emotion knowing that you made a difference to someone's life, that you were needed.

When she pulled up outside Tickle Cottage and parked on the road – with Maggie's car on the drive there wasn't room for hers – she switched off the engine and thought of what Lawrence had said at breakfast that morning, about putting her house on the market. Her immediate reaction was that she wasn't ready to sell it yet. 'Why not wait until the market has really picked up?' she had replied. 'Meanwhile I could rent it out.'

A piece of toast in his hand, he had kissed the top of her head as he passed her on his way out of the kitchen to go to work. 'Whatever you think best,' he'd said. 'It's your house; I was only making a suggestion. Alexis,' he called upstairs, 'this is your final warning. If you're not down here in two seconds you'll have to walk to school.'

'I think you'll find she's still in bed and fast asleep,' Ella had said. 'It's the Easter holidays, remember?'

He'd groaned. 'Now you see how hopeless I am without you?' He'd kissed her again, this time on the mouth, leaving her with crumbs and the tangy taste of lime and grapefruit marmalade on her lips.

Maggie had the front door open before Ella had even got out of the car. On the one hand it was a welcoming gesture, but on the other it was weird because nothing could have made Ella feel more like a guest in her own home. It was compounded further when Maggie said the kettle had just boiled and did she want tea or coffee?

But the feeling was soon forgotten when Maggie, after thanking her yet again for letting her stay, said, 'Ella, something happened here last night that I think you should know about.'

Maggie had been in two minds about telling Ella. Ethan had said he didn't want his wife to know, but he hadn't said anything about keeping it from Ella. And anyway, if Ella had been here, she would have seen and heard him for herself.

'You're joking,' Ella murmured, her eyes wide. 'Please tell me you're joking.'

Maggie shook her head. 'Sorry, but it really did happen. It was quite funny really. Well, not the bit when he banged his head. I was terrified he'd killed himself.'

'Another stunt like that and I'll kill him myself!'

'Oh, don't say that.'

'But what the hell did he think he was doing?'

Maggie smiled. 'Serenading the woman he loves, I suppose.'

'That man doesn't know the first thing about love. Honestly, I could ... I could throttle the stupid idiot! What was he singing? Something insufferably trite, I bet.'

'It was that Coldplay song, Viva something or other. He said in the car afterwards when I was driving him home that you liked to dance to it. He said that was why he chose it.'

Ella frowned. Then she felt her face blushing and her expression softening. 'Whatever am I going to do with him?'

'Search me. But I know this, I'd give anything for Daryl to do something like that for me.'

'Maybe if he knew that you were interested in him again, he would.'

Maggie shook her head. 'I can't get the picture of that woman on his boat out of my mind.'

'What about your husband? Have you heard anything from him?'

'Not a peep. Just goes to show, he didn't give a rat's arse for me. Excuse my language.'

Ella smiled. 'No apology required. You know you can stay here for as long as you need, don't you?'

'Thank you, but I'm going to get myself organized. I'm done with crying. Tomorrow I'm going to start looking for a small place to rent. I've got my bingo winnings safely tucked away in a building society account, so it's not like I'm penniless. By the way, what was it you rang me for yesterday?'

Ella had to think. 'Oh my goodness!' she exclaimed after a few moments. 'I'd forgotten all about that, what with being so concerned about you. But thinking about it, this might just be an answer to a prayer for you.'

'Really? I could do with some good news.'

'A client of mine needs someone to run the domestic side of his life – a sort of informal housekeeper if you will, someone to shop and cook and take care of all the things he doesn't have time for. I'll warn you, though, it's a big house, so you'd have your work cut out.'

'A general dogsbody, is what you're saying?'

'I don't think he'd view it that way.'

'What's he like?'

'He's great. Young, not married, and one of the most considerate people I've ever worked for. And the best bit is, there's separate accommodation available so you could live in if you wanted. What do you think?'

'I don't know. I've never done anything like that before. What about all my other cleaning jobs?'

'I wouldn't like to say. The thing to do would be to meet him and discuss exactly what he requires and what the wages would be. Maybe you could work solely for him.'

Maggie thought about it. 'No more Mrs Edwards,' she said quietly. 'No more Mrs Paxton. That alone means it's definitely worth a punt.'

When Ella let herself in at Mayfield, there was no sign of Lawrence, but Alexis was in the kitchen. She was stirring the contents of a large mixing bowl. It was a classic scene of domestic bliss and added to Ella's thoroughly good mood.

She had left Maggie far happier this evening than she had last night. With the prospect of a potentially well-paid job at Belmont Hall – Ella was convinced Hal would not be stingy when it came to money – Maggie had something positive to think about now. Ella had to admit that she had got ahead of herself a little, as Hal hadn't actually said anything about anyone living in, but really there was a lot of sense in having someone on site permanently.

'What are you making?' Ella asked.

'Chocolate brownies,' Alexis answered her. 'I've decided I need brain food, you know, to help me revise.'

'An excellent idea if ever I heard one. Where's your dad?'

'Playing squash with Jonty.'

'He didn't mention that this morning. Have you eaten?'

'I made myself some scrambled eggs on toast earlier. Dad's going on to the pub for something to eat after his squash game. Could be a late night for him. You know what he and Jonty are like when they get together. Oh, he told me to tell you he's made an appointment for an estate agent to take a look at your house tomorrow. Around lunchtime, I think he said.'

So much for it being her house and doing whatever Ella thought was best. 'I don't think that's entirely convenient for me,' she said, her good mood leaching away and replaced with something she would rather not put a name to. She went over to the fridge. Scrambled eggs sounded the perfect supper dish for her as well.

'I hope you're not looking for any eggs,' Alexis said. 'I've used the last of them for the brownies. We're running low on loo rolls as well; you and Dad need to hit the supermarket tomorrow.'

Ella closed the fridge door, disappointed.

'Why isn't it convenient tomorrow?' Alexis said as she tipped the brownie mixture out of the mixing bowl and into a non-stick baking tray; it was one of those rubbery silicone trays, the type Ella had never tried using – they gave her the heebie-jeebies for some unaccountable reason.

'I'm working at Belmont Hall again tomorrow,' she said, 'and it's nowhere near my house, ergo, it'll take up too much of my valuable time to schlep all that way just to meet an estate agent.'

'Maybe Dad could meet the agent instead of you.'

Fiddling with a screwed up tea towel that was on the table where Alexis was now smoothing the surface of the brownie mixture with a knife, Ella could feel herself growing restless with annoyance. What was the hurry to sell her house? Why was everyone being so quick to help her do it? It was *her* house. She would sell it when she was good and ready. She watched Alexis open the oven door and place the baking tray inside – the rubbery baking tray that defied the natural laws of baking; surely it should combust?

Which was probably what she would have done had she been at home last night when Ethan had carried out his ridiculous song and dance routine. Really, what had he been thinking? What if she hadn't moved out and Lawrence had been there with her?

After leaving Maggie and driving back to Mayfield, Ella had begun to see the funny side of what he had done. Or more precisely, the funny side of the exact moment he realized his performance had been watched by the wrong person. What a shock he must have got when he looked up into Maggie's face.

But thank God Maggie had promised not to tell a soul about her late-night visitor. The last thing Ella needed – and presumably Ethan, too – was someone blabbing to all and sundry that Ethan was crazy about her. Crazy being the operative word.

She would have to speak to him. She would have to make it very clear that if he couldn't be trusted to behave himself like a normal human being, she would have to take steps. What steps exactly, she had not the slightest idea. But he had to be made to understand that he could not go around making such grandiose gestures. It had crossed her mind more than once that had she thrown herself at him from the outset, he would have got her out of his system a long time ago. Right now he was like a child obsessed with something he wanted and could not have.

Well, tough luck sonny Jim! I'm definitely something you can't have.

'Hel-*lo*, anyone at home?'

Ella roused herself from her thoughts. 'Sorry, Alexis, what were you saying?'

'I was just saying,' she ran her finger round the inside of the mixing bowl and licked it with undisguised pleasure, 'that maybe Dad could meet the agent for you tomorrow.'

'I'll speak to your father later when he gets back. But I really have no intention of selling just yet.'

Alexis stopped licking her finger and looked at Ella. 'Why? Are you already regretting your decision to move back in with us?'

The sharp tone to Alexis's question took Ella by surprise. 'Of course not,' she said. 'I just don't think now is the best time to sell. I want to investigate the rental market first.'

'You know, don't you, that so long as you have your house, Dad'll always be worried that you'll run off again.'

Again Ella was taken by surprise by the girl's directness. Although, of course, given their inglorious history, she should never be surprised by anything Alexis did or said. 'I didn't run off, Alexis,' she said coolly. 'I've never run away from any-thing in my life. If you remember, I was more or less pushed out of this house. You made it very clear that I wasn't wanted or needed. You wore me down and I gave in. You got what you wanted. At the time,' Ella added, to counter the harshness of her words.

Alexis's dark eyes flashed warningly. 'I knew it! I knew it all along. You're never going to forgive me, are you?'

Ella sighed with tired exasperation. How had they got into this? She had been looking forward to a pleasant problem-free evening with Lawrence, dinner with a nice glass of wine (that was one thing with Lawrence you could guarantee), a chat and maybe something interesting on the telly to watch together, and what had she got instead? Nothing to eat and questions and accusations that would put the MPs' expenses inquiry to shame. 'We've discussed this before,' she said, straining to be patient. 'Naturally neither of us can forget what happened, but we've put it behind us, haven't we?'

When Alexis didn't reply, Ella said, 'I wouldn't be here if I didn't believe you wanted me back permanently.'

'Prove it to me. And to Dad. Sell your house.'

In his office at home – leaving Francine and Valentina to the brain-rotting delights of *All New America's Next Top Model* – Ethan was still trying to come to terms with what he had done last night.

What a crackpot idea he'd come up with. With the laser logic of the man who'd drunk too much he'd really excelled himself. Every time he thought of what he'd done he felt like throwing himself under his desk and hiding there for ever, or at least until the worst of his crippling shame had passed.

Parts of the freak show he'd put on for Ella's benefit were lost to him. For instance, he couldn't really remember entering her garden or how he had ended up hitting his head. Maggie had said he'd been spinning like a top and had simply lost his balance and thwacked his head against the edge of a large terracotta pot.

He remembered very clearly, however, how excruciatingly embarrassed he had felt when he'd been sitting in Ella's kitchen drinking coffee with Maggie. He would have to find a way to thank her. Only he didn't want her to think he was trying to buy her silence; that would make it look like he didn't trust the promise she had made to keep quiet. He had no reason to doubt that she would be discreet when it came to his wife, but he would put money on it that she would let Ella know what had taken place. They had probably already had a jolly good laugh at his expense.

But he could hardly blame them. *And the winner for Most Stupid Act of the Month goes to Ethan Edwards!* It was quite possibly the most out-of-character thing he had done in his entire life. Never before had he gone to such lengths to show someone how much he cared about them. And he really did care for Ella.

Okay, let's not beat about the bush. When he used the word 'care' what he meant was, he was in serious danger of falling in love with her. Maybe he already had. All he knew was that he couldn't stop thinking about her. In particular he couldn't stop thinking that she was making a terrible mistake taking up where she had left off with that Lawrence character. The thought of them in bed together was driving him mad.

But what could he do to stop her? He was in no position to offer her what in an ideal world he would want to offer. To do that he would have to give up everything he had spent a lifetime working for.

Why couldn't he just forget he had ever met her? How had she got under his skin to the extent she had? Perhaps he should do what poor Maggie's bloke had done: go out and find someone new to distract him.

A pinging sound from his computer announced the arrival of an email. He sat up straight when he saw that it was from Ella. Oh shit, he thought. This could mean only one thing. He opened the email and saw that he was right.

All it said was: *WE NEED TO TALK*. She had used capital letters, leaving him in no doubt just exactly what it was she wanted to discuss with him.

Chapter Forty-five

At Belmont Hall Ella was racking her brains trying to come up with a suitable meeting place.

She had narrowed it down to two options: a) somewhere they would be as well hidden as a couple of pebbles on a beach, a place in which if they were spotted, it would be quite reasonable to explain the situation as being nothing more than a chance meeting. Just as it had happened in Abersoch. Or, b) an isolated place so off the beaten track no one they knew would chance upon them.

Another ten minutes of brain-racking whilst moving dust-sheets and mixing paint and she decided on option b. She texted Ethan accordingly and resumed work.

She really wasn't cut out for a life of deception and skulduggery. Unlike some people she could mention. Ethan bloody Edwards for one! Now there was a man who had turned sneaking around into an art form.

And now it seemed Lawrence wasn't above some sneaking around of his own. She was still rattled that he had arranged for an agent to value her house without speaking to her about it first. 'I just thought it would help get the ball rolling,' he'd said late last night when he was back from his evening out with Jonty and they were in bed. 'I didn't realize it would be any kind of a big deal to you. I'm sorry.'

'It isn't a big deal,' she had responded as airily as she could.

'So why are you sitting there with your arms folded and with that look I know all too well on your face?'

She had unfolded her arms and said, 'What look? I didn't know I had a look.'

Laughing, he had taken one of her hands and put it to his lips. 'You have a vast range of looks, all of which I am fully acquainted with. This one says I overstepped the mark. It also says that only a fool would have blundered into an area that was so clearly signposted "Private – Trespassers Will Be Shot!" I'm sorry. Am I forgiven?'

He had defused the situation so effectively it would have been churlish of her to pursue the subject. Or to raise with him what Alexis had said, that maybe he needed rock-solid proof – in the form of selling her house – that she wasn't about to leave him again. But did such a thing exist? Was there any such thing as rock-solid certainty in life?

Ethan was waiting for her in the car park of the Cat and Fiddle Inn. Located on the infamously dangerous road between Macclesfield and Buxton, it was an uninspiring-looking pub, primarily known for being the second-highest point in England.

That she had found time to come here but not to meet the estate agent troubled Ella to a degree, but right now Ethan was her priority. She would sell, or indeed rent out her house all in good time, but Ethan had to be dealt with urgently.

'You picked a nice day for it,' he said cheerfully when she got out of her car and he came over.

'A nice day for what exactly?' she snapped, determined to strip him of any cheerfulness and the opportunity to make light of the trouble he seemed intent on causing her.

'For giving me a rollicking.' He turned abruptly and looked out across the vast expanse of moorland. The sky was clear and the sun bright. Annoyingly, he was right; it really was a beautiful day. 'You know, it's years since I've been up here,' he said. 'I know the plan was to hide ourselves away inside the pub whilst you take me to task, but since I'm a condemned man, allow me a final request: let's walk. By the way, are you armed?'

'Heavily,' she said as she fell in step with him and they crossed the road towards a well-trodden path.

'I knew I should have put on my bulletproof vest this morning.'

'Something that's probably seen a lot of action over the years, I shouldn't wonder,' she replied stiffly. Was he doing it deliberately, being so damned jolly? 'You do realize, don't you, that you've become a gold-plated nuisance in my life. It has to stop. As of now. I simply won't tolerate any more of your idiotic behaviour. You've—'

'You're right.'

'You've crossed so many lines I don't even know where to start. I can't begin to think what passes through your mind when—'

'You're right.'

'Please don't keep interrupting me. I'm trying to make you realize just how—'

'And I'm just trying to save you a lot of bother,' he interrupted her again. 'You're absolutely right. I've behaved appallingly. And I'm sorry.'

She hadn't expected him to take this line and wrong-footed, she said, 'Well, good, that's good, I'm relieved that you're being reasonable at last.'

'I've always been reasonable, Ella.'

'Then you have a curious understanding of the word. Try looking it up in a dictionary one day. I'm sure it doesn't include making a complete fool of yourself in the middle of the night by singing and dancing whilst drunk in my garden.'

'Please don't remind me of that.'

'What else am I supposed to do? Forget it ever happened?'

'It would help.'

'And it would help if you left me alone. It would be too embarrassing all round for me to have to take out a restraining order on you.'

He gave a short laugh. 'I'd like to think that's a joke on your part, but I wouldn't like to put it to the test.'

'You're a wise man.'

'I'm glad you finally think so.' He slowed his pace, put a hand on her arm and stopped walking. 'I am genuinely sorry,' he said. 'The last thing I ever wanted to do was annoy or upset you.'

She looked at his hand and slowly raised her glance to his face. There were lines around his eyes as he frowned into the brightness of the sun. She wanted to tell him to remove his hand, but unaccountably she couldn't. She found she couldn't stop looking into the intense darkness of his eyes. She noticed there were two crescents of puffy shadows beneath them. He looked like a man who wasn't getting enough sleep. He also still struck her as having lost weight.

'You'd rather I didn't do that, wouldn't you?' he said. 'Touching you is breaking one of your cardinal rules.'

'It makes me feel uncomfortable,' she murmured.

'I know. It makes me feel uncomfortable, knowing that you feel uncomfortable.'

'Then perhaps you shouldn't do it.'

'You're probably right, as you so often are.'

Finally she managed to tear her gaze away from his. 'No *probably* or *often* about it,' she said.

He smiled and took his hand away. They walked on. For something to say, and having noticed the plaster, Ella said, 'How's your head? Maggie told me you gave yourself quite a nasty bump.'

'Please don't offer me sympathy; I'm liable to burst into tears. You know how fragile I am.'

In the distance a couple of serious walkers appeared. Stooped and moving fast, their shoulders bent to the miles they were clearly hell-bent on covering, they were dressed in ready-for-any-eventuality-when-walking-the-hills attire, laden with rucksacks and jabbing the ground with what looked like skiing poles. As they passed Ethan and Ella, they let out a merry 'hello' but their expressions said, 'Look at the state of those two: not a walking boot between them!'

When they were alone again, Ella said, 'We'd better not go any further. I don't have much time.'

To the right of them Ethan indicated an area of flattened grass and some conveniently sized rocks on which they could perch. 'How about we stop here for a while?'

As soon as they were settled, Ella said, 'I want you to promise me you'll leave me alone, that there'll be no more midnight pranks.'

'If that's what you want.'

'It is. I'm back with Lawrence now; I've moved in with him, so it really wouldn't be appropriate to have a friend like you loitering in the background.'

'You keep using that word, *appropriate*.'

'That's because it's … entirely appropriate. You are taking this seriously, aren't you?'

'Earnestly so. I can't think of anyone less appropriate than me to have as a friend. I'm there rubbing shoulders with Bin Laden, Radovan Karadzic and Peter Mandelson. Can I ask you something?'

'Depends what it is.'

'If Lawrence hadn't resurfaced and we had continued with our friendship, would you have enjoyed meeting for an occasional drink or meal?'

'You know I always had a problem with the fact that you were married, so that tended to colour things for me.'

'That's not really answering the question, is it? Were there times when you enjoyed yourself?'

'Yes,' she said after a long pause. 'Yes I did. And that's why I don't want to see you any more.'

'So I was right. There was an attraction between us?'

'That's not what I said.'

'But it's what you've always felt and what you've always fought to deny.'

Ella's mouth fell open. 'Your arrogance is breathtaking at times.'

'It's not arrogance, Ella; it's merely stating a fact. Can I ask you another question?'

She sighed. 'As if it would stop you if I said no.'

'If I wasn't married, and if there was no Lawrence, would we be more than friends?'

'I've never approved of hypothetical questions. They're meaningless and futile.'

'I disagree. I think the answers to them can be most revealing.'

She turned and looked at him. 'Okay, well, here's a hypothetical question for you. You're obviously a man who's used to getting his own way when it comes to women, so if I had gone to bed with you at the outset of all this nonsense, would that have got me off the hook? Would you have satisfied yourself and moved on to someone else to pester?'

He frowned. 'Is that how you see me? A sex pest?'

'Answer the question.'

'I may in the past have behaved in a way that would rule me out of ever becoming Husband of the Year, but I'd humbly suggest that sex pest is going too far.' He banged the heel of his shoe against the rock on which he was sitting. 'This may sound like I'm spinning a line, but since I met you, I've changed. It was only when I started to get to know you that I realized that what I've really been looking for all these years is someone I can feel close to – a friend and confidante and yes, a lover. It'd been so long since I'd experienced a genuine emotion, I didn't know initially that was what I was beginning to feel. You made that happen. You've made me feel real again. I'm sorry if the idea of that is repellent or offensive to you, but it's the truth. And nobody is more surprised by that than me. It's why I behaved so badly in Abersoch. I was as jealous as hell at the thought of you with another man. It made me realize just how strongly I felt about you. The thing is, Ella,' he turned and looked at her, 'I've fallen in love with you.'

She swallowed. 'I don't know what to say.'

He shook his head slowly and his shoulders slumped. 'Given our circumstances, I don't think there is anything either of us can say. Other than,' he suddenly smiled, 'if things don't work out with Lawrence, can I have first refusal?'

She smiled as well. 'You're impossible.'

'But we're okay now, aren't we? If I promise to do exactly as you say and stay away from you, you'll forgive me?'

'Yes, I forgive you.' Her words were an echo of what she'd said last night to Lawrence.

'You see, that's what I've come to understand since meeting you,' Ethan continued. 'That if you love a person you want them to be happy and, Ella, if it makes you happy never seeing me again, then so be it.'

He stood up and held out his hands to her. 'Come on,' he said. 'We both need to get back to work. Where are you working at the moment?'

'At a place called Belmont Hall.'

'I know the house; it's colossal. I remember it being on the market last year. Are the new owners well-behaved clients?'

'It's just the one owner, and he's impeccably behaved,' Ella answered, trying hard to match her tone to that of Ethan's. He'd gone from nought to sixty, laying himself painfully bare to conducting an entirely normal conversation in a single heartbeat. 'I'm hoping there might be the chance of a job there for Maggie,' she added.

'Really? It's a big house for her to clean all on her own. It would be like dusting the Forth Bridge.'

'The job may turn out to be full-time.'

'I don't like the sound of that. Francine won't be happy to lose Maggie.'

'Then she should have been nicer to her and not treated her like dirt.'

'Is that what she's done?'

'Oh, come off it, Ethan, that can't be a newsflash for you.'

He shrugged. 'I suppose not.'

'You know, you really can't go on living the rest of your life with your head in the sand.'

'I'm not sure I'm brave enough to live it any other way.'

'You don't mean that.'

They were now level with the main road. They waited for a lorry to thunder past and then crossed over to where they had left their cars. There was now a motley collection of vehicles in the car park, including a tractor and a rather flashy Mercedes sports car that had its engine running at a low growl. It was silver and spotlessly showroom smart and stood out effortlessly from everything else, if only because it had trade plates and tinted windows and made Ella think of overpaid footballers.

Ethan saw her to her car. She had the door open when he said, 'I suppose this is goodbye, isn't it?'

'I suppose it is.'

'A shame it feels so awful.'

She smiled and in a gesture that felt wholly natural and right, she kissed him on the cheek. 'You take care now, won't you?'

'You too.' His voice was scarcely audible.

They looked at each other for a moment and then with the subtlest of movements, Ethan kissed her on the mouth. His lips hardly touched hers and lasted no more than a second yet she felt the connection as surely as she would a two-thousand-watt jolt. She briefly closed her eyes and when she opened them, she found herself staring into an expression of such profound sadness she caught her breath.

'Goodbye,' he said. 'I really hope Lawrence makes you happy.'

She drove away without looking back.

Five minutes later, and giving Ella time to get well ahead of him, Ethan drove off in the same direction.

Two minutes later the silver Mercedes pulled out of the car park.

The driver's face was set like stone. Who would have thought that test-driving the latest Mercedes and agreeing with the salesman – a smarmy young lad called Aaron – to take the Cat and Fiddle Road to put the car through its paces, would lead her to this?

If the salesman hadn't asked if she could pull into the pub car park as he had drunk too much coffee that morning and was in the embarrassing position of having been caught short, she would never have spotted them.

It was while Aaron was inside the pub that she had seen Ethan and Ella appear from across the road. Shocked, but thinking fast, she had whipped out her mobile and photographed the exact moment when Ethan had kissed Ella. The question was, what was she going to do with the photograph?

'So, Mrs Paxton, how do you like the car?'

'I'll be honest with you, Aaron, I hate it: it's been a real let-down.'

'Oh,' he said.

Yes, I thought that would knock the smarmy look off your smarmy little face. She drove back to the dealership, venting her fury on the car, taking the bends of the moorland road so fast that when she came to a tyre-squealing stop on the forecourt, Aaron's face was ashen.

Chapter Forty-six

Now that her suspicions had been confirmed and she had real evidence that Ethan had been having an affair, the hatred Christine felt toward Ella Moore was beyond anything she had ever experienced. Every time she thought of the photograph she had on her mobile, her body shook with fury.

Ethan, *her* Ethan ... how could he do this to her? And with that pathetic nobody of a woman! Oh, and how well Ella had played her part. A real butter-wouldn't-melt-in-her-mouth type. She may have fooled Francine and that boyfriend of hers, but she hadn't fooled Christine. Oh, not by a long chalk. She had got Ella's number right from the start. Now all she had to do was decide how to teach Ella a lesson she wouldn't forget in a hurry. Revenge would be sweet.

Maggie was getting ready to leave when she heard the front door opening. She had hoped to leave before Mrs Paxton came home, but that wasn't going to happen now. Now she would be subjected to a list of criticisms and complaints about how badly she was doing her job. It never failed to surprise her how women who hadn't lifted a finger in years to clean their own houses could be such experts when it came to anyone who did it for them.

'Thought you'd finish early today, did you?' Mrs Paxton said. She stood in the doorway of the kitchen and there was no getting away from how narked she looked. Never a picture of sweetness at the best of times, her face was lashed with hatred and her voice sounded sharp enough to cut through toughened glass.

'It's the time I always finish,' Maggie said, flicking her gaze over to the clock above the Aga.

'Is it indeed? I hope you've done a better job this week of cleaning the shower door in my bathroom. Last week you left it covered in smears. And I see you haven't cleaned this floor properly. Look at the state of it. I don't pay you to sit here on your backside watching the telly all day, you know.'

'I've tried getting those stains out, Mrs Paxton, but that's the trouble with limestone tiles; if they're not treated regularly and properly, they absorb everything in sight.'

'Suddenly you're an expert on floor tiles, are you, Maggie?'

I know a hell of a lot more than you do, Maggie thought as Mrs Paxton came towards her. 'I have to know things like that for my work,' she said.

'And you presume to lecture me about it, do you?'

'I'm just saying, that's all.'

'No, Maggie, what you're saying is that you know better than I do. So let's just get one thing clear: I pay your wages, which means you do as I say, and if I say it's possible to get those marks out, then you'll bloody well do it. Do you understand me?'

Maggie swallowed. Just how much more of this woman was she going to take? Was she really going to stand here and let her get away with being so rude? She needed the money, and never more so than now. But there was the chance of a new job just around the corner. Thanks to Ella, an hour from now she was meeting the owner of Belmont Hall. If it was a full-time job and the pay was good, as Ella hinted it might be, she wouldn't need Mrs Paxton's money.

'Are you listening to a word I'm saying, Maggie?'

Maggie swallowed again and from somewhere deep inside her came the courage to stand up for herself, just as she'd done with Brenda and Shelley. 'Yes, Mrs Paxton,' she said, 'I'm listening all right, and seeing as I'm such a useless cleaner, perhaps I shouldn't work for you any more. And you know what? I'm sure you'll have no trouble getting those stains out of the tiles yourself. One drop of acid from your poisonous tongue should do the trick.'

If it was possible, Mrs Paxton looked even more furious. She now looked like she could throw something at Maggie. Which Maggie wouldn't put past her.

'How dare you speak to me like that,' the woman hissed.

'Oh, I dare all right! I just wish I'd got the hang of standing up to folk a long time ago. You know what, you look the part of a lady, but you're nothing of the friggin' sort. You're a rude, foul-mouthed bitch. You and my mother-in-law would get on like a house on fire.'

Then hitching her bag over her shoulder, her head held high, Maggie made her exit. She willed herself not to trip over anything on her way out and spoil the effect.

Shaking with a mixture of triumph and shock – had that really been her putting Mrs Paxton in her place? – Maggie drove to Belmont Hall, following the directions Ella had given her. She hoped she hadn't burnt her bridges. If she didn't get this job, she would need to find a new client; she really couldn't afford to be a client down.

She was almost at Belmont Hall when she realized that she was only a mile or so from the canal and Daryl's boat. Her heartbeat immediately quickened as she thought of him.

Being so close to Daryl's boat was surprise enough, but the real surprise was Belmont Hall. She had seen places like this in magazines and on the telly, but had never dreamed she would one day get to go inside a house that was so big. Again she followed Ella's instructions and at the electric gates, she pressed a button on a small panel and as if by magic, after a tinny version of Ella's voice said, 'Hi, Maggie!' the gates slowly swung open. As she approached the house along the long, long drive, she knew that it had to be worth a small fortune. Or a very large fortune. She suddenly felt nervous. This wasn't her world.

But then what was her world? Where did Maggie Storm belong?

She didn't seem to belong anywhere. She didn't fit in with Dave and his family, that much was obvious. Her son hardly ever spoke to her and as for her mother, well, where to begin with Lou? She didn't even have any real friends. She was one of life's loners. A misfit.

There still hadn't been any word from Dave. She could imagine he was well under his mother's thumb now, under orders not to make the first move. The plan would be to force Maggie to be the one to crack first. He and Brenda would have a long wait.

She felt a wave of relief when she saw the enormous front door of the house open and Ella appear on the doorstep.

'You found it all right, then?' Ella said after she had pointed to where Maggie should park, next to Ella's car.

Maggie looked about her in awe. 'It's difficult to miss! I mean, it's huge.'

Ella smiled. 'Don't worry, you soon get used to the size of it.'

Despite her smile, Maggie thought Ella didn't look her usual self; she looked tense, as if there was something on her mind. She wanted to ask if she was okay, but just then a car came tearing up the drive as if it was being chased. It came to a stop in front of the house, churning gravel as it did so. The top was down and a fair-haired lad wearing sunglasses was sitting behind the wheel. He waved over to them. Perhaps he was the son of the owner, Maggie thought. Although Ella hadn't mentioned anything about there being a family to look after. In fact, she'd said he wasn't married.

'That's Hal Moran,' Ella said quietly.

'You're kidding! He's just a boy.'

'He's older than he looks. And twice as smart. That car's his latest new toy. He only got it last week.'

'He's got to be smarter than paint to afford all this. The new toy's a Bentley, isn't it?'

'Well spotted.'

Maggie laughed. 'Maybe *I'm* smarter than I look.'

'I'm sorry I'm late,' Hal Moran said as he bounced over to them. He seemed to have so much energy. He took off his sunglasses and held out his hand to Maggie. No potential employer had ever done that to her before. 'I got caught in traffic,' he said. He winked at Ella. 'I know what you're thinking, all that money on a car and I still can't beat the traffic.'

'Not your fault, Hal,' Ella said. 'You just need the rest of us mere mortals to get our annoying little cars off the road and the highway would be all yours.' She doffed an imaginary cap at him.

He laughed and then winked at Maggie. 'This is the kind of abuse I'm subjected to – can you believe it? Now then, how about I make us some tea?' He held up a box tied with a ribbon. 'Look, I've bought us some cakes, and then you and I can get down to business, Maggie. Is it all right if I call you Maggie?'

You can call me anything you like, she thought. All her nervousness had now gone and more than anything she wanted to come and work here. She would spend her every waking minute cleaning Belmont Hall and she would be as happy as Larry.

It was all settled and she couldn't believe her luck. Amazing! The perfect job and with accommodation thrown in. Talk about an answer to a prayer. Not that she went in for praying, but maybe from now on she would.

When Hal – he had insisted on her calling him by his first name – had shown her the two flats above the garage block and told her to choose which one she would like to live in, she had wanted to throw herself down on the floor and weep. The one she chose was perfect in every way. There was a nice lounge that opened onto a kitchen and she could picture herself sitting at the small breakfast bar beneath the window that overlooked the front garden and drive. A narrow corridor with a row of built-in cupboards led to a bedroom and a bathroom. There was even some furniture. Hal had apologized for the state of the carpet and the lack of curtains but she had at once said she could easily make new curtains and a rug or two would cover up the stains on the carpets.

The job itself would be flexible, Hal had explained. He needed someone to keep the house in order. Him, too. She would be in charge of all the domestic details he didn't have time for. He had a part-time contractor taking care of the garden for now, but that was going to change just as soon as he had found a suitable full-time gardener. The cleaning side of things would be a challenge while there was still so much work being done to the house, but she had assured him she would keep on top of things for him. When asked what kind of meals she would cook for him, she had been honest and said that she didn't do anything very fancy, but she could learn. He'd said that home cooking without any frills would suit him well enough.

The best bit of all was that she would be paid a lot more than she was currently earning. She had quickly worked out that even after paying what she guessed would be the running expenses on the small flat, she would be miles better off than she was right now.

When Hal had offered her the job she had blurted out, 'But don't you want things like references?'

'Ella has given me all the assurance about you that I need. When can you start?'

'Next week if that's what you would like,' she'd said.

'Great, you're hired!'

She would work the rest of the week with her existing clients, but then that would be it. She felt guilty that she was letting some of them down at such short notice, but she didn't give a tinker's cuss about Mrs Edwards. Seeing the back of that woman would be as welcome as it had been to put Mrs Paxton in her place earlier that afternoon.

She hadn't felt this happy or positive in a long time.

Not since that day when she had been with Daryl on his boat and they had ripped the clothes off each other and made love for the first time.

Immediately her thoughts took a turn for the worse and she paused at the end of the long drive. If she took the right turn, the road would take her down to the canal. But did she want to risk catching Daryl in bed with that woman again?

No, she couldn't put herself through that.

She decided instead that there was something she had to do that couldn't be put off any longer. She couldn't go on hiding.

'Well, well, *well*. Look who's come crawling back. Just as I knew she would.'

'Hello, Brenda, I see you've lost none of your charm.'

Maggie stood in the doorway of the lounge. Nothing seemed to have changed. The telly was on as usual and Dave was in his usual seat on the sofa, feet up – plaster cast on his left leg and crusty toenails sticking out – beer can in hand. 'How are you, Dave?' she asked.

'Like you care!'

'Brenda, I was talking to Dave. Why don't you make yourself useful by putting the kettle on while I have a word with him on my own?'

'What, and leave you to worm your way back in here? I didn't arrive on the last trolley bus, you know. I've got my eye on you, my girl. I know what your game is. You think you can march out of here any old how and then expect to come back and pretend you've done nowt wrong. Our Dave, I told you that's what she would do. Didn't I say, she'll come back bold as brass and just as cheap, thinking she can take up where she left off. The nerve of her. It fair takes my breath away!'

'Do me a favour, Brenda: get your breath back and then shut up! The only reason I'm here is to collect the rest of my things and to tell Dave that I want a divorce. I'm sorry, Dave, I wanted to say that to you in private, but since you don't have the guts to tell Brenda to mind her own business, you gave me no choice. Is there anything you want to say to me?'

He looked at her as though she was a stranger. But then wasn't that exactly what she was to him? That was the whole problem: he didn't know the first thing about her. He put his beer can down. 'A divorce?' he said. 'Why? What did I ever do to yer?'

'Nothing is what you did. You never paid me any attention and you did nothing to stop Brenda from always putting me down. She did it all the time, right under your nose and you never once stopped her.'

Brenda snorted and took out a cigarette.

'Yer've changed,' Dave said flatly. 'You're not the Maggie I married. The Maggie I married would never have spoken like that.'

'You're right. And that was my mistake. I should have stood up to you and your mother a long time ago. Can you honestly say you've missed me these last few days? Did you even notice I wasn't here?'

'Course I noticed yer were gone; I'm not stupid. And for yer information, I thought of yer only yesterday.'

Yesterday? Oh big, massive deal! 'What made you think of me?' she asked.

'I couldn't find any clean cacks,' he said. 'Mum had to wash some for me.'

Maggie forced herself not to react. 'Then it was lucky good ol' Brenda was here to help you.'

Forty-five minutes later she had all the things she needed in three large black bin liners. She wrote a note for Dean, left it in his bedroom and went back downstairs. Brenda was in the kitchen standing over the cooker, a cigarette dangling from her mouth, a length of ash about to drop into the pan of beans she was stirring. On the floor, in his basket, a pitifully bald and partly bandaged Evil Sid stopped licking himself and gave Maggie one of his surly looks. See, she thought, even he couldn't be grateful that she had saved his life.

She left the house without saying goodbye. She bundled her things into her car and set off. But then she changed her mind.

One more call to make.

She rang Mrs Oates's doorbell.

'Saints alive!' Mrs Oates exclaimed when she opened the door. 'It's been such an age since I saw you last. Where have you been hiding yourself?'

'It's a long story.'

'Then you'd better come in and tell me all about it. I've got news for you, too. Jack's asked me to marry him!'

Over a supper of comforting shepherd's pie and apple crumble for afters, Maggie listened to Mrs Oates's news – how Jack had taken her away for a romantic weekend in Llandudno over Easter and had then surprised her with an engagement ring hidden in a napkin during dinner. The wedding was to take place in August. 'I know what you're thinking, my dear,' Mrs Oates had laughed. 'That it's all a bit quick, but at our age we can't hang about.'

Then Maggie had told Mrs Oates about her awful Easter and everything that had happened since, including her new job at Belmont Hall.

'Goodness,' was all Mrs Oates could say whenever Maggie paused for breath.

'But you're sure you want to divorce Dave?' she asked finally.

'Yes. I know it's drastic, but why should I stay? What is there to stay for?'

Mrs Oates patted her hands. 'Is there anything I can do to help?'

'Yes, stay in touch with me.'

Mrs Oates smiled. 'I wouldn't have it any other way.' Then she looked serious. 'You haven't mentioned Daryl. Does he know about you and Dave?'

Maggie shook her head. 'I ended things with Daryl after that terrible night here when you found us in the kitchen. I haven't spoken to him since. Anyway, he's found someone new, Mrs O.'

'Has he? Jack hasn't said anything about that.'

Maggie told her what she'd seen on board the *Bohemian Rhapsody*.

Mrs Oates frowned. 'Are you sure?'

'Oh, very sure. You can't get something like that wrong.'

'But you must have. Daryl hasn't been around these last few weeks. He's working on a cruise ship. Look, I had a post-card from him only yesterday. He says his act's been going really well.' She went over to the mantelpiece and picked up a card that Maggie had noticed earlier; it showed a picture of the Leaning Tower of Pisa. 'He's in the Mediterranean,' Mrs Oates said, giving the card to Maggie. 'He's on a three-month contract.' The old lady sat down again, but she was still frowning. 'So,' she said slowly, 'whoever you saw on Daryl's boat, it couldn't have been Daryl.'

No, thought Maggie. And when she really thought about what she'd seen that day, she hadn't seen Daryl, had she? Only the woman. She stared at the card, at the tower that was tilting so dangerously and felt, if not the whole world was tilting, her little bit of it certainly was.

'I think you should ring him, dear, don't you?'

Maggie looked up. 'But I don't have his number any more.'

The old lady smiled. 'I'm sure we can get that from Jack without too much trouble.'

Maggie couldn't speak. Instead, she threw her arms round Mrs Oates and hugged her.

Chapter Forty-seven

He was cursed. There was no other explanation. Why else would his day have panned out the way it had, with him now forced to endure an evening with Francine's parents and Alan's interminable looks of undisguised contempt?

His crime – the latest in a long list of heinous misdemeanours in the eyes of his father-in-law – had been to return home late from work having forgotten all about tonight's dinner to celebrate Alan's birthday. Late for a bloody dinner – anyone would think he'd committed genocide.

He had been delayed because a much-valued customer, a customer who had traded with Ethan for sixteen years, had telephoned just as Ethan was switching off his computer and calling it a day. Everyone else had already left and taking the call he had recognized Jim Hilton's voice straight away. He had switched his computer back on to open Jim's client file, knowing all too well the Hilton account still hadn't been cleared for the last order. Twenty thousand pounds was owed. Adopting his most casual and genial manner, Ethan had made all the usual noises about how great it was to hear from Jim and how was the weather down there in Bristol? At first Jim had played along, but his jittery voice was giving him away big time. It was evident that he had called with bad news; the man's depression was palpable. And then it all came tumbling out. Unable to weather the storm ... bankruptcy ... so sorry ... no money left to settle the account ... the sound of sniffing ... the awful sound of a fifty-six-year-old man crying ... so sorry again ... he hoped Ethan would understand.

Ethan tried to. But twenty grand's worth of understanding was stretching it. Why the hell had Jim placed such a large order last month when he must have known at the time he couldn't pay for it? Because, just like the rest of them, he had convinced himself it would all come good in the end, if he could hold his nerve and pretend everything was just fine. It was what they all did. It was the hope that Ethan himself was desperately hanging on to. When it came down to it, it was the only thing there was to do. That and recite the classic self-empowerment mantra of all those business books: *I've been down before; I can bounce back.* He just had to keep on convincing himself he could do it. Just as he had tried to convince Jim that bankruptcy would be a temporary glitch, that he would soon be back in the game, and yes, of course, Ethan would always be willing to do business with him. For now, though, Ethan knew that Jim would be a pariah within the industry. No one would want to go near him for fear of being infected by failure.

Now as Ethan drank his after-dinner coffee, he observed his wife, his mother-in-law and his daughter as they hung on Alan's every word about the charity golf tournament he was organizing. Never mind poor old Jim being ostracized by the industry; Ethan was a pariah in his own home.

Today Ella had accused him of living with his head in the sand and told him he couldn't go on doing it. But what else could he do? He looked about him at the walls of the dining room, at the utopian landscape Ella had created and felt her presence as keenly as if she were here.

The thought of what he'd promised her – never to get in touch with her again – depressed the hell out of him and just as he was remembering how he'd steeled himself to explain how he felt about her, a sudden searing pain had him catching his breath and pressing a hand to his stomach. With nobody paying him any attention, he excused himself from the dining table and left the room. At the foot of the stairs he gasped and doubled over at the pain; he had to put a hand on the newel post to steady himself.

In the bathroom, the door closed, he didn't bother measuring out the suggested dosage into the small plastic cup provided, but put the bottle to his lips and tossed back several mouthfuls of the gloopy liquid.

Too much red wine, he thought. That and too much anxiety. His and Francine's joint credit card statements for Visa and MasterCard had arrived that morning and the amounts owed were mind-boggling.

He looked at himself in the mirror above the basin and didn't like what he saw. His face was drained of colour and beads of sweat had broken out on his forehead. Closer inspection told him that he had acquired more grey hairs. Quite a lot of grey hairs. Where had they sprung from? Same place as the others, he thought bitterly. Life wasn't just passing him by, it was hurtling past at supersonic speed.

Hoping that the worst of the pain was over, he fumbled with shaking hands to replace the lid on the bottle of medicine and returned it to the shelf in the cabinet. The bottle was almost empty. He would have to remember to buy some more. Especially as the attacks were becoming more painful and prolonged. He ought to make an appointment to see a doctor, but as with so much in life he kept putting it off, convincing himself that it would pass; he just had to hang in there.

He couldn't face going back downstairs yet, so he lowered the toilet lid and sat down. He closed his eyes, tried to block out the burning pain still flaring in his stomach. When exactly had his life turned to shit? He had started out with such determined ambition, driven by an unshakeable belief that he could achieve whatever he put his mind to. He was going to be The Man, a Man of Substance. That was what his father had said a real man strove for – to be a Man of Substance – because that was how his worth was measured. A golden rule of his father's was never to display an ounce of hesitation: hesitation was weakness; weakness was failure.

How ironic was it that it looked very much as if Ethan was going to end up the way his father had: dead and with nothing to show for the years of hard work he'd put in. At least Francine and Valentina wouldn't be left entirely without money, thanks to the life insurance policy he had taken out, not because he'd been anxious about dying any time soon, but because it had seemed a sensible thing to do. That was in the days when he was carefully placing the building blocks on top of each other, building the foundations of a life he would be proud of. Now he had to accept that those foundations had been built on shifting sand. But then everything was. Nothing came with a cast-iron guarantee.

He opened his eyes. The pain had all but passed. He felt almost lightheaded with relief. It was a sensation that re-minded him of another moment during the day when he had felt similarly affected. It had been the high spot of his day. Albeit a bittersweet high spot. It was when he had kissed Ella. He hadn't meant to, but like a heat-seeking missile homing in on its target his mouth had suddenly made contact with hers. Then just as suddenly it was over. A moment so fleeting he could have believed it hadn't happened. For the rest of the afternoon – until Jim Hilton had phoned – he had felt lightheaded and a little like he was walking on air. Absurd. But that was how it had affected him.

Did Lawrence feel the same when he kissed Ella? Ethan wondered. If so, he was a lucky man. To experience that sen-sation every time you kissed the woman you loved, there was nothing to compare to it. Did Lawrence really feel that? Did he get it? Did he realize just how bloody lucky he was to wake up every morning with Ella beside him in bed? Ethan couldn't think of anything that would give him more pleasure.

But that was never going to happen and it was pointless to dwell on something he couldn't have. Better to enjoy the memory of the softness in Ella's eyes when she had kissed him on the cheek and told him to take care. Better to store away the memory of the light touch of his lips against hers.

He inhaled deeply, stood up and braced himself for another round of happy families downstairs. Back to the trenches ... Once more unto the breach, dear friends ...

It was twelve forty-five and sitting up in bed in Ella's spare room, Maggie pressed send.

If she'd got it right, it would be one forty-five in the morning where her text message was heading. She could have waited until tomorrow, but she couldn't wait that long. Hopefully Daryl would have finished work but wouldn't be asleep yet. He used to say that with working the clubs up and down the country for so many years and driving home in the early hours he had become a night person through necessity.

Two minutes passed.

Then three.

Then five.

She had never sent a text abroad before. She knew it was more expensive, but did the long distance cause a delay?

Six minutes.

Then ten agonizing minutes.

Oh well, she thought. At least she'd tried. Maybe he'd reply tomorrow. About to switch off the bedside light, she nearly jumped out of her skin when her mobile beeped.

Gr8 2 hr frm u. Ive msd u lots. x

Her heart surged and she tapped in her reply. *Ive msd u 2. x* She pressed send and waited.

Four minutes later her mobile burst into life again, but this time it wasn't a text, it was Daryl calling her.

Chapter Forty-eight

'May is the perfect month to put a house on the market,' the estate agent had assured Ella. 'All properties look better in May. Nothing like a bit of sun and some colour in the garden to get the punters in the right frame of mind.'

Five weeks had passed since Ella had moved back to Mayfield and although she had originally been resistant to the idea of selling her house, two factors had persuaded her to change her mind. One was personal, and the other was basic economics – she would sell if she could get the right price and make a worthwhile profit. She was quietly confident that she would. Having done her homework, she knew that the market was picking up and having lifted Tickle Cottage out of the décor doldrums – nothing had been done to it for years when she'd bought it – she knew she had improved the property beyond recognition and turned it into an attractive and saleable commodity.

She was now showing a young couple round the house. Lawrence had said she should leave the viewings to the agent, but Ella knew that the best person to sell her house was her and not a pushy twenty-something-year-old dressed in cheap shoes and a dodgy suit and reeking of aftershave and cigarettes.

The young woman – the wife – was already convinced that the house was exactly what they were looking for. She had said as much after only seeing the downstairs, but her husband was going to great lengths to play it cool by shaking his head and picking out everything he considered wrong with the place.

He wanted a detached property, not an end of terrace. He wanted a sitting room at the rear of the property, not at the front. He didn't like the long thin garden; he wanted a square garden. He wanted a garage. He had amateur negotiator written all over his face and was deluding himself if he believed his clumsy negative comments would drive down the price. The house was fresh to the market and Ella had no intention of giving away her beautiful home to the first person through the door who made her an offer below the asking price.

She politely waved them off ten minutes later and went through to the kitchen to make herself a drink. She no sooner had the mug of tea in her hand and was opening the back door to go outside to her workshop when the phone rang.

It was Lawrence.

'How did the viewing go?' he asked.

'So, so,' she replied, stepping out into the garden.

'That doesn't sound very positive.'

She explained about the husband playing the negotiator hand and how his parting words were to say it wasn't really what they were looking for. 'But I guarantee he makes an offer in a couple of days. An offer well below the asking price.'

'Not to worry; it's early days. Are you on your way home now?'

'No. I've got some stuff to do in my workshop.'

'But I'm doing salmon. With lime and coriander. The way you like it.'

'Can you put it on hold for a couple of hours?'

'Not really. Alexis wants to eat now. You know how stressed she is with the exams – she wants to eat early so she can spend the rest of the evening revising. It's history tomorrow.'

'Then cook for you and Alexis and I'll do something for myself when I get in.'

'That's two nights running you've done that. I don't understand why you don't move your workshop things back here. It would be so much easier for you. I've said I'll help you do it. Unless ...' his voice trailed off.

'Unless what?'

There was an ominous silence down the line. Ella looked about her, waiting for him to answer. On a branch of the lilac tree a perky little robin was eyeing Ella steadily.

'Lawrence?' she repeated.

'Unless you're having doubts ... perhaps you're not really committed to our relationship.'

Ella took a deep breath. There had been a lot of deep breaths in the last ten days. She put it down to Alexis winding them up over her GCSEs. 'Where's this come from?' she said. 'I've moved back in with you and I'm selling my house, just as you wanted. What more can I do to prove how committed I am to you and our future?'

'I ... I don't know. I just feel that I'm unlucky when it comes to women. I lost Abigail, then I lost you and—'

'You lost me temporarily,' she cut in.

'But what if I lose you for good?'

'That's not going to happen. Besides, the reasons you lost me before no longer exist.'

'Yes, but— Oh, just ignore me. I'm being silly.'

'Yes you are.' Her voice was light. 'Now go and cook that salmon for you and Alexis and I'll see you later.'

'I love you, Ella.'

'Love you right back.'

She cringed and ended the call. *Love you right back.* Did she really just say that? And as if he too couldn't believe what he'd heard, the robin flew off into Phil's garden next door. I don't blame you, she thought. And she really didn't blame Lawrence for needing reassurance from her. She was doing her best, and not just with him; there was Alexis to reassure and keep calm during these stressful weeks.

Alexis was her 'personal' reason for deciding to sell Tickle Cottage. Ella had suddenly realized one morning whilst driving her to school and trying to keep her calm before a French conversation exam, that it wasn't so much for Lawrence's benefit that she had to do it, but for Alexis's. The girl needed the stability of knowing that Ella would be there for her. In short, Alexis wanted to rely on Ella but could only do that if she could trust her.

She had made it as far as her workshop when this time her mobile rang; she fished it out of her jeans pocket. She didn't recognize the number on the screen.

'Is that Ella Moore?'

'It is.'

'It's Christine Paxton here.'

Oh hell!

'Now I know you said you had more than enough work to keep you busy, but I simply won't take no for an answer.' The voice was jarringly chirrupy. 'And you can't be that busy, as I saw your advertisement in this month's *Cheshire Life*.'

How was she ever going to get this woman to back off? 'That advert was placed several months ago,' Ella said patiently, 'but I'm afraid my diary is still as full as ever. I can recommend another specialist painter to you; I know several who are extremely good.'

'No, that won't do at all. I've seen what you're capable of and it's you I want.' Something in the woman's tone put Ella on her guard.

'Do you have your diary to hand? I'm free tomorrow after-noon. Let's say three thirty, shall we?'

'Mrs Paxton, that really isn't convenient for me. I'm cur-rently working on a large project and I can't break off just like that.'

Laughter came down the line. Humourless laughter. 'You had plenty of time not so long ago to break off from work to enjoy a lunchtime ramble up at the Cat and Fiddle, didn't you? Although I think you were doing more than just ram-bling.' Another humourless laugh.

Ella's mouth went dry. 'I don't know what you're talking about,' she said with studied calm.

'I think you do. And I have a very interesting photograph that captures the moment perfectly. Tomorrow it is, then. I'll see you at three thirty. On the dot. Don't be late,' she added in a sickeningly saccharine tone.

The Sisters of Fun couldn't believe it.

'I've said it before, chuck, and I'll say it again: you're a dark horse and no mistake.' Mo's surgically enhanced eyes were wide and her eyebrows practically in her hairline.

'Ooh, I'm that jealous,' Betty said.

'Good luck to you,' Peggy said. 'Here's to you and your new life.'

They all raised and crashed their glasses together. 'To you, chuck,' Mo said. 'The world really is your scampi in the basket!'

'Don't you mean oyster?' asked Peggy.

Mo laughed. 'A nice bit of scampi in the basket beats an oyster any day in my book.'

The only person who didn't seem to be happy for her was Lou. When Maggie had moved into her little flat at Belmont Hall last month, she had called Lou to fill her in. 'You've really left him, then?' Lou had said flatly.

'Yes, I've told him I want a divorce.'

'More fool you. Just so long as you don't expect me to bail you out.'

Maggie had then explained about her new job and that she wouldn't need to be bailed out.

Lou's response was glum. 'Some people get all the luck.'

'What's up, Mum?'

It turned out Gordon had helped himself to the contents of her purse and done a runner.

Now, as Lou's friends were begging her to tell them all about Daryl, Lou said, 'I wouldn't get too excited about him. Take it from me, con men are easy to come by, unlike a decent husband.'

'Who says I want another husband?'

'But every woman wants a husband,' Peggy said. 'Otherwise

who else is going to fix the leaky tap or work the DVD player?'

'Dave never did any of that anyway.'

'Does he know you've left him for someone else?' Mo asked.

'I didn't leave Dave because of Daryl.'

'Yeah, and the world isn't round.'

'I'm being honest, Mum. I left Dave because I didn't love him any more. I don't know if I ever did. I probably married him for all the wrong reasons. I wanted something he couldn't give me.'

Lou rolled her eyes. 'You don't have to love someone to stay married to them. You just have to learn to put up with them.'

'Never mind about love and marriage, Lou – what about the sex? Come on Maggie, tell us all. Is Daryl any good in bed? Is he super, smashin', bloomin' marvellous?'

'Mo! I can't answer that with Mum sitting next to me.'

'Get away, chuck, course you can. So what's the answer? Is he sextastic?'

Maggie smiled shyly. 'He's amazingly sextastic!'

'I knew it! Is that why you bought all that fancy underwear at my party?'

Maggie nodded, embarrassed.

'You dirty devil!' roared Mo and everyone laughed and raised their glasses again.

When the laughter had died down, Lou said, 'I s'ppose some good will actually come out of this; at least I won't have to put up with Brenda any more.'

Another toast was made. 'Here's to the back of Brenda!'

'So when do we get to meet your new fella?' asked Betty.

'Not for a bit. Not until his contract runs out.'

'Well, just you make sure we have the chance to get our hands on him.'

*

Maggie left her mum and friends at the pub and drove back to Belmont Hall. To her new life. Her new and wonderful life.

Every time she caught sight of the house she got the biggest thrill. She still couldn't get over how lucky she was. Hal really was the perfect boss. He trusted her to get on with whatever needed doing and was always complimenting her on the meals she cooked – unlike Dave, who had always been able to find something on his plate to grumble about.

Every Monday morning Hal would give her a list of meals he fancied for the week ahead and just as he'd said during her interview, his taste was for plain, simple food, apart from the occasional curry. She had never cooked curry before – Dave had said it rotted his gut – so she had bought a cookery book and followed the recipes carefully.

Lunches were always the same: ham and mustard sandwiches with an apple on a tray, which Hal ate whilst sitting in front of one of the many computers in his enormous office overlooking the lake. Every now and then he would join Maggie and Ella in the kitchen for lunch. When she remembered the awful way Mrs Edwards and Mrs Paxton used to treat her, she had to pinch herself. Was this really a job? Was this really work? Or was it a dream? Was she going to wake up and find herself back in her old life? Okay, it was a nightmare trying to keep the dust at bay, what with all the work that was going on in the house, but it didn't matter how exhausted she was, she always felt a sense of pride at the end of the day.

And how she loved her evenings, alone in her cosy flat either watching television – actually watching a programme she was interested in – or reading quietly. She no longer read only romantic novels, but, at Hal's suggestion, she was borrowing from his shelves. Sci-fi and fantasy were completely new to her but she had to admit, she was hooked. All those strange parallel universes where anything was possible. But when it came down to it, the stories were still basically about good versus bad and people falling in and out of love.

And on top of having such a brilliant job and place to live, she had Daryl. There wasn't a day that passed without a message or a phone call from him telling her that he loved her. He said he was counting the days until he could fly home to be with her. The only thing troubling him was that his Freddie Mercury act was going down so well, the ship's entertainment officer wanted him to sign up for another contract. Maggie had been firm with him: 'Don't pass up such a great opportunity just to come back here.'

'But I want to be with you,' he'd said.

'You also need to work and you're enjoying what you're doing, aren't you? So stick with it whilst you can and let's see how things turn out.'

'You've not got someone else there, have you?' he'd asked.

She'd scoffed at that and told him not to be so daft. 'It's more likely you who's got someone else. Odds on there's an army of women chasing you on that ship.'

'None of them's a patch on you, Maggie. Believe me.'

That was the funny thing; she did believe him. For years she had doubted she was worthy of anyone's love, but Daryl always made her feel special. He could put a smile on her face without trying. She had told him about the day she had gone to see him at his boat only to discover a naked woman on his bed and how she had reacted. It turned out that a friend had been keeping an eye on Daryl's car and the boat and he must have done more than just check that no one had broken in. 'So you came to see me?' Daryl had asked. 'Any reason why?'

'Because I missed you,' she'd answered.

'That's nice.'

'No, it was horrible. I'd had the worst ever Easter, I'd left Dave and all I could think about was turning to you for help. I hated myself for that. It seemed wrong, like I was using you.'

'I wouldn't have thought that for a minute. I'd have done all I could to help you. But it looks like you've done just fine on your own.'

'With a lot of help from Ella. She was the one who got me the new job and somewhere to live. I don't know how I'll ever repay her. It was also Ella who encouraged me to get in touch with you.'

'In that case, I don't know how *I'll* ever repay her.'

Maggie was still thinking this when she saw a car parked in front of the electric gates at Belmont Hall. Her heart sank. It was Dave's car and he was leaning against the side of it. She wished she had never told him where she was now living and working. But thank God Hal was away down in London for a couple of days. The last thing she needed was for Dave to kick up a stink and get her sacked. She got out of her car and walked towards him.

'I see you've got the plaster cast off now,' she said, looking down at his ankle.

Ignoring her comment, he said, 'What the hell's this?' He pushed a letter at her, almost in her face.

'What do you think it is?' she said, glancing briefly at it. 'It's a letter from my solicitor saying I want a divorce.'

'Come off it, Mags, yer don't want a divorce. Yer're just upset, having a funny turn. It's what you women do. Yer've made your point. Now it's time to stop messing about and come home.'

She shook her head. 'You just don't get it, do you?'

'I tell yer what I do get. It's this: I've always provided for yer, put food on the table, a roof over our heads; yer wanted for nowt. Okay, we don't have a fancy house like Vernon and Shelley, but not everyone does. I've done the best I can, Mags. What's it gonna take to make yer happy? What about if we got that extension done and a downstairs loo put in?'

She would have laughed if he hadn't looked so pathetically serious. 'A downstairs loo isn't going to fix our marriage, Dave,' she said. 'And if you think it would, then it only confirms that I've done the right thing in leaving you. What's more, it wasn't just you putting food on the table; I was doing that too. Not only did I cook every bloody thing you ate, I paid for a lot of it. You never gave me credit for what I did. "Oh, Mags is *just* a cleaner," I heard you telling someone at the pub once.'

He suddenly looked about him, as if seeing where he was for the first time. He stared through the gates at the big house in the distance. 'What the hell are yer doing here, Mags? This isn't our kind of place.'

'It might not be your kind of place, but I feel very at home here.'

'What kind of work do they make yer do? Yer some kind of servant, or what? A maid? Do yer have to curtsey when some poncy git speaks to yer?' He couldn't have put more scorn in his voice if he had tried.

'I'm a housekeeper. What's more, I'm respected for what I do. I'm paid and valued. Does that mean anything to you? Probably not, because you never once valued me during our marriage. All I ever was to you was your unpaid skivvy. And your mum's as well.'

'Yer always have had it in for Mum, haven't yer? She reckons yer're jealous.'

'You're talking rubbish. Why don't you go home and tomorrow find yourself a solicitor. You're going to need one.'

'I don't want a divorce. I just want my wife back where she belongs.'

'And where's that, in the kitchen?'

'Mum and Shelley think yer've got some bloke poking yer. I told them they were wrong.'

'Why? Because you think no one else in their right mind would find me attractive?'

'Not to put too fine a point on it, take a look at yourself, Mags. You're not exactly Jordan are yer?

'Thanks a bunch! Nice of you to drop by and insult me.'

'I'm just speaking the truth, because let's face it; your're just not the type to have an affair. Yer don't even like sex.'

'And what would you know about what I like or dislike?'

'I know you. You've been my wife for—' he broke off.

She could practically hear the cogs of his brain grinding as he tried to remember just how long they'd been married. Give him any more time and he'd start adding the years up on his fingers.

'It'll be eighteen years in October,' she said helpfully. And you know what? I'd have got less for murdering you instead of marrying you. Ever thought that maybe I didn't enjoy sex with *you*?' she said. 'Ever thought that you were no good at it and that with the right man I might be mad for it?'

His jaw dropped.

'Yes that's right, Dave. I now know what good sex is all about. No, strike that. I now know what *great* sex is. For once your mum and Shelley got something right; I have been seeing someone else. Someone who really appreciates me. So like I just said, why don't you go home and find yourself a solicitor because this divorce is really going to happen. And if it makes you feel better, you can divorce me on the grounds of whatever you want. It makes no odds to me. Just so long as I'm free to get on with the rest of my life.'

Chapter Forty-nine

'All I need is another twenty days, then I'll have the money for you. Come on, Ethan. We go way back. You know you can trust me. You know I'll come through for you; it's just this month's so bloody tight. If I had the money it would be yours. You know that.'

'But things are tight for me, Desmond.'

'Fifteen days, then. Give me fifteen days and I swear you'll have it. I'm not asking for much, just fifteen days. You know how tough this last year has been for me. And not only with the business.'

It was hard to argue with a man whose wife had been diagnosed with a brain tumour last Christmas and who was yet to be given a clean bill of health, so reluctantly Ethan agreed to wait the requested fifteen days and after telling Desmond to pass his best wishes on to his wife, he rang off.

He stared at the piece of paper in front of him. He had marked five of the figures in the column on the right-hand side with an asterisk. The total of these figures came to £105,000. It was money owed to him that wouldn't be arriving in his bank account any time soon. The phone call to Desmond was the last in a morning of ringing round these customers and nudging them to pay up. Each call had more or less started and finished in the same way: *Funny you should get in touch, Ethan. I was about to ring you ... Bit of a cash flow problem this end ... I need more time.*

What could he do, other than give them more time? To play the heavy hand with these customers, as Francine's father was continually telling him to do, would ultimately backfire and they would take their business elsewhere when times were good.

The bank had been in touch first thing that morning and whilst the manager at the other end of the phone had not been without sympathy, the bottom line was that the account had to be replenished. And soon. When Ethan had explained that in order to pay his employees' wages this month he was going to have to temporarily extend the overdraft facility, the manager had suggested Ethan came in to the bank to discuss the matter in more detail. An appointment had been made for tomorrow morning.

Meanwhile, Francine was continuing to spend money they didn't have on the new house in Abersoch. She had given up on the idea of commissioning Ella to do any of the work and was currently investigating other specialist painters. Having been introduced to the world of specialist paint finishers, Francine was no longer prepared to consider employing the services of a mere work-a-day decorator, a decorator who would simply slap on some paint or wallpaper as instructed. If Ethan had the time he'd drive over to Abersoch and do the bloody decorating himself!

Come to that, he would clean The Lilacs if he had the time. Perish the thought that Francine would spare a single minute from her hectic shopping and spa life and do it herself. He had been in the kitchen when she had answered the telephone and received the news from Maggie that she would no longer be cleaning for them. Francine had been livid. Ethan couldn't believe what he was hearing when Francine, in no uncertain terms, informed Maggie that she wasn't ever to expect a reference from her. 'Don't even think about it, unless of course you want me to tell a prospective employer that you're not only unreliable but appallingly rude.'

It wasn't just what Francine had said that shocked Ethan – it was the tone of voice she used. Ella had been right; Francine did treat Maggie like dirt. When he'd queried his wife on why she had accused Maggie of being rude, she had said, 'Ask Christine. Maggie was downright offensive to her. That's the trouble these days. These people don't know their place. You give them an opportunity and what do they do? They take advantage.'

Ethan had found it impossible to believe that the woman who had looked after him that night when he'd made such a fool of himself in Ella's garden and who had then driven him home could be at all offensive. It was a far easier proposition to imagine it being the other way round, that Christine had been ill-mannered and offensive to Maggie. And as for anyone in this day and age being kept in their place, that was offensive beyond belief.

He had been so disturbed by Francine's behaviour he had secretly found Maggie's mobile number in his wife's address book and called her the next day to apologize. She had been surprised to hear from him and after he'd said he would have no hesitation in writing a good reference for her whenever she needed one, she'd told him where she was now working and that she was seeing Ella almost on a daily basis. 'I'm glad you've phoned,' she'd then said. 'I wanted to thank you for giving me the courage to get in touch with Daryl again. And you know what, it wasn't him on his boat with a woman, it was a friend of his.'

Ethan remembered Maggie telling him about leaving her husband and there being another man involved somehow, but as to giving her any advice, his mind was a blank. He hadn't admitted that, though. 'Does that mean everything's okay between the two of you?' he'd asked.

'More than okay.' She had laughed. 'I've never been happier. I feel like I've been given this amazing second chance, and I'll tell you for nothing, I'm not going to let it go. You know, you and Ella were a great help to me.'

Oh, so Ella had given the same advice, had she? Great minds and all that.

In the days that followed Ethan often thought of the sheer delight in Maggie's voice – *I've never been happier*. He envied her. Not just for the turnaround in her life and good fortune, but for being brave enough to change the status quo. Not many did. Too many, like him, sank further and further into the quicksand of their miserable lives until there was no hauling themselves out. God, how he hated self-pity.

Suddenly it felt like a blowtorch was being taken to his guts, as if his self-pity was a full-blown disease nestled in the pit of his stomach. He yanked open the top drawer of his desk and groaned. Damn, he was out of antacid. He checked the next drawer down. Nothing.

With dread he waited for the pain to build. It did, and with a ferocious intensity that had him clenching his fists. Breathless and nauseous, he suddenly felt hot. He closed his eyes and in the distance, in another world, he could hear Pat, the receptionist, answering the phone in the small outer office. Lightheaded, he tried to get his breath. Sweat was pooling between his shoulder blades and under his arms. He really should see a doctor. He couldn't go on like this.

Eventually, the pain subsided and he was consumed with tiredness. He hadn't been able to sleep last night – his mind had been racing, his heart pounding, but now, overcome with exhaustion, he felt like he could sleep for a week.

He was just wondering if he could get away with shutting his office door and stealing a discreet nap when he remembered his mobile had buzzed earlier while Desmond had been on the phone pleading his case. He dug out the phone from his jacket, which hung on the back of his chair. There was a text. *Please call me.* URGENT! *Ella.*

Ella was at Belmont Hall. Unusually the house was quiet. There was no one drilling, hammering, or sawing. There was no Hal either. Not that he ever made any noise in the house. After a hastily eaten lunch with Maggie, she was now back in the drawing room anxiously waiting for Ethan to reply to her text.

She climbed back up the scaffolding and tried to focus on the task of adding the gilt detail to the ceiling rose in the centre of the room. As distractions went, it was failing miserably.

She had spent most of last night and this morning trying to decide what to do. Her initial thought was to deal with the matter on her own, which was how she always did things. Asking for help or bringing in back-up troops was not something she ever favoured. But in this instance it wasn't just her who was involved. If she mishandled things she could land Ethan in all sorts of trouble. Part of her thought he had brought it on himself and therefore had only himself to blame if the consequences were not to his liking.

But selfishly, what bothered her more was what could happen if Christine Paxton decided to make trouble for Ella by contacting Lawrence. Just as important and equally puzzling was why the woman clearly disliked Ella so much. Surely she wasn't going to do anything as far-fetched as try to blackmail her, was she? Did she, for instance, think this might be a way to get Ella to work for her for free?

And what of the 'interesting photograph' Christine Paxton had referred to? A photograph that apparently captured the moment perfectly. Was it the moment when Ella and Ethan had been standing by her car, when she had innocently kissed him goodbye on the cheek? Or when he had kissed her on the mouth? That hadn't seemed so innocent at the time, and it certainly didn't now. How to explain that away? And how on earth did Christine come to have that photograph? Had she been following Ella? Or had Ethan been her target? But why? Why, why, why? What was Christine up to?

Whatever was going on inside Christine's head, Ella knew that she had to talk to Ethan. The response to Christine and how she should be dealt with could not be unilaterally decided; it affected both her and Ethan.

With a terrible sense of foreboding, she checked her watch. In two hours' time she was due in Lilac Avenue.

Her mobile rang, making her jump. It was Ethan. At last. Thank goodness.

Chapter Fifty

Just what in hell's name was he going to do about Christine? What did she want from him? And what exactly did she know? Or think she knew?

In his car, driving to meet Ella, he couldn't help but be horribly reminded of Collette. Collette had been the woman with whom he'd had the affair, the woman who had turned nasty when he'd ended things, the woman who had, to spite him, informed Francine that she was pregnant by him. He'd been effectively a prisoner of his marriage ever since, and it didn't bear thinking what would happen this time round if Christine behaved as maliciously.

But what could Christine tell Francine? The truth of the matter was he had done nothing wrong. Yes, he was guilty of fantasizing about Ella, but if guilt by thought alone was ever made a legally punishable offence, then there would be a pretty long queue of offenders.

Yet even as he justified his actions to himself, he knew that he was guilty of so much more, and Francine would know that. She would believe whatever Christine told her. Besides, there was a photograph. Or so Christine had told Ella. What if she was bluffing and there wasn't a photo? As chilling as it was, he suspected she wasn't bluffing.

But why was she doing this? Was it simply to get back at him for turning her down? He recalled the night she had been in the kitchen at The Lilacs and coming on to him and he'd had to make it very clear nothing was ever going to happen between them. She had warned him, hadn't she? She had said he was making a big mistake.

The worst of it was that he had got Ella involved. Understandably she had sounded uptight on the phone, anxious that Christine might try to cause trouble for her and Lawrence. Poor Ella. She didn't deserve this. She had done nothing wrong. He wished he could think of a way to extricate her from the situation.

Not for the first time he wondered why Christine had approached Ella and not him. What was her game? He was beginning to wonder whether Christine was mentally unbalanced. What if she was so obsessed with him she was prepared to hurt someone she believed he cared about? It would be one way of exacting maximum revenge, wouldn't it? The only retaliation he could come up with was to say that he would tell Francine what kind of friend Christine was – the kind of friend who thought it was perfectly acceptable to make a play for a best friend's husband behind her back.

It didn't seem much of a retaliation when he really thought about it. He didn't think for a minute Francine would believe him. Even if she did, what did it gain him? If there was a photograph of him with Ella, how was he ever going to explain that?

He winced and then groaned as a wave of agonizing pain gripped his insides. It was so bad, he had to pull over and stop the car.

When at last he felt able to drive, he started up the engine and drove on to Belmont Hall.

Alone in the house with Ethan – Hal wasn't due back from London until tomorrow and Maggie was at the supermarket – Ella was shocked at the sight of him. He looked exhausted. His skin was deathly pale and there were dark bruise-like shadows under his eyes. She was so concerned by his appearance that she couldn't bring herself to let rip at him for the invidious position he had put her in. She took him through to the kitchen and was about to offer him a drink when he suddenly gasped and bent over as if he'd been kicked in the stomach.

'Ethan?'

He didn't respond. Alarmed, she put a hand to his back. 'Ethan,' she repeated, 'what is it?'

He straightened up slightly and started to cough, a hand covering his mouth. He sounded like he was choking. To Ella's horror she saw blood seeping through his fingers. He staggered towards the sink and leaned over it. Blood gushed out of him. She had never seen anything like it.

Terrified, she dialled 999 for an ambulance.

Chapter Fifty-one

Wound tight with pent-up rage, Christine was furious; she hadn't anticipated a no-show. Just who did Ella Moore think she was? The woman had made a serious error of judgement. The gloves were off now. It was time for Ella to find out exactly with whom she was dealing.

Taking the number from the business card that Ella's dupe of a boyfriend had given Adam in Abersoch, and which Christine had removed from his wallet, she tapped it into her mobile.

A minute later and a feeling of calm satisfaction came over her. Really, the stupid woman had only herself to blame. First, Ella should never have got involved with Ethan. Second, she should have agreed at the outset to do the work for Christine. And third, she should have kept their appointment this afternoon. Their meeting was to have made it crystal clear that Ella was to stay away from Ethan. If she had refused then her boyfriend would receive the photo of Ella kissing Ethan.

Now he had received it. She smiled. How she would like to be a fly on the wall when that little bomb exploded in Ella's face. It served her right. She should never have made a move on Ethan. Ethan wasn't to blame. What healthy red-blooded man would refuse a woman who threw herself at him so obviously? Even a charmless woman like Ella.

The more Christine thought about it, the more she realized that Ethan had been right not to succumb to her own feelings for him. Given the circumstances, he had shown great tact and great strength of character in refusing her, and she admired him for that. An affair with his wife's best friend and neighbour wasn't on. Anyway, she wanted more than an affair. She didn't want to share Ethan with Francine; she wanted the whole of him.

But things between Ethan and Francine would soon change. When the time came for Christine to show Francine the photograph, the marriage would be over and Ethan would be free. He would be free to discover just how much Christine loved him and what a wonderful life they could have together.

Ella was so glad to have Maggie's company at the hospital.

Returning to Belmont Hall from the supermarket shortly before the ambulance had arrived, poor Maggie had walked into a scene of unimaginable horror. The kitchen looked like a chainsaw massacre had taken place; there was blood everywhere. Ethan's face, clothes and hands were covered in it, as were Ella and the floor, and some of the cupboards. Poor Maggie had let out a petrified, piercing scream and dropped the two bags of shopping she'd been carrying.

Ella had gone with Ethan in the ambulance while Maggie had followed behind in her car. Ethan had been fully conscious during the journey but in great pain as the blood continued to pour out of him. Not knowing what was wrong with him, Ella had been terrified. She was still terrified sitting here in the hospital waiting area. She couldn't rid herself of the awful memory of all that blood. How could anyone lose so much and still live?

The limited information they had received from the medical staff so far was that he was now undergoing emergency surgery for suspected peritonitis, a perforated peptic ulcer. How long had Ethan been suffering from a stomach ulcer? Had he even known he'd had an ulcer? Once or twice he had mentioned that he occasionally had stomach problems, usually made worse when he was stressed. According to Maggie there had been a selection of antacid products in the bathroom at The Lilacs for nearly a year.

Footsteps had her looking up. It was Maggie. She had gone outside to use her mobile. 'Mrs Edwards will be here soon,' she said. 'You ought to go.'

'I know.' But Ella didn't move. Her stomach was jittery, her chest tight and tears were pricking at the back of her eyes. It was shock, she supposed. The shock of seeing Ethan so ill. He had been in such pain in the ambulance. Even the paramedic seemed shocked by what was happening.

Maggie sat in the chair next to her. 'I'll let you know how he is,' she said. 'I promise I'll call you. But if Mrs Edwards finds you here, she'll want to know why and that will cause all sorts of problems for you and Mr Edwards.'

'Remind me of our story.'

Their story had been hurriedly concocted while they waited for the ambulance to arrive.

'I was driving back from the supermarket and spotted Mr Edwards' car in a lay-by not far from Belmont Hall where I now work,' Maggie explained. 'He was out of his car and didn't look well to me so I stopped and asked if he was okay. When he said he didn't feel well enough to drive, I offered to take him to Belmont Hall until he was feeling better. That was when he started coughing up blood. I then phoned for an ambulance.'

'And his car?'

'You're going to sort that out when you leave here. You're going to drive it back to the lay-by and then walk the short distance back to Belmont Hall. You've got the keys, haven't you? I gave them to you earlier.' Ella nodded.

'And there's no mention of me working there?'

'No mention of you at all. Now go. I'll call you when I know something.'

Ella smiled weakly. 'I'm glad one of us is thinking straight; my brain seems to have gone into meltdown mode. Thank you.'

Maggie returned the smile and gave her an unexpected hug. 'It's the least I can do after everything you've done for me.'

Ten minutes after Ella had left, Maggie heard the clickety-click of heels and an unmistakable voice: Mrs Edwards had arrived and was demanding to see her husband. The young nurse sitting behind the desk at the nurse's station was on the phone; she covered the receiver with her hand and spoke to Mrs Edwards, then pointed towards the waiting area. That was when Mrs Edwards saw Maggie. She came over. 'Do you know how he is, Maggie?' she asked.

'Only that they're operating on him. It sounds like he had an ulcer and it exploded or something. I don't really know the details.'

'An ulcer? That can't be right. I would have known.'

You wouldn't have noticed if he'd collapsed right under your snooty nose, you uncaring bitch, thought Maggie. 'Can I get you a drink, Mrs Edwards?' she asked politely. 'There's a vending machine not far away.'

The other woman shook her head. 'Tell me exactly what happened and how you came to be with my husband.'

When Maggie had finished talking, Mrs Edwards sat down and rummaged through her handbag. She pulled out her mobile phone.

'I don't think you're allowed to use that in here,' Maggie said.

Mrs Edwards gave her a look that could have frozen the sun. 'I'll do what I damn well please,' she snapped. 'Valentina needs to know about her father.'

She made the call, but from what Maggie could hear, she wasn't able to speak to Valentina and had to leave a message. She was about to make another call when the young nurse who had directed Mrs Edwards to the waiting area hurried over, her shoes squeaking on the shiny floor. 'I'm sorry,' she said, 'mobile phones aren't allowed.'

Mrs Edwards looked murderous. 'And I suppose someone having the good manners to tell me whether my husband is alive or not isn't allowed either?'

'As I said earlier,' the nurse replied, standing her ground, 'Mr Edwards is still in theatre, but just as soon as I know anything I'll let you know.'

When they were alone again, Mrs Edwards looked at Maggie. 'There's no need for you to stay. You can go.'

No longer an employee of Mrs Edwards, Maggie wasn't going to be pushed around by her. 'For peace of mind I'd like to stay until I know Mr Edwards is all right,' she said firmly.

Mrs Edwards looked at her suspiciously. 'I didn't know you cared so much for my husband, Maggie.'

'He's always been very good to me.'

'Really?'

'I just want to stay until I know he's okay,' Maggie repeated.

Mrs Edwards shrugged her shoulders. 'Oh well, if you are going to stay, maybe I will have that drink after all. Coffee, black, no sugar.'

With a touch of arsenic perhaps, thought Maggie.

The front door slammed. 'Mum! You'll never guess what's happened!'

In the sitting room, Christine put down the magazine she was reading. 'Katie, how many times have I told you not to slam doors and shriek like a fishmonger's wife? It's most unladylike. Is that chewing gum in your mouth? And why have you got ink all over your hands? Haven't those teachers taught you how to use a pen properly yet?'

Katie puffed out her cheeks and rolled her eyes. 'Mum, just listen to me, will you? When we were on the bus coming home, Valentina got a message from Francine; Ethan's been rushed to hospital.'

Christine was on her feet. 'Hospital? What's wrong with him? Has he had an accident?'

'No, but he's had to have an emergency operation.'

'Oh my God, no! What kind of an operation?'

'I dunno. Valentina's ringing for a taxi to go to the hospital.'

'Where is she?'

'Next door. Where else would she be? We've just got back from school.'

'For heaven's sake, Katie, why are you standing there like an idiot? Go and tell Valentina to cancel the taxi. I'll take her.'

On her own, Christine closed her eyes. Her precious Ethan. In hospital. She couldn't believe it. An emergency operation. What if he died? Oh, it was so unfair! Why couldn't it be Francine who was in danger of dying?

Christine wrapped her arms around Francine. 'Darling, how is he? Tell me he's all right. Tell me he's not in danger.'

'They've finished operating on him. That's all I know.'

'Poor Ethan. I can't bear to think of him suffering.' She let go of Francine. 'And you, Francine, how are you bearing up?'

'I'd feel a lot better if there was something more palatable than vending machine coffee to drink. The one Maggie got me earlier was undrinkable.'

'Maggie? What was she doing here?'

'She was with Ethan when he was taken ill. She was the one who called an ambulance for him.' Francine looked about her. The waiting area was empty, save for the two of them and Valentina and Katie. 'She must have gone. She was here a minute ago. I told her to go, but she insisted on staying until there was news.'

'Really? What was she doing with—'

'Mrs Edwards?' interrupted a woman's voice from behind them.

Both Francine and Christine turned and looked into the doughy face of a young nurse. Francine said, 'I'm Mrs Edwards. How is my husband?'

'He's back from theatre and whilst he's still very poorly, he is stable now.'

'Poorly? Stable?' repeated Christine, wanting to take the

nurse by the shoulders and shake the uselessness out of her. 'What exactly does that mean?'

The young nurse gave her an enquiring look. 'I'm family,' Christine said, in case the stupid girl had any ideas about excluding her from hearing any information by claiming 'family only'. 'I'm Mr Edwards' sister.' She gave Francine a meaningful glance. 'Isn't that right?'

Francine nodded. 'Please tell us in plain English just what's going on with my husband. And when can we see him?'

'I'm afraid he won't come round from the anaesthetic for some hours yet but there was a complication during surgery.'

'What kind of complication?' asked Francine.

'Because he'd lost so much blood, your husband's blood pressure dropped and he went into cardiac arrest.'

Christine gasped. 'Cardiac arrest!' she cried.

'But he's all right now?' asked Francine.

'As I said, he's stable now. But you have to bear in mind he'll be quite weak for a while. He's had to have a blood transfusion as well. He'll need to rest. I suggest you take a break and go and find yourselves something to eat. There's a cafe on the ground floor.'

'You think we're capable of eating at a time like this?' Christine snapped at the nurse. 'Just how insensitive can you be?'

'I understand you're all very upset but—'

'Trust me, you cannot possibly understand how we're feeling.'

Francine put a hand on Christine's arm. 'Perhaps we could manage a sandwich,' she said, 'if only to pass the time.'

The nurse walked away.

'I could eat more than a sandwich,' Valentina said. 'I'm starving. How about you, Katie?'

'Oh, why go to the bother of asking her?' Christine blasted. 'Let's face it, if eating was made an Olympic sport Katie would be a gold medallist!'

'Mum!'

'For God's sake, doesn't anyone care about Ethan? Are you all more concerned with food than you are with him?'

The pressure of Francine's hand increased on Christine's arm. 'Shush, Christine, people are looking.'

'I don't care; let them look!' She glared at a couple who had just joined them in the waiting area, daring them to keep staring. They didn't. 'You go and get something to eat, Francine,' she said, taking a deep breath and realizing that she had to get a grip on her emotions. 'I'll stay here just in case there's any more news.'

'Are you sure?'

'Perfectly sure. That's what any good friend would do. Go on, take the girls and stay as long as you like. I'll hold the fort here. Don't you worry.'

With Ethan's car now parked in the lay-by, Ella was back at Belmont Hall cleaning the kitchen. Dazed and numb, she scrubbed at the gruesome darkening splashes of blood. Some of the stains refused to budge from two of the cupboard doors; she would have to repaint them.

Now having locked the house securely and switched on the burglar alarm as Hal had shown her, she was driving to Tickle Cottage to change her clothes. She could hardly turn up at Mayfield covered in Ethan's blood.

She was five minutes from home when her mobile rang. She saw who it was and pulled off the road.

'Ella, it's me, Maggie. You okay to talk?'

'Yes, what's the news?' As she asked the question she felt time stand still. Please let him be all right, she silently prayed.

'They've finished operating on him and he's now on a ward sleeping off the anaesthetic. But he gave them all a right scare at one point – apparently his heart stopped.'

'No!' Ella felt her own heart almost stop. Her hands began to shake.

'Don't worry, he's all right now.'

'You're sure? You're absolutely sure?'

'That's what the doctor said.'

'Did you speak to the doctor?'

'No. But as luck would have it, after Mrs Edwards arrived I recognized one of the nurses – we'd been at school together. Anyway, she turned a blind eye to the usual rules about "family only" and filled me in.'

'Thank goodness for old school friends.'

'I'll see you at work tomorrow, then? By the way, you sorted the car out, did you?

'Yes, and I've left the keys in the kitchen, as agreed.'

'Good. I'll let Mrs Edwards know she can collect the car when she wants to. Which means you'll have to keep yours hidden for a while.'

'You're right, I hadn't thought of that. Thanks for everything you've done today, Maggie. You've been great.'

'No problem. You have a nice evening. Try and relax.'

But a nice evening was the last thing in store for Ella. When she let herself in at Mayfield, she found both Lawrence and Alexis in the kitchen waiting for her. The grim expression on Lawrence's face told her something was dreadfully wrong.

'I'm sorry I'm so late,' she said, thinking that maybe this was what was bothering them.

Lawrence stepped towards her. 'I suppose you're late because you've been with your boyfriend?' He picked up his mobile phone from the table, fiddled with it, then thrust it towards her.

She glanced at it with trepidation. 'It's not what you think,' she said.

Chapter Fifty-two

He was on a boat and drifting. The sky was blue, the water calm. There was no wind. He could feel the hot sun on his face and his body. Ella was lying next to him, the fingertips of her right hand touching the fingertips of his left. It was the merest whisper of contact between them but it was enough. It was all he needed. Just knowing she was there beside him was enough.

The boat continued to drift on the calm water and the sun continued to soothe his tired and aching body. But then, as if a cloud was passing over the sun, he felt a shadow above him. It was Ella and her face was inches above his. She kissed him on the mouth. Her lips were warm and soft and he lost himself in the kiss, not wanting it to end.

Gradually the pressure of her mouth against his increased and she was pressing down on him. He began to feel stifled; he couldn't breathe. He tried to turn his face away but his body wouldn't react – it was as if he was paralysed. 'Stop it,' he tried to say, 'please stop it.' He didn't want her kissing him like this. There was no tenderness to it. He forced his eyes open and saw that it wasn't Ella kissing him; it was Christine. Sickened, he recoiled and tried to push her away, but again his body wouldn't move; his arms were like lead weights. She was smiling at him now and telling him not to worry, that he was going to be all right and she would take care of him because she loved him so very much. He wanted to call for help and to shout at her to go away, to leave him alone, but everything began to go blurry and he felt himself slipping into the depths of a warm darkness.

Christine stroked Ethan's cheek. 'Sleep, my darling,' she murmured. 'Sleep all you can and let me take care of you and our future. Just leave everything to me.'

Ella was a mass of conflicting emotions. At times she was angry with Ethan. Other times she was angry with Lawrence for being so short-sighted. But mostly she was furious with herself.

When she was thinking rationally she promised herself she would not hold Ethan accountable. But right now, when she was feeling anything but rational – Alexis had just sent her another vicious text message – she held Ethan absolutely accountable. For the simple fact he *was* responsible. He *was* to blame. He was the reason she was now held in such contempt. Because of him she had been cast in the role of liar, cheat and betrayer. Even Toby, her normally staunch and faithful supporter, had given up on her after Alexis had made it her business to send him the photo on Lawrence's mobile. After that, what else could Toby do but think badly of her? A picture cannot lie, after all.

She had repeatedly explained to Lawrence the innocent nature of the photograph and how it had come about, but he had refused to believe her. In the end, her head metaphorically black and blue from being beaten against the brick wall of Lawrence's blinkered anger, she had simply given up. She had packed her things and left Mayfield. For ever. There was no going back.

That had been two days ago and whenever she thought of Lawrence's implacable refusal to hear her out, or recalled the look of hatred in Alexis's face or replayed the disappointment in Toby's voice – how she hated knowing that she had lost his respect – she thought, Thank you, Ethan Edwards. Thank you for ruining my life. For making me appear guilty when I'm innocent.

Her innocence, however, was built on decidedly shaky

foundations. *Hypocrite!* Shouted the voice of her conscience. *Self-righteous hypocrite!* Much as she wanted to be in the right, she wasn't, not when she remembered how she had felt at the hospital when she had watched Ethan being rushed to the operating theatre. In that moment, seeing him so helpless and so dangerously ill, the true extent of her feelings for him could not be denied. She had been overwhelmed by the need to hold him, to reassure him that she would be there when he woke up. Leaving the hospital, not knowing if he was going to live, had been one of the hardest things she had done.

In her workshop at Tickle Cottage, her mobile started to ring. Presumably it was Alexis wanting to abuse her verbally now. But the number was withheld. A client, perhaps?

'Ella, it's me, Ethan.'

'Ethan? How are you? And where are you?'

'I'm okay, but I'm still stuck here in hospital. They're not letting me out until the day after tomorrow, and only then if they're convinced I'm well enough. I've been going crazy wanting to ring you, but Francine confiscated my mobile and told the nurses I was banned from using a hospital phone in case I phoned work. I managed to sweet talk one of the nurses into letting me make this call, though.'

Ella almost smiled. 'How like you that sounds.'

'Believe me, I wouldn't bother for anyone else. But Ella, I have to thank you for what you and Maggie did. The surgeon said that if you hadn't got me here as fast as you did, I could have died. Something about a ruptured artery.'

'I heard that things got worse when you were on the operating table.'

'I heard that, too. Perhaps a part of me didn't think life was worth living any more.'

'Don't say that. Not ever.'

There was a pause, and then: 'Sorry, I'm being melodramatic. Blame it on all the drugs they're pumping me full of. So how are you?'

'In better shape than you,' she said lightly.

'I certainly hope so. You should see the massive scar I'm going to be left with.'

'Does it hurt?'

'Only when I laugh. Which isn't often. I can't tell you how good it is to hear your voice.'

Ella swallowed. 'It's good to hear yours as well.'

'Do you mean that?'

'Yes ... there was a moment when I thought I might not hear it again.'

Her words hung in the ether between them. She heard him sigh and then clear his throat.

'There's something else I need to thank you and Maggie for,' he said. 'The story about how I ended up here. I got the gist of it from Francine and played along.'

'That's good.'

'Is it? I'm not so sure. If things were different, I might—' His voice broke off.

'Carry on,' she urged him.

'No. No point. Water and bridges. How's Lawrence?'

'Angry.'

'Why? What's he got to be angry about?'

She told him about the photograph Christine had sent and how Lawrence had reacted.

'Oh shit, Ella. I'm sorry. Is there anything I can do? When I get out of here, would it help if I spoke to him?'

'There's nothing you could say that I haven't tried saying already.'

'But I'd tell him the truth. That it was me who kissed you.'

'It doesn't explain everything else, does it?'

'But I'd tell him that no matter how hard I pursued you, you didn't give in. I'll swear that you were the epitome of propriety.'

'I don't think he would believe you.' Why should he, she thought, when she didn't really believe it herself?

'Don't you want me to try?'

She hesitated. And continued to hesitate. Would there be any point? A short while ago she had been wholly committed to rebuilding her relationship with Lawrence. She had genuinely believed it was what she wanted, but on top of his previous behaviour towards her, his instant dismissal of her and his adamant refusal to listen had left her wondering just how committed he really had been to her. Had they both merely been going through the motions of what they thought was the right thing to do, to reclaim what they had once had because it was better than nothing? Without doubt, Ella had come to realize in the last couple of days that she had used Lawrence. She had hidden behind him as a way to avoid admitting her true feelings for Ethan.

'Ella? Are you still there?'

'Yes,' she said tiredly, 'I'm still here.'

'Can I ask you one of my irritating questions?'

'Go on.'

'Did you hesitate just then because you're not sure Lawrence is the right man for you? Is there a chance you think there's someone out there, not a million miles away, who might suit you better?'

Despite everything, Ella laughed. 'All I can say is that it's a shame the doctor who had you on the operating table didn't remove your massive ego when he had the chance.'

'It's because I was on that operating table that I'm asking the question, Ella. Life's too short to mess about, so I'm just going to come right out and say this: I love you and want to be with you. I know that when I'm with you I feel happy, that life feels worth living.'

'But I don't want a married man to love me.'

'I know that. I know that all too well. Oh, sod it, I'm going to have to go. Francine's arrived. I can hear her haranguing one of the poor nurses. Goodbye Ella.'

'Goodbye Ethan. You take care now.'

Chapter Fifty-three

It was the middle of July, school had finished and Francine had taken Valentina and Katie to Abersoch for the week. If the weather proved to be good, the week might turn into two. Ethan could only hope a miracle might happen and the good weather would continue for three weeks. Today was Monday and though he had been charged with joining them on Friday evening, the rest of the week stretched invitingly ahead of him.

In his office, supposedly 'taking it easy' on his first day back at work, he was dealing with a limited amount of paperwork. It was strange being back. He felt distanced from it all, as though in the big scheme of things everything that had mattered so much to him before meant nothing now. Whilst he'd been forced to recuperate at home, Chris had kept him regularly updated. A surprising number of clients had been in touch to pass on their best wishes, but less surprising was that the large amounts of money owed still hadn't been paid.

He swivelled his chair and turned to look out of the window. It was a beautiful day, the kind of summer's day that could lift the weariest of spirits. Even his. He had been warned that he might suffer from occasional bouts of depression following his operation, that it was quite common, especially after a skirmish with death. He didn't think he was depressed, but he could be happier, that much he knew. But that had been the case for many years.

During his stay in hospital he'd learned that if only he had gone to the doctor when he'd first experienced problems, the ulcer in his stomach wouldn't have perforated. The surgeon had explained that what had happened to him was quite rare these days, if only because most sane people went to see their GP at the first sign of trouble.

To help his recovery he was under strict orders not to drink any alcohol and to avoid caffeine; he also had to stick to a low-fat diet. He missed an occasional glass of wine of an evening, but it was the caffeine he really missed.

Staring out of his office window at the cloudless blue sky, he decided to take a risk and go home; he would sit on the terrace and finish the paperwork there.

It was a risk because ever since he'd come home from the hospital, he hadn't chanced spending any time alone in the garden for fear of Christine 'popping' round. He hadn't felt safe alone inside the house either and whenever he was on his own he was paranoid about the front and back doors being locked. The moment Francine left the house to go to her spa or the shops, he would check there was no way Christine could get in. He'd frequently heard the front door bell being rung or the sound of knocking at the back door, but at all times he stayed upstairs where Christine wouldn't be able to peer in through a window at him.

His paranoia stemmed from the gruesome recurring dream he kept having. Nearly every night he dreamed that he was back in the hospital, in a bed, unable to move, with Christine kissing him and then whispering in his ear that she loved him and would take care of him. Sometimes he dreamed she was stroking his face. Always he would wake from the dream with a chilling sensation that it had really happened, that when he was still under the effect of the anaesthetic Christine had been there at his bedside. He couldn't get it out of his head that she had done something to him. It was a sickening thought and so bothered him he knew that he would have to tackle her about it. But not yet. For now he didn't want to be anywhere near her. She was a dangerous woman, a woman who had deliberately wrecked Ella's relationship with Lawrence and who knew what she would do next? Hopefully she didn't have anything in mind for today. As far as he knew, from Francine, she was down in Dorset with Adam, which meant he should be able to enjoy some peace and quiet in the garden at home.

He had been in the garden for no more than half an hour listening to U2 playing through the open French doors when he heard his name being called.

With a bottle of champagne and two glasses in her hands, Christine emerged from the side of the house. She was dressed in a white linen shift dress; it was unbuttoned low enough to show her lacy bra and unbuttoned high enough to very nearly show her crotch. Right, the subtle approach.

'Hello, Ethan,' she said. 'I thought maybe you'd like some company, seeing as Francine has abandoned you and you're here all on your lonesome.'

'I thought you and Adam were house hunting down in Poole,' he said without getting up.

She smiled. 'That's what I told Francine. Adam's down there, but as you can see, I'm very much here.' Ignoring the carefully ordered papers and laptop on the glass-topped table, she plonked the bottle and flutes in the middle of it. 'Do you want to do the honours, or shall I?'

He forced himself to stay calm, to hide his revulsion. 'It's very kind of you to think I might be lonely,' he said, 'but as you can see I have plenty to occupy me.'

She sat in the chair next to him. 'Oh, don't be silly, no one's working on a beautiful day like this. Come on, darling, open the bubbly and then we can talk. It's been so long since I last saw you.'

He cringed at the word *darling*. 'I'm sorry,' he said, 'but I'm not allowed to touch alcohol these days.'

'How very boring. But I'm not restricted, so open the bottle, pour me a glass and tell me how you're feeling. You know, I don't think I'll ever get over the shock of seeing you in that hospital bed. I was there while you slept off the anaesthetic, you know. Francine left you all alone to go in search of something to eat. I couldn't believe she could do that. But I was there for you, Ethan. I stayed devotedly by your side, waiting for you to wake up.'

He tensed. 'How odd,' he said mildly. 'I thought I'd dreamed that. So you were really there?'

'Do you remember anything else?' She tilted her head and smiled. It was a knowing smile that sent a chill running through him.

He looked straight at her. 'Was there anything else to remember?' he asked. He felt like he was looking into the eyes of a deadly snake.

'We shared our first kiss, darling. I was hoping it might wake you up. You looked so weak and vulnerable lying there in that bed. Quite helpless.'

He swallowed. He'd been right all along. He'd *known* something had happened. 'Please don't call me darling,' he said.

'How about sweetheart? Do you prefer that? Goodness, you still haven't opened that champagne!'

He suddenly cracked, couldn't keep the mild-mannered pretence up any longer. 'Forget the champagne, Christine! Just tell me why you're here and what it is you want from me.'

She settled back in her chair and crossed her long, tanned legs, causing the front of her dress to part yet further. 'I would have thought that was obvious. I want to make you happy. You deserve to be happy, don't you? You've been through so much and I just know that if you were to accept that your marriage is over, you and I could be happy together.'

'Who says my marriage is over?'

'You don't need to pretend with me, darling. I know marriage to Francine is about as fulfilling as—'

'As your marriage?' he interrupted her scornfully.

She either didn't catch his tone or deliberately chose to

ignore it. 'Adam simply isn't the man you are,' she said. 'He bores me in bed. And out of bed, come to that. Whereas you, Ethan,' she leaned forward, put a hand on his forearm and ran her nails the length of it, 'you would never bore me. Quite the reverse. I think you and I would have plenty in common; we would be perfect bedfellows. Don't you agree?'

He removed her hand from his arm. 'No. I don't think we would ever have the slightest thing in common. In or out of bed.'

'That's because you're playing the part of dutiful husband. But I know the truth of your marriage. I've known it for ages. And I know all about your little indiscretion from way back when and that you only stay with Francine because she'll take you to the cleaners if you try to leave her. She'll take your business and you'll be left with nothing. That's why you stay with her. She really doesn't deserve you. You see, I know everything. And let's not forget what I know about you and Ella. I suppose you dallied with her because you felt sorry for her. But I can forgive you for that.'

She sounded every inch the madwoman he had begun to suspect she was. 'Why would I feel sorry for Ella?' he asked carefully.

Christine laughed. 'Come off it, Ethan. It's perfectly obvious she was a courtesy shag that got out of hand. She came on to you and you politely gave in and then she wouldn't let go of you. I know how women like her operate.'

'You couldn't be more wrong. And don't you dare ever criticize Ella. She's an extraordinary woman. She has more ethics and principles than you or I will ever have.'

'You'll be calling her a paragon of virtue next. Which I would find hard to believe, knowing what I know.'

'You know nothing, Christine. Whatever you've convinced yourself of, you could not be more wrong. Ella and I have only ever been friends. We have not had an affair. And nor will you and I ever have an affair. It will never happen. Not in a million years. Not even if we were the last two people on earth and it was down to us to keep the human race going.'

She sharpened her gaze on his. 'You know, I'm not getting a good feeling from you right now. I don't think you've quite grasped the situation and what it is I'm offering you.'

He stood up abruptly and moved away; he needed to put some distance between them. 'Oh, I've grasped the situation all right. You think you've got some kind of hold on me and as a consequence I'll do whatever you ask.'

'I'm offering you a way out, a chance to be free. But if you turn my offer down, well, let's consider what would happen if, for instance, I showed Francine the photograph I have of Ella kissing you. Francine would wipe the floor with you, wouldn't she? Is that what you want to risk?'

'And the alternative? Your offer?'

'You come to your senses and admit that your marriage is over and you leave Francine for me.'

'Francine would still take everything from me.'

'Darling, you'll have me, and after I've divorced dull old Adam, we'll have enough money for the two of us. You'll be able to start a new business. You'll be free, Ethan. Don't you want that?'

He pushed his hands into his pockets and walked to the edge of the terrace. He stared at the monstrosity of a water feature that Francine was so proud of. He turned to look back at Christine. 'You've put a lot of thought into this, haven't you?'

'When I want something, I go all out for it.'

'So all my problems would be over? I'd have the love of a woman who adores me, and sufficient financial security to start up a new business? Is that how you see the future?'

'*Our* future. And yes, that's exactly how I see it.'

'I have to hand it to you, Christine. It's a tempting offer, an offer only a fool would refuse. It's certainly something to think about.'

*

It was two months since Maggie had last seen Dean and he seemed as much of a stranger to her today as he had always been.

This was her son, she had to keep reminding herself. She had given birth to him, she had fed him and dressed him and she had changed his revolting nappies. She had taken him for walks in his buggy; she had taken him to playgrounds; she had taken him to school and brought him home. She had watched him grow, every chunky inch of him. But somehow it didn't seem possible that she had had anything to do with him or that he was her son. She could see nothing of herself in him. With his pale scalp showing through his buzzcut hair, his slightly too-fat lips and his Nana Brenda's pale eyes, he was one hundred per cent his father's child. He had his dad's sweet tooth as well and as he tipped a third sachet of sugar into his mug of tea and began stirring it, Maggie pictured the thick, gravelly bottom of the mug being dredged like the seabed.

When she'd been pregnant with Dean she had secretly wanted a daughter and when he was born – after the midwife had taken the decision that the only way to get the baby out was for Maggie to have a caesarean with an epidural – she had burst into tears when she was told that she was now the mother of a big, bonny boy. The midwife, along with Dave, had put her tears down to tiredness and relief. She had never told anyone of her disappointment – she had felt too guilty to admit such a thing. She had promised herself that she would be a good mother to Dean, but it hadn't been easy. He hadn't been a huggy baby. He'd been a proper howler, a screaming, angry, colicky baby. He'd never wanted to be comforted or cuddled. In the end she had given up trying to hug him, tired of being pushed away all the time.

Would she have been a better mother if she'd had a daughter? Would things between her and Dave have been better had she got her wish? But the chance to have a daughter had been lost to her when something had gone wrong with her body two days after Dean's birth. She'd never really understood what had happened – something about an infection in her uterus – all she knew was that she had to have an emergency operation in the middle of the night and when she woke up the next morning she was told that she wouldn't be able to have any more children. She had cried and cried. For days. For weeks. And always on her own. She rarely allowed herself to remember that time; it hurt too much to dwell on it.

She fought off the painful lump in her throat and said, 'So what did you want to see me about, Dean?'

He had texted earlier that day to say he wanted to see her. She had agreed to meet him this evening before he started his shift at the supermarket where he stacked shelves. Sitting in the supermarket cafe now, Dean had already made short work of a plate of egg, sausage, hash browns, beans and chips she'd bought for him and he was now onto his second mug of tea and an iced bun. He had a new tattoo on the side of his neck, a small spider's web just below his pierced right ear. He had always been a thickset lad and enjoyed his food, but he looked bigger than when she'd last seen him. If he carried on eating the way he was, it wouldn't be long before he was the same size as Dave. She pictured the spider's web stretching to keep pace with his expanding neck.

'It's Dad,' he said.

'What about your dad?'

'He's been made redundant.'

Shocked, she said, 'I'm sorry.' And she *was* sorry. Dave had always loved his job at Talbot's Garage. Over the years he'd moaned like everyone else did about the poor pay and the long hours, but he'd been there man and boy and had taken it for granted that he'd be there until he retired.

'Are you sorry?' Dean said. 'You don't look like you care.'

'I do. But what do you want me to do about it? What can I do?'

'You can stop all this crap about getting divorced. You've made him suffer enough. Come home.'

'Did he ask you to come here?'

Dean stared at her as he slurped his tea. How many times had she told him not to slurp, that it was bad manners? 'Why do you ask that?'

'It seems likely, that's all.'

'Would that be such a bad thing? He needs you, Mum. *We* need you. He's had to sign on for benefits. We're getting next to nowt. It's not fair. The shame's killing him. He just sits there on the sofa all day with the curtains shut. I caught him crying the other day. He won't go out. Not even to the pub. He's going tonto.'

'I'm sorry.'

'Yeah, you said that already. Don't you care about us any more? Have you forgotten us?'

Anger and resentment spilled out of Maggie. 'No more than you forgot about me. How many times have you called me since I left? How many of my messages have you actually replied to? I'll tell you how many. None! Not one.'

He shrugged and picked up his teaspoon. He started to bend it. She wanted to snatch it out of his hands and throw it across the cafe. 'I was angry with you,' he said.

The spoon was now bent out of shape. 'And now you're not?'

'I just want you to come home and make everything right again. Even Nana Brenda wants you to come home. She says she'll forgive you if you come back.'

That's big of her, Maggie thought bitterly.

He tossed the ruined teaspoon aside with a clatter and drained his tea with a long noisy slurp. 'Will you come back, then?' he said. 'Will you forget about divorcing Dad? He needs you. He says he'll do whatever you want him to do to make things work like they used to. If you want him to take more notice of you, he'll do that. If it's candles round the feckin' bath you want, he'll even do that for you.'

To hear Dean pleading on Dave's behalf, Maggie couldn't help but be touched.

When she didn't say anything, Dean said, 'At least think about it. You owe him that much. Don't you reckon he deserves a second chance?'

Chapter Fifty-four

Saturday morning. It was seven o'clock and the roads were quiet. Another hour and Ethan would arrive in Abersoch. It had been a busy week. A week of decisions. Big decisions. He had Christine to thank for that. He had done the very thing she had wanted him to do: he had come to his senses. And God bless her for that!

The consequences of the decisions he'd made were going to be cataclysmic, but he didn't care. If that awful day at Belmont Hall had taught him anything, it was that life could end when he least expected it. He might live to be a hundred and end his days in a depressing nursing home. Or he might not. He might die next week. Next year. Who knew? Whatever time was left to him, he was damned well going to make the most of it. No more living a lie. No more living with his head in the sand, as Ella had rightly accused him of doing.

The house was quiet when he let himself in. Francine and the girls were yet to rouse themselves. That was fine by him. He quietly went about the business of making himself some breakfast in the recently fitted kitchen. He felt cavalier about the expensive granite surfaces, the slick built-in TV, the tap that provided instant boiling water, the induction hob, and the handmade units. A week ago he had been worried sick at the thought of how he was ever going to pay his father-in-law back for it all. Now he didn't give a toss.

He took his mug of tea and plate of grilled tomatoes on toast out to the raised decking area that overlooked the sea. The builders and garden landscaper had done a fine job here, too. He raised his mug and toasted his father-in-law. 'Nice work, Alan! Way to go!'

He was onto his second mug of tea when Valentina and Katie appeared. Both dressed in pyjamas – a combo of vest tops and shorts – and rubbing the sleep from their eyes, they plonked themselves down at the table. They both bore traces of last night's make-up and had a distinctly pale look about them. *Rough* wasn't putting it too harshly.

'Morning you two,' he said cheerfully.

'Hi,' Katie murmured. She looked worryingly like she might be sick.

'When did you get here?' Valentina asked, helping herself to his tea. 'Mum's gagging herself mental that you didn't come last night.'

'And a good morning to you, Valentina.'

She waved his sarcasm aside. 'Yeah, whatever. And, Dad, if you could, like, keep your voice down we'd appreciate it.'

'Out late were you?'

'There was a party on the beach,' Katie said.

'Sounds fun. Meet anyone nice?'

'A few nice—'

Valentina cut Katie off. 'Hel-*lo*, boring alert!' she said to Ethan. 'Could we, like, just skip the Q and A session?'

'Just trying to make conversation.'

'Well, don't bother. Not until at least this afternoon.'

'I've missed you too, sweetie.'

She looked at him as though he'd just sprouted a second head. 'What's with the sarky rip?'

He reached across the table and took back his mug of tea. 'I guess that's the mood I'm in.'

She rolled her eyes in a familiar withering gesture; it had been learned at the knee of her mother from an early age. 'Weird,' she said. 'You're acting, like, seriously weird, Dad.'

'Feels good to me.' He finished his tea. 'Right, I'm off for a walk.'

'A walk? You never go for walks.'

'I do now. I'll see you later.'

When he returned Francine was sitting in the chair he had oc-
cupied earlier. Prada sunnies in place, she was drinking a glass
of orange juice. Without saying anything, she held her cheek
out to be kissed. He ignored it and took the chair opposite.
'The new kitchen is looking good,' he said. 'Are you and your
father pleased with it?'

'Very pleased.' She lowered her sunglasses and looked at
him. 'Valentina says you're in a strange mood.'

'I prefer to think of it as a decisive mood. Where are the
girls?'

'They've gone to see Mum and Dad.'

'Good, that gives me the opportunity to talk to you on
your own.'

'I don't like the sound of that. You're not going to go on
about money again, are you?'

'There's a lot you're not going to like the sound of in the
next few minutes, and some of it will be about money. And
I'd be grateful if you didn't say anything until I've said all
that I've come here to say.' He reached across the table and
removed the glass of orange juice from Francine's hand. Better
for there not to be anything close by for her to throw at him.
'First,' he said, before she could ask him what he was doing,
'you need to know that Christine is not your friend.'

'What are you talking about?'

'Christine hates you. She thinks you're a manipulative bitch
who doesn't deserve me. Frankly, she has a point. You are
manipulative and ninety-five per cent of the time you are a
bitch.'

Francine's jaw dropped.

'Save the shock for later. There's worse to come. As for
whether you don't deserve me, I'm inclined to be generous
and say we deserve each other. I've not been the perfect
husband and you certainly haven't been the perfect wife. So

let's say we're quits in that department. No, don't try to say anything – I'm far from finished. For ages now Christine has been coming on to me. No,' he said as once again she tried to speak, 'still not the moment for you to say anything. I know you think Christine is your closest friend, but would a true friend ask me to leave you so I could be with her? I don't think so. She says she loves me and wants to divorce Adam so she and I can be together. She says she wants to set me free from the hold you have over me. You know, you should never have told her our private business. There, your turn now to say something.'

Francine removed her sunglasses and with a face as pale as Valentina's and Katie's had been earlier, she said, 'I don't believe you. I don't believe any of what you're saying.'

'Why would I make up something like this?'

'Because … because. Oh, I don't know. Maybe you've gone crazy after being ill. That can happen. I've read about people undergoing personality changes after a big operation.'

'What I went through was certainly a reality check. It made me rethink how I want to live my life. Christine has also played her part in helping me decide what to do next.'

Francine visibly stiffened. 'Oh, my God, you're going to try and leave me, aren't you? That's what this is about? How typical! How bloody typical! But then a man never leaves his wife unless he thinks he has a better option lined up.' She suddenly leaned forward, the colour back in her face. Ethan could see she was ready to fight him now. 'You know the score,' she said. 'You leave me, you lose everything. And I mean *everything*.'

He raised his hands. 'That was the deal you made all those years ago and I stand by it. You get the lot. Lock, stock and empty barrel.'

'What do you mean, empty barrel?'

'Poor Francine, you really have no idea, do you? The business is in serious trouble. You're welcome to it.'

'Don't be ridiculous.'

'Ask your father. Ask to see the accounts. The accounts don't lie. Not unless your father has been up to professional mischief.'

'But if it's that bad, why didn't you tell me?'

'I've dropped hints and a lot more besides that things weren't going well, but your beloved father made me promise that I would never come right out and worry your pretty little head about such things. That's his philosophy in life: protect the womenfolk from anything unpleasant. Keep them living in cloud cuckoo land.'

'But this house …' – she cast her gaze about her, at the pristine decking, the shiny glazed earthenware pots of cordyline, and the no-expense-spared custom-made oak French doors from the kitchen – ' … how are we going to repay my father?'

Ethan shrugged. 'Not my problem. I'm just going to walk away from it all.'

'What? You really have gone mad.'

'If this is madness, then it's the sanest I've felt in a long, long time.'

'You're seriously going to leave me to be with Christine?'

'Good God, no! I'd sooner gouge out both my eyes than be with that woman.'

'But I don't understand. You said that she helped you to decide to leave me.'

'She did. She made me realize just what a prisoner I was being married to you. Okay, a prisoner of my own making, I admit, but when Christine started telling me of the plans she had in mind for me, how she could set me free from you, by effectively swapping one life sentence for another, I knew I had to do something drastic. Oh, and you'd better prepare yourself for a retaliatory blow from Christine. When she knows I'm not going to take her up on her generous offer, she'll send you a photograph of me kissing another woman.'

'Another woman? Who? Do I know her?'

'Yes. It's Ella Moore.'

A look of incredulity swept over Francine's face. 'Now I've heard everything. You and Ella Moore. *Ella?*' She laughed nastily. 'Couldn't you do better than her? Don't tell me you're losing your touch.'

'As it happens, Ella is as good as it gets.'

'So you're leaving me for her?'

'No. She doesn't want me. She's got more sense.'

'And what about Valentina and me? How are we supposed to manage without you? What about her school fees?'

'Gosh, Francine, you might have to get a job and support yourself.'

This was clearly going too far. She jumped to her feet. 'You bastard!' she hissed. 'You absolute bastard!'

'Hey, but hang on, you've got a ready-made business to run, haven't you? Good luck with that.'

'But you've just said it's not doing well.'

'Here's another idea: sell The Lilacs and use that to shore up the business until things improve.'

'Sell our house? Our home? You can't be serious.'

'Trust me, I'm being deadly serious.'

She put her hands on her hips, breathed in deeply, then let out her breath slowly as if centring her anger. 'Well, don't think for a minute that I'm going to let you have anything,' she said at last. 'If I have to sell the house, you won't get a penny.'

'I don't want anything, other than my freedom. But if you have any wits about you, you'll let me carry on running the business and then, given time, and with the wind blowing in the right direction, you might not need to sell The Lilacs. Discuss my suggestion with your father. I'm sure he'll agree that this is the best way forward for you.'

She stared at him. 'I can't believe you're doing this.'

'Me neither.'

'Don't you care at all what this will do to Valentina? She's your daughter, your only child.'

'I doubt she'll care that much. Yes, she'll miss the Bank of

Daddy, but that's about all. You and your parents have seen to that. That's my biggest regret – that I've been complicit in spoiling Valentina. But I promise to do whatever I can to support her financially. As you say, she is my daughter and I'm not about to shirk my responsibility.'

Her bejewelled flip-flops slapping against her well-pedicured heels, Francine paced the length of the sustainably produced decking. Ethan could feel the teak boards springing beneath him. She then whirled round. 'Why the hell can't you have a normal mid-life crisis like any other man?'

'What, go out and buy myself a sports car and start dressing like a teenager? I don't think that would fix things, do you?'

She retraced her steps back towards him. 'What if I said I would forgive you?'

'For what exactly?'

She didn't answer him. 'No marriage is perfect, Ethan. There has to be give and take, on both sides. I forgave you your affair all those years ago. I could do it again.'

'Why? Why would you want to forgive me? Why would you want to stay married to a man who doesn't love you? We should have divorced years ago. You know that's true. Our marriage has been nothing but a sham, and can you really say you forgave me for what I did back then, that you haven't held it against me ever since? And can you honestly say you love me and that if I had died last month you would have been heartbroken?'

She came to a stop and put her hands on the back of the chair she'd been sitting in earlier. She looked at him across the table. She pursed her lips and narrowed her eyes. 'I'll tell you what I can honestly say to you, Ethan. I've given you the best years of my life only now to be dumped. And for that I hate you. I always will. A day won't pass without me wishing you had died when your stomach ruptured, or whatever it did.'

'Don't be too hard on yourself, Francine. You've got plenty of good years ahead of you yet. You're a very attractive woman; you'll find someone else in no time. Who knows, you might even be happy.'

'Go to hell!'

'And on that cheerful note, I'll leave you to enjoy the rest of your holiday here. I'm going home now. But don't worry, when you return I won't be there. I wouldn't inflict my presence on you unnecessarily.'

During his return journey to Cheshire, Ethan was one part exhilarated, one part terrified. There was no going back. The wheels of his new life were oiled and already turning. The one thing he didn't feel was regret.

He had called Francine's bluff with regard to the business and if she did decide to seize control and find someone else to run it, then so be it. The risk was worth taking. One of the things he had done this week was to call in all the money owed to him. It hadn't been easy, but he'd refused to take any more stalling tactics. So now he had cash flow. Amazingly, he even had somewhere to live – a one-bedroom flat in the centre of Kings Melford. It was no great shakes, a bit crumby really, but the rent was cheap and it was a roof over his head. For the foreseeable future he needed no more. All that was important to him was that he was now free.

He lowered the car window, turned up the volume on Radiohead's 'Exit Music (For a Film)' and sped on. No more pursuing the hopeless course.

Chapter Fifty-five

The sudden heavy downpour of rain forced Ella to make a dash for shelter inside the bookshop in Kings Melford. She stood for a moment in the doorway to catch her breath. It had done nothing but rain on and off for the last ten days. What had happened to the heatwave they'd been promised for August?

She rolled up her umbrella and browsed the piled-high tables of books. She spotted a new Kate Atkinson novel. The sticker on the front offered her the chance to buy three for the price of two. She didn't want three. She only wanted one. Life was like that. Always trying to push you in a direction you didn't want to go, always trying to make you feel dissatisfied with what you already had.

Determined not to be manipulated, she took the book over to the cash desk, bracing herself for the inevitable sales pitch that was designed to make her feel she was missing out on the chance of a lifetime. There was a woman in front of her with a gaggle of lively children and while she was being served, Ella unearthed her wallet from her bag. The woman and her offspring now gone, Ella moved forward and did a double take. 'Toby!'

He was able to take his lunch break ten minutes early and they sat at the back of the shop in the small cafe area. The woman with the children was seated at a nearby table. She looked tired and harassed, a woman on the edge. Who could blame her? More than a month into the school holidays, and given the horrendous weather they were having, she was probably fast running out of ways to occupy her children. She certainly appeared to have no control over them, was powerless to stop them pushing and shoving and spilling their drinks over each other. They wriggled and squirmed so much they resembled an overexcited octopus.

Settled quietly at their own table with two mocha lattes and a plate of carrot cake for Toby, Ella got the conversation going by asking when he'd started work at the bookshop.

'At the end of term I went on holiday with a group of friends and when I got back I hit lucky and heard there was a job here for the rest of the summer.'

'And it's going well?'

'It's great. Miles, who owns the shop, is pretty cool and let's face it, it beats flipping burgers. How've you been?'

Touched by his question, she took a moment to reply. 'I'm okay,' she said.

'Only okay?'

'You might not believe me, but I still feel bad about what happened.'

'So do I. I wasn't very nice to you. I've felt guilty about that ever since. I'm sorry.'

'Oh, Toby, you have nothing to be sorry about. And guilty is the last thing you should feel.'

'But I didn't really give you a chance to explain what happened. You said at the time that it wasn't how it looked. But the photo that woman sent Dad wasn't faked, was it?'

'No, it wasn't faked. That situation did arise, but think about it: someone could take a photograph of the two of us sitting here and make it look altogether different, couldn't they?'

Toby didn't look convinced.

Wanting him to understand, Ella then poured out the whole story, how she and Ethan had met, how trapped and unhappy he was, and how Christine Paxton had maliciously stirred things up for her own ends.

'So she'd caught you in a moment when you were trying to get Ethan to leave you alone?'

'Exactly. The kiss was nothing more than him wanting to say goodbye in a way that was …' she hesitated, trying to come up with the right words, 'that was meaningful to him,' she said at last.

Toby looked directly at her. 'Was it *meaningful* to you in any way?'

She had never lied to Toby and couldn't bring herself to do so now. Again she struggled to find the right words. She took a sip of her coffee. But before she could say anything, Toby said, 'He did mean something to you, didn't he, Ella? I can see it in your face. Come on, you can be honest with me.'

'Okay,' she said. 'Yes, against my better judgement I was attracted to him, but the fact that he was married precluded doing anything about it. And then your father wanted us to try again and everything looked like it was going to work out. Except Ethan kept popping up at just the wrong moment.'

'Dad says that with hindsight he can now see that you were dragging your heels about committing to him again. It was when you didn't want to move back in, and then when you didn't want to sell your house. Do you think that's true?'

'In some ways, yes. You have to remember, I'd been badly hurt by Lawrence before, when he stood back and let Alexis destroy our relationship, and a huge part of me was worried it might happen all over again. I needed to take it slowly.'

'You don't think Ethan figured in your hesitation?'

'Goodness, Toby, you're really giving me the third degree, aren't you?'

His expression turned even more solemn. 'I'm not having a go. Please don't think that. I'm just trying to get you to admit how you really feel. I don't think you've been truly honest with Dad or yourself.'

'When did you get to be so wise?'

His face brightened with a smile. 'I've seen enough good and bad relationships going on around me amongst my friends to learn a thing or two.'

The harassed mother of the children was trying to round

them up; in the process chairs were being knocked over and cups and plates sent flying. When they'd finally departed, leaving a scene of carnage, the cafe seemed very quiet. Lowering his voice, Toby said, 'Ella, you've always been like a real mother to me; I never once thought of you as a substitute. You were the real deal, always willing to help with any problem I had, always there when I wasn't sure about something, and best of all you could always make me laugh.'

'Yes,' she said with a smile of fond remembrance, 'I recall you laughing at my awful pronunciation when I was helping you revise for your Latin exams.'

'I got an A-star thanks to you.'

'Rubbish. It was all down to your hard work.'

'But you made it possible. I don't think you ever really appreciated just how much you did for us as a family. For Dad especially.'

'Mm ... but not so much for Alexis.'

'Who knows, perhaps my sister would have turned out a lot worse had it not been for you.' He finished the last of the carrot cake and licked his fingers. She remembered a similar moment, a long time ago. It had been his first birthday with her at Mayfield and she'd made him a cake that resembled the cover of the latest Harry Potter book. She had never made a cake like that before, but she'd given it her all. It had been a wonky masterpiece, a triumph of enthusiasm over any real skill, but Toby had been delighted with it. He had eaten two slices of it in quick succession and licked his fingers clean, as well as the plate.

'Can I ask you a personal question?' he asked. 'If Dad asked you to try again with him, would you?'

She shook her head. 'No. Absolutely not. Whatever we had has gone. It just wouldn't work now. I'm sorry if that upsets or disappoints you.'

'This isn't about me being upset or disappointed, Ella, it's about you. What if Ethan turned up and said he was now single? Would you give a relationship with him a go? And be honest.'

Ella looked away. She thought of Ethan at Belmont Hall when he'd been so violently and dangerously ill. She remembered how she had felt at the hospital, how scared she'd been that he might die. She thought of the times when she had enjoyed his company and how she had known in her heart, despite kidding herself otherwise, that she was playing with fire. She thought, too, of how she occasionally found herself missing him.

'The thing is,' Toby continued, 'the little I saw of the man over in Abersoch, he seemed okay. I saw him looking at you a couple of times and I have to admit, I wondered then whether there was something between the two of you. His wife, on the other hand, seemed a total nightmare. Along with that friend of hers.'

'I had no idea you were being so observant that evening.'

'I like to think there's not a lot that gets past me. So what are you going to do?'

'About what?'

'About Ethan, of course.'

'Nothing. He's married. I don't need the hassle of someone like him in my life. And can you imagine that daughter?'

Toby laughed. 'She would certainly give Alexis a run for her money in the race for most difficult stepdaughter.'

Ella laughed too. 'It's been so good talking to you again, Toby. I've missed you. Can we stay in touch, like we used to?'

'Yes, I'd like that.'

'Now tell me how Alexis is. Has she had her exam results yet?'

With only five minutes left of his break, Toby quickly filled her in on his sister's clean sweep of A-stars and subsequent A-level plans, and in turn Ella told him of her own tentative plans.

Chapter Fifty-six

Christine would never forgive Ethan. She had offered him the chance of a perfect new life and he'd thrown it away. He had ruined everything, destroyed all her hopes and dreams. Thanks to him Adam had moved out, taking Katie with him, and had instigated divorce proceedings.

When Ethan had done his utmost to humiliate her by saying he'd given her offer all of his serious consideration and concluded that he'd sooner go through the experience of a perforated ulcer again than be stuck with her for the rest of his life, she had carried out her threat and sent Francine the photograph on her mobile. Within hours, Francine had arrived home from Abersoch with Valentina and Katie. She had stormed into the house and screamed at Christine that she was a conniving, two-faced whore for trying to steal her husband. Her behaviour was that of a madwoman and she had started throwing things at Christine – a cut glass vase from the windowsill, a decorative plate from the wall, even the fruit from the bowl on the kitchen table. She had only stopped when Adam had heard the commotion and had come rushing in from the garden and tripped over an apple that was rolling around on the floor. 'What the hell's going on?' he'd roared.

'Ask your scheming bitch of a wife!' Francine had yelled back at him.

By this stage, Katie was crying and had run upstairs and Valentina had disappeared next door. All in all, it had been a very undignified scene.

At first Adam had refused to believe any of Francine's accusations and had asked her if she was drunk, but then Francine had removed any doubt from his mind. 'Why else would Christine have sent this photograph to me?' she had screeched, holding her mobile up for Adam to see. 'If she was a real friend, wouldn't she have tactfully told me to my face that she suspected my husband of having an affair? But no, she deliberately sent this to stir things between Ethan and me! What's more, she promised Ethan a new future with her, and guess what? She was going to use your money to do it, Adam. Yes, I thought that would stop you in your tracks.'

Since then the house had gone on the market and Adam was swearing she wouldn't get a penny from him if he could help it. He was talking nonsense, of course. He knew as well as she did that she was entitled to at least half of what was in the pot. A lot more if she had anything to do with it. She had a new life to get on with. She would show both Adam and Ethan that she could do perfectly well without them.

Now, as she parked her car in Manchester and set off for her appointment to meet her divorce lawyer – the bachelor son of a friend of her mother's who had so far sounded very agreeable on the telephone – she knew that whatever she had once felt for Ethan was now dead. She hated him. She hated him as much as she had once loved him.

Maggie had never been to an airport before and she followed the signs carefully. Just parking the car in the right terminal had been challenge enough, but that was mostly because she had been all but shaking with excitement.

Ahead of her she saw a sign that said she was now in the Arrivals Hall. It was so packed out with people she had to slow her pace. Which was more than she could do with her heart. If it was to beat any faster, she would keel over. She checked her watch. Did she have time to find a toilet and check how she looked? Looking her best wasn't enough. Today she had to look better than her bestest best.

She noticed a crowd of people staring up at a row of screens. Curious, she went over to see what they were so interested in. It turned out to be information about flights. She scanned the screens for one flight in particular. Her heart leapt. The plane had already landed! She was so excited she wanted to turn to the people all around her and tell them the fantastic news. *He's here! He's here!* Instead, to keep herself calm, she went in search of the toilets.

She was in and out of the cubicle as fast as possible and was then fiddling with her hair. But it didn't need fiddling with. It was fine. She'd been to the hairdresser's first thing that morning and her hair had that lovely silky shine that she could never manage herself. She dabbed on a bit more lipgloss, then decided it was too much. She took it off and put just a tiny bit on.

She studied herself in the mirror. Did she look better than her bestest best? Close to it maybe. But the important thing was, she was happy with the person staring back at her. This was the new Maggie Storm. The old Maggie Storm was long gone.

After that evening with Dean, she had gone to see Dave to see if there was anything she could do to help. She had been shocked by the change in him and had offered help in the only way she could. Or the only way she was prepared to help. She had offered him the bulk of her bingo winnings to tide him over until a job came along. Brenda had been all for accepting the money, but with a flash of pride Dave had thrown it back in her face. 'Yer can stick yer charity,' he'd said, barely glancing at her, his eyes on the can of Special Brew in his hand. 'I want none of it.'

'Suit yourself,' Maggie had said, trying not to wrinkle her nose at the pong in the room. It wasn't just Evil Sid who whiffed – Dave smelt none too fresh either. He was a proper mess from top to toe. His clothes were crumpled and stained and his greasy hair hadn't been cut in a long time; it wasn't even combed. He hadn't shaved in ages and his slippers were worn to threads. If she had seen him on the street, she might have thought he was a homeless man living rough. 'How are you getting on with finding another job?' she had asked.

'Oh, I like that,' he'd rounded on her. 'Yer barge in here chucking your money about like Lady Bloody Muck while I'm brickin' it with worry and then yer accuse me of not looking for a job. Bloody nerve of yer!'

'I didn't accuse you of anything of the sort,' she'd responded. Although fair play to Dave, that was precisely what she had implied. He looked about as lively and motivated as a piece of week-old cod and was never going to be anybody's first choice if jobs were being handed out.

Leaving him and Brenda to bad-mouth her, she had driven back to Belmont Hall determined not to feel upset or guilty. She had tried to help Dave but he hadn't wanted it. It wasn't her fault that he had lost his job, or that he didn't appear to be doing anything about getting a new one. Hal often said that people made their own luck in life, and he should know – he'd done brilliantly for himself. But he worked hard, that much she knew. He frequently worked until gone midnight and started again at six in the morning. He was no slacker. You wouldn't catch him slumped on the sofa watching the telly all hours of the day. He was a good boss as well, and was quite happy for her to take the odd day off here and there if she ever needed to.

Such as today.

Back out in the Arrivals Hall, Maggie inched her way through to the barrier where suntanned holidaymakers were streaming through a pair of automatic sliding doors. As she watched them being greeted by friends and family, she felt stupidly choked up. Everyone was so cheerful and so glad to see each other. There were dreadful things going on in the world, but here, right now in this busy place, everyone was happy.

She returned her attention to the sliding doors. The stream of arrivals had slowed to a trickle. She suddenly felt anxious.

What if he wasn't coming? What if he had changed his mind? She thought of all that she had done to welcome him home and how much she had enjoyed doing it. She had spring-cleaned his boat, had filled the fridge and cupboards with food, including two fillet steaks and a bottle of sparkling wine for tonight, and made him a chocolate cake.

The trickle of arrivals had dried up now. The doors closed and then remained closed. Her anxiety increased and she became aware of everyone around her drifting away. He'll be here, she told herself. He promised. He promised he'd be back for Jack and Mrs Oates's wedding tomorrow morning. He wouldn't break his promise to them and to her, would he? She crossed her fingers and hoped.

Minutes passed and then the doors opened and, partly hidden behind a couple with a trolley stacked with luggage, there he was. He'd never looked more gorgeous. He was wearing jeans and a pale blue shirt that was open at the neck and his dazzling blue eyes were as bright as stars. He spotted her straight away and his tanned face lit up with the widest of grins. Her heart bounced with joy and from then on it was all a dizzy blur. He was holding her and kissing her and lifting her off the ground, spinning her round and round. 'Put me down, you daft beggar!' she said breathlessly, but not meaning it.

'You've got to be kidding,' he laughed. 'I'm not letting you go for at least twenty-four hours.' His hands squeezing her waist, he kissed her again. 'Come on,' he said, his lips brushing against her cheek, as she breathed in the wonderful smell of him. 'I've waited long enough. Let's go home and you can have your wicked way with me.'

Chapter Fifty-seven

Ella loved the month of October. She loved the chilly fresh-
ness of the mornings, the glittery brightness of the light, the
rich, earthy scent in the air. Most of all, she loved the tangible
sense of change that autumn brought with it.

It was a crisp Saturday morning and at the top of a ladder,
Ella was fixing a leaking gutter. It was a simple enough job,
just a matter of replacing a screw that must have come loose
and dropped out from the cast-iron guttering. She was giving
the replacement screw one final turn when she heard a voice.
She looked down into her neighbour's garden, expecting it
to be Phil. There was no sign of him. She turned to look the
other way and saw someone she hadn't expected to see ever
again. Certainly not standing in her garden at the bottom of a
ladder. She was so taken aback she dropped the screwdriver.
It missed him by a few inches.

He retrieved the screwdriver from behind a flowerpot.
'Your aim is lousy,' he called up to her.

'And your timing is lousier still.' She stayed where she was,
wanting – *needing* – time to recover.

'Should I move out of throwing range, or am I okay to stay
where I am?'

'You're fine.'

'Anything I can do to help? Shall I come up there with the
screwdriver?'

She tried to keep her voice as normal as possible. It wasn't
easy. 'No thanks, I've finished with it now. What brings you
here?'

'Toby thought it would be a good idea.'

'*Toby?*' Shocked, she clung to the ladder.

'He arrived, quite out of the blue, in my office one day; he tracked me down on the internet. He said he needed to talk to me. He said if I cared about your happiness as much as he did, then I should listen to what he had to say. He's an astute and persuasive young man. Are you going to come down any time soon?'

'I'm not sure I want to.'

'It would be nice to have this conversation without the neighbours listening in. There's something important I want to tell you.'

She stayed where she was. 'I think I'd prefer to talk this way.'

He raised a quizzical eyebrow. 'Do you really mean that?'

'Yes.' The truth was, she felt safer up here. Even after all this time, Ethan still had the same effect on her. It was deeply unsettling. 'When did you see Toby?' she called down to him.

'A couple of weeks ago, not long before he was due to return to university.'

'But that can't be right. I saw him before he left for Durham; he never said a word about seeing you.'

'That was the general idea; he was going behind your back.'

'The sneaky devil! Just wait till I speak to him.'

'Look, this is absurd. Are you sure I can't tempt you to come down? I'm getting a crick in my neck looking up at you.'

'I'm staying put.'

'In that case, you leave me no alternative. And I want you to know I wasn't going to do this, I really wasn't – I'd made up my mind to try and get you out of my head, that's why I never contacted you again, but after Toby's visit I knew I had to give it one last shot. You see, you're there all the time in my thoughts. I keep imagining the many things we could do together. I imagine how extraordinary it would be to wake up next to you in bed every morning. I imagine all sorts of other things that might be nice to do in bed with you, but given the open-air nature of this conversation I won't risk going into that now.'

'Yes, if you don't mind I'd be much obliged if you kept that kind of thought to yourself.'

He laughed. 'You know, I'd be very much obliged too if you'd come down.'

She gripped the ladder harder still. 'I'm quite happy up here, thank you.'

'Then I suppose I shall just have to come up there.' He moved towards the ladder and put a foot on the lowest rung. 'You wouldn't believe how much I've missed you, Ella, and how many times I've wanted to call you. And don't even ask me how many times I've wanted to kiss you again, like I did that day at the Cat and Fiddle.' He placed his other foot on the next rung up. The ladder wobbled.

'Stop it,' she said.

'Too late, I can't. I'm on a mission now.' He took another step up. 'Do you want to know one of the things I'd love to do with you?'

'No, I just want you to stop messing about.'

'I want to dance with you. I want to dance to "Viva La Vida" with you.' He moved onto the next rung; the ladder shook and wobbled alarmingly.

'Okay,' she said, 'I give in. I'll come down.'

'There's no need. I might be terrified of heights, but I'd walk on hot coals for you, Ella.' He climbed another rung.

'Oh, stop being ridiculous, Ethan! If you're scared of heights you shouldn't be anywhere near a ladder. Now go back down before I get extremely cross with you. Honestly, I've never known anyone as irresponsible as you!'

He looked up at her. 'You remind me of my old friend the Dragon Slayer. She had a scorching tongue on her.'

'You'll be on the receiving end of it again if you don't do as I say. Now get down.'

'Only if you promise to come down so we can talk properly.'

'All right, I promise.'

When she had both feet firmly on the ground, she turned and found herself within touching distance of him. She immediately wanted to shimmy straight back up the ladder. Just as she always had, she felt the extraordinary physical pull of him. It was what had always been so dangerous about him. Wearing jeans and a cinnamon-coloured cashmere sweater with a chocolate-brown scarf tied loosely around his neck, he looked well, but then when she'd last seen him he had been close to death.

In the months since, she had oscillated between feeling proud of herself for having got through another week without succumbing to the desperate urge to get in touch with him – just to know that he was all right, to know that he had made a full recovery – and hating herself for her iron will, for doing the right thing. Because the right thing was to forget Ethan. He was married. He would always be married. At the start of the year she had promised herself that her head would rule over her heart, that she would never again make the mistake of wasting time and energy on a relationship that would take everything from her and give nothing in return. But seeing Ethan again, seeing him so well recovered, all the emotions she had battled to suppress were being stirred up.

From the safety of the top of the ladder it had been easy to avoid his gaze, but standing so close the physical pull of him was compelling her to look into his face. She did. It was a mistake. His dark eyes were on hers, the expression in them so intense, so penetrating, she caught her breath.

'What are you thinking?' he asked.

'I was thinking you could have got us both killed messing about like that on the ladder,' she lied.

'Are you sure that's what you were thinking?'

Her cheeks flamed. 'I see you still haven't cured yourself of your outrageous arrogance. You presume far too much.'

'Only when I'm convinced I'm right.'

She cleared her throat and stepped away from him. 'Okay then, tell me what was I thinking.'

'You were thinking that what this tricky situation needs is a nice cup of tea to take the edge off things. Am I right?' He was smiling at her.

She smiled too. 'What d'you know, you've turned into a mind reader. And please don't be tempted to say that you've always been able to read my mind.'

'As if I'd say anything as crass as that. Shall I do the honours and make some tea for us? Or would that be presumptuous of me?'

'That would be the least presumptuous thing you've ever done. So go ahead and do that while I put the ladder away.'

'That doesn't sound right – you hefting such a heavy bit of kit around on your own. You do the tea; I'll do the ladder.'

'I shift heavy things around the whole time with my work. Go on, you put the kettle on.'

They sat at the circular stone table at the end of the garden, the autumn sun on them. 'It's very peaceful here,' Ethan said. 'But then I've always liked your house. Especially the name.'

'Thank you.'

'I moved out of The Lilacs more than two months ago.'

He said it so matter of factly, she could have easily missed the importance of what he'd said. 'Really?'

'Yes, battle lines have been drawn up and Francine and her divorce lawyer are doing their worst. Christine and Adam are getting divorced, too. Your coming to The Lilacs certainly put the cat amongst the pigeons. Not that I'm saying you're responsible.'

'I should hope not. But you've really left your wife?'

'Yes. The house is up for sale.'

'How's Valentina taking it?'

'Badly. She's refusing to have anything to do with Katie, as if the poor girl is to blame in some way for her mother's awful behaviour. And as for me, I no longer exist. Which, given the enormous influence Francine and her parents have over her, is more or less what I expected to happen. '

'Maybe with time her attitude will change.'

'I'd like to think so.'

'And the business?'

'Francine's sticking to her original threat and taking it.'

'I'm sorry.'

'Don't be. It was time to shake things up. No more head in the sand for me. Just as you said.'

'How are you managing?'

'For now I'm still running things, so I'm okay for the short term. But I'm tired of it. I need a change.' He turned and looked at her. 'I don't suppose you'd like to take on an apprentice, would you? I'm a lot handier than I look.'

She smiled. 'You'd be no good up a ladder, though, would you?'

'Actually I lied about that. I'm not at all scared of heights.' His expression suddenly became earnest and he took her hand. He laced his fingers through hers. 'The only thing I am scared of is losing the chance of being happy.' He paused. 'Now that I'm officially heading for the divorce courts and singledom, is there anything I can do to make you reassess the situation between us? For you to consider a potential *us*?'

She regarded his hand on hers, then raised her gaze and studied his face. Once again she felt drawn to his eyes, the dark, alluring intensity of them. 'That rather depends on what you think about long-distance relationships,' she said.

A frown creased his brow. 'What do you mean?'

'I'm leaving. It's why I was fixing the guttering. I had thought I'd sell, but I've decided to rent it out instead. Hedging my bets.'

His eyes widened. 'Where are you going?'

'Back to Italy. I've found a wreck of a house to restore. I signed the contract last week. I'm sure it will be a total nightmare but I'm in need of a challenge. A fresh start.'

'Sounds like a big job.'

'It will be.'

'I don't think I'm a fan of long-distance relationships,' he said flatly.

'That's a shame.'

'Why, is that something you'd consider doing with me? Late night phone calls, emails, webcam chats? Is that what you'd like?'

A crazy idea popped into her head. Her pulse quickened. But why not? Now that things had changed for him, why not be a little crazy? 'Yes and ... no,' she said hesitantly. She swallowed. 'The thing is, now that your situation has changed, I can be honest about my feelings for you. And before I say anything else, don't you dare say, "*I knew it!*"'

He smiled. 'But I did know it, didn't I? There was something between us right from the start.'

'Yes, it was your wife.'

'I didn't mean that. So what is it that you want to say?'

She summoned all her courage. 'If you genuinely are handier than you look, perhaps you could help me.'

'How?'

'Come with me to Italy. Help me restore this house I'm buying.' There, she'd said it. And it didn't even sound that crazy.

'Are you offering me a job?'

'No, I'm offering you the chance to do something completely different. To have some fun, maybe.'

'Are we talking actual real-life fun? I don't think I can remember what that feels like.'

'Don't get carried away with the idea. It won't always be fun. There'll be times when we'll be utterly exhausted and so miserable we'll be throwing ourselves on the floor and howling like a couple of babies.'

'That still sounds like a hell of a lot more fun than I've had in a long while.' He sighed and shook his head. 'You're an extraordinary woman, Ella. I knew that the night we met.'

'And I knew you would be trouble.'

'Nice trouble?'

She smiled. 'We'll see.'

He put his arm around her and for the very first time she allowed herself to relax into his embrace. It felt wonderful. She rested her head against his and breathed in the delicious scent of him.

'Would this be an appropriate moment to ask if I could kiss you?' he asked softly.

She raised her head from his shoulder. 'I can't think of a more appropriate—' But she broke off, and led entirely by her heart, she stood up abruptly. In for a penny of spontaneous craziness, in for a pound of it. She held out her hands to him. 'Perhaps it would be more appropriate if you kissed me inside the house.'

Ethan took his time undressing Ella, and she the same with him. In silence they lay on the bed and as he kissed her, he touched and stroked her lightly, exploring her body. He watched her intently; he so badly wanted to please her. He had wanted her for so long and now his wish had come true, he didn't want anything to spoil it.

He moved on top of her and she wrapped her arms and legs around him, her hands sliding from his shoulders to the nape of his neck, her fingers warm and sure on him. His desire intensified but he was determined not to rush. And there was no anxiety in him. He knew that the problems he had encountered in the past would not happen with Ella. He loved Ella. With her it would be different. It would be everything he wanted.

He was right. When they both climaxed together in an explosion of profound intimacy and he looked down into her face, he was overcome with an emotion he'd never before experienced. He held her closely, his heart filled with a sense of coming home, of finally being at peace.

They lay in silence.

'Were you serious about me joining you in Italy?' he asked eventually.

'Why, chickening out already?'

He stroked her hair away from her cheek. 'Not a bit of it. I'm giving you the opportunity to change your mind. I don't want you to regret any rash decisions.'

She turned onto her side, her face thoughtful. She traced a finger lightly over his scar – the scar that had changed everything. 'What could be more boring than a life without surprise, passion or rashness? And anyway, nothing in life is carved in stone. All I'm saying is come to Italy for the fun of it. Let's not make any promises. Let's just see if it works between us.'

'But you realize, don't you, that after Francine has finished with me, I'll have precious little to offer you. Nothing of any substance. Only myself. Is that enough?'

She pressed a finger to his lips. 'Quite enough. Now stop worrying. It'll be fun. It'll be an adventure.'

'An adventure,' he echoed softly. 'I like the sound of that.'

'Me too.'

He moved her hand away from his mouth and kissed her. And went on kissing her.

Chapter Fifty-eight

For the first time in living memory Maggie wasn't cooking Christmas lunch. Daryl was in charge and her job was to do nothing more than set the table and rearrange things so that there would be room for their guests, Mrs O and Jack – although of course, ever since August Mrs O had become Mrs P.

Until a week ago Maggie's mum had said she'd be joining them for Christmas day, but then she and Mo had got a last-minute deal and had scooted off to Lanzarote for five days. And with Hal away with his parents in Australia, visiting his sister who had recently had a baby, Maggie was officially on holiday until his return. Hal had offered her and Daryl the use of the Hall over Christmas if they fancied having more room, but as nice as the thought was, they were happier to be on board the *Bohemian Rhapsody*.

They had decorated the boat together, stringing up cards and twinkling lights at the windows and amazingly they'd managed to squeeze in a miniature Christmas tree. Whenever she was on the boat, Maggie felt as if the rest of the world didn't exist. It was a lovely feeling. And today, with everything so wonderfully Christmassy, she felt it even more. She just knew it was going to be the best Christmas ever – nothing like the miserable ones she had experienced before.

But she wasn't going to think about those days. She didn't want to be reminded of what she'd allowed herself to become during her marriage. She'd been nothing but a doormat and really she had only herself to blame. Not only should she have been more honest with Dave years ago, she should have stood up to Brenda right from the start. She had thought she was doing the right thing sticking it out, but really she'd been a coward.

Hers wasn't the only life to have changed in the last few months. A Christmas card had arrived from Italy yesterday morning; there'd been a letter and a photograph with it. The photograph was of Ella and Ethan looking as grubby as a pair of navvies while standing next to a cement mixer. Their grinning faces and arms wrapped around each other told Maggie all she needed to know: they were happy. She had never seen Ethan look so well or so cheerful.

It was a shame Ella was no longer working at Belmont Hall, but the girl she had found to replace her was lovely and Hal certainly liked her. If Maggie didn't know better, she'd say that Hal was sweet on her. Well, good luck to him; he deserved somebody nice in his life. He spent far too much time alone, in her opinion. She looked over at Daryl as he opened the oven and checked on the turkey roast – he was humming 'Silent Night' to himself. Her heart did that funny skippy thing it always did when she looked at him. She would miss him in the New Year when he rejoined the cruise ship he'd been on before, but six weeks later she would be joining him in the Caribbean for ten days.

Less than a year ago she had been flicking through the pages of a holiday brochure dreaming of the impossible. Now nothing seemed impossible to her. Who knew what the coming year would bring her? The world really was her oyster.

Or her scampi in the basket, as Mo would say.

CherryPicks
Our books.
Your choice.